THE DEMI-SEXES
&
THE ANDROGYNES

JANE DE LA VAUDÈRE was baptized Jeanne Scrive and was married to Camille Gaston Crapez, who began styling himself Crapez de La Vaudère after inheriting the Château de La Vaudère from his mother. Her prolific literary work is very various but she was assimilated to the Decadent Movement firstly because of two scandalously scabrous Parisian novels, *Les Demi-Sexes* (1897) and *Les Andrognyes* (1903), and, more pertinently, because of a series of accounts of *moeurs antiques*, some of which—notably *Le Mystère de Kama* (1901)—set new standards of excess in their exotic eroticism and fascination with torture.

BRIAN STABLEFORD has been publishing fiction and non-fiction for fifty years. His fiction includes an eighteen-volume series of "tales of the biotech revolution" and a series of half a dozen metaphysical fantasies set in Paris in the 1840s, featuring Edgar Poe's Auguste Dupin. His most recent non-fiction projects are *New Atlantis: A Narrative History of British Scientific Romance* (Wildside Press, 2016) and *The Plurality of Imaginary Worlds: The Evolution of French* roman scientifique (Black Coat Press, 2016); in association with the latter he has translated approximately a hundred and fifty volumes of texts not previously available in English, similarly issued by Black Coat Press.

Jane de La Vaudère

THE DEMI-SEXES
&
THE ANDROGYNES

Translated and with an Introduction by

Brian Stableford

THIS IS A SNUGGLY BOOK

ISBN: 978-1-943813-62-9

CONTENTS

INTRODUCTION

This is the first of six projected volumes translating fiction by Jane de La Vaudère (15 April 1857-26 July 1908). Five of those volumes each contain two of her short novels, while the second in the series, *The Double Star and Other Occult Fantasies*, contains a selection of her short fiction. The present volume contains translations of *Les Demi-Sexes*, originally published by Paul Ollendorff in 1897, and *Les Androgynes, roman passionel*, originally published by Albert Méricant in 1903 and reprinted posthumously by the same publisher as *Folie d'Opium* [Opium Madness] in an undated edition that is mistakenly dated 1900 in some sources.

The third volume in the series, *The Mysteries of Kama and Brahma's Courtesans*, contains translations of *Le Mystère de Kama, roman magique indou* (Ernest Flammarion, 1901) and *Les Courtisanes de Brahma* (Flammarion, 1903). The fourth, *Three Flowers and the King of Siam's Amazon*, contains translations of *Trois fleurs de volupté, roman javanais* (Flammarion, 1900) and *L'Amazone du roi de Siam* (Flammarion, 1902). The fifth volume, *Syta's Harem and Pharaoh's Lover*, contains translations of *Le Harem de Syta, roman passionel* (Méricant, 1904) and *L'Amante du Pharaon, moeurs antiques* (Jules Tallandier, 1905). The sixth volume, *The Witch of Ecbatana and the Virgin of Israel*, contains translations of *La Sorcière d'Ecbatane, roman fantastique* (Flammarion, 1906) and *La Vierge d'Israel, roman de moeurs antiques* (Méricant 1906).

Jane de La Vaudère was baptized Jeanne Scrive; she was the daughter of a doctor, who was the Surgeon-General of the French

Army during the Crimean War; he died while she was still a child, in 1861. Her mother, who also died when she was still a child, was the sister of Louis Loew, a magistrate who was appointed president of the appeal court in the 1880s and became famous in 1899 for overturning the guilty verdict originally issued against Alfred Dreyfus.

In the social class to which her family belonged, which might be described as the "upper bourgeoisie," just a fraction short of the aristocracy, the standard practice when a young girl was orphaned at an early age was to put her in a convent, where she would be educated until her teens, and then marry her off as soon as possible. That appears to be what happened to Jeanne Scrive and her elder sister Marie. It is necessary to say "appears" because almost nothing is known for sure about Jane de La Vaudère's personal life and death, all of it now being covered by an obscurity that remains virtually impenetrable, save for the statements she made in a few newspaper interviews and a few objectively determinable facts. Even in those instances there are elements of doubt; she apparently shaved a few years off her age later in life and sometimes reported the year of her birth as 1860, an incorrect figure that is still cited in many sources.

In one interview, which formed the basis for a copiously illustrated profile in the *Revue Illustrée* for 15 June 1904, La Vaudère said that while she was resident in the convent of Notre-Dame de Sion she seriously considered remaining there permanently, the idea of living as a nun having a certain romantic attraction, but she soon abandoned the idea. In fact, shortly after leaving the institution, when she apparently went to stay for a while with Marie, by then married to a military surgeon, she was married herself to Camille Gaston Crapez (1848-1912). He inherited the Château de La Vaudère in Parigne-L'Éveque in the Sarthe from his mother and styled himself thereafter Crapez de La Vaudère. The name with which she signed her books was not, therefore, as many sources report, a pseudonym, although she deleted the Crapez and anglicized her forename.

In the early years of her marriage, Jeanne Crapez had one child, a son named Fernand, who eventually became Maire of Parigne-L'Éveque. Fernand apparently stayed with his father when his mother went to live in Paris, where she seems to have lived alone, initially in an apartment at 39 rue La Boétie (Eugène Sue had once lived at number 41) and later at 9 place des Ternes. Although she was never divorced, and her body was taken back to Parigné-L'Éveque for burial after her death in Paris, the separation appears to have been complete; no newspaper reports of her appearances at social events or interviews conducted at her home ever mentioned the presence of her husband. Nothing was reported about the circumstances of her death, although neither her husband nor her son appear to have been with her at the time; the unusual brevity of the death notices and the conspicuous absence of the customary post-mortem eulogies are suggestive of a diplomatic silence, but we can only speculate as to what it was that was deliberately not being said about her sudden death at a relatively young age.

The circumstances of Jane de La Vaudère's early life evidently had a profound impact on her literary work, especially her prose fiction, to which she turned a trifle late in her career. Before she began writing, in her thirties, she had attempted to make a career as an artist and exhibited at the Paris Salon; when she decided that her real vocation was literary she first began writing poetry, and then wrote for the stage, those genres being more prestigious at the time than fiction. Her first collection of poetry, *Les Heures perdues* [The Lost Hours] (1889) appeared in the same year as the production of her one-act comedy *Le Modèle* [The Model]. Her early poetry was praised by Victor Hugo and Charles Leconte de Lisle, and she later acknowledged that she had received particular encouragement from Alexandre Dumas *fils*. Her verse is Romantic and might have seemed a trifle old-fashioned at the time of its publication; she was certainly not unaware of contemporary trends in Symbolist poetry, but she was a very voracious reader and her influences were eclectic. *Le Modèle* was the first of many frothy and frivolous one-act comedies, many in verse and often performed with musical accompaniment—fifteen of them were eventually collected in *Pour le Flirt! Saynètes modernes* [approximately: Just For Fun, modern satirettes] (1905)—but she also wrote longer comedies and dramas.

She continued to write poetry and plays alongside her prose fiction, but there are very striking differences between her works in the three genres, and her prose work also shows sharp generic divisions. It is not unusual for writers to manifest seemingly different personalities in their prose fiction and work for the stage, especially if the latter mostly consists of vaudevilles written as pure entertainment while the former is more earnest and detailed, but in La Vaudère's case the difference is extreme. That is so even in her contemporary "Parisian novels," which often feature female characters not unlike those routinely portrayed in her stage comedies—young socialites, actresses and artists' models—but is very marked in the remarkable series of exotic novels set in far-flung places and times that make up the last four volumes of the present series of translations.

La Vaudère's first novel, *Mortelle étreinte* [Mortal Embrace] (1891) is the story of a young orphan brought up in a convent who then goes to live with a relative, where she continues to live in virtual seclusion, in the psychological environment of her vivid imagination and the books she reads in abundance. She knows nothing about the real world and is utterly unready to cope with her own hectic emotions when she is first attracted to a man—a man who is also greatly attracted to her, but is, from every other viewpoint, quite unsuitable and incapable of providing her with the existential anchorage and security that she needs and desires.

The basic features of that storyline were to recur again and again in the author's work, almost to the exclusion of any other, even in the most bizarre décor. Its melodramatic intensity is inevitably restrained in *Mortelle étreinte*, as it in *Les Demi-Sexes* and *Les Androgynes*, by the conventions of the society in which it is set; when it is removed to ancient India or ancient Babylon, however, in the author's accounts of *moeurs antiques*, such shackles no longer apply and the pitch of that intensity is turned up to a level perhaps unequaled in the work of any other writer of the era. The sensation of having been brought up in an artificial environment, with little or no parental guidance, and then thrust into a world equipped with hopes and expectations that are certain to be betrayed, is developed in story after story, in variants that are extraordinarily wide-ranging, often wildly exaggerated, and almost always brutally tragic.

La Vaudère might well have begun writing short fiction before working on her first novel and her first vaudeville, but it was not until the latter works had given her the beginnings of a reputation that the short stories began appearing in periodicals, often as short serials, including "Amour Astral" (1890-91; tr. as "Astral Amour") in *L'Univers illustré*, "Terka" (1891; reprinted as "Nihiliste") in *Le Matin*, "L'Anarchiste" (1892) in *Le Figaro* and "Le Centenaire d'Emmanuel" (1892; tr. as "Emmanuel's Centenary") in *La Nouvelle Revue*. Some of those items were collected, with others, in *L'Anarchiste* (1893). The references in her early stories reveal that she had become intensely interested in contemporary research in physiological psychology, especially hypnotism, and the possible connections between hypnotism and the magic and mysticism of the occult revival; although the intensity of that interest declined somewhat over time, it continued to exert a strong influence on some of her more exotic works of fiction, several of whose plots have central supernatural elements.

La Vaudère probably attended spiritualist séances in the 1890s, led by curiosity rather than belief, but we can only speculate as to how closely she was acquainted Camille Flammarion, the brother of her principal publisher, whose weekly salon played host to many of the most celebrated mediums of the day, as well as writers, and the activities of which often included experiments in automatic writing and drawing. One of the stories in *L'Anarchiste*,

"L'étoile double" (also reprinted as "Dans une étoile"; tr. as "The Double Star") is clearly based on Camille Flammarion's ideas, but La Vaudère had surely read his bestselling *Uranie* (1891) and might well have picked them up from there. The question is of some interest because La Vaudère's fiction, which rarely stands up to rigorous rational analysis, often gives the impression of having been written in a self-induced alternative state of consciousness. One can, of course, say that about all fiction, but La Vaudère's more exotic work seems to have been exceptionally disconnected from rational preplanning, ongoing self-censorship and prudent afterthought. All of her novels seem to have been made up as she went along, with relatively little advance planning, and often meander or change direction in response to her contemporary reading or her mood, routinely lacking continuity, consistency and coherency.

Following the publication of her second novel, *Rien qu'amante* [Only a Lover] (1893), La Vaudère devoted her principal effort to long fiction, although she contributed weekly articles to *La Presse* between 1897 and 1901 which included a great many short stories, often no more than a few hundred words long and she then went on to supply another long sequence of unreprinted short stories to the weekly supplement of the daily newspaper *La Lanterne* in 1901-3. She published a good deal of poetry, much of it in the same newspapers, and several further poetry collections. As well as her solo work for the theater she adapted a short story by Émile Zola for the Grand Guignol and collaborated with a number of other writers on theatrical work, including Félicien Champsaur and Aurélian Scholl, as well as the composers who supplied music for some of her comedies.

Once begun, her literary production rapidly became unusually prolific, and she published more than twenty novels between 1894 and her death in 1908. Seven more appeared posthumously under her name. It is unclear why she wrote in such unusual profusion, and although she might well have needed the money her books earned, that was surely not her only motive. She certainly seems to have been avid for success, trying out several popular formulae in her varied fiction, as well as deliberately plowing new literary ground in order to fish for *succès de scandale*, but if her motives had been purely commercial she would surely have made more effort to pander to popular tastes and expectations than she did.

The conventional theory of literary marketing holds, with good reason, that the great majority of readers like "happy endings" in which the heroine and the hero are united and nasty characters get some kind of chastisement. Although La Vaudère did do that occasionally, the vast majority of her works are not merely tragedies but horror stories, in which falling in love, at least for her heroines, is the prelude to inevitable mental agony and ultimate destruction—not a formula that most publishers would have considered to be calculated to please the public. Nevertheless, some of her books enjoyed enormous success in spite of their apparent disregard for conventional audience expectations, her more exotic works routinely selling between fifteen and thirty thousand copies—which makes it all the more remarkable that they are now almost completely forgotten, many of them almost impossible to find.

The most striking direction that La Vaudère's work eventually took—although it was always multifaceted—seems to have been largely defined by the success of her first bestseller, the highly controversial *Les Demi-Sexes*, whose *succès de scandale* she tried hard to repeat in more than one of the strands of her subsequent work, to considerable effect. Equally important, however, was the evident inspiration she took from the novel that was the great bestseller of the era, Pierre Louÿs' *Aphrodite, moeurs antiques* (1896), which sold three hundred thousand copies and, inevitably, launched a bandwagon chased by many Parisian publishers, including Ernest Flammarion and, more especially, Albert Méricant. The latter became La Vaudère's second major publisher in the last few years of her life, and the publisher of most of the posthumous works signed with her name.

That *Aphrodite* was the bestselling book of the *fin-de-siècle* in France was probably a great surprise to its author—a leading light of the Symbolist and Decadent Movements whose work was generally considered to be esoteric and decidedly highbrow— and to its delighted publisher. The novel carried forward a rich tradition of feverish antiquarian erotic fantasies begun with Théophile Gautier's "Une nuit de Cléopâtre" (1838; tr. as "One of Cleopatra's Nights") and continued by Gustave Flaubert's *Salammbô* (1862; tr. as *Salammbo*) and Anatole France's *Thaïs* (1890; tr. as *Thaïs*). *Aphrodite* demonstrated in no uncertain terms that erotic extremism was more acceptable to the contemporary French literary audience, presumably because it seemed more plausible as well as less offensive, if its exemplars were set long ago and far away, in the context of a culture where moral standards and expectations could be presumed to be very different from those of the contemporary Parisian bourgeoisie.

Pierre Louÿs was by no means alone in making that attempt; writers such as Jean Lombard, the author of *L'Agonie* [The Death-Throes (of the Roman Empire)] (1888) and *Byzance* [Byzantium] (1890), and "Jean Bertheroy" (Berthe le Barillier), the author of *Cléopâtre* (1891) had already tried it, and Bertheroy, not unnaturally, was one of the first writers to leap on to the bandwagon that Louÿs inevitably started rolling, in *La Danseuse de Pompei* [The Dancing-Girl of Pompeii] (1899) and *Les Vierges de Syracuse* [The Virgins of Syracuse] (1902), while Lombard, who had died in 1891, enjoyed something of a posthumous revival of interest. One of the more prestigious of the writers who followed suit was J. H. Rosny (Joseph Boëx), although he signed *Amour etrusque* (1898; tr. as "Etruscan Amour") and other works in a similar vein with the pseudonym "Enacryos," in order to distance them from the Naturalist novels for which he was better known. Another was La Vaudère's sometime collaborator Félicien Champsaur, in *L'Orgie Latine* (1904; tr. as *The Latin Orgy*).

La Vaudère's first venture into exotic erotica, the Java-set *Trois fleurs de volupté* (1900; tr. as "Three Flowers of Sensuality") is not set in the distant past, and owes something to the French genre of "travelogue fiction," but its successor, *Le Mystère de Kama* (1901) pulled out all the stops in a remarkable extravaganza of eroticism—Kama is the Hindu god of amour—which is also remarkable for some gruesome scenes of bloodshed. In the works recorded in *Trois Fleurs de volupté* as "en preparation," *Les Amours d'un fakir*, which was presumably the working title of *Le Mystère de Kama*, is listed second, after *L'Amazone du roi de Siam* (1902), which might, therefore, have been written earlier, or perhaps simultaneously. If it was the publisher who chose to issue the India-set novel first, it was a wise move; even more controversial than *Les Demi-Sexes*, *Le Mystère de Kama* was the first of La Vaudère's novels to sell thirty thousand copies, and it set a pattern that was continued by a series of novels, initially issued at the rate of one a year, all featuring the same garish eroticism and many of them displaying a similar fascination with physical torture.

Although La Vaudère continued to publish "Parisian novels," similarly at the rate of one a year, their sales—as indicated in the preliminary material to some of her later novels, including *Le Harem de Syta*—were far more modest, and four of the last five books that she published during her lifetime were accounts of *moeurs antiques*. The last of them, *Rêve de Myses, roman d'amour de moeurs antiques* (1908; "The Dream of Myses") is only a short story, the slender book being filled out with photographs of naked women, and might have signified a decline of energy, although the close association of its theme and background with the 1905 *L'Amante de Pharaon*, several sections of whose text it reproduces, suggests that it might have been written some time before its publication. Unfortunately, the last full-length novel published during the author's lifetime, *Les Prêtresses de Mylitta, roman babylonien* [The Priestesses of Mylitta] (1907) is now completely unobtainable—although one contemporary newspaper article alleged that it sold twenty thousand copies in the first few weeks after its publication—and I was unable to include it in the present series.

※

At first glance, the perverse fascinations displayed in La Vaudère's erotic fantasies might seem odd on the part of a small, apparently frail, upper-class woman in her forties. To some of her contemporaries, at least, they seemed shockingly indecent, strangely perverted and frankly sadistic, although the politeness with which they were reviewed by the daily newspapers of the day, almost always in gushingly complimentary terms, also seems a trifle odd in retrospect. One reviewer described *Les Courtisanes de Brahma* as a "charming idyll," somehow neglecting to notice, let alone to report, that the later phases of the story are a virtual bloodbath, replete with murders, massacres and violent rapes, and even the tender scenes of loving sexual intercourse are confused by the involvement of a female black panther.

It seems probable, in retrospect, that *L'Amazone du roi de Siam*—which was surely planned, if not actually written, before *Le Mystère de Kama*—was partly a reaction to another notorious Decadent novel of the era, which, although it did not sell nearly as well as *Aphrodite*, certainly attracted a lot of attention: Octave Mirbeau's *Le Jardin des supplices* (1899; tr. as *Torture Garden*). There is a fleeting reference to a "jardin des supplices" in *Trois fleurs de volupté*, but no actual torture; *in L'Amazone du roi de Siam*, however, the author seems to have deliberately set out to describe a torture garden that would make Mirbeau's look tame, producing a series of atrociously horrific images, some of which were to recur frequently in many of the subsequent works in the series, most conspicuously and melodramatically in *Le Vierge d'Israel*.

That recurrence is more suggestive of psychological obsession than a straightforward repetition of a narrative move that had proved capable of generating sales, and the same is true of certain other recurrent features of La Vaudère's account of exotic mores, most obviously her accounts of childhood sexuality. The works in the sequence of *romans de moeurs antiques* are obsessed with dancing girls, and in particular with dancing girls kept and raised in closed religious communities dedicated to the worship of female deities. The images in question are highly fanciful, often bizarre, but it seems apparent, with the aid of hindsight, that their imaginative bedrock is the author's own experience of having spent her childhood and early adolescence in a convent, feeling the loss of her parents very keenly. It is possible, of course, that her frequent depiction of very young girls obsessed with sex is completely imaginary, as is her frequent suggestion (but not depiction) of the routine brutal sexual exploitation of those same young girls by priests; nothing like those allegations features in her novels of contemporary French life, in spite of occasional ventures in pushing the envelope of the conventionally unmentionable. On the other hand, it would perhaps be surprising if such imaginations did not have psychological roots of some kind.

Exploring the possible psychological roots of garish imaginings is always a speculative and problematic business in which certainty is far out of reach and even plausibility is difficult to obtain, but that does not reduce the temptation. La Vaudère's employment of physical torture in her novels is presumably symbolic—although she was never admitted to the Symbolist Movement's almost exclusively male club, she uses symbolism far more extravagantly and graphically than many of its members, partly because she has no permissible language with which to describe sex acts except the symbolic vocabulary of insects and flowers—it is not immediately obvious what the symbolism in question might be masking.

There is an inevitable temptation to charge writers describing scenes of gruesome torture as "sadistic," and it is necessarily the case that such scenes credit sadistic motives to the characters responsible for the described torture, but that rush to judgment skips over the crucial question of whether the author is inviting the reader to identify with the torturer or the victim. Invariably, in La Vaudére's case, her narrative voice shares the distress of the victims and witnesses of torture, especially when they are her heroines, and offers the same facility to her readers. The most extreme deployment of atrocious imagery—the extensive torture of Kali-Yana in *L'Amazone du roi de Siam*—is certainly a compassionate nightmare, not a sadistic one, and the same is true of the ordeals to which many of her other heroines are subject, which frequently feature extravagant and exotic mental torment even when no blood is shed. Significantly, the few who avoid mental torment entirely—most conspicuously the children who are the heroines of *Trois fleurs de volupté*—usually end up dead regardless, although the pain of torture and dying is often anesthetized by their boundless amour, and the death frequently saves them from inevitable agonies to come.

Almost all of La Vaudère's literary work focuses intently on the literary mythos of amour: the idea and the ideal of an exclusive, omnipotent, all-consuming and indestructible passion, which surely has no existence in reality. Her work represents that ideal with an intensity and extremism that might be impossible of attainment for someone not brought up in perceived and keenly felt isolation from "the real world," in an ambience of assertive religious pretense. For La Vaudère, perhaps to a greater extent than any other writer of her era, the idea of extreme amour embodies both the idea of Paradise and the idea of the Inferno; it is simultaneously the most sublime exaltation and the ultimate torment, the only really worthwhile desire there is, but an essentially deceptive and self-destructive desire, opening a gateway to damnation and eternal, inextinguishable fire.

In Jane de La Vaudère's literary world, "kisses" (the French *baiser* [kiss] is the standard literary euphemism for sexual intercourse) always burn, and erotic excitement usually consists of imaginary fire coursing through the veins. In that hypothetical world the endurance of physical torture is a natural extrapolation of the masochism of amorous commitment—for women. It is taken for granted, in the literary world in question, that men are different, unfitted for heaven or hell, whether they are nice, nasty, or merely careless. It is not quite taken for granted that conventional "happy endings" are beyond the bounds of possibility—two of the ten novels in the present series feature tokenistically contrived narrative moves of that kind—but it is very obvious in those exceptional cases that the author cannot bring herself to believe in them, whereas the endings in which the heroines die, whether or not they are still cradled by their delusions, seem to carry her complete conviction.

In view of these circumstances, the complaint that La Vaudère's novels often do not make any sense is largely irrelevant. Unlike her anecdotal vaudevilles, they are not representations of the quirks of real life, even when they seem to be naturalistic. They are, in essence, dream fantasies, flights of what the author referred to as her "chimera," of which an extraordinary but perhaps symbolically accurate picture is painted in "L'Étoile double." The claim made in the preface to *La Sorcière d'Ecbatane* that the story was dictated to her by a spirit cannot be taken literally—although she did claim in a subsequent interview that the séance described therein was one that she really had attended—but there are features of her work that are strongly suggestive of a writer letting her imagination wander freely, with only a minimum of conscious strategic direction.

Les Demi-Sexes was the first of Jane de La Vaudère's novels seriously to test the boundaries of the conventionally unmentionable, which it does forthrightly, in its first chapter, when its heroine, Camille, asks a doctor for "an operation." It is difficult for modern readers to realize just how shocking that would have been in an era when, in spite of the alleged moral decadence of *fin-de-siècle* Paris and its literature, the greatest of all unmentionable topics was contraception. Few of La Vaudère's readers would have been in doubt, even before Nina Saurel explains its purpose, exactly what Camille's "operation" is intended to achieve, given that she is neither ill nor pregnant, but very few of them would have had any idea what it might actually entail. Indeed. La Vaudère only seems to have the vaguest notion herself, which is odd, given that it could not have been difficult for her to find out, and it seems more likely that her evasiveness and falsification was a diplomatic move, a matter of deliberate self-censorship.

In fact, once the barrier had been breached, it only took two more years before a practicing physician, André Couvreur, took up the baton of the moral and political cause espoused in *Les Demi-Sexes*, in a far more detailed account of the medical scandal that it was ostentatious in "exposing." In *Le Mal necessaire* (1899; tr. as *The Necessary Evil*), Couvreur makes it perfectly clear that the surgical operation that had allegedly become popular not merely among the *demi-mondaines* but also the *mondaines* of Paris, as a contraceptive measure, was a hysterectomy. La Vaudère eventually describes Dr. Richard's procedure as an ovariectomy, but the narrative voice seems to be under the illusion that such an operation would leave no visible trace, in the form of a scar, and the vague descriptions of what the operation entails suggest that what is being imagined is more akin to the kind of abortion that back-street amateurs once used to attempt with the aid of a knitting needle.

In fact, *Les Demi-Sexes* is not the only novel by La Vaudère to feature characters rendered "demi-sexual" by an "operation," and it might be significant that *Les Courtisanes de Brahma* contains an account, based on actual (but clearly unreliable) pseudo-anthropological accounts, of the masculinization of female children by a combination of genital mutilation and an "injection," by means of a long thorn, of a plant extract that causes the ovaries to atrophy, administered by a Brahmin, in order to adapt the victims in question to a religious role. La Vaudère might not have read those pseudo-anthropological reports in 1897, but if she had, it might have been an adaptation of that imaginary method that she credited to Dr. Richard.

Unlike Couvreur, however, La Vaudère is not really concerned with surgical details, but only with matters of motivation: specifically, a particular kind of feminism (emphatically not her own) which leads women deliberately to mutilate their sex organs in order to free themselves from the danger of pregnancy, thus giving themselves free rein to practice a kind of libertinism previously judged to be the sole prerogative of the male sex. That is why, in her novel, the perceived demand for the operation is coupled, a trifle paradoxically, with another form of libertinism, which was also widely perceived by moral alarmists in 1890s Paris to be becoming more popular and oddly fashionable: lesbianism. Nina Saurel thus becomes a corrupter of young women in two entirely different and contradictory fashions, and Camille an uneasy and eventually regretful victim of both persuasions.

Largely by virtue of precedents set by Charles Baudelaire and robustly renewed by Pierre Louÿs, lesbianism was by no means as unmentionable in literary works as contraception, but it was not until after the turn of the century that the exploits and publications of notorious Parisian "amazons" gradually began to popularize and mythologize it as an attractive lifestyle choice. Thus, although the novel was by no means groundbreaking in that respect, the allegations made in *Les Demi-Sexes* were still perceived as rather shocking. The particular use of lesbianism in the text in question is conventionally disapproving, but it is worth noting that other novels by La Vaudère offer a very different view. In particular, the characterization of the lesbian Xali in *L'Amazone du roi de Siam* is entirely positive, and it is asserted with conviction the love she has for Kali-Yana is not only "true" but infinitely preferable to Kali-Yana's heterosexual obsession, and in *L'Amante du Pharaon*, Zelinis is saved from fatal despair by a lesbian relationship that only has positive consequences for both parties.

The controversy occasioned by *The Demi-Sexes* was complicated when La Vaudère was accused of not only having borrowed its theme but sections of prose from Guy de Maupassant's last novel, *Notre coeurs* [Our Hearts] (1890), which tells the story of an amoral and heartless socialite, in a rancorous and misogynistic fashion. *La Nouvelle Provence* published an article in its 15 avril 1897 issue that printed short passages from the two texts in parallel to illustrate the copying in question. In fact, it is by no means difficult, now that we possess search engines, to find passages in many of La Vaudère's novels that are paraphrased from other books, usually non-fiction books that she was using for background research, but sometimes novels. It appears to have been an intrinsic element of her writing method to import material in that fashion, presumably by way of a crutch, in order to keep her production flowing.

The two illustrative passages quoted from *Le Demi-Sexes* as appropriations from *Notre coeurs* are utterly trivial and there is no earthly reason why anyone would have bothered to plagiarize them, but there are much more startling examples in other works, notably in *La Vierge d'Israel,* where the concluding section of the climactic chapter is manifestly imported from a novel by F. Marion Crawford. The principal observation to note in this regard, however, is that the slight dependency of *Les Demi-Sexes* on *Notre coeurs* was merely a springboard, for a long leap into the unprecedented, and that the originality of the ensemble is not in question.

Superficially, at least, the moralistic position that the narrative voice of *Les Demi-Sexes* takes up, stridently defending the ideal of exclusive and obsessive heterosexual amour and protesting against various trends of modern moral "decadence," is conventional, but even without the hindsight provided by the author's subsequent works, it is obvious that the narrative voice is fascinated by the things about which she is supposedly complaining, and that the protest is somewhat suspect. That element of fascination becomes far more obvious in *Les Androgynes*, obviously written as a companion-piece to *Les Demi-Sexes*—perhaps commissioned as such by its publisher—and blatantly intended as a bid to repeat the specific scandalous success of the earlier novel.

Whereas *Les Demi-Sexes* holds up Nina Saurel as a female paradigm of villainy, *Les Androgynes* casts Jacques Chozelle as a male equivalent, although his attempts to corrupt the hapless hero, André Flavien, by making him a pawn in homosexual orgies only achieve a very limited success. The cost of that evasion, however, is that André throws himself wholeheartedly into escapist opium-smoking—another habit whose supposed rapid spread had been an object of popular anxiety in the 1890s—and retreats into a world of nightmare fantasy.

In much the same way that *Les Demi-Sexes* proved to be at the forefront of a trend, if only by a short head, *Les Androgynes* appeared a year before Claude Farrère's *Fumée d'opium* (1904) renewed the literary fashionability of opium-smoking in no uncertain terms, although it had never gone away completely since the days when the experiments of "Le Club des Haschischins" (1846) had been so memorably publicized by Théophile Gautier in his famous documentary fiction. La Vaudère's narrative voice, quite conventionally, represents opium-smoking as an exceedingly dangerous habit, as *Trois fleurs de volupté* had done previously, but nevertheless exhibits an intense interest in the imaginative description of its supposed hallucinatory effects.

Les Androgynes has an extra dimension of controversial interest by virtue of the fact that, whereas Nina Saurel was an entirely hypothetical character, Jacques Chozelle seems to be modeled, in part, on a real and recognizable individual: Jean Lorrain. The representation is blatantly slanderous—unlike Chozelle, who is devoid of talent and hires André to write the books and articles that he signs, much as "Willy" (Henri-Gauthier-Villars) was widely known to do, Jean Lorrain was a writer of great ability, who did all his own work—but the most interesting thing about the characterization is that all the criticisms leveled against Chozelle's writing by the characters and the narrative voice could equally well be leveled at Jane de La Vaudère instead of Jean Lorran. Chozelle is charged with being fascinated by the morbid and the perverted, of having a strong liking for unusual terminology and a marked distaste for clarity, but La Vaudère was certainly no less guilty of those "faults" than Jean Lorrain, and took those affectations to an unparalleled extreme in her more exotic novels.

The plot of *Les Androgynes* includes an episode in which a dancer maliciously attacked by Chozelle in one of his articles seeks to strike back at him, which might lead one to wonder whether Lorrain, a notoriously vicious reviewer, had made unkind remarks in print about one of La Vaudère's books, or even about her (his prolific writings—he needed the money—often strayed into the kinds of society reportage that would later become the stock-in-trade of newspaper "gossip columns"). If he had done something of that sort, however, the insult must have been a trifle old by the time *Les Androgynes* appeared; his health having been wrecked by using ether as a stimulant, Lorrain had left Paris in 1900 to live in the Midi, although he was still sending copy as fast as he could to the Parisian newspapers. It is possible that *Les Androgynes* had been written some years before it appeared, and that it was not commissioned by Méricant but taken up by him after Flammarion declined to publish it, but that is pure speculation. Another possibility is that Lorrain had based a character in one of his works of fiction on La Vaudère—or that she thought that he had—and that her move was a deliberate tit for tat. If that is what it was, though, the gesture was spectacularly outshone by the time the novel came out; in May 1903 the artist Jeanne Jacquemin sued Lorrain for libel because of a relatively innocuous portrayal of a character recognizably based on her in one of his stories, and won enormous punitive damages, effectively bankrupting him.

Whatever the reason for the apparent caricature was, however, the fact that traces of Jean Lorrain are so clearly evident in the character of Jacques Chozelle does reflect the fact that Lorrain had become, by 1900, the effective figurehead and emblem of the entire Decadent Movement, of which Jane de La Vaudère was very obviously an affiliate, albeit an offbeat and rather downmarket one. As a calculated exercise in Decadent scandalousness, in fact, *Les Androgynes* seems very modest by comparison with *Le Mystère de Kama*, which might be another reason for suspecting that it had been written beforehand. The seeming eccentricity of a Decadent writer assailing contemporary decadence was, however, by no means unusual. Indeed, exceedingly few works of Decadent prose actually went as far as approving of moral decadence, even while admiring the esthetics of decadent lifestyles and lauding the achievements of decadent art.

The titular image of *Les Androgynes* was probably borrowed from the writings of Joséphin Péladan, a self-styled Rosicrucian magus who wrote a long series of novels railing against the decadence of contemporary western civilization and calling for a renaissance of the Hermetic tradition as the only possible cure. The plot of *Les Androgynes* has some striking similarities to the plot of the fourth novel in Péladan's series, *À Coeur perdu* [The Heart Lost] (1888), in which a sculptor named Nebo, who is intent on achieving the incarnation of the Androgyne—which he regards as a crucial step in human spiritual evolution—takes a Russian princess under his educative wing and dresses her in male clothing so that they can tour the brothels of Paris together, observing the perverse workings of contemporary desire.

If the seeming paradox of Decadent novels attacking decadence is so commonplace as to be virtually characteristic of the entire Decadent Movement, however, there are other paradoxes on display in *Les Demi-Sexes* and *Les Androgynes* that are more peculiar to La Vaudère, one of which is revealed by repetitions that occur in the two novels. In chapter VI of *Les Demi-Sexes* Camille recalls her childhood by means of a nostalgic description that concludes with the lament that she has since become "the hasty and morbidly blooming flower of extreme civilizations." That description is paraphrased in chapter XX of *Les Androgynes* as an account of Fiamette's childhood, with a similar concluding judgment. Both accounts also include a lament repeated elsewhere in *Les Demi-Sexes*, where it is attributed in Chapter VII to the biography of Nina Saurel, describing her corruption by "bad books, boarding school confidences and the first sensual breath that deflowers the purity of virgins"—phraseology repeated almost exactly by Philippe in his final bilious rant, to describe Camille.

What is odd about the repetition is that it assimilates characters who are supposedly completely different—the corrupt Nina, the unfortunately corrupted Camille and the defiantly innocent Fiamette—who surely cannot all be type-specimens of "extreme civilization." Camille is, of course, only incompletely corrupted, and the vile Philippe's venomous account of her character in describing her to poor Julien is horribly unjustified, but the fundamental innocence that likens her to Fiamette is surely exactly what makes her atypical of *fin-de-siècle* moral decadence, and not akin to Nina Saurel at all. In all probability, the repetition is not the result of a calculated attempt to assimilate the two heroines but a coincidence resulting from the author drawing upon a nostalgic memory of her own, and the person she really has in mind, plaintively, as a "hasty and morbidly blooming flower of extreme civilization" is herself.

La Vaudère's contemporary, Rachilde, who might have provided a little of the inspiration for *Les Demi-Sexes* in *Monsieur Vénus* (1884; tr. as *Monsieur Venus*) and *La Marquise de Sade* (1887; tr. as *The Marquise de Sade*), was fond of saying that she had once been an innocent country girl before she had been corrupted by the luxury and lust of Paris, but Rachilde actually lived a respectable and seemingly contented life once she was married to the staid Alfred Vallette, saving all her scandalous decadent fantasies for her books. It is by no means obvious which "bad books" La Vaudère had in mind as possible corrupting influences on Camille, Nina Saurel and Fiamette, but the two Rachilde novels cited might well have sprung to the minds of many of her contemporary readers, as well as Catulle Mendès' calculatedly scabrous *Méphistophéla* (1890), another possible influence on *Les Demi-Sexes* and *Les Androgynes*, the heroine of which is a probable model for Nina Saurel.

The confusion between Camille, Nina Saurel and Fiamette, with regard to their supposed typicality of their era, is the tip of a much larger iceberg that runs through the entirety of La Vaudère's work, and is crucial to any attempt to understand it. With the wholehearted endorsement of the narrative voice, Camille comes to believe, and Fiamette always believes, in common with all of La Vaudére's heroines, that the ideal of wholehearted and exclusive amour is the only thing worth striving for in life, and the only thing that can make life worthwhile, even though it leads inevitably and inexorably to disaster. Clearly, La Vaudère did not think that the paradoxical combination in question was a personal idiosyncrasy on her part, or even a frequent accident, but that it was a product of a particular pattern of experience in a particular social milieu, in which regard *fin-de-siècle* Paris was, as the adherents of the Decadent Movement affected to believe, recapitulating a state of "extreme civilization" attained many times before, in overripe empires on the brink of collapse.

It is interesting to compare and contrast *Les Androgynes* with the other two novels that La Vaudère published in 1903 (a cluster which might, once again, suggest that it was left over from an earlier year). *L'Expulsée* [The Expelled] is a historical novel set in the 1790s, when the Revolutionary government dismantled the religious apparatus of the realm and expelled the residents of many convents forcibly. It is the most piously moralistic of all her novels, and has an uncharacteristically triumphant happy ending, but the heroine's saintly mentor and spiritual guide, the ailing Sister Bénédict, still has to endure a kind of Hell on the way there. The third 1903 novel *Les Courtisanes de Brahma*, an obvious attempt to repeat the success of *Le Mystère de Kama*, is also a historical novel, set in the final year of the reign of the Mogul Emperor Shah Jehan, and it also provides the heroine and her lover with a happy ending of sorts, but in other respects it could hardly be more different, and the heroine's fortunate outcome is literally bought with innocent blood, in a fashion that casts her moral entitlement to that reward into grave doubt.

Fiamette, too, not only survives her ordeal, but in a sense, gets what she wants so fervently—but again, at what a terrible cost!

All three novels, therefore, weigh the very notion of a conventional happy ending in the balance, and find it wanting in more ways than one—just as *Les Demi-Sexes* had done in a different and more flamboyant fashion—and it is less surprising, having compared them, that La Vaudère had an obvious long-standing preference for tragedy. In both the novels included in the present volume the rhetoric trumpeted by La Vaudère's narrative voice and the characters to whom it is most sympathetic is not merely undermined but almost obliterated by the tacit argument of the plots, which luridly advertise the utter impossibility of achieving the advertised ideal—and that is entirely typical of almost of all her work in the prose medium.

The sum of all these peculiarities might not recommend Jane de La Vaudère as a writer of great literary merit, in any conventional sense, but it certainly helps to make her work intensely interesting and intriguing. When her imaginative reach is at its most extravagant—and she was not one to be sparing with extravagance, sometimes giving the impression that she was unfamiliar with the meaning of the word "excess"—she is a very effective writer, possessed of a considerable flair for the grotesque and the macabre as well as the erotic. Had her prose and her plotting been more rationally meticulous, more polished and more coherently organized, she would surely have lost a good deal of the raw power that her best work has; although her oeuvre is something of a curate's egg, it is not merely good in parts but quite spectacular in parts, with a peculiar but unique brilliance. Although the two short novels contained in the present volume cannot have the same shock value today that they had in 1897 and 1903, they still have the ability to surprise and to provoke thought, and their zestful mixture of tragic lamentation and ostentatious outrage ensures that they remain captivatingly readable.

※

The translation of *Les Demi-Sexes* was made from the London Library's copy of the Ollendorff 1897 edition (which is marked "second edition" on the title page). The translation of *Les Androgynes* was mostly made from the copy of *Folie d'Opium* reproduced on *archive.org*, but one page of that scan is missing, containing about 750 words of the first chapter (recent print-on-demand reprints taken from that scan are thus incomplete). I am extremely grateful to David Deiss of Elysium Books, who kindly supplied a scan of the missing text, taken from a copy of the exceedingly rare 1903 edition, which enabled me to complete my translation.

—Brian Stableford

THE DEMI-SEXES

PART ONE

I

"Mademoiselle! Mademoiselle!" cried Miss Ketty, fearfully. "What are you going to do here?"

"Shut up," replied Camille, lowering a thick violet-white veil over her features. "You haven't heard anything or seen anything . . . it's necessary not to disturb anyone."

"Are you suffering, then?"

"Yes, for several days, and I desire to consult Dr. Richard, who has been recommended to me especially."

"What will Madame Luzac, your grandmother, say?"

"Who could tell her, dear Ketty? You won't betray me. I repeat that it's nothing serious; a few days' treatment and it will be gone."

The young woman went into the concierge's lodge.

"Dr. Richard, if you please?"

"First floor, facing door."

That response had been made in an obliging voice, in which there was concern for the tenant and curiosity for the visitors.

"Let's go," said Camille to Miss Ketty, who seemed hesitant. "It's necessary not to miss the consultation." And she went up the stairs, which were covered with a thick scarlet carpet, holding on to the rail with a clenched hand. Her heart was hammering; in spite of her decisive manner, her courage was beginning to abandon her.

As soon as she had rung, the door opened, and she found herself in the presence of a black-clad valet, grave and clean-shaven, so perfectly dressed that she thought she was mistaken.

"Is this where Dr. Richard lives?"

"If the ladies would like to go into the drawing room . . ."

Camille, losing her aplomb again, felt herself go red with dread; she was breathing hard.

She was about to take a big step, embarking on a singular, long-anticipated, dreamed-of existence . . .

With Miss Ketty on her heels she took a few steps into an antechamber cluttered with furniture and carpeted with heavy fabric, and went into a well-lit room filled with shrubs, with wall-hangings and curtains of sea-green satin. A number of women were waiting there, riffling through brochures. A singular odor floated over everything and eventually became vaguely intoxicating.

Camille and Miss Ketty sat down in large, flexible plush armchairs. They felt themselves sink in, supported and gripped by the caressant furniture, the padded backs and arms of which sustained them delicately.

The young woman looked around with surprise, contemplating the portrait of the doctor, who seemed to be smiling at the red ribbon in his buttonhole, in a large golden frame.

She had very pale, faded blue eyes, and the shiny, round, black pupils rendered her expression strange. With its thin nose, strong lips and willful chin, her irregular and passionate face emitted a strange seduction. It was one of those female faces in which each line reveals a mysterious grace, seemingly significant, every movement of which might communicate or hide something. The gaze, above all, spoke of morphine dreams or, perhaps, more simply, the artifice of belladonna. She was slim, elegant, supple, slightly hesitant and feverish in her gestures.

There were whispers in the antechamber, a rustle of dresses, and the physician opened a crack in the drawing-room door. Immediately, one of the women got up and went into the other room.

That had happened so rapidly that Camille had not been able to examine Richard. She fell back into her reflections, without paying any heed to the fearful expressions of the governess.

Increasingly, she had the sensation of being in a hothouse full of heady perfumes. Large palm trees opened their lanceolate foliage in the four corners of the room, rising all the way to the ceiling; on both sides of the fireplace, other plants contributed a lively and cheerful note. There were no strikingly bright colors; one felt surrounded by soft, but nevertheless disquieting, things.

One by one, the women who were waiting got up and went into the doctor's study. Their faces betrayed no emotion, but Camille noticed that their feverish eyes had large dark circles, that their stride was languid and that their hands were agitated by slight tremors.

When the physician opened his door one last time to make her a sign, Miss Ketty was asleep, and the young woman quit the drawing room furtively, her heart beating rapidly.

The room in which she found herself did not differ greatly from the other. The same low seats were found there, the same drapes; one breathed the same strange and penetrating perfume there.

Richard examined his client curiously, waiting for an explanation.

Very troubled, she began: "I've come on the part of . . . Madame Saurel."

"And you desire?" he asked, in a glacial tone.

She breathed forcefully.

"I desire an operation."

"An operation? How old are you, then?"

"Eighteen . . . but age has nothing to do with it."

"Certainly . . . but still, it requires serious reasons."

"I have all the reasons possible."

"Oh? What are they? Permit me to take account of them."

Camille felt an impulse of recoil, quickly suppressed. "Yes, that's true . . . I'm not ill, Doctor, not suffering."

"In those conditions . . ."

"I'm not suffering . . . but all women, eventually, are attained by fatal, original sufferings . . . by maternity. I want to escape those miseries, you understand . . ."

Richard smiled within his blond beard, and his interrogative gaze, imbued with a feigned compassion, had occasional steely glints.

"The role of a woman . . ." he began.

"Oh, no, Doctor, I beg you, don't repeat what I know better than anyone . . . rather say that you consent . . ."

"A decision of this gravity cannot be taken without serious examination."

"Certainly, we'll both reflect. However, the operation isn't very dangerous . . ."

"I only operate on women genuinely afflicted."

"Let's suppose that there's a necessity for me, as for the others."

"At your age?"

Richard continued to examine her with the sharp gaze that undresses souls. In a lower voice, he asked a question. She blushed, and her eyes flashed briefly.

"I'm a virgin," she said.

"Oh, I beg your pardon."

"You had a right to make that supposition, and I can't take offense."

"Believe, Madame, that I sincerely regret . . ."

"Oh, no, don't refuse me, I beg you . . ." She put her hands together, pleading in a coaxing voice.

Richard went on: "In any case, there might be a risk . . ."

"What does that matter to me?"

"You're doubtless closely monitored by your family?"

"I no longer have any family . . . only a grandmother."

"Several of my colleagues have been troubled recently. Public opinion is unfavorable to us . . . quite wrongly, I assure you. We only employ great means when the matter is urgent. For instance, many women who believe themselves to be perfectly well are often wounded in the utmost depths of their being, and it requires all our science to save them from an imminent death."

"You see . . ."

He was sitting facing her, seemingly trying to read her thoughts, to penetrate her intentions, and everything that she dared not say. Then he began to interrogate her, as a priest in the confessional might have done, asking precise questions that made her blush and stammer.

When he had constrained her to talk in that fashion for ten minutes, he said: "That's fine. Now it's necessary for me to examine you."

"Oh! Doctor . . ."

"It's necessary. Have no fear . . ."

When she got up again, her face crimson with dolorous shame, and her eyes full of tears, he said: "No complication is to be feared. Come back to see me again in a few days. I dare not engage myself lightly, you understand . . . but everything leads me to believe that the response will be as you desire."

Still smiling, he accompanied her to the door.

She went out, stammered a few vague thanks, and woke Miss Ketty, who was sprawled in her armchair.

When she found herself in the street again, she felt sad and ill-at-ease, haunted by the obscure sensation of a chagrin and a remorse. She walked rapidly, wondering why that sudden melancholy had overtaken her, when she had been so determined a few moments before. She could not explain that new mental disposition, but the doctor's precise speech was still resonating disagreeably in her ears, causing her to sense the impression of chill and desperation that even a glimpsed triviality or a minimal incident is sometimes sufficient to give us. And it seemed to her that that man, for whom she had little esteem, had the right to hold her in even lower esteem.

II

Camille lived with her grandmother in a small house between a courtyard and a garden in the Faubourg Saint-Honoré. Two rooms on each floor overlooked the street, two others overlooked a tiny garden contiguous with a sort of park planted with superb trees. The neighboring house being almost always closed, one could enjoy its carefully maintained lawns and flowerbeds in complete liberty.

The Baronne de Luzac's reception rooms were on the first floor. Firstly there was a very large drawing room, longer than it was broad, with three windows overlooking the trees, the leaves of which brushed the shutters, and then two smaller drawing rooms overlooking the street, and a boudoir hung with soft and precious fabrics of an especially affected femininity.

She had garnished all those rooms with exceptionally rare and carefully wrought objects and furniture, of charming taste and great value. Everything—the chairs, tables, the shelf-units, the dainty candy-dishes, the porcelain figurines under glass, the statuettes, the paintings and the vases; the entire décor of the apartment in fact—attracted the eye by virtue of its form, its antiquity or its elegance. In order to create that elegance, of which she was proud, she had sought long and hard, rummaging at auction sales and bric-à-brac stores, in the company of a few knowledgeable friends.

Camille dismissed her governess and went into one of the drawing rooms without waking two valets who were dozing on chairs. In the little boudoir, four respectable ladies were chatting quietly around a circular table bearing cups of tea. Baronne de Luzac, extended on a chaise longue, was listening to the light chatter of her visitors and smiling vaguely.

"There you are, child," she said, on perceiving the young woman. "You've come from your singing lesson?"

She leaned over and kissed the old lady's white hair in a distracted manner. The latter, her sight troubled and her mind befuddled, did not notice either Camille's shining eyes or pale complexion.

"Serve the tea, darling. We've been awaiting your return impatiently."

The conversation resumed. The topic was the cold weather, which was becoming violent, but not enough to halt the epidemic of typhoid fever that was claiming numerous victims. Everyone gave her opinion regarding the insalubrity of the Parisian climate; then they expressed their preference for the azure land where perpetual spring reigns, with all the banal reasons that linger in the minds of old women like dust on furniture.

A slight noise made Camille turn her head, but she had a disappointment. A fat woman had just arrived at a slow pace, breathing heavily. As soon as she appeared in the boudoir, one of the visitors got up, shook the Baronne de Luzac's hands, kissed the young woman and withdrew. When the agitation of that arrival and departure had calmed down, they talked spontaneously, without transition, about the new play and the massacres in Armenia. The ladies discussed those things from memory, in the voices of studious schoolgirls.

Camille, whose features were increasingly contracted, responded graciously to the questions that were addressed to her, never hesitating over what she ought to say; her opinion, in that society, was always ready in advance. But she perceived that night was falling, and she rang for the lamps.

When the valet had withdrawn, she mingled in the conversation again, which was still flowing like a stream of marshmallow, while her anxious gaze watched the door to the deserted drawing rooms.

To a superficial observer she seemed sage and calm; her correct intelligence, devoid of surprises, gave the impression of being laid out like a French garden, with beautiful straight pathways and baskets of selected flowers. Her reasoning seemed delicate, discreet, sure and slightly ironic, as befits the daughter of a good family. Mothers cited her as an example; young men flocked around her with a keen interest that her coldness maintained within the limits of respectful flirtation.

Baronne de Luzac, impotent and idle, left her the stewardship of her large fortune, of which she took good care, like a businessman. Orphaned very young, Camille had learned to do without advice and protection, and to maneuver in life with the aplomb and skepticism that youth acquires so rapidly nowadays. She was used to discussing her interests, managing a house and doing the honors of it. Among its habitués were several artists, who had formed her judgment and sharpened her naturally independent spirit.

Then, when she was grown up, she had made a selection among her former acquaintances, in accordance with her tastes. The first ones admitted became intimates, forming a basis, and attracting others, giving Baronne de Luzac's drawing rooms the allure of a little court to which everyone brought a name or some special title. Requests for presentations and invitations flowed; the Thursday dinners became famous. The debuts of actors, artists and young esthetes had taken place there. Inspired and hairy neurasthenic pianists replaced Hungarian violinists and epileptic chanteuses.

Camille had already abandoned her slightly Bohemian penchants, while remaining correct in her whims and moderate in her audacities. Fundamentally, she was one of those contemporary crackbrains who have too many nerves to follow the beaten paths of human mediocrity. Already, she was solicited by a thousand contradictory fantasies that did not rise as far as desire. Without ardor and without enthusiasm, she seemed to combine the caprices of a spoiled child with the dryness of an old maniac.

From a very old and very good family, Baronne de Luzac had therefore found herself, involuntarily, at the head of a small cenacle, in which amiable and witty people met. There, as in a few rare Parisian houses in which the traditions of conversation have been conserved, nothing in the evening recalled newspaper articles or political speeches, the two vulgar molds of present-day thought. Intelligence shone there in sparkling and lively witticisms, light and profound, and even in simple intonations, expertly graduated.

But the interesting people only arrived at dinner time, and Camille, in the midst of her grandmother's old friends, was beginning to find the time terribly long.

The bell rang again, and the valet announced: "Madame Saurel."

The woman in question was a brunette with an almost gilded complexion, with shiny hair, orange-tinted eyes mingled with changing streaks, like Florentine gems, and broad shoulders, which her hips did not surpass in width. Her eyebrows were prolonged to her temples, like those of certain Asiatics. The expression of her face was simultaneously passionate, ironic and sensual; in the flare of her nostrils, as expressive as her eyes, there was a supreme decision, like that of a bad deed, or even a crime.

She came in slowly, with a smile addressed to the young woman. Her somber, very simple, tight-fitting dress molded her from head to toe, amorously embracing the lush forms of her body.

When she was in the boudoir, Camille shook her hand forcefully and, under the pretext of showing her a remnant of lace, took her to her bedroom on the second floor: a large room hung with soft fabrics, limply draped, with furniture and a bed in pale green lacquer.

"Well?" asked Madame Saurel, when they were alone.

"It's done."

"You've seen the doctor?"

"Yes."

"He consents?"

"Almost . . . at the cost of a struggle."

"Undoubtedly. You're content?"

"Oh, darling! How can I thank you?"

"Don't thank me. What I've said to you I would have said to others, if I had other friends."

Camille took a cigarette from the mantelpiece and lit it.

"What a dream! To be a woman and no longer to have anything to dread! You didn't suffer, did you?"

"Very slightly. During the operation one doesn't feel anything . . . it's only after awakening. But it's quite supportable. Don't worry."

"There's no great danger?"

"There's less at your age than at mine . . . the younger one is, the better it is."

"How did you have the idea?"

"It was my lover who . . ."

"Ah!"

Madame Saurel took a cigarette in her turn, and recounted the adventure indifferently. It was a long time ago . . . others had come . . . many others. What can one do in those conditions? Was a woman not the equal of a man, who never deprives himself? The moment one suppresses the consequences, there is no further reason for feminine virtue. The two sexes are equal.

She spoke volubly, blowing out threads of smoke, which initially emerged in a straight line from her lips, and then broadened out and evaporated, leaving occasional gray streaks in the air, a kind of mist reminiscent of cobwebs. Sometimes, with a sweep of her open hand, she effaced those slight traces, and Camille, thoughtfully, followed all her gestures, all her attitudes and all the movements of her body and her features. She felt reassured now, almost joyful.

"Do you believe sincerely," she asked, "that two women can love one another absolutely . . . completely?"

"No, it's not absolute amour. Women love one another in hatred of men, not otherwise. Amour between women is more comfortable, more durable, and less deceptive. Women love one another better and don't love one another as well. Would you appreciate a dinner in which there were only *hors-d'oeuvres*?"

Camille started to laugh.

"And tell me, after having passed through Dr. Richard's hands, is one as much a woman as . . . before?"

"More, perhaps . . . and the reason is easy to understand . . ."

The young woman leaned toward her friend and, even though they were alone in the bedroom, the latter whispered a few words in her ear.

But a valet opened the door and announced solemnly: "Mademoiselle is served."

III

There were several people at Baronne de Luzac's table that evening, as there were almost every evening. Camille was seated between Madame Saurel and Julien Rival, a slightly timid young man who was making his debut in society. She had invited him for his fine moustache, his mat complexion, his beautiful teeth and the adoration of his large velvety eyes. He scarcely spoke, and contented himself with gazing at her dazedly, a language almost as clear as the most passionate of declarations.

She had resumed her impassive expression, and her neighbor made himself very small in order not to touch her dress. For him, she was only an imposing image, an idol above his ambition and his desire. He scarcely dared pass her the salt or pour wine into her glass.

Camille did not seem to pay any attention to him, and what she said, always very correct but insignificant, gave him no idea of the character she might have. But then, what did it matter? He might have spent his entire life without thinking of the possibility of an intrigue with Mademoiselle de Luzac, if an unexpected event had not suddenly disrupted his soul and his senses.

Seven guests surrounded the brightly lit and florid table in addition to Julien and Nina Saurel: Maurice Chazel; Duclerc; the stout Perdonnet, a young philosopher, a very fashionable man of the world; the Comte de Naussion, celebrated for his paradoxes, his complicated erudition and his eccentric attire; Paul Tissier, a scientist destined to add nitrogen to the conversation; Michel Gréville, a politician recently fallen from the tribune without doing himself any harm; and, finally, Philippe von Talberg, a rather enigmatic Austrian who had only recently been received.

The last-named was, in appearance, a man of about thirty, but hot sun, unknown fatigues, or perhaps passions, had attached to his physiognomy the mask of a man of forty. He was not handsome, but his features had a very particular expression of irony and bitterness. His uniform forehead had audacity, his lips and his chin determination. When he smiled, his gaze remained serious, and he rarely abandoned himself to a sincere gaiety. His face was long and hollow-cheeked, deeply tanned by the habitude of travel, and his eyes, darkly gleaming and close together, were discomfiting in their persistent fixity. Seated at the table, he seemed taller than he really was, by virtue of a slight lack of proportion in his upper body, for he was of medium height but very well made, with a vigor and dormant suppleness similar to that of a tiger. He spoke French without the slightest accent, and sometimes threw an original note into the conversation, conspiring slyly against all opinions without taking sides with any.

There was little talk over the soup, and then one of the men said: "Have you heard about the latest scandal?"

And they discussed a case of flavorsome adultery that had already become a topic of conversation in salons. The faces took on the intensity that denotes a suddenly stimulated interest. Spurred on by one another, those temporarily torpid intelligences were unfrozen, and sparkled with their own petty gleam.

They did not discuss things as they are discussed in the bosom of families; they did not become indignant or astonished by events; instead, they searched for secret causes with a benevolent curiosity, and an absolute indifference for the crime itself. They tried to discover the origin of the action, to explain its genesis, its determining causes.

Other recent events were examined with the same amiable and mildly ironic skepticism.

Julien was still gazing at Camille, without daring to address a word to her. Her slender wrist, ornamented by a circlet of gold, from which a ruby hung like a drop of blood, seduced him. Finding nothing to say to her, he attended to the dishes, serving her devotedly. The young man had a new heart and a fresh soul. Like all overgrown children, he secretly aspired to ardent and tender amours. Among young men of his own age he had encountered braggarts of a sort who went around with heads held high, spouting trivia, sitting down without trembling next to the women who seemed to them most imposing, saying impertinent things while chewing the end of their cane, and prostituting to themselves the prettiest mistresses. They claimed to have put their head on every pillow and to have refused many favors, and they considered the haughtiest women as easy prey.

However, the conquest of power and renown seemed to Julien to be a triumph easier to obtain than a success of the heart. He found in the troubles of his timidity, in his sentiments and in his irresistible worship, a complete discord with the maxims of society. His boldness was in his desires, not in his actions. Unfortunately, many women, who are unable to divine the mute admiration of the delicate, belong to fools who scorn them.

How many times, mute and motionless, had the young man admired the ideal of his dream surging forth in festival fashion? Then devoting his existence, in thought, to eternal tenderness, he expressed all his hopes in a gaze, allowing himself, in his ecstasy, a naïve idolatry that was already running toward disappointment. At times he would have given his life for a single night of intoxication, but he had not found the pillow on which to cast his passionate words, the heart on which to lay his own heart; he had battled in all the torments of an impotent energy that devoured itself, either for lack of opportunity or lack of experience. He despaired of making himself understood and trembled at being understood only too well: an excess of tenderness, but also an excess of pride.

The dinner was very good and served expertly. Although Julien scarcely ate anything, the majority of the other guests devoured like ogres.

Sometimes, Madame Saurel leaned toward Camille, and they laughed discreetly, without raising their eyes.

At intervals, a domestic paused behind the chairs, offering wines: "Corton? Château-Laroze?" And the men allowed their glasses to be filled every time.

Julien now felt himself invaded by a complete well-being, a well-being of mind, body and soul. Unconsciously, he allowed himself to touch Camille's arm, and that slight contact, extracting him from his torpor, seemed delightful to him. Decidedly, he was not the conceited Lovelace that all very young men are, to a greater or lesser extent, who believe themselves to be irresistible because they have harvested sheaves of kisses from the mouths of their mothers' chambermaids. He still had a fear of sensuality and dared not even confess his ecstasy to himself. In any case, Camille de Luzac was not one of those that one could desire outside of marriage, and he deemed himself too modest and too obscure to dare to raise his sights as far as her.

Talberg, silent and preoccupied, had appeared for some time to be alarmed by the whispers of Nina and Camille. As the domestic made the tour of the table, he stood up and proposed a toast to the imminent marriage of Mademoiselle de Luzac.

Everyone inclined toward the young woman and dissimulated a grimace of discontent, and Julien, a trifle gray, dropped his glass, which broke on the tablecloth. He thought he had felt Camille's knee brush his, and the emotion had been so strong that he almost started trembling. A more vigorous blood suddenly ran through his veins, and an infinite hope came to him. He had never experienced anything like it. And as he turned his head, he encountered the eyes of Madame Saurel, which seemed to be encouraging him with a malicious gaiety.

All the men were talking at the same time, with gestures and vocal outbursts, without worrying overly about the women, as happens in social gatherings in which political and social questions are being agitated after a good meal.

"Do you hear them?" asked Camille.

And Nina Saurel, shrugging her beautiful shoulders, simply uttered the words: "The imbeciles."

They left the dining room in order to take coffee in one of the drawing rooms. A valet rolled out Baronne de Luzac's armchair; she was already somnolent.

Little groups formed. Talberg, approaching Camille, joined in the conversation, which revolved around the mystery of certain existences.

"The most beautiful romances of life," he said, "are realities that one has touched with the elbow. You French only pay heed to the things that concern you directly, and you don't even take the trouble to dissimulate your sentiments. The secret of Parisian existences is only too transparent for an observer."

"What do you mean?" asked Camille, with a certain anxiety.

"Your society, which was hypocritical yesterday, is merely cowardly today, and there is not one of us who has not been witness to those strange instances of passion or folly that change an entire destiny, those dolorous heartbreaks over which society puts its indifferent silence . . ."

She smiled disdainfully.

"Oh, I scarcely understand the imprudence of passion."

"You're so young!"

"I'm more resigned than you think, but I've never been in love."

"You will be."

"I hope not. Life's too short, and there's no place in mine for suffering."

"Oh!"

"No, there won't be, in my poor womanly existence, any of those cruel dramas, those bloody dramas that are, indeed, played too frequently behind the curtain of private life. What emerges from those terrible events is so sickening that the mere thought of it makes me shudder."

"How can you affirm, however, that you will never fall in love?"

"I do affirm it. Oh, of course, I inspire mad passions. Men suffer for me and because of me. What men are so often for the unfortunate women who listen to them, I shall be for them."

"What do you have to reproach men for, then?"

"Me? Nothing. I shall avenge the others."

"Be careful; you can ruin yourself at that game."

"I won't have the imprudence of allowing myself to be caught."

"And what if I were to tell you that one of those you scorn so much would be happy to give you his name, to surround you with cares and affection, to sacrifice himself for your happiness?"

"I would thank him for his generous thoughts . . ."

"And?"

"And I would refuse to link my life with his."

Philippe's features contracted. "Why?" he asked in a stifled voice.

"Because I don't want to marry; because I shall never marry. Yes, my situation and my person have already seduced a few young men, I've received declarations that would have been able to satisfy my self-esteem, but my heart has remained mute. And as I've told you, I firmly believe that it will always observe the same discretion. Men might perhaps belong to me, but I shall never belong to a man."

She expressed herself with the composure of an advocate or a notary explaining to his clients the progress of a lawsuit or the articles of a contract. The clear and seductive timbre of her voice did not display the slightest emotion, but her face and her stance took on a coldness and diplomatic dryness that confounded her interlocutor.

"However," he went on, with a hint of irony, "in order to have addressed such fraternal warnings to me, it's necessary that you're afraid of dooming me, and that assurance might satisfy my pride. But let's leave personality aside. You are certainly the only young woman with whom I can discuss philosophically a resolution so contrary to the laws of nature. Permit me to tell you that, relative to other individuals of your sex, you are a phenomenon."

"I pride myself on it," she replied, smiling.

"Well, Mademoiselle, let us seek together, in good faith, the cause of that abnormal psychology. Does there exist in you, as in many women proud of themselves and amorous of their perfections, a sentiment of refined egotism that causes you to be horrified by the idea of belonging to a man, of abdicating your will and being submissive to a conventional superiority?"

"Precisely."

He replied with an aggressive vivacity, but his sarcasms did not extract from Camille a single word or movement of chagrin. She listened to him, maintaining on her lips the habitual smile that she had for her friends, simple acquaintances or strangers.

Then, judging that the conversation had lasted long enough, she saluted him slightly with a nod of the head and rejoined Madame Saurel.

"Another one who'd like to marry me," she said. "He finds the family suitable, the daughter pretty and the dowry sufficient. It's the final consideration that decided him."

"Yes, be assured that he consulted his notary first. After six months of marriage he'd have a mistress, perhaps two."

"Don't worry, Nina, I'm shielded from Monsieur von Talberg's petty intrigues. I want to choose my lovers, I want to be the man in my liaisons and vary them in accordance with my whim."

Julien Rival had approached. There was disturbance and interrogation in his dark eyes, but Camille's had become as calm, mute and indifferent as usual. He was seething with curiosity, anxiety and dread, and no longer understood the coldness of the young woman who had just testified to him at least a certain sympathy. He was so emotional that he no longer feared weighing upon the impenetrable gaze the supplicant and inflamed gravity of his own. He waited for a word, a sign or anything to encourage him, and, as it did not come, he threw himself into mad ideas, everything that was most absurd in the situation.

Finally, Camille seemed to perceive him, and he sat down next to her at a gesture from Madame Saurel, who was examining him and smiling. Nina was telling a story to which Michel Gréville seemed to be listening with prodigious attention. In reality, he was digesting. She had a facile and banal way of speaking, charm in her voice, a great deal of grace in her gaze and an irresistible seduction in the carriage of her head.

Julien and Mademoiselle de Luzac chatted in their turn about indifferent things, as if they scarcely knew one another: Paris, the banks of the Seine, the waterside towns, pleasures, the summer, and many other topical subjects about which one could converse indefinitely without fatiguing the mind. Camille related anecdotes with the communicative enthusiasm of a woman who knows how to please and always wants to be interesting. More familiarly, she placed her hand on the young man's arm, and lowered her tone to say trivial things that thus took on a character of intimacy. He was excited by touching Mademoiselle de Luzac, who deigned once again to take an interest in him. He would have liked to accomplish some chivalric prowess, to devote himself, to have to defend her in order to prove his gratitude to her. But Talberg approached and, out of discretion, he yielded his place to him.

Once again, then, he felt sad, ill at ease, and haunted by the obscure sensation of a mysterious chagrin. Philippe's severe face displeased him; it seemed to him that a danger was menacing Camille, that she was wrong to listen to that foreigner. The arrival of that man, breaking up such a pleasant conversation, to which his heart had already become accustomed, had caused the impression of chill and anxiety to pass through him that an overheard word, a gesture or a glance is sometimes sufficient to cause. It also seemed to him that without him being able to divine why, Philippe had been discontented to find him there.

Camille was frowning. She would have preferred to keep Julien beside her, and did not feel anything for the newcomer but aversion—an aversion that was even beginning to turn into hatred.

"I see what's happening in you," he said, when they had been left alone, by virtue of a kind of tacit understanding. "You're cursing me for having interrupted such a charming conversation."

She did not reply.

"You're wrong to hold it against me," he said. "I'm your friend, your best friend. If you permitted it, I could give you good advice. You're alone, abandoned in life at an age when one needs support and protection . . . oh, I know, you're very reasonable, in appearance at least, but the calm you affect only reassures me in part. Thanks to your exceptional education, you suspect in the world more passions and disillusionment that one generally suspects at your age. You're one of those curious young women who instruct themselves by listening at doors and dream so much about what they've overheard. However, it isn't in this drawing room, assuredly very correct, that you've been able to make serious studies. Who, then, has taken charge of enlightening you?"

And Philippe's gaze went to Nina.

Camille made a gesture of impatience. "What does it matter to you?"

"It matters a great deal to me, because I love you."

"You've already said that."

"And I repeat it. I want to make every effort to retain you on the brink of the gulf . . . for the danger attracts you and you're looking into the void. You aren't one of those young women, however, whom the modesty of their dowry forces to torment themselves in the catacombs of celibacy. You have a name and a fortune, but you have, above all, the beauty and the seduction that permit you to believe that the miracle of a loving marriage will be produced for you without compromise. Is it of Julien Rival that you're thinking?"

"No more of him than anyone else."

"If you'd like to marry him, I'll stand aside for him."

"I repeat to you that I don't want to marry."

"What do you want, then?"

"Nothing."

"Or too many things, perhaps. Be careful; you might break your bones in the fall."

Camille stood up angrily. Philippe exercised upon her a kind of involuntary magnetism, to which she was subject in spite of her resistance. Sentiments have their secret hierarchy and it is not rare to find, in individuals who are seeking their path, unconscious fears that nothing positive or demonstrable can explain, and which make it understandable that young people require masters, like the peoples that, in spite of their age, always remain children.

Talberg had rendered himself indispensable to Baronne de Luzac, who adored playing cards, and scarcely woke from her torpor any longer except to play whist. The young woman had therefore found that same face at the card table every evening, and had ended up paying a certain attention to it. Unconsciously, he acted upon her imagination with the power that exceptional beings have over other exceptional beings, because vulgarity protects one from superior influences and renders one as invulnerable as the best of armor. She contemplated that tormented face with curiosity, those curt dark eyes, and those tight lips: all the marks that unknown passions had left on the person of the foreigner, and which rendered him simultaneously significant and disquieting for a seeking mind.

As for him, he had loved her since the first day. He had allowed himself to be captured by the mystery of her smile, the penetrating charm of her voice, and the sadness of her gaze. How can one describe, in any case, the transitory hints of sentiment, the priceless trivia, and the details, insignificant for the profane, that express everything for initiates?

For hours he remained plunged in a silent reverie, uniquely occupied in *seeing her*. It seemed to him that the light of the lamps caressed her, uniting in her, or that light more vivid than light itself emanated from her pale face. Sometimes, a thought seemed to be painted on her forehead. Her eyelids flickered, her features were transformed and the reflection of her hair cast amber gleams over her temples. Every nuance of her beauty gave new feasts to Philippe's gaze, revealing unknown things to him. He wanted to read a sentiment, a hope, in every phase of that delicate visage. Those mute speeches must, he thought, penetrate from soul to soul like a sound and its echo; he experienced temporary joys that left him with profound expressions. It was no longer an admiration or a desire but a charm, a fatality. The hardened skeptic had become the most ingenuous of believers.

And while her mute adorer played the cards negligently, she was thoughtful, ripening her culpable project. Until this evening, Talberg had not allowed her any prescience of his impressions and she conserved, with regard to him as to other men, the singular calm that rendered her so different from other young women of her age. She and he were two abysses placed in confrontation, and attracting, as all abysses do.

Now, he had spoken, and she was a little scornful of him for having revealed the depths of his soul.

Maurice Chazel, Duclerc and the stout Perdonnet had already gone. Paul Tissier and Michel Gréville had launched into an interminable discussion of Panama, and Arton's revelations.[1] That miry subject had caused them to fall, from one pothole to another, into the secret cloacas of politics, and they were wallowing there with an increasing animosity, the outbursts of which woke Baronne de Luzac. She sat up in her wheeled armchair and asked what time it was.

That was the signal for withdrawal.

"People are leaving," said Camille. "It's late."

Philippe bowed coldly.

"Very well. Do you desire that I don't come back again?"

"What does it matter to me?"

"You're cruel, Mademoiselle. However, I can hope that all is

---

1 Émile Arton, or Aron, was perpetually in the news in the 1890s for his criminal role in various financial scandals, including the financing of the troubled Panama Canal, although it proved difficult to convict him conclusively in a series of trials.

not lost for me . . . that you will do me the honor of reflecting on the request that I've just made you, and that later . . ."

"Listen," she said, less harshly. "I will never be your wife, but I will never be the wife of anyone else."

"Not even Julien Rival?"

"Not even Julien Rival. I want to be free in life, powerful and happy. Don't seek to understand; it would be futile. Adieu, Monsieur."

IV

She lay on her bed for a long time with her eyes open, in a reverie of pride and fear. A mysterious enchantment held her rational thoughts in suspense, and the critical sense and haughty irony that were within her capitulated in their turn before the will of the obsession. She was now living her life in the indefinable emotion of the unknown, of something irreparable that she was about to accomplish, albeit without regret or remorse. She had come a long way since the time when the fresh impression of faith had fallen into her tender heart, when everything in her mind was sweetness and caress, when she commenced to respect all the affections of family, household and amity. Her mother, having died too soon, had not been able to instil her profoundly with the beliefs that give a woman detachment and resignation, in order to pass through the miseries of the world and remain invincible.

She had not been similar to other children, who hold on to the maternal skirt with one hand and pick flowers from hedge-rows with the other. She had scarcely known the enveloping voice, the familiarity of ideas and words, and the gracious and facile images that cradle the weakness of the very young. She had made her first communion, like all girls of her age, but the English protestant governess who took her to catechism had not been able to favor the blossoming of religious thought within

24

her. Now, she no longer prayed. No formulae of faith, invocation or pious recitation ever rose to her lips.

If she lingered sometimes in church, in a vague idleness of mystical contemplation, there was no sincerity in it. Her idle reverie, abandoned to the amour of the Jesuit art, spread and dissolved like the caress of a sensual hand in the magnificent work of the décor. She loved to see, over her head, the vaults of cathedrals crowded with ornaments, cavities and arabesques, and scintillating like a golden ark. She loved the blazing festival of tabernacles and the gray smoke of incense; that animated magnificence, that palpitating milieu in the half-light of stained-glass windows through which slid darts of multicolored light. She loved the groups at prayer in the mysterious shelter of chapels, the passionate languor of attitudes, the avalanche of happy forms and the aureoled heads of paintings in which dwelt the smile of a population of the blissful dead.

She associated herself with everything that seemed tremulous among things, as if, in those monuments of marble and precious stones, she found herself in the domain of ideal amour.

At present, in the soft shadow of her silky curtains, she was thinking about the two magic words of all human destiny: *will* and *power*.

She was about to place her life, not in the heart that breaks, nor in the senses that soften, but in the brain, which is not used up as quickly, and ought to scorn the heart and the senses.

She told herself that she would be the equal of men in thought and action, and that the miseries of womanhood would no longer afflict her. Henceforth, she would be able to obtain anything, because she would be able to disdain everything. Her sole ambition would be to see. To see—was that not to know and to enjoy intuitively? Was it not to discover the very substance of events? What remains of a material possession? An idea.

How beautiful, then, ought to be the existence of an individual who, able to imprint all realities in her thought, draws freely from the wellspring of terrestrial joy?

She would know everything, but tranquilly, without passion and without desire; she would stroll through life as in a garden or a habitation that belonged to her. What women called disappointments, dolors, remorse, humiliations and follies would not exist for her, who would be above her sex. She would be amused by the chagrins of others, without fear of ever experiencing them; and she would find companions in pleasure like Nina Saurel, who had informed her of the sovereign remedy. She would have young, witty friends devoid of prejudice, as joyful and as pretty as her . . . and she would know endless kisses without peril, kisses without punishment.

The image of Julien Rival presented itself to her mind.

And why not? she said to herself. *He will be my first lover. And he will suffer, for he is all sentiment, that young man! He has too much naïvety for an artificial society that lives in the light, that renders all its thoughts in conventional phrases or words that fashion dictates. He doesn't know how to talk while being silent, or to be silent while talking. He keeps fires within him that burn him, and he has a soul similar to the one that so many women want to encounter; he's prey to that exaltation for which they're so avid, and he'll attach himself fatally to a creature unworthy of him. Oh, the poor child, who only thinks he's alive in order to love and to give happiness. The poor child, who will foolishly cast his treasures under the feet of an insensible coquette!*

She laughed lightly; then her ideas followed another course.

Certainly, I've reflected a great deal, she said to herself, *and I've read a great deal. The love of reading, which, since the age of seven until my entry into society, has occupied my life constantly, has endowed me with the facile force with which I'm able to render my impressions and march hastily in the field of observations. The abandonment to which I've been condemned, the habitude of suppressing my enthusiasms and showing myself with a mask, have invested me with the ability to compare and to meditate. Hasn't my sensibility been concentrated to become the improved organ of a will higher than the will to passion? I desire to avenge myself on the society that condemns us, women, because we're weak; I desire to possess the souls of men while subjugating their intelligence and scorning their scorn.*

Men are habituated, by virtue of I know not what mental inclination, only to see the faults in an honest woman and the qualities of a whore. They experience a great sympathy for the turpitudes of prostitution, which are a perpetual flattery for their own indignities, while the intelligent and upright woman does not offer them enough incense to compensate for her merits. Delicacy of sentiment is a crime that all lovers condemn, for they want to find in their mistresses a reason for the satisfaction of their vanity. In them, they only seek shameful complaisance, which they exploit and criticize by turns. Instead of carefully maintaining the chaste ignorance of their daughters, parents ought to prepare them for the struggle, put them on guard against their excessive sensibility, and unveil for them human aridity, cruelty and hypocrisy.

Camille nourished ideas absolutely contrary to received ideas; she had already suffered, and found herself without protection or support, alone in the middle of the most frightful desert: a paved, animate, thinking, living desert in which indifference was more murderous than hatred. In those conditions, the resolution she had taken was natural, although foolish. She was building herself a tomb, as chrysalides do, in order to be reborn brilliant and glorious. She was going to risk dying in order to live!

V

The next day, Nina came to find her, and they went to see Dr. Richard together.

There was no one in the waiting room as yet, and they were introduced into the physician's presence immediately. Amiable and correct, as usual, he invited them to sit down.

"I've reflected, Monsieur," the young woman declared, "and I persist in my resolution."

He shook his head and exchanged a rapid glance with Madame Saurel. "I too have reflected . . ."

"You accept?"

"No, I refuse. The matter is truly too serious; I don't want to risk losing my position."

"You know full well that we won't talk . . ."

"Undoubtedly; but afterwards, there will be need for rest, assiduous care . . . the convalescence might be long . . . and if another physician is called . . ."

"I no longer have anyone but my grandmother, Monsieur," said Camille, "and I swear to you that she won't notice anything. Nina is my intimate friend, my confidante; we'll give the pretext of a voyage to the Midi, and I can be cared for at my leisure in her home. Once healed, no one will suspect the truth, since the operation won't leave any apparent trace."

"Indeed, it will be a secret between the three of us."

"In that case, it's agreed. It only remains to fix the day. Shall we say a week today?"

"A week today, so be it."

"And I'll be courageous . . . you'll see."

"No suffering, in any case . . . we'll put you to sleep. Only the consequences are sometimes to be feared."

"Bah!" she said. "If there were no risk, the thing would be truly too tempting. You'd no longer be sufficient, Doctor, and the world would end."

"No," said the doctor. "There would still be poor people, whom the cost would frighten."

"After the reign of the bourgeois, then, would come the reign of the proletariat. It seems to me that we're favoring the new ideas. And see how tranquilly things would happen: no struggle, no revolution, no bloodshed . . . the rich would extinguish themselves, very decently and very politely, without progeny."

"They've already begun."

The physician had escorted the two women to the door of the apartment, and they went downstairs laughing, fresh and pretty in their morning apparel.

When they were in Camille's little blue coupé, tightly squeezed together, Nina murmured, in a kiss: "Listen; it's necessary to act with extreme prudence."

"Isn't everything already settled? You'll simulate a departure for Nice and you'll come to look for me in traveling costume. Grandmother, as you know, permits me escapades that are frequently renewed. My chest is delicate, I need southern air. Instead of leaving, I install myself in your house; I have the operation and I wait patiently to heal, while forming plans for the future.

"What a beautiful existence I'll have, darling! And how I shall mock henceforth the inherent miseries of my wretched sex! I'm solitary, without real friends, without support, an atheist in amour, believing in nothing, because I've read too much and gazed too much. Life is vile, because society is defective. Today, my good Nina, I can confide my reflections to you, talk to you with an open heart, but once, I only had for my expansions the mocking complaisance of a chambermaid . . .

"Realizing those fabulous characters who, according to legend, sold their soul to the Devil in order to obtain the power to walk through life without shackles, I want to trade my salvation—if religion isn't a hoax, like everything else—in exchange for all enjoyments and all pleasures. Instead of flowing for a long time between two monotonous banks, I want my life to seethe and precipitate like a torrent. The material caress is doubtless to the body what mystical dreams are to the soul. The intoxication of the senses must plunge into even greater ecstasies. I shall know all intoxications and all ecstasies."

"Yes," Nina continued, "you'll be equal to those men who think they have the right to dispose of us, and you'll choose the most seductive among them. The brutal satisfaction of the beast, in the depths of which the conscience drowns itself deliciously, is followed by charming torpors, after which the futile intelligence of bored individuals sighs . . ."

"Yes, we sense the necessity of complete repose, and excesses of all sorts are taxes that superiority pays to human nature."

"All individuals who are not voluptuous are paltry."

"For certain deceived destinies, heaven or hell is necessary," said Camille. "I choose both!"

"And how will you pay for such a service? Richard will be very demanding."

"Oh, I've thought of everything. The sum is ready; I've taken it from my personal fortune. Baronne de Luzac is only concerned with questions of interest. I could dissipate her wealth and mine if I wanted to."

A gleam passed through Madame Saurel's eyes. "All is for the best, then?"

"Yes, yes—I'll give him the sum immediately. It appears that that's customary."

"Indeed."

"One sometimes dies, doesn't one?"

"What an idea!"

"It's necessary to anticipate everything. I'm risking my life, I know, but I'm not frightened by that; the fate that awaits us isn't enviable enough. If I have to vegetate, like all the women I know, I prefer to finish it immediately. I believe that I have too much pride and not enough courage to support abasement and sacrifice . . . and if that fortunate disposition should change one day, I won't suffer any consequences, for my precautions will have been taken."

The two friends spent the day together. They were seen in the Rue de la Paix, in the Bois, everywhere that it is good form to show oneself in one's new dress. Their contrasting beauties brought out the best in one another; they knew that and had a very keen, undissimulated liking for one another.

In the evening, a few intimate friends were gathered at Baronne de Luzac's whist table, as usual. Camille had to support the suspicious gaze of Philippe, which seemed to want to penetrate the veil of indifference with which she enveloped herself and infiltrate the depths of her soul. He was meditating profoundly, and only opened his mouth to pronounce the sacramental words "tricks" and "honors," the only expressions that dedicated players ought to permit themselves.

Camille felt vaguely anxious, in spite of the Comte's apparent impassivity. Absorbed by his game, he seemed to have the profound, reflective attention that is exerting itself in plans regarding the fall of the cards, and, after the first hour, he seemed to forget the young woman entirely. Compared to him, sphinxes crouching in the lava of their basalt would have seemed full of confidence and expansion. And Camille, involuntarily, came back to that motionless face, interrogating it with an almost pleading gaze.

Not once, however, did he deign to perceive the anxiety he had awakened, and not once did he respond to the mute prayer of those closed lips with a nod of the head or a smile.

Under that icy appearance, he understood her very well, and he desired her with all the force of his being.

VI

Before the great day, Camille spent very agitated nights. In her struggles, hopes and fears, the surges of heat that rose to her temples, and the prostration of her brain following the excitement of the day, still had a dolorous charm.

She allowed herself to be lulled by those enervations, comparable in their bleak languor to the sometimes-sweet abandonment to wellbeing that precedes a fainting fit. Then shaking it off, emerging from that slackness, she resumed her ardor, her strength and the exasperation of her will. On the pillow, the agitations of thought returned to her body again; the hallucination of the imminent torture passed repeatedly behind her closed eyelids. They reignited the anxious thought that had dozed off, and fears came furtively to install themselves at her bedside. The hours dragged painfully, only bringing a little repose at first light.

She saw once again, then, the landscapes of childhood: a stony path full of cicadas and mulberries, fields of blond wheat into which she plunged shoulder-high in order to pick cornflowers. She saw herself walking, with her skirts heavy with flowers, stopping to breathe under a vault of high, dense, somber verdure pierced here and there by little rays of sunlight shining like streams of dew. Behind a few frailer trees to the left she perceived hedges of sorb, ravines velveted with grass, luminous clumps of golden furze and patches of tremulous shadow through which black insects were passing.

She resumed her route under the more tightly packed branches, and it was only at the bends in the path that she perceived the sunlit countryside or the wall of a farm building, which, framed in a gap, seemed to fill in the sky. She walked more rapidly in order to escape the silence and solitude that impressed her childish thoughts, and only recovered confidence in the park of her dwelling. She lay down under an enormous, solemn oak, which had a metallic patina on its bark and the roughness of the hide of a centenarian beast.

In front of her, a sheet of bright red geraniums stuck bloody flowers on the warm velvet of foliage. In the middle of a green carpet the marble of a statue was animated by a dazzling supernatural life; further away, stone hemicycles rounded capriciously under the bite of ivy, and the freshness of a fountain springing forth underneath seemed to be draining the light again.

Sometimes, she went to the end of the garden, toward a regular colonnade of tall Italian pines, addressing the majesty of their nave to the daylight, and as she advanced beneath the monumental wood, the resinous trunks and the interwoven parasols of violet branches, with a warm fur of moss and gray ash, she felt full of an inexpressible wellbeing.

Thus her early years had gone by in the midst of the smiles of nature, the protection of people and things. She now evoked with regret the dream of an impossible happiness. Gradually, by virtue of her imprudent reading, by the frequentation of her perverse companions, evil had entered into her and had withered the roses of her heart. Disillusioned before having lived, lost before having loved, she was definitely the hasty and morbidly blooming flower of extreme civilizations.

After a number of other people, Nina had whispered in her ear the confused words that make the souls of virgins shudder, and she had succumbed, avid to know and to inform in her turn.

Madame Saurel, ten years older than her, was spending without counting a fortune whose origin was rather mysterious. Since the death of her husband, of whom nothing was said, she had led a luxurious and vagabond existence. They had met in society and had talked, attracted by a reciprocal sympathy that was to awaken, in natures that were very different, similar undersides and sentiments.

The following evening, Nina had taken Camille to the Bois in her carriage. It was a night devoid of winds, one of those steam-bath nights when the overheated air of Paris enters the lungs like the vapor of a furnace. An army of fiacres was bringing a population of lovers beneath the immobile branches of the trees. The two women amused themselves gazing at the interlaced couples, tenderly united in the immodest confidence of obscurity. It was like an ocean of amour flowing toward the discreet pathways under the hot and starry sky.

The loving couples abandoned themselves, mute, clasped against one another, buried in the hallucination of desire, breathless in the expectation of the imminent embrace. All those united beings, intoxicated by the same reckless ardor, left in their wake a kind of troubling sensual breath.

Camille sighed, without knowing why, and Nina, with an arm round her waist, hugged her tenderly against herself.

"What are you thinking about, darling?"

"Nothing. I'm happy."

"Happy to be with me, aren't you, and to hear the beating of my heart?"

"Yes, happy . . . very happy . . ."

As they arrived at the turning that follows the fortifications, they clasped one another more tightly and kissed.

The great current of carriages had separated at the entrance to the thicket. The fiacres were spaced out more widely, but the perfumed darkness of the trees, the air vivified by the humidity of streams chattering in the shadows, gave the lovers' kisses a sweeter and more penetrating savor. They kissed again. And Camille no longer struggled against the obsession that was haunting her mind and troubling it delectably. She felt caught, as if in a net, enmeshed, numb in the arms of the temptress who had conquered her, without her knowing how.

It had happened so rapidly that she never understood how she had yielded without a struggle, almost without surprise; and the next day, when she woke up, exhausted and feverish, in her girlish bed, she had no regrets.

Soon, Nina became indispensable to her. They met up at the dressmaker's, at exhibitions, at street corners. Camille sent Miss Ketty away and climbed into her friend's carriage.

One day they stopped in front of a tall house, of a somewhat equivocal appearance.

"Where are we?" asked the young woman.

"Get down and enter without dread. I have a *pied-à-terre* here; we'll be more tranquil."

"But . . ."

"Would you be afraid to come home with me? This is my bachelor apartment, which I only show to initiates."

Camille was about to go upstairs. She caught her by the arm. "It's here on the ground floor. Sometimes I receive friends. You'll see, we'll have a good time . . ."

In fact, other women had come in the following days, even young girls who made their governesses wait in the antechamber.

On the door, an engraved plaque said: *Madame Berton, drawing teacher*. Only women were seen there, and no one in the neighborhood found anything to say about it. All those students with waists that were still slim, fresh temples and delicate faces, looked at one another with the imperturbable assurance of their pure, untroubled eyes, without disturbance and without revolt.

They seemed ignorant of evil, ignorant of amour, and came from a church where they had gone to pray to the angels for the remission of the sins of others.

Only in Paris does one encounter those pretty creatures with candid faces who hide under the appearances of the most virginal chastity the depravity of ancient courtesans.

Camille left in Nina's abode all the whiteness of her conscience. She admired that cold, voluptuously cruel corruption, which was strong enough to commit a crime and irresponsible enough to laugh at it. Nina would have had tears for the funeral procession of her victim and joy in the evening for the reading of the will. She was, at the same time, the soul of vice and vice without a soul.

They had mad escapades. Nina put on a blonde wig and Camille a brunette one. Eyebrows blackened, features hidden under red and white greasepaint, they were unrecognizable. They could have been seen in all the places where people amuse themselves, and no one would certainly have taken it into their heads to name Mademoiselle de Luzac on seeing that provocative creature with the sharp gaze, lips parted in an audacious smile. They ran around to little theaters, ballrooms and students' brasseries, at random.

When they went into smoky rooms they huddled against one another, fearful and content, watching the prostitutes and the men. Then, from time to time, as if to reassure one another against an ever-possible danger, they moved closer to the municipal guardsman, who did not even seem to see them.

Their series of excursions in all the shady places where people amuse themselves went on for months, and they had a passionate taste for that dangerous vagabondage. The acrid vapors of alcohol and tobacco numbed their nerves; they watched without surprise the tribe of whores and pimps prowling the corridors of circular promenades, and heavily made-up, shop-soiled women enthroned behind counters selling drinks and amour.

Sometimes, Camille, too violently insulted, murmured: "Let's get out of here." And they went, heads bowed, at a slow pace, between drinkers with elbows on the tables, who watched them go by suspiciously. Once outside, they uttered a deep sigh, as if they had just escaped some terrible peril. However, there were all castes and all professions there: bank employees, shop assistants, civil servants, reporters, officers in civilian dress, elegant individuals who were coming from dinner at a tavern or going to the Opéra—but the rabble was dominant, a noisy and aggressive rabble.

They showed themselves thus in all the ballrooms of the barrière, clad in somber costumes with little bonnets. They went in with rapidly beating hearts, and advanced between the poles supporting the hall, in the center of which an octagonal platform bore the orchestra. Along the walls, green-painted tables with wooden benches awaited customers. On the dance floor, under the harsh gaslight, women in faded dresses with dirty corsages frayed at the seams displayed in their tangled hair a coral comb or golden pins and around their neck a brightly colored ribbon, but underwear was lacking. The skirts had old mud-stains; all the faces, in spite of the smiles, conserved something sad, extinct and earthen, a vaguely sinister appearance in which the return to the hospital and the return to the pawnshop were mingled. The men had overcoats, kiss-curls under their caps and flamboyant neckerchiefs. They all leapt and quivered in a reek of warm wine and old clothes.

Toward midnight, Camille and Nina, returning to the fiacre that was waiting for them at the door, quit their disguises. Sometimes, in front of them, the moral brigade carried out horrible, savage, blind raids, taking the gigolettes and whores to the Depot in the "salad basket." The two friends drew very close together in their cab, seized by a sudden anxiety. Whistle-blasts cut through the air and the menacing horde surrounded their human prey, which screamed and struggled in the brutal hands. There was a mad race of vague forms under the frost-covered trees; then everything suddenly returned to order outside the cafés and cabarets in jubilation.

Sometimes, they had lost their vehicle, had gone astray, and had walked, ashamed and dirty, under the low sky, in the suspect darkness of a barrière avenue. The red houses of merchants succeeded the trellises of the guinguettes: low, leprous and sinister dwellings. They went past sordid, sealed and dark shops, mysterious stretches of wall, infernal pathways that seemed to lead to abodes of murder. Tiny gardens resembled corners of cemeteries in which the poor are buried. There were shards of broken bottles everywhere and a vague reek of poverty. From time to time, at an abrupt turning, alleyways opened that seemed to sink suddenly into a hole. And incessantly, underfoot, there were peelings and mud.

They went along, trembling and anxious, often insulted by the hoarse voice of a drunkard or a pimp. They crossed the whole area in which the drunken rabble of the locale finds its amours, and, out of strength, stopped in front of a hospital or an abattoir. Sordid prostitutes stared at them, and men advanced their hands brutally to seize them. In spite of their fatigue, they fled, and ended up finding a fiacre, which had gone astray, like them, and plunged into it, exhausted, more dead than alive, looking out of the window to see whether anyone was following them.

Gradually, the streets became less sinister; the shops of the wine merchants no longer seemed like dens of murderers. Kitchen ranges, bowls of punch and bottles of multicolored liquids were visible through the oozing window panes. The hotels had less frightful entrances, the streets became bright and clean. Camille and Nina were reassured, and, pale-faced, they laughed madly at their adventure.

The next day, in order to procure different sensations, they went to the Opéra ball, masked to the teeth. Elbows on the edge of the box, they saw a swarm of heads beneath them, and above them the marvelous ceiling, a dazzling veil of white lights, the golden garlands of balconies; and then, above and below, set against the red background, white cravats, faces congested by heat, black suits, the shadows of women muffled in lace capes. Down below, between the fearful municipal guardsmen, floods of masks circulated, which collided, complimented one another, abused one another or caressed one another. The eyes became tired following the fluttering of head-dresses, colors, spangled skirts and leotards in that ocean of capricious dancing flames. Over all of that floated the outbursts of brass, the rumbling roll of drums, the thunder of the entire orchestra, mingled with the cries, kisses and hoots of a delirious crowd.

Camille and Nina fell silent, hypnotized by that fog of radiance, by that concert of rumors, by that bestial vapor, the dust and sweat of the Sabbat. Then they left, insensible to the propositions of men, taking a few pretty girls picked up in passing to supper with them.

At the tavern, avalanches of waiters rolled down the stairways; the tables were full and it was only with great difficulty that they succeeded in encasing themselves in a minuscule booth. The heat of the gas, the acrid smoke of cigars, the odor of sauces, the popping of champagne corks and the hoarse voices all testified to the matinal hour. They squeezed in as best they could, or, for want of anything better, went to Nina's silent ground floor. At nine o'clock, Camille, chastely coiffed, her appearance modest, returned home and kissed Baronne de Luzac with her habitual tranquility.

In a moment of uncertainty, she had asked her friend whether the future had never frightened her, and Madame Saurel had started to laugh.

"The future? What do you call the future? Why would I think about something that doesn't exist yet? I never look backwards or forwards. Isn't it fatiguing enough to occupy oneself with one day at a time? In any case, we know the future: it's annihilation."

"Oh! Nina . . ."

"Well, what's so frightening about annihilation? Isn't sleep, every night, annihilation for us? Death is eternal, peaceful sleep, devoid of visions and nightmares. I don't fear it, and it will come to efface my sins . . . not too late, I hope. When we're neither mothers nor wives, when old age puts a withered mask on us, paralyzes everything that there is of the woman in us and dries up the joy in the gaze of our lovers, what will we be able to regret? Nothing will any longer be seen in us but the caricature of cold, arid, futile humanity. The prettiest dresses become rags, and if there's still a heart underneath those ruins, everyone insults it, without even admitting the memory of a lost beauty.

"What does life matter then to those who can no longer live their dreams? What does wealth or poverty matter to someone who only has unrealizable dreams? Sweeping the steps of châteaux with satin or the streets with a broom seem equally painful to me. Old women, you see, have nothing left to do but die, for man has not made a place for them in existence."

"Better times might come for us."

"No. We're too weak or too generous; we'll abandon the struggle."

Nina had two ground-floor apartments. The first only received students, the second was reserved for teachers. Madame Berton became Madame Laval for the initiates.

For a long time, Camille hesitated to follow her friend's advice and go to see Dr. Richard. Any violent action frightened her; she was really only audacious in imagination and recoiled before the means. It was the long, burning gazes of Julien Rival that decided her, not because she experienced amour for the young man, but because he had at least been able to awaken her curiosity. Then again, she thought that she would then be able to raise herself up in her own eyes from a constitutional inferiority, and ensure the definitive triumph of her will.

VII

Camille had made all her arrangements. Baronne de Luzac had accepted without astonishment the pretext of a voyage to the Midi, and the next day, Nina was to come to fetch her friend.

The trunks were packed and already placed in the antechamber. Surely, no one suspected anything. Except that the piercing gaze of Philippe conserved its disquieting fixity—but Philippe could not have discovered the two women's secret. How and by whom could he have been informed?

As soon as she was alone that evening she began to reflect. She was too troubled for her thoughts to settle; one single idea returned confusedly—*Tomorrow; it's tomorrow!*—without that certainty awakening anything in her other than a sort of awkward astonishment. A tremor agitated her hands. After having made a few tours of her bedroom, she sat down and started to reflect, trying to see clearly into her sensations.

Gradually, the terrible scene that she was about to play became more precise in her mind. She saw herself panting, inanimate, covered in blood, and uttered a muffled exclamation. The sound of her voice frightened her; she looked around anxiously, drank a glass of water and went to bed. She was very cold in the sheets, although it was warm in the bedroom; it was in vain that she kept her eyelids obstinately closed; somnolence did not come.

She turned over and over, sometimes on her left side, sometimes on her right. Her heart began to beat madly at every familiar noise in the apartment; even the tick-tock of the clock was painful for her. *I'm afraid!* she said to herself. *Frightfully afraid.* And yet, she was resolved to go on to the end; she was fully determined not to tremble at the decisive moment.

A singular desire suddenly came to her to get up, in order to look at herself in the mirror. She relit the candle, lifted it above her head and approached the looking glass. When she perceived her features reflected in the polished glass she scarcely recognized herself, and it seemed to her that she had never seen herself before. Her eyes seemed larger, of a different color, profoundly sunk in their orbits, and she had certainly never been as pale.

Abruptly, a thought gripped her in a terrible fashion: *This time tomorrow, I might be dead.*

She turned toward her bed and she saw herself distinctly, lying on her back, with the hollow face that the dead have and the meager rigidity of the hands folded over the breast.

Then she was afraid of her bed, and, in order no longer to see it, she went to the mantelpiece and knelt down in front of the fire in order to reanimate it. She picked up the tongs and poked it for a few moments. A nervous tremor agitated her body; her head reeled; spinning, dolorous hallucinations and a strange intoxication invaded her brain, as if she had been drinking. And incessantly, she asked herself: *What will I become?*

Then she thought that nothing was forcing her, that life was as beautiful for her as for others, that she was young, robust, full of years and future. What was the point, then? Why tempt heaven? But she was afraid of her weakness. Had she, then, less willpower than Nina, who decided immediately? Had she not been told that, by reason of her great youth, the risks for her would not be as grave? What was wrong with her, becoming emotional like this?

Her teeth chattered in her mouth with little dry clicks. She wearied her thoughts imagining the slightest details of the torture, and her body vibrated, traversed by staccato shudders. She tightened her lips in order not to cry out, with a crazy need to agitate, to run, to break something. There was a small bottle of Melissa water on the mantelpiece; she seized it and emptied it in a single draught. A heat like a flame immediately burned her stomach and spread into her limbs, reaffirming her soul by numbing it. Her skin suddenly burning, her limbs more supple, she went back to bed toward dawn and finally went to sleep, heavily.

When Nina came to fetch her a few hours later, she had forgotten the terrors of the previous day.

"Is everything all right?" the young woman asked, after having kissed her.

"Yes, fine."

"You're calm?"

"Entirely calm."

"It's for the best. I didn't think I'd find you so brave. In any case, you won't feel anything, absolutely nothing. And you'll be so content afterwards. Oh, darling, what riddance!"

Camille ran to say goodbye to Baronne de Luzac, whom she found plunged in reading Perrault's tales.

"You're taking Miss Ketty, aren't you?" asked the old lady.

"What's the point, grandmother? I won't go out without Nina, and since she wants to chaperone me, I can't, out of delicacy, impose the presence of a third party on her."

"Do as you please, child. I know that you're reasonable enough to take care of yourself. You'll write to me often?"

"Yes, grandmother."

"Don't stay longer than a fortnight, and above all, don't tire yourself out."

"The weather will cure me of this wretched chill. It's so cold here!"

"Yes, yes, go distract yourself, it's your age. Oh, if only I could get out of this frightful armchair!"

The luggage was already in the carriage, and Nina ordered the coachman to go to the Gare de Lyon; but two minutes later she put her head out of the window.

"To my house," she shouted, "and quickly!"

VIII

Officially, Madame Saurel lived in a large apartment, with a high ceiling, but much obscured by thick curtains that were closed over white silk blinds. The chairs were lacquered, with silk and feather pillows attached to the backs by ribbons. The wall-hangings and door-curtains allowed their soft Corah pleats, patterned with large yellow and mauve flowers, to fall from the friezes. Screens, shrubs and a few watercolors signed with well-known names completed the pleasant interior.

When she went in, Camille was astonished not to find any domestics.

"Are we alone?" she asked.

"It's more prudent, you see. Richard will bring two of his nurses, women who won't talk. Would you care to come into my bedroom? Everything is ready."

On the threshold, the young woman made a movement of recoil. The drawn curtains allowed a bright daylight to penetrate. The bed had been moved next to the windows. Compresses, forceps, wadding and steel instruments of redoubtable form, whose gleam attracted the gaze, were displayed on the furniture.

"What, you're afraid? Since I tell you that there's nothing to fear . . . !"

"Will they be here soon?"

"Undoubtedly. There will be three of them. It's necessary."

Camille took banknotes from her pocket.

"Here, I've brought the money. If I die . . ."

"That's all we need! In my home! That would be a fine scandal! You can imagine that if I've consented to keep you here it's because I'm certain that everything will work out marvelously. Let's go, my darling . . ."

In her life full of hypocrisy and cunning, Nina had only ever had the curiosity of evil. Married very young, she had brought into her household, for amour and tenderness, all the perverse instincts that are awakened in certain precocious girls by bad books, boarding school confidences and the first sensual breath that deflowers the purity of virgins.

None of what women put around the man who has possessed them—loving words, the imaginations of pious affection—existed in her. A lover was only a plaything for Nina, and a man's passion appeared to her only as something forbidden, illicit, curious and droll, an excellent matter for amusement and irony. Her smile, in intimacy, was always mocking and impertinent. There was almost cruelty in the two corners of her red lips, so well adapted, however, for kissing. On her beautiful face, in her expressive features, decision, boldness, energy and insouciance were mingled with all sorts of vivid sensations, which were tempered at certain moments by an expression of feline seduction. With her shiny black hair and her almost masculine costume, she was simultaneously charming and terrible in her disquieting allure.

No one, in any case, had yet discovered the secret of her life, and her manners were correct enough not to shock anyone. Since being widowed, she had been received everywhere, without anyone seeking to fathom the mysterious side of her existence, so true is it that everything is pardoned in Paris if one does not overtly challenge public opinion.

Camille had let herself fall into a chair and remained silent, while her friend lit a cigarette and formulated future projects.

"You'll see how nice it will be, our little household. To begin with, you won't be ill for long. In a week, there'll be no further danger, and we'll be able to go out for short excursions in a carriage. We'll receive reliable friends, those who have passed through the same proofs. For we're numerous! You can't imagine how many poor women there are in Paris who have wanted to free themselves from the inconvenience of their sex!"

"Without necessity, like me?"

"Of course, they don't admit it, nor the physicians either, but as it's impossible to determine afterwards whether it was necessary or not, they can always say what they want to."

The doorbell rang, and Richard came in with his two assistants.

Calm and resolute, Camille put up no resistance. In any case, the chloroform very quickly reckoned with her thought. Her eyes flickered, partly hiding their pale velvet orbs under their long lids. She was now talking in a changed, singular voice that had never been hers. Her speech had something vague, palpitating and suspended about it, with great silences of respiration and words exhaled like sighs. She seemed to be groping for memories of the past and passing her hand over faces.

Words were audible:

"Oh, never again . . . No, I wouldn't say that . . . There was snow on the trees . . . But he'll love me . . . !"

44

Her breast heaved; she breathed in an effluvia of spring.

"Look, apple trees . . . apple trees in flower . . . alongside the flowers are fruits . . . they've ripened very quickly, very quickly . . . ! No, I can't eat any more . . . That odor is making me feel sick . . . ! There are worms in the apples . . . ! Oh, something stung me . . . ! Look, there's blood . . . ! It's rising, rising . . . take it away!"

✳

Nina was mistaken in her prediction; Camille did not have the strength of resistance that she had supposed; complications appeared that put her life in danger.

For five days, wrapped up in bed, she had the strength to combat her terrors; she wanted to live and clung on to hope with a desperate energy. On the sixth day she abandoned herself to her suffering; a chill passed into her soul, and she told herself that everything was finished. The glaucous hand that Death places on your shoulder had already gripped her, livid specters were already running along the curtains. Without resigning herself, she nevertheless yielded to the irresistible, telling herself that she had merited the punishment.

Then she became delirious, and talked without stopping for an entire night. What escaped her, what she spilled in the halting and inconsequential words, was the regret of a bad deed, repentance, the desire to re-enter grace. And, as she confessed, her language became so grave that her voice was transposed into notes of dream. Continually, the word "die" escaped her tremulous lips, vibrating in a sinister fashion. Then, suddenly sitting up on the edge of the bed, she threw back the covers, attempted to flee, and fell back, overwhelmed, vanquished by the effort. All sorts of black things, with something like wings, and voices, battered her temples. Vague, somber temptations arising from crime and madness caused a bloody light to pass before her eyes, like murderous lightning.

Nina did not understand it at all. She had suffered so little from the operation that she wondered whether the surgeon might have made a mistake, committed some imprudence. The situation, in being prolonged, became worrying for her. If Camille died, there would be an investigation, research would be carried out, everything would certainly be discovered. What a bore! If she had been able to foresee such complications . . .

Camille no longer expected anything of chance; a great indifference had come to her. What was the point of living? Life, in spite of everything, wasn't worth the fatigue of such a struggle. For all human beings it was the same route of tortuous and difficult misfortune, the shame-shadowed road that leads who knows where . . .

But as she was very young, thoughts still traversed her at times that made her heart beat faster and made her look ahead, beyond her present. It seemed to her that she might still be happy, and that, if certain things happened, she would be. Death would have pity . . . At her age, one didn't go just like that, because of a little bloodshed . . . She would live, because she was still alive; life had already remade life . . .

Leaping from one extreme to another, she arranged accidents, fortunate or unfortunate changes; she connected the possible and the impossible. Her enfevered desire set about creating singular, marvelous events on the horizon; then, by an abrupt reversal of her mobile thoughts, she told herself that nothing of what she had dreamed could happen, and she remained reflective, her eyes vague, her lips taut, for entire hours. Sinister temptations were reanimated of their own accord, agitating in her mind. Obsession returned, persistent and penetrating . . .

In the end, she was horrified by her crime, and judged herself unworthy of forgiveness.

Soon, the nervous dislocation of these continuous assaults was reflected in a commencement of disturbance in the young woman's perceptions. Her consciousness went astray; what remained of resolution, energy and courage vanished under the sentiment, the desperate conviction, of her impotence to save herself. She felt now as if she were in the current of a river which was drawing her away, limp and irresistible. She no longer summoned to console herself the sweet memories of her childhood; she judged herself unworthy of such an evocation and told herself that she was one of those unfortunates who spoil what nature has given them and condemn themselves to an eternity of moral misery. If life triumphed in her, she would only know happiness by envying it in others . . .

She nourished herself and fed herself on that thought, hollowing out its irremediable sadness indefinitely. Motionless, feverish and livid, she vegetated in the slack inquietude in which the unexpected is feared as a calamity, and through every door that opens a frisson passes, all the way to the utmost depths of being.

✳

One morning, after Richard's visit, Nina came to kiss her, as she had not done for a long time.

"No more dread, darling, you're saved!"

"Saved?"

"Yes, all danger has disappeared. All the same, you can boast of having given us a great emotion."

"You thought that I wasn't going to come back from it?"

"Yesterday, we still weren't certain. But rejoice, then! One might think that the good news didn't give you any pleasure."

"That's true. I'm astonished by my indifference."

"You have happiness before you, though."

"Do you think so?"

"Eighteen years old, youth, beauty, fortune . . . you can't imagine what you'll be able to realize henceforth in life!"

"And if I no longer have any desires?"

"Get away! You're still under the influence of dread. You're not appreciating things at their true value. Tomorrow you'll be grateful to me for the good I've done you."

"Perhaps. I don't know any more. I'm so tired. Let me sleep."

PART TWO

I

Baronne de Luzac continued to vegetate, resignedly and placidly, in her large armchair. At nine o'clock she was rolled into her bedroom, and Camille, completely recovered, as fresh and pretty as before, accompanied her friend Nina into society or to the theater.

That evening, they had a box for a new ballet, and under the fire of opera-glasses admiringly directed toward them, they abandoned themselves to the pleasure of sensing themselves envied and caressed by so many connoisseur gazes. In the monumental fame of the Opéra, in that blaze of white light, their contrasting beauties shone with an exceptional splendor. Behind them, Julien Rival and Michel Gréville sat attentively.

Throughout his life, Julien was to recall the moment when, in the intoxication of the voluptuous music and the prestige of an admirable décor of enchantment, he had felt the young woman's little hand seek his and keep it, in the shadow of the box.

During the intermission there was a procession of black suits: Maurice Chazel, Duclerc, the stout Perdonnet and Paul Tissier came to pay their respects to Mademoiselle de Luzac, who had an amiable word and a pleasant smile for all of them. Nina's friends were more numerous and more eager. The young, after a few banal phrases, went away regretfully, still too timid, not daring to persist; the old took their place and spouted gallantries.

That evening, Camille was truly charming; from her soft and fine hair to her small arched feet she seemed to be made to respire the incense and adoration of an entire amorous population. She wore an ivory satin dress veiled with old lace, to which admirably sculpted opals were attached at intervals. Her slender figure was braced against the velvet of the armchair; she was nonchalantly sniffing a large bouquet of white carnations that Julien had given her.

He had not quit his place behind her, and gazed at her ardently, without her appearing to pay any heed to it. He was still under the charm of the incredible sensation that he had just experienced in sensing the audacious hand of the young woman seek his own. That had been as unusual as it was unexpected. All his blood, ignited by that grip, had hastened to his heart, as if sucked in by it. He had become frightfully pale, and thought he might lose consciousness. Now he dared not speak, wondering whether such an improbable happiness could be real.

In the artificial glare of the electric lamps, Mademoiselle de Luzac's face was idealized by whiteness, and the pale blue of her eyes had aquamarine reflections. He contemplated her, tortured and delighted. What had he done to be distinguished by her? Camille spoke to him, and he did not know how to respond, in the desire that he had to proclaim his joy and drag himself in the dust at her feet.

She kept him by her side because he was handsome, naturally elegant, and many of her friends found him seductive. Half hidden behind her, he was still the focal point of twenty pairs of feminine opera glasses.

Nina smiled at a few women that she would find again at the exit: Rose Mignot, pale and frail, with the air of an indolent virgin; Comtesse Delys, whose short hair and monocle underlined an almost masculine costume; Delphine de Belvau, always languid, fatigued by sterile shocks, who, in the penumbra of her box, was searching in her pocket for the indispensable Pravaz syringe; Marguerite d'Ambre, splendid with youth and freshness, a new recruit scarcely divorced.

The final act commenced, and again, Camille's hand had fallen upon the hand of the young man, who squeezed it with the ascendancy of the pleasure that she was conscious of provoking. Prey to the thousand frissons that the clasp shot through his entire body, he was nevertheless fearful of betraying what he was feeling by a tremor in his voice and the alteration of his facial expression. He had never felt a comparable emotion.

The performance was over. The spectators hastily put on their fur coats and made for the exit. Julien went down the steps of the grand staircase behind Nina and Michel Gréville, pressing Camille's bare arm, poised on his, against himself, and in a sudden impulse of his entire being, he murmured in her ear: "I love you! I love you!"

She did not reply, but her eyes suddenly changed expression, filling with anger. Philippe was before them, somber and tragic, his face so contracted that Julien, in spite of his inexperience, sensed a sharp pain in his heart.

The young woman had stopped.

"Do you want to speak to me, Monsieur von Talberg?"

"Yes, but not here. Tomorrow evening, at your home."

"Oh."

"I'll be playing whist with Madame de Luzac."

Camille had recovered all her calm. "You've been missed in recent times, Monsieur. Why do you no longer come to play the habitual game?"

"I'll tell you the reason for that . . . tomorrow."

He bowed very low before the young woman, and did not appear to perceive the presence of her companion.

Nervously, Camille drew Julien away.

"Come on, Nina's waiting for us."

"And shall I see you again?"

"Soon."

"Oh, yes, soon," he begged. "How can you expect me to live far away from you now?"

"Shh! Someone might hear you."

At the foot of the staircase, on the right, the carriages were arriving one by one. With the aid of the footman, Camille found Madame Saurel, already huddled in the cushions of the coupé.

50

When they were warmly installed beside one another, with the glass raised and their feet on the foot warmer, Nina asked, laughing: "It's done?"

"What?"

"Haven't you and Julien written the prologue to your little romance?"

"Oh, you saw?"

"Do you take me for an idiot?"

"Have I chosen well, for my debut?"

"He's polite and he'll be discreet. In our situation, you see, only one thing is indispensable: the discretion of the lover. Search, therefore, among the men you meet, for the most honorably known and the most worthy. When we want to amuse ourselves like gigolettes, we'll put on costumes and render ourselves unrecognizable."

"It's singular that your reputation is intact everywhere; no one suspects a thing."

"Because I've been able never to attach myself. Don't you think that, if I had the desire to do so, I could marry in almost unhoped-for conditions of fortune and situation?"

"You're beautiful enough . . ."

"Yes, I'm beautiful, but I have what trumps beauty: skill."

Camille reflected momentarily.

"Julien won't talk; he loves me sincerely."

"Also mistrust grand passions . . . they're very encumbering in our existence. Don't give that child the time to become attached. He's still at the age when one loses one's head."

"I'll show myself to him in the most unfavorable light."

"And he'll love you all the more. What do you expect? The apprenticeship is difficult. If you don't have the intuition of things, you'll commit irreparable imprudences. I'm sometimes tempted to say: 'Resume the straight route, get married . . .'"

"Then, frankly, it wouldn't have been worth the trouble."

"Bah! Who would know? You'll still be delivered from a worry."

The carriage had stopped, Camille leapt down.

"You're going to supper, then?"

"Yes, with Rose, Delphine, Marguerite and a few other pretty women."

"Is Richard presiding?"

"We owe him too much gratitude not to reserve him that honor. I hope that you'll be with us, next time?"

II

Mademoiselle de Luzac had completely transformed her grandmother's drawing room. A casual animation reigned there that would have astonished the good lady a few years before. Now, impotent and passive, she was as incapable of praise as of criticism, and allowed herself to be rolled meekly to her bedroom when the regulation hour had chimed.

Men and women, grouped in pairs, were chatting in the corners. The conversations, tender, light or ironic, fluttered discreetly; a murmur of private discussions buzzed everywhere, sometimes allowing a louder expression to appear, a witty remark underlined by laughter.

There was nothing any longer of the correct and chilly society of old, the tedious and polished society in which the men dreaded allowing a personal idea or an original opinion to show. Everyone at Madame de Luzac's was at ease and in confidence. The cordial grace and communicative liberty reigned in the drawing rooms that only the kind of women known as "new women" give to social relations. Liberated from habitual conventions, lies and grimaces, Camille's companions spoke, thought and laughed as they liked, and did not recoil before true expression. An honest bourgeois who had taken his daughter there would have been disconcerted by the vivacity of speech, the liberty of customs and a thousand trivia habitually proscribed by familial traditions.

There were also many young artists in Camille's abode. One had just revealed an original talent that, miraculously, had succeeded without the charlatanry of renown; another had hazarded, the day before, a remarkably conceived and written book that did not offend modesty too much. Further away, a sculptor, whose rude face displayed a vigorous talent, was chatting with one of those cold mockers who, according to circumstances, sometimes did not want to see any superiority anywhere, and sometimes saw it everywhere. Here, the cruelest of our caricaturists was seeking a type to add to the tragic grotesques of the "pleasant land"; there a young orator, often booed, was distilling the quintessence of political thought, or condensing, playfully, the spirit of a fecund writer. An influential critic, as incapable of a good article as of praise, was replying to him. Oh, how he would have pulverized all the works of present times if his talent had had the power of his hatred! Both were trying adroitly to mask the blackness of their souls by addressing mutual eulogies to one another.

Young authors devoid of style were standing beside young authors devoid of ideas, prose writers full of charm beside poets devoid of harmony. Camille had coupled all those incomplete beings mischievously, who would, in any case, have sought one another out voluntarily, disdaining the women. And one saw the separation into two hostile groups of the esthetes with long hair, slender figures and bulging chests and the women with short hair and flat, asexual chests.

Among those men, five had arrived, ten would obtain some temporary glory, and the others, those who displayed their pomposity most extravagantly, were destined to disappear, after a few beats of the big drum, into the crowd of mediocrities.

In the middle of her guests, the majority of whom were unknown to her, Mademoiselle de Luzac had the anxious gaiety of a troubled conscience. From time to time, her gaze strayed impatiently toward the door of the large drawing room. Julien, meanwhile, remained by her side, hearing nothing and seeing nothing, so absorbed by his amour that real things no longer existed for him. Camille was too certain of his submission, however, to accord him the slightest importance. She was waiting for Philippe, whose conduct seemed to her to be singularly disquieting, for, in spite of his promise, he had not reappeared since the evening at the Opéra. The antipathy she had for him was augmented by the terror that he was beginning to suspend over her, and she would have given a great deal to know what his apparent impassivity was hiding.

The piano resonated; silence fell. A young chanteuse, chastely décolleté, stiff and straight, sang a few of the ditties of a laboriously inappropriate humor that would have been the preferred entertainment of Paris a few years before. Then men pastiched Bruant and people smiled at the most expressive argot terms.

Perdonnet had approached Michel Gréville with a soft malevolence on his lips.

"What a change, my dear! I no longer recognize more than two faces in this drawing room, once so correct. Oh, our fine games of whist!"

Michel sighed. "Madame Saurel is a very dangerous friend for the de Luzac child."

"Do you know something?"

"My God, no, but the beautiful Nina must be one of those professional deflowerers who don't recoil before any experience. Oh, demi-virgins have made progress recently, and the fraction of purity that remains to them is very minimal."

Massaged professionally by the technical tongues of their lovers or their friends, the women would have astonished a stranger who spoke French perfectly by their singular Parisian expressions. From time to time a risqué word emerged from the factory or the newspaper office appeared in their speech. Their attire also had the unprecedented, capricious and whimsical note that one only finds in Paris.

Julien did not understand the young woman's new attitude at all. Since the evening at the Opéra he could no longer sleep. Camille was in his brain and in his heart. She had ignited an inferno in his veins, and had then stolen away, like an incendiary who does not even turn his head to see the apotheosis that he has unleashed.

At home, in his modest student bedroom, he remained on the alert for entire days, for she had told him that she would come, and he perpetually thought he could hear the light rustle of her dress along the corridor. He went home quickly in order to wait for her, and stayed there, dreaming of her blonde beauty. After attempts to work or to read, he paced back and forth in his six-feet-square room, like a lion cub that scents fresh meat, and he adored her all the more as she made him desire her more. He was now so violently exasperated that he ended up no longer fearing compromising himself by gazing at her, imposing on her impenetrable blue eyes the desolate and inflamed menace of his own. Was her conduct a game? Was it coquetry? Bewildered, he waited for a word, a sign, a trivial remark uttered in a low voice before all those indifferent individuals who did not even seem to see him.

"Be careful," Nina whispered, going past Camille.

"Why?"

"Julien is exasperated; he's going to do something stupid."

"That's true . . . I'd forgotten him."

"Say something nice to him. He needs something, the child, in order to be patient until tomorrow."

"Tomorrow I don't have the time."

"When you wish, then." The young woman shrugged her shoulders, carelessly.

"I thought I was interested in him . . . but this evening, it's no longer there."

"Him or another . . ."

"Yes, I have no preference. All men resemble one another. One quickly makes the tour of their egotism and vanity. Have you seen Philippe?"

"Not yet. Does he please you, then?"

"How can you think so? I hate him!"

"So?"

"I hate him, but he scares me."

"You know that you can attach yourself to him henceforth, as to anyone else."

"Never!"

"If he isn't handsome, he's singular. And then, I believe he loves you."

"He does love me, and that's why he'll do me harm."

At three o'clock, people were having supper at little tables. A few women, leaning on one another, were no longer hiding their preferences.

It is ordinarily joy and a thirst for amusing oneself, that supper gives; but here it was curiosity, regret and the desire to know new sensations; it was almost ennui, ennui in fancy dress, hidden under smiles and marvelously armed for combat.

Jealous of their lost empire, Camille and Nina's friends nevertheless displayed before the weary gazes of the men, all that they had of beauty, wit, resources, adornment and power. Each of them doubtless had a hidden drama to recount; almost all of them brought the chagrin and rancor of broken promises, and joys ransomed by disgust.

Laughter burst out; the murmur augmented; voices were raised; folly, tamed momentarily, threatened at times to re-awaken. A painter was inclining his brown moustache so close to his neighbor's cheek that one would not have been able to say whether the attitude concealed a confidence or a kiss. An eminent critic was talking to a young poet as pale as a wax Christ and, from time to time, putting his hand on his affectionately. Delphine de Belvau was somnolent under the influence of morphine. Comtesse Delys had taken a very young woman on her knees, who was laughing, and presenting her with glasses full of champagne.

Others, with dry throats and moist eyes, were slumped back in their chairs and remained silent.

III

One evening, Julien was sitting next to his lamp, reading a book that did not interest him, his mind fully occupied with Mademoiselle de Luzac. More infatuated than ever, and profoundly unhappy, he had asked her to marry him, but she had put her slender hands over his mouth.

"One does not marry me, Monsieur Rival. I don't want to marry."

"Why not?"

"The explanation would take too long . . ."

"I beg you . . ."

"Abandon all hope." As he stood there, dejected, she had added in a lower voice: "I permit you, even so, to love me. Love me with all your heart, all your strength."

And since then, he was possessed, as the devout must be, by the Devil.

Amour is always amour, but it has various eccentricities, particularities and follies, in different individuals. If, in certain respects, in terms of spontaneity, vivacity and the thunderbolt, Julien's passion was like everyone else's, it was his own by virtue of a rare nuance; he loved, perhaps, more by means of the heart than by the senses. It was not so much the woman in Camille that spoke to him as the incomprehensible character.

However, she had the living form and charming life of his chimera; she was his imagination personified, the creature of his dreams, translated and glorified in exquisite flesh.

Delicate and distinguished by nature, Julien possessed, to a high degree, the sensitive tact of impressionability. He had within him an almost dolorous perception of the things of life. Everywhere he went, he was affected, as if by an atmosphere, by the sentiments that he encountered, or which disturbed him. He sensed sympathies or hostilities in the air, good or bad news. And all of his interior perceptions were so nearly a presentiment that they almost always became reality. A gaze, the sound of a voice, or a gesture, spoke to him and revealed to him what they hid from almost everyone else. He sincerely envied those who passed through events without seeing anything of what was shown to them and who remained until death without the mask of their illusions being removed. An item of furniture was a friend or an enemy to him; a hue, the form or the color of a fabric pleased him or offended him; a false note in a conversation or a melody was sufficient to cure him of a caprice or an admiration.

For the very reason that he was in love, however, all the subtle senses of his being were now numbed. That nervous sensibility, that continual shock of impressions, had abruptly ceased, for he was no longer living anywhere but within himself, in the intoxication of his dream. His little apartment, at the back of a courtyard, was as silent as a well. He could only hear the drip of the rain on the pavement, and the regular ticking of his clock.

Suddenly, without any sound of the catch that might have alerted him, his door swung silently on its hinges, and remained half open. He raised his eyes and put down his book, thinking that it as a visit from a friend. Then he put his hand to his breast, so strong was his emotion. Camille was on the threshold, calm and resolute in spite of the pallor that covered her face.

The most supernatural vision could not, at that moment, have given Julien the kind of nervous shudder, an almost dolorous palpitation, that he felt when he saw the young woman coming toward him.

With an energetic gesture, she repressed the cry of delight that was about to escape him, and she listened momentarily, her ear against the door, to see whether anyone had followed her. Then, looking at him with her impenetrable blue eyes, she took him in her arms and sought his lips. Fastened in the fiery kiss that penetrated him, intoxicated by the breath that he respired recklessly, he carried her to his bed, no longer knowing what he was doing.

In the bosom of the joy that she had come to seek and offer, she remained silent, and he, now kneeling before her, addressed all the insatiable "whys" of his amour to her. But she made no reply; her ardent mouth remained mute to everything except kisses.

He thought that a moment would arrive when she would deliver her soul to him as she had delivered her body, and he interrogated her again with tenderness and obstinacy.

"Don't ask me anything," she said, finally. "I've come . . . isn't that enough for you?"

"I love you, Camille, I adore you. Tell me, do you want, now, to be my wife?"

"No more than yesterday. I'm your mistress. Aren't you happy, then?"

"Oh, so very happy!"

"And do you want that happiness to last?"

"All my life!"

"Then obey me without ever interrogating me."

He told her, slowly, with almost solemn words, that he gave her his existence forever, in order that she could do with it as she pleased.

She shrugged her shoulders as she replied: "Don't promise too much, my little Julien."

He turned toward her completely, and, looking into the depths of her eyes with a penetrating gaze that resembled a touch, he repeated what he had just said, at greater length, more ardently, and better still.

Everything that he had thought, in so many exalted reveries, he expressed with such fervor that she listened to it as if in a cloud of prayer and incense. She felt caressed in all her womanly fibers by that adoring mouth, more and better than she had ever been in her culpable intoxications.

And yet, a slightly ironic smile remained at the corners of her lips. There was so much naïvety in that amour, so much passionate candor. She understood the enjoyment of the mystery in the complicity that makes lovers and conspirators.

Camille, in herself and in society, became impenetrable again, and Julien cradled proudly and almost sensuously in the innermost depths of his consciousness the idea that all that magnificent indifference hid an infinity of tenderness, for him alone, and that nothing could henceforth darken his joy. No one on earth but the two them knew of their dementia . . . and that thought was delicious.

From the day when she had brushed him at table until the moment when she had surged forth like an apparition in the frame of his open door, Camille had not haggled with his emotion. Her embraces had a languor and force that for him was better than a language, and he told her his dementias and intoxications. He talked endlessly, providing the questions and the responses, no longer seeking to make the sphinx confess. Amour had gripped his heart as an eagle seizes a prey in its claws, and he did not struggle, only too glad to have been caught. He lived in sunlight, in golden ideas, his soul warmed, his mind cradled and bathed by light, in an ardent peace.

She was not satisfied. Her fall already horrified her. Oh, that mute, interior agony, with no other witnesses than the self-esteem that bleeds and weakens. The shameful agony that she had not foreseen! Would it be necessary always to suffer that? Would the amour that she poured so generously not also warm her up and bring her forgetfulness?

She had an entire month of discouragement during which she felt, all the time, an indifference and an immense disgust, with an unhealthy need for action. Then she yielded to one of the stupors consequent on too forceful a shock to the organism, which repose without curing.

IV

One evening, when Camille was sitting next to Baronne de Luzac at the whist table, in one of the fits of sadness in the current of which she vegetated, abandoning her will to her instinct and her thoughts to the whim of hazard, she suddenly shivered. The valet had just announced Comte von Talberg.

Since the evening at the Opéra she had not seen him again, in spite of his promise, and she was beginning to reassure herself as to the possible consequences of his imprudence. Had she not wearied Philippe's rancor by her indifference, and had he not renounced the futile struggle?

She did not know that somber and inflexible nature well enough to comprehend that it was only a temporary suspension of an ever-present menace. While the game recommenced, more doggedly and more silently, she thought: *What does he want with me now? What is he going to say to me? Nothing, surely . . . why fear complications?*

She was a little pale, a little thinner, but still charming, and perhaps even prettier, with her more delicate appearance.

Baronne de Luzac scarcely woke up any more except for her cherished games; a bad cold had aggravated her illness, and her bedroom reeked of tisane, fever and tar. When Philippe came in she murmured, in an extinct voice: "Ah, my dear Monsieur, you've done well to come back. I was despairing of seeing you again in this world." As he protested, she went on: "Let it go, let it go, don't spoil my last pleasures. Sit down here, Comte, and replace Monsieur Perdonnet, who only does stupid things."

She was breathing in a rapid, shallow fashion, and sometimes uttered a long sigh of lassitude.

It was March. The evening was mild.

"Give me some air," she said to Camille.

"Be careful," the young woman replied, "it's late; you might catch cold again, and you know it gives you coughing fits."

But the sick woman made a febrile gesture of discontentment with her right hand and murmured, with the grimace of a dying woman, which showed the thinness of her lips, the hollowness of her cheeks and the projection of all her bones: "Open it, open it, I'm suffering . . ."

She obeyed, and opened the window-door that gave access to the balcony. The breath that entered surprised them like a caress. It was a soft, warm, peaceful breeze, a spring breeze, already heady and intoxicating.

There was a long silence, a dolorous and profound silence. The sky was a somber blue, dotted with stars; a vague rumor rose from the street.

Camille looked outside, and did not move, her face stuck to the pane. She had not understood, until that day. Now, an unknown, atrocious anguish entered into her, as if she had sensed very close by, raised over the armchair where her grandmother was panting, the hideous hand of Death. She had a desire to weep, but the rebel tears would not flow.

Paul Tissier, Michel Gréville and Perdonnet soon left, the game having become impossible, and only Philippe remained with the two women.

For a long time they remained thus, sometimes pronouncing some futile, banal remark, as if there were a danger, a mysterious danger, in allowing the silence to go on too long, in letting the mute air congeal in the room where the implacable specter of death was beginning to prowl.

But the Baronne's head slumped on to the back of the chair, and she fell asleep almost peacefully.

Philippe, who seemed to have been waiting for that moment, drew nearer to the young woman.

"My presence here astonishes you, doesn't it?"

"In fact, I'm no longer accustomed to seeing you . . ."

"And you're wondering what motive has brought me back?"

"I'm not wondering anything. I'm satisfied . . ."

"No, you're not satisfied. You're afraid. I can read in your eyes that you're afraid."

She laughed nervously.

"Of what would I be afraid? What could you have against me? And then, I don't suppose you have any intention of doing me harm?"

"And what if I had that intention?"

"With what end would you have it?"

"Vengeance is very sweet."

"One doesn't avenge oneself on a woman."

"That depends."

She raised her head proudly. "In sum, what are you getting at?"

"Why did you reject me, when . . . ?" He searched for words, dared not, and recoiled before the brutality of the confession.

She shrugged her shoulders. "I didn't love you."

"That's possible, but you didn't love anyone. So, as well me as another."

She shivered under the insult.

"You have no right to speak to me like that."

"Do you think so? You don't know that I hold your destiny in my hand, that I could doom you if I wanted to."

"Doom me?"

"Yes," he said, weighing his cruel gaze upon hers. "I know everything."

Very pale, she stammered: "What do you know? It's impossible!"

"Oh, in Paris it isn't difficult to obtain information. There are agencies that take responsibility for investigating the most mysterious existences. It's simply a matter of price."

She contemplated him, distraughtly.

"You haven't done that! That would be despicable!"

"Why? Don't I have a right to know? Everything that concerns you is of the keenest interest to me. If I'd been able to employ a nobler means, I'd have done so, but I had no choice."

"What infamy!"

"You can't judge me, for, of the two of us . . ."

She closed her eyes in rage, in order no longer to see the person who had just spoken to her in that fashion. She hated him; she struggled against his strength, impotent to pronounce a word. She was like a beast in a net, tied up and thrown at the feet of the man who dared to challenge her.

And now, in that drawing room, next to the dying woman, she felt weaker, more abandoned, and even more lost, than she had ever been before. However, she struggled desperately; she defended herself, calling for help with all the force of her soul, desiring to die rather than fall thus, she who had never recoiled before anything.

Finally, she stammered: "Will you keep quiet, Monsieur?"

"That depends on you."

"On me?"

"Yes. You've refused me as a husband, take me as a lover."

"Oh! But no . . . you don't know anything! I'm well able to support your insults and threats. Get out!"

He laughed scornfully. "Get away! Soon you'll be begging me to stay. Listen, I know about your relations with Madame Saurel . . . your culpable relations . . . your excursions to all the places in Paris where people amuse themselves . . . and the two very discreet ground-floor apartments to which the young girls bring their governesses. I also know about your visits to Dr. Richard and the pretended voyage to Nice that was the consequence of them . . ."

"Shut up!"

"Do you still want me to go?"

"No, no . . ."

She understood that it was finished, that the struggle was futile. She did not want to give in, however, and she was seized by one of the nervous crises that throw women to the ground, palpitating, howling and writhing.

She was trembling in all her limbs, sensing that she was about to fall and roll on the carpet uttering shrill cries.

"Finally," he went on, implacably, "I know that you're the mistress of young Julien Rival."

"Oh," she moaned, unable to do anything, anything at all, against that man.

"You detest me, eh?"

"With all my being!"

"But you're no longer chasing me away?"

"Go on, then, recount what you know. No one will believe you."

"Yes, they'll believe me, because people always believe evil."

"Well, what do you want me to do? I'm in your power, I no longer have any will."

He drew nearer to her, his hands trembling.

"Camille . . . ! Camille . . . !"

She felt a surge of disgust.

"I won't talk, I swear to you . . . Simply let me love you, and tell you so. My passion has been augmented by all the tortures you've made me endure . . . Yes, I know, lovers have anguishes about which they are not permitted to talk to the women who live in a kind of cruel unconsciousness . . . Optimists by virtue of egotism, unjust by virtue of habitude, they exempt themselves from reflection in the name of their enjoyment and absolve themselves of their sins in the enthusiasm of pleasure. If amour has to plead its cause by means of great sacrifices, it also ought to cover them adroitly with a veil and bury them in silence. You won't have to repent of having been good. I'll be your slave, you'll see!"

He pressed himself against her and sought her lips.

But she showed him her grandmother, asleep.

"Yes," he murmured. "In your bedroom, then . . ."

She tottered, and her limbs weak and her hands feverish, let herself fall into a chair.

"For pity's sake!" she murmured.

He took her wrist, rudely.

"Come . . . come."

He opened a door, and they found themselves in the small drawing room, almost dark. Then he fell at the feet of the young woman and rolled his face in her dress.

"You see, I'm not demanding anything . . . only imploring."

She pushed him away with her extended arms, and, divining that he was losing by begging, he got up, put his arm around her waist, and, while that revolted body was agitated by spasms, he said to her, so close to her face that she felt the contact of his lips: "It's necessary that you be mine. You really thought that I would resign myself?"

He held her tighter; she felt herself carried toward the sofa, and the idea that she was about to be taken in spite of herself, possessed by force, gave her a new energy. With her hands, her legs violently crossed, she resisted and defended herself. But he seemed insensible to the bites and scratches . . .

Exhausted, she resigned herself, weeping with impotent rage.

When they went back into the drawing room, Madame de Luzac was still asleep.

"Trust me, Camille," he murmured. "I won't say anything . . . ever . . . not ever. It will be sufficient for me to see you every day to be happy, very happy." And, as she looked at him uncomprehendingly: "Yes, every day; I want to see you every day. Here, at my home . . . it doesn't matter . . . you choose."

"But it's impossible!" she cried. "I don't want to! I hate you!"

He laughed, silently.

"So be it," she said. "I give in. You can see me whenever you wish. Now, get out!"

And as he drew away, she put her hands over her face, to hide her tears.

V

"Bah!" said Madame Saurel, the next morning, when Camille had recounted the evening's events. "You're very tormented for such a little thing. You couldn't buy this Talberg's silence any other way."

"There, in my home, next to my sick grandmother!"

"She doesn't know anything and never will know anything."

"Certainly."

"Well then, what are you afraid of?"

"My life horrifies me!"

"Already?"

"I foresee a long series of lies, treasons, and cowardly actions. It will be necessary for me to walk that terrible road, without looking back, until the punishment—for there will doubtless be a punishment."

"Come on, don't be melodramatic, my little Camille. Evil doesn't exist, any more than good. There's only nature, and we're not culpable for following the penchants that are in us."

"You scare me, Nina!"

"Let's love one another, Camille. There's nothing good but amour, you see, and our life of amour is so short, as women! Take advantage of your youth, your beauty!"

She drew her toward her on the chaise longue, and slipped off her white silk peignoir.

But Camille pulled away, gently. "No, leave me alone. I'm sad today, frightfully sad."

"You're bored. If you like we can go out this evening . . . I know amusing places that you haven't seen yet."

"No, not this evening."

"Tomorrow, then?"

"Not tomorrow, nor afterwards. Your pleasures no longer tempt me. What kind of woman are you, to give yourself thus to anyone who comes along? How can you throw yourself into all the arms that close around you? Even the fury of your exceptional or sick senses isn't sufficient to explain such a dementia! You're not at the beginning of your horrible life of error, to throw yourself into it with such fury . . ."

Nina shrugged her shoulders. "I don't know. My body is mad enough to render the madness contagious. And then, you see, in what is called pleasure there are abysms as profound as in amour. Only the vulgar know them. You aren't the first that I've formed in my image. Many women, even young girls, have followed your example. But I've loved you more, because you were more difficult to conquer."

"For me, the humiliation of it is all the greater!"

"Fie!"

"Forgive me, Nina . . . forgive me! I don't have your serenity, you see; I'm weak. Go away, leave me alone."

"Are you going to see Julien and Philippe today?"

"I don't want to see either of them."

"Go on, you will. Don't forget our supper, will you? The supper of the demi-sexes?"

"I won't forget. Haven't I come punctiliously every month, since . . . since I've been one of you?"

Camille remained alone with her remorse. *No, I won't go*, she said to herself. *I won't go any more. Is my existence doomed then? Will I not find the remedy alongside the evil?*

She insulated herself against external things and distractions, in intimacy with disenchanted impressions and memories. She spent two hours leaning on the arm of her armchair, dreamily riffling through the ever open pages of that poem with a hideous energy. Her naturally meditative mind revealed to her, by intuition, everything that she would have to suffer subsequently if her life came to be known.

And yet, society tolerates and forgives vice more readily than dolors or miseries, which it fears like contagion. Vice is a luxury that flatters self-esteem. However majestic a misfortune might be, it always ends up by being ridiculous. Society, like young Romans in the circus, never accords mercy to the gladiator who falls. But Camille was too young to have lost all candor. She imagined in good faith that her crime would be unforgivable, because there was no excuse for it.

Reflections flowed into her mind with the promptitude of waves breaking on a shore. She looked around her and felt the sinister chill that evil distills, and which grips the soul more sharply than the December wind chills the body. She folded her arms over her chest, tilted her head and fell into a profound melancholy.

She thought about the scant happiness that is found down here. What is it, then? Amusements devoid of pleasure, gaiety devoid of joy, feasting devoid of enjoyment, delirium devoid of sensuality—in sum, a hearth devoid of flame and sparks. She did not have the kind of consciousness that steals away from suffering out of habit and by virtue of the sort of insouciance in which a woman vegetates, naïvely furtive. In her, a morbid sensitivity, a mental disposition always agitating in bitterness, and a moral sense that had baulked after each of her falls—all the gifts of delicacy and election—united to torture her and to bring back even more cruelly in her despair the torment of what was so little to Nina.

Camille gave in to the allure of pleasure, but as soon as she had given in, she held herself in scorn. Even in the intoxication of her senses she could not forget herself entirely and lose herself. As she abandoned herself and descended in her pride, she did not sense immodesty arriving in her. The degradations into which she plunged did not fortify her against disgust and horror for herself; habitude had not hardened her. Her soiled conscience rejected its soiling, struggled against her shame, and did not leave her even a second of the full enjoyment of the vice, the entire numbness of the fall.

At two o'clock in the afternoon., she received a letter, which she opened tremulously. It was from Philippe, and only contained the words: *Five o'clock at my home. Don't forget that you belong to me as I belong to you.*

She went, with anger and disgust.

VI

That day, Julien waited in vain in his room, full of the flowers that she loved. In vain he pressed his forehead against the window and interrogated the dark courtyard that she had to traverse. Camille did not come.

At eight o'clock, unable to stand it any longer, he went to the Faubourg Saint-Honoré and asked for news. He was told that

Baronne de Luzac was a little better, and that Mademoiselle had gone out immediately after dinner. Disorientated, not knowing what to think, he went home in the hope of finding a letter, but Camille had not written.

That silence was inexplicable, and the young man tortured his imagination in a thousand ways. Without her, henceforth, life was impossible; never had he felt that so forcefully. And yet, if their lips were united, nothing united their thoughts. When he sought to associate himself with the action of her mind, he encountered an insurmountable barrier. They were not brought together either by the same will or the same goal. In the violent paroxysms of his passion, however, he had not dissected his sensations, analyzed his pleasures or calculated his heartbeats as a miser examines and weighs his gold coins. The experience of evil had not yet cast its lugubrious light over defunct events. He was so young that memory scarcely existed for him. More learned, he would have understood that Camille was passionate and not affectionate. She played her role, to begin with, as a consummate actress; then, suddenly, her tone, a glance or a word betrayed her ennui.

Julien's amour was painted entirely in his eyes, but she sustained their radiance without the clarity of her own altering, for they seemed, like feline eyes, to be lined with a sheet of metal. Since he possessed her in his home, heart to heart, every day, he believed that he was happy. Society and its cold politeness no longer separated them; he told her all the follies of his imagination. Sometimes, he even thought that he was her husband, and admired her, occupied with minimal details. He loved to see her take off her feathered hat and her long cloak lined with ermine. He offered her delicacies and Spanish wine. He placed himself beside her in front of the fire blazing in the hearth, drank from her glass, choosing the place where she had placed her lips. And when he sensed, so close to him, that adorable young woman, whose beauty would become famous, that Camille, so proud, which rendered her the object of all attention, all coquetry, his voluptuous felicity became almost painful, so much did he dread seeing it end.

They gave one another a thousand caresses, a thousand kisses, and, in order to prolong his ecstasy, he would gladly have traded two years of his life for each of the hours that she was prepared to grant him.

He had broken with his studious habits of old. He went into society frequently in order to encounter his mistress there, and he tried, in order to dazzle her, to surpass in appearance the fops and the heroes of coteries who paraded themselves before her. Happiness had given him self-confidence; he crushed his rivals, passing for a young man full of seductions, prestigious and ir-resistible. Psychologists said, on seeing him: "A fellow as skillful as that will have his way made by women; it's the surest way nowadays." Charitably, they praised his artfulness at the expense of his honesty.

He was, however, amorously stupid in the presence of Camille. Alone with her, he was no longer able to do anything but stammer his tenderness. Sometimes, he was as sadly cheerful as a courtesan who fears displeasing. He tried to render himself indispensable to her life, to her joy and to her vanity. He seemed a plaything, a slave, incessantly at her orders, and she truly was the male in the couple.

He had employed all his time, effort and science of obser-vation in penetrating further forward into the impenetrable character of his mistress. Thus far, hope and pride in his success had influenced his opinion; he saw in her, by turns, the most sentimental or the most cheerful of his entourage.

That evening, after having waited for her all day, he knew true despair. The most insensate projects passed through his mind. He did not sleep, and spent the night turning back and forth in his sheets.

At nine o'clock in the morning, Miss Ketty, who was now the confidante of their meetings, came to tell him that he ought no longer to count on Camille's regular visits, the Baronne de Luzac having been suffering a great deal since the previous day.

Julien did not reply, but he remembered that the young woman had spent the previous evening out of the house; her grandmother was therefore not as ill as she wanted him to believe. Many little details returned to his memory, and for the first time, a sentiment of jealousy pierced his being. Sinister gleams illuminated events that had remained obscure until then.

Camille was justifying all his dreads: she was insensible and cruel. He had not yet surprised tears in her eyes . . . at the theater, a tender scene found her cold and ironic . . . she reserved all her finesse for herself and did not divine either the sadness or the happiness of others. One evening, she had humiliated him in front of Nina by one of those gestures, one of those glances that no words can depict . . .

A thousand small forgotten events presented themselves to his memory, illuminated with a singular clarity.

He often accompanied Camille to the Opéra with indifferent individuals. There, close to her, entirely given to his amour, he contemplated her with bewilderment, drawing from his soul the double pleasure of loving and finding the movements of his passion rendered well by the inspiration of the musician. His ardor was in the air, on the stage; it triumphed everywhere—except in his mistress.

As on the first evening, when he had been so happy, he expected Camille's hand to fall upon his. But she remained motionless, and he was the one who took, tremulously, the indifferent little hand, studying the young woman's features and eyes, soliciting a fusion of their sentiments, one of the sudden harmonies that, awakened by the notes, make beings come together in unison. Alas, the hand remained mute and the bright eyes said nothing.

When the fire of amour proclaimed by all Julien's features struck her too forcefully, she darted him a constrained and fatigued smile. The divine pages of Masters did not seem to move her, no sentiment translated the poetry of her life. She appeared there as a spectacle within the spectacle, and her vague eyes wandered tiredly from box to box.

He told himself—unjustly, in fact—that she was the victim of fashion, that her dress, her flowers and her carriage were everything to her, and that, apart from her royalty, nothing else existed. He pleased himself now attacking his idol, in denying her, and insulting her. Reflection suddenly tore the veils from his tenderness. Camille was nothing but a falsehood; nothing good had ever germinated in her heart; her soft words were not the expression of kindness; her pretentious exaggeration in certain matters was only snobbery. He saw her clearly now; he had stripped her hidden personality of the thin bark that was sufficient for society, and he was no longer duped by her grimaces!

When a simpleton complimented her and praised her, she smiled, and he was ashamed for her . . . Oh, what a great fool he was, who had hoped to melt her ice under the wings of a poetic amour! He had loved her as a man, a lover, an artist, when it would doubtless have been necessary to disdain her in order to please her. A pretentious fop, an egotist or a vile calculator would have triumphed in that more easily. Vain, artificial and hypocritical, she would certainly have understood the language of vanity, intrigue and flattery, would have allowed herself to be wrapped by the gilded nets of deception.

No, there was still something else: incomprehensible, Camille lived far from humanity, in a sphere of her own, an inferno or a paradise.

In sum, that mysterious female, clad in soft silks and furs, brought all human sentiments into play in his heart: pride, tenderness, indignation, anguish and despair.

After Miss Ketty's visit, he nearly went mad in the intensity of his distress. Any thought that was not of Mademoiselle de Luzac became odious and chimerical to him. Five times, in the days that followed, he presented himself at the house in the Faubourg Saint-Honoré; always he was told that Camille had gone out and that the Baronne was no longer receiving.

Julien's condition was indescribable. He cursed Camille with all the force of his being, and he had never cherished her so much . . .

VII

After a week of struggles and tears, at the moment when the young man was thinking seriously about suicide, his door suddenly opened and Camille came in with the lovely undulating stride that he knew so well.

He wanted to be dignified, but she threw her arms around his neck with the tender words of contrition that leave no room for reproach, reflection or second thoughts.

She told him that she was foolish, that she had tried to forget him, because their amour was culpable, that she had not been able to succeed in it, and that she had come back more loving than ever. Tears, promises and confessions were punctuated with kisses and smiles like sunbeams in a downpour.

For an hour she played that adorable comedy of amorous repentance. For an hour she was a great actress, she was a she-cat, she was a woman. Then, when she saw her lover's last rancor dissolve under her caresses and her regrets, the prayers that disarmed him were succeeded by the laughter that made him forget.

"Why did you lie?" he asked, with a residue of mistrust.

"I didn't lie."

"Oh, how can you say that? Miss Ketty claimed that you were caring for your grandmother, but you weren't at home."

"Yes I was, but I wasn't receiving."

"You didn't go out during that week?"

"Since I tell you . . ."

"You could have come to see me, if only for a minute . . ."

"Come on, Julien, it's necessary not to be too demanding. You can see everything that I've already sacrificed to you. What other young woman would have done as much?"

Calmed down, he returned to his idea, tenderly insistent. "Why don't you want to be my wife, my darling? We'd be so happy!"

"I've already told you that I don't want to marry."

"However . . . an accident might happen . . . if . . ."

"What?"

"If you perceived that . . ."

"Oh—yes, I understand."

"Well?"

But she had the mysterious smile that troubled him so much.

"Don't worry, my Julien. That won't happen. Don't think about such things . . ."

She made fun of herself and of them, their foolishness—his, above all—when they had everything in order to be content, young and free with the future before them. What folly it had been to create torments and chagrins, to have made their amour weep! How had that come about? What had impelled her? For it was all her fault. She was wicked, a tease, a bad girl not to have written polite little letters that would have soothed his annoyance, made his waiting easier. He was too good, too weak; he must have become angry, not seeing her . . .

And the flow never dried up of the charming words of a woman pretending to be a little girl, asking to be scolded for not being good.

Their beautiful romance recommenced.

Camille's entire occupation during the days that followed was consoling Julien.

She really was fonder of him since she had made two parts of her personality and was prostituting herself to another man every day. For some time, she even had the illusion of a veritable amour. She no longer seemed to have any regard or any thought for anyone but him. They shut themselves away in their room, made a thousand plans, never wearied of repeating their mutual tenderness.

Julien had created a charming interior. He had bought a delicate Chinese silk from a second-hand dealer, slightly passé, with a design of golden butterflies and mauve flowers, to cover the walls of his bachelor apartment. Tables trimmed with lace bore an entire set of brushes and blonde tortoiseshell boxes for Camille's toilette, and the flowers that she loved blossomed around her.

He only lived in memory and expectation, heaping her when she was there with caresses, kisses and sensualities. Every day, all their felicity returned in that fashion in an instant and possessed them, while, side by side, bathed in moist warmth, they smiled at one another before gazing at one another, slowly reborn to themselves while taking care not to lose the last wing-beat of ecstasy as it flew away.

It was such a sweet embrace! Half-dressed, still quivering, hair undone, she nibbled the cakes that he had prepared. Their chairs soon came together; they took one another by the waist and she held some perfumed fruit between her lips. Her moist mouth fled Julien, attacked him and fled him again. Finally, near to being taken, she pressed her cheek to his and slowly, shared her booty in a kiss.

Those insatiable delights filled the whole tiny apartment. Their tiny paradise was scarcely vast enough for their amour, and the world scarcely far enough away for their happiness. There was nothing around them that was not themselves, no gaze between their gazes, and no voice between their voices.

Outside, bad weather, days without light in which the sun seems drowned in a muddy pool, glacial rain and wind whipping the windows left them indifferent.

He no longer went out, spending his days waiting, for in his home everything once again spoke to him of happiness. There was nothing that was not the confidant or the relic of an hour of intoxication. In the evening, when she had gone, his hearth lulled him like a melodious voice. The fire filled the room with a soft warmth; the lamp shed a white light, brightening a corner of the table, an armchair, or a patch of carpet. The rest was in warm shadow, cheered up here and there by a golden snag on a picture frame, a glimmer of silk or a gleam of copper. In the semi-darkness, his feet stretched out on the fire-irons, he reviewed his memories of the afternoon deliciously.

She had forbidden him to accompany her to the theater, as he once had, and he had yielded, without seeking to know what her caprice concealed, he had so much new confidence in her.

What more could he have wanted? Every day he undressed her, pin by pin, lingering over the soft whiteness of her lace, the silk stockings held in the palm of his hand, and when, of all her attire, scarcely anything was left but the woman, Camille extended her arms to him, abandoned herself, and he picked her up and carried her to the bed like a child.

When she was weary of his caresses, he gazed at her, remaining in contemplation: in the lamplight, her fine, cloudy hair had the radiance of moonlit dust; her visage was languid on the whiteness of the pillow, and all that was visible there were the long dark eyelids lowered over the ecstasy of a dream.

And in that sweetness and that ticklishness, in that wellbeing, he let time go by like a wave between open hands, not wanting anything more. The hours pushed the hours, memory succeeded hope, and in the moment of her dear presence, everything else was abolished. There was no bitterness, no dread, no worry, no doubt, no menace . . . he believed in his mistress as he believed in God.

And when she emerged from those embraces, Camille went to meet Philippe.

VIII

"Come on, Camille, let's go! We're only waiting for you!"

"Philippe didn't want to let me come."

"Why, if you please?"

"For some time he's been insupportable. I've had to promise him to get him an invitation to our supper."

"But we don't want men! We only admit Richard . . . on special occasions."

"Just for once?"

"No, no—no men!" cried twenty women grouped around a table already served. "We don't want any more of them . . . there are too many of them already. Mercy for this evening, at least!"

"So be it," said Camille, calmly. "You can throw the Comte out. If you knew how little it matters to me!"

"Take Richard's place—our dear Richard, the liberator of our suffering sex."

Adorable were the adornments, but more adorable still were those wearing them. Their passionate eyes had disquieting gleams, their ring-laden hands were agitating in feverish impatience. Marguerite d'Ambre proudly displayed the magnificence of her young bosom. Delphine de Belvau had combined the insidious transparency of silk muslin with the pale tones of her flesh, and seemed naked under the light corsage that a simple thread of stones retained at her shoulders. Rose Mignot, a white and chaste figure descended from the clouds of Ossian, resembled a wax Madonna. She was enlaced with Claire Delys, whose boyish beauty formed a striking contrast with hers.

There were flowery springs there, splendid and savorous summers, and lush autumns; dazzling breasts prominent on the silky edges of corsages, and, under jewels, snowy shoulders, and soft and powerful arms made for gripping and caressing. There were frail dolls there, invented and created by the Devil himself for the damnation of big, bearded children. One had a dreamy gaze of celestial blue, veiled by heavy, modest eyelids; another had long, thin eyes, slightly curled up toward the temples, like those of the Chinese race. Their green enamel gaze slid between the black lashes that veiled the mystery of thought. Bright hair with silvery silky reflections brushed dark hair with blue reflections of charcoal. The voices had crystal vibrations, and unexpected, mordant ideas of a particular turn, mischievous and droll, retained a destructive charm. The cold and corrupting seduction, and the morbid complication of all those neuroses, troubled passions and violent agitations reciprocally.

There were extravagant socialites of true society there, whose husbands went everywhere, affable and great lords who appeared to see nothing. Were they blind, indifferent or complaisant? All opinions had free rein on that matter; some went as far as insinuating that they profited from the secret vices of their wives and did not suffer therefrom, having very strange tastes themselves.

Motionless, pale beneath her heavy black hair, staring straight ahead, Nina waited . . . In her immobile face, in the entirety of her disquieting being, there was something new, like the threat of storms that one divines in burning skies.

They were almost all Parisiennes, those women vain in regard to their attire and their bodies, supple and hard sirens, heartless and devoid of weakness, who knew how to create the treasures of voluptuousness and counterfeit the accents of passion. Laughing, they crowded around the table like bees around a hive. Soon, a few cries burst forth; the noise was augmented, the voices became shrill . . .

One of the most charming ideas of that supper had been to have it served by women, in order that it could not be said that anything disturbed the harmony of a feast at which women alone were the queens. The table setting was a masterpiece of taste, delicacy and fortunate expertise. It is ordinarily desire and the hope of amusement that supper produces; here it was recognition, disdain, irony and cruelty, but in fine clothing, concealed beneath smiles and witty quips. They had accumulated all the opulence of their lives there; they brought, for themselves alone, all that they had of beauty, intelligence, resources and power. Floating everywhere was the warm scent of fabrics, removed furs and flesh; the gleam of chandeliers gripped, at their feet, the silvered buckets in which pale Aï wine was chilling; orchids, lilacs and anemones covered the lace tablecloth entirely and fell on to the knees of the guests in perfumed clusters.

As bold as pages, they exhibited an incomparable verve and brio, for they felt superior, above society and prejudice. The gladness of that discovery, the mental influences that are so decisive over nervous beings, the glare of the lights, the enervating odor of flowers that were swooning in the overheated atmosphere, the spur of vehement wines, and the thought of their complicity in the petty crime of such a gathering, all acted at the same time, plucking the frail harp of those delicate organisms and making it vibrate excessively.

The rockets of bursts of laughter mingled with harmonious sallies struck at random on the piano by light fingers. Soon there were confessions and vague kisses . . . They had eaten the turtle soup, the grouse, the crayfish . . .

Camille stood up, her eyes half-closed, a glass of champagne in her slender hand. That evening, she was wearing a very pale silvery velvet skirt, and her hair hung down below her waist in two superb wavy tresses.

"Dear friends," she said, in a vibrant voice, "dear models of all the reprehensible virtues, always rise to the height of yourselves: be charming, irresistible and heartless. Distill desire and desperation, enfever mere mortals to the point of frenzy, and, fearing nothing, remain pitiless!"

The baskets of fruits had been ravaged. Coffee was now fuming in transparent cups. Nina was enveloped by swirls of white smoke, like a goddess in a cloud. Voices swelled, the tumult increased. There were no longer any distinct words now. The most cunning were whispering their secrets to the curious, who were not listening; the melancholy were smiling like dancers who have just bowed to the audience; intimate friends were insulting one another; enemies were hugging one another convulsively.

Nina and Camille had just placed between them a tall, well-proportioned girl who seized attention by virtue of vigorous contrasts. Her black hair, broadly curled, fell over her shoulders. She had long, curved eyelashes and a sensual red mouth. Her breasts and arms were well developed like those of the beautiful young women of the Carrachis; nevertheless, she seemed extremely supple and her vigor implied an almost feline agility. She was not laughing, scarcely amused by Nina's advances, and, like a prophetess agitated by the Evil Spirit, awoke a perverse curiosity. All expressions passed like glimmers over her mobile features; she must have delighted the base, excited the desires of intellectuals and skeptics, reawakened the indifferent, the incapable and the disdainful.

"Do you think I'm pretty?" Camille asked.

"No, it's me she prefers!" exclaimed Nina.

"Come on, darling, answer."

"Answer," Nina repeated, nudging the girl's arm.

And the latter, playing with Camille's necklace, said: "Oh, how I'd love to have one like it."

It was late—which is to say, early. Against the ceiling, and at a certain place in the hermetically sealed curtains, a drop of opal was seen to appear and round out, like a growing eye: the eye of the daylight, which had the indiscretion to peep at what they were doing in that diabolical salon.

A certain languor was beginning to weigh down the female knights of that Round Table, like flowers leaning over on their stems. They had emptied a large number of glasses of champagne to the glory of their liberation, and they were rolling in the bosom of the delectable limbo in which the lights of intelligence are gradually extinguished. Some, arrived at the threshold of drunkenness, were still occupied in seizing a thought that offered evidence of their own existence; others, more expansive, were holding forth in mocking speech about the absent sex. Intrepid oratrices were talking about the rights of woman and the defects of man. A few pearly roulades ended in frenetic bursts of laughter. Silence and tumult were bizarrely coupled. Drunkenness, amour and forgetfulness of the world were in hearts and on visages. Here and there, groups of enlaced figures seemed to be posing for some masterpiece of bronze or marble.

Camille hugged the tall brunette whom she had conquered, rolling her head in the loose curls of her hair. Although the two lovers still preserved a kind of deceptive lucidity in their ideas and sensations, a last imperfect simulacrum of life, it was impossible for them to recognize what there was of the real in the strange fantasies, or of the possible in the supernatural sensualities, that were being accomplished before their weary eyes. The stifling heaven of their dreams, the ardent phantasmagoria of their visions and ever unslaked desires, assailed them so vividly then that they mistook the play of those embraces for the caprices of a nightmare in which movement is soundless and cries are lost for the ears.

Rose Mignot, next to Claire Delys, whose dress she was ripping, was reciting verses to her. Delphine de Belvau, intoxicated by morphine, was asleep on the knees of Marguerite d'Ambre, who was cradling her like an infant, gently refreshing her with the flapping of her fan of feathers.

The candles were beginning to go out, causing their crystal holders to explode. The flowers were crushed on the tablecloth. Nina suddenly pushed Claire away and, throwing herself on Rose Mignot, tore away the light corsage of lace that was only held at the shoulder by a string of pearls.

"What are you doing?" asked Claire, astonished.

"Let it go, it's a game."

Rose's skirts, corset and all her fleecy undergarments fell under the table. When she was naked, Nina lifted her up in her powerful arms and slid her over the tablecloth, knocking over the bottles and glasses.

Shaken by nervous laughter, Rose did not defend herself. She was surrounded by flowers, lifted up on cushions.

"Now," said Nina, "let's drink to woman, let's drink to ourselves, let's drink to the abolition of the slavery that has kept us curbed for so long in shameful submission! Let's drink to the glory of our commencing reign!"

And they all took communion from the same cup . . .

IX

"Don't disturb yourselves," said a grave voice. "It's me."

"What, it's you!"

"We've forbidden the door!"

"It's an indignity!"

"Your soubrettes are lying on the tiles. As there was no way of doing otherwise, I employed violence."

"It's daylight, we're going to go to bed."

With one bound, Rose had stood up, and Claire Delys had enveloped her in her fur coat.

Philippe von Talberg examined them with an ironic expression.

In spite of her composure, Camille had been unable to help going red with anger. "Why have you come?" she demanded. "I thought it was a joke! Your place, my dear, isn't here!"

"My place is everywhere that you are."

"Get away! I'm free. I don't have to account for my actions to anyone."

"Do you think so?"

"I believe it so firmly that I order you to retire."

"Oh," said Nina, "he's scarcely inconveniencing us. What more can he see than he's already seen?"

"That's true—what more could I see?"

And, still calm, Philippe poured himself a glass of Russian eau-de-vie and spread caviar on a slice of bread, while gazing at the golden thread of his dessert knife.

"Then again," he continued, "I'm an enemy of the household, for I know your secret."

"Our secret?" they asked, fearfully.

"Of course! The visits to Dr. Richard, the mysterious little operation followed by a fairly long convalescence, the escapades, timid at first, until they become customary, the rendezvous in Madame Saurel's ground floor, the habitual procession of . . .

acquaintances—in sum, the permanent fête, veiled under the appearances of the most perfect correctness."

As they looked at him in consternation, he went on: "Have no fear; I'm too much a gentleman ever to betray you; however, I'd be excusable, since none of you has taken me as a confidant. Think of the success that such revelations would obtain! The newspapers are full of scandals that aren't worth as much as that one! Oh, don't protest, there are young girls and minors among you, and that's serious. What are they doing here, those dear children? They ought to be fast asleep, tucked in by maternal hands, with a glass of orange-blossom on their table! You're going to go home now, my beauties, with the pretext of an innocent ball. Out there in the antechamber there are three complicit governesses asleep on benches. Truly, their remorse will keep them warm! Look at yourselves! You're livid, unrecognizable. And what a lugubrious return journey! The rain is falling, mingled with snow: a rain as glacial as your hearts, a rain of Lent and funerals!"

All the pretty faces had paled further, the eyes misted by a vague expression of distress. No, this was not a playful man, this chance guest. His features and his bearing certainly did not lack the conventional distinction that makes people tolerable, his speech was not tedious, but no sympathy emanated from his person, which remained disquieting even in contentment.

Camille hated him more and more, and yet he weighed upon her by virtue of a sort of occult magnetism that she could not avoid. He captivated her attention by means of a special bizarrerie. His conversation, without being beyond the pale in the intrinsic value of his ideas, maintained one alert by means of a vague implication, which his secret preoccupations seemed to slide into it involuntarily. Fundamentally, she did not know whether he wished her good or evil, so much did his affection sometimes resemble intimacy. He was undoubtedly scornful of her, but that scorn, at the same time, must be a stimulant to his blasé imagination.

"Yes," he went on, after a momentary pause. "I won't say anything. You have nothing to fear from me."

"For the moment?" Camille interrogated, anxiously.

"It's certain that I love you too much to resolve myself to ruin you, but that if ever you attempted to escape me . . ."

She tried to laugh. "You want to frighten me, I suppose? A gallant man never betrays a woman, especially when that woman had confided herself to him. In any case, I won't have to leave you, my friend. You'll weary of me as all men become weary after the possession. I only have to give you the time . . ."

"You're one of those of whom one does not weary."

"Thank you for that gallantry. It's a trifle banal, but when one spends the night being witty, it's necessary not to be too difficult when day dawns."

"Are we leaving?"

"Yes."

"You'll permit me to take you home?"

"It's necessary."

Nina put her long velvet, ermine-lined cloak over her shoulders, and, after having kissed her, whispered in her ear: "Your Philippe will do you a bad turn . . . beware!"

The young woman shrugged her shoulders with ennui. "Bah! When the life is no longer possible, I'll find a means of getting out of it. Nothing is worth the trouble of an effort, even in pleasure."

And, indicating her companions whose wan faces were contracted with fatigue and enervation, she added: "Truly, don't you find our little fêtes very droll?"

X

When they were in the carriage, Philippe wanted to take her lips, but she shoved him away almost harshly.

"Oh, no! I'm weary of kisses and caresses. I'm drowsy . . . horribly drowsy. I'd like to sleep for an eternity."

And as he contemplated her with the hard stare she knew so well, she said: "Yes, I can't be disciplined. You won't change me; I have my instincts, my vanities, my revolts. I'm devoid of respect and devoid of pity; I make a game of everything and I don't believe in anything."

"In fact," he said, "you're the ultimate product of our morbid civilization. You resemble people who jib under domination and no longer want to be saved, even by God."

"You still believe in something, then?"

"Although I'm lacking all dogmatic religion, I've conserved an intellectual religion for which I struggle and suffer: the will. I go forth, I march, already old, my temples gray, bilious and paled by age, but I hold firm and I persevere."

"Why that great effort of will? You're rich, and you only have to let yourself live. Will is only useful to the disinherited . . . and even then, most of the time, it only serves to prolong their misery. A knife, a gas oven or a rope would serve them better."

"You're mistaken. It's precisely my fortune that has doomed me. Labor, and labor alone, exists and sustains. By means of labor, a man escapes the flesh and detaches himself from it; he no longer feels hunger or cold; his vision no longer sees, except within himself; his ear, filled with the music of his ideas, no longer hears the vain noises of existence; time falls silent and, no longer having any indicative needle, is only measured by dawns and dusks. All the petty external worries, disappointments and dreads cease to affect him. He savors the sublime lethargy of the human machine annihilated in the effort of the brain, the riddance and the escape from the body that is given to the mind that has fled from thought into the immaterial world of abstractions. Oh, if I could possess that blissful fever, I'd be saved. For me, the weeks would pass like days; I'd have entire months devoid of ennui, without the spleen that seizes, after a long repose, the mind habituated to exercise and wrestling with itself; months in which the egotism of intelligence would deliver me from all caprice and all sentiment."

"Sentiment?" Camille queried. "What has sentiment to do with this? Is it for the sake of amour that you've taken me, then?"

"Certainly."

"And yet you're scornful of me."

"My amour, unfortunately, supports that humiliating juxtaposition very well. I don't seek to magnify it; I offer it for what it is. Now, my dear Camille, permit me to tell you that you're calumniating yourself. You're perverted, but not perverse. Beneath your poses, beneath the bragging of your mask, you still have the blushes, naïveties and timidities of a little girl. Behind the false shame of illusions, of devotions, of all social pieties, behind your affectations of skepticism and your ferocious paradoxes, there's a disgust for your failed existence, a fear of the future and a regret for a host of puerile little things, which swells your heart. Be careful, there are still illusions that will doom you . . . and, who knows, perhaps even amour."

"Amour?" she said, in a mocking voice. "I see, my friend, that you don't know me at all, in spite of your science of the feminine soul. I've never loved, and I never will."

A flash passed through Philippe's eyes, a nervous contraction twisted his lips, but he made no reply.

The carriage stopped outside Mademoiselle de Luzac's house.

"Adieu," she said.

He held her back by her cloak. "No, not yet. Come home with me."

"You can't think so? I'm exhausted by fatigue."

"What does it matter?"

"I'd be in an execrable humor."

"Too bad."

"After what happened last night?"

"So much the better!"

"You horrify me."

"That's already something."

"I detest you."

"That will make it even more piquant."

Already he had seized her, holding her down on the cushions, and, putting his head out of the window, he shouted to the coachman: "Home!"

XI

Baronne de Luzac was improving, but Camille, coming home with Nina from one of her mad nocturnal escapades, caught a pleurisy that nearly carried her off.

Spring had been uncertain, rainy, tormented by sudden variations and abrupt winds. The young woman, who did not deign to look after herself, retained a bad cough that continued to exhaust her. There were insistent and convulsive fits of coughing that stopped momentarily and then resumed more furiously, coughing fits whose silences left in the ear an anxious expectation of what might be about to recur, and which always did recur at regular intervals.

The physician, however, could not find any affliction of the organs essential to life. The lungs were certainly a little ulcerated, but youth accomplished miracles without the aid of science. The miracle of that life of disorder and surprise was that it did not burst forth. Camille did not allow any of it to emerge; she did not let anything rise to her lips, nor did anything show in her physiognomy. Baronne de Luzac, always confined to bed now, was scarcely occupied with anything but her own torments, but the friends and acquaintances who succeeded one another in the invalid's bedroom, might have been able to see with more clairvoyance.

After the pleasures, after the most lunatic intoxications, the young woman retained, even in sleep, the incredible strength to contain everything and suppress everything. Of her real nature, no word or phrase ever escaped that might ignite a glimmer of enlightenment. Disappointment, disdain, scorn and rancor all remained within her, silent and stifled. The rare weaknesses that gripped her, in which she seemed to be struggling, always ended up speechlessly in a greater melancholy. Even malady, with its enfeeblements and enervations, did not get anything out of her.

Crises of nerves extracted cries from her, but nothing except cries.

She thus led two existences; she was like two women, and by dint of skill, energy and diplomacy, with an ever-present composure, she succeeded in separating those two existences and living them both without mixing them up. Close to her grandmother she was the proud and noble heiress that no one suspected; she emerged from her orgies without bringing away a taste for them, and showed, when she quit her lovers, an almost puritan reserve. There was neither a word nor a glance that awoke suspicion of her clandestine life. Nothing in her betrayed her nights. When she set foot in the house in the Faubourg Saint-Honoré, in the company of Baronne de Luzac, she adopted the speech, the attitude and the chaste modesty that removed a woman even from the thought of a man's approaches. She was as severe on the faults and shame of others as a person beyond reproach.

However, all that deceptive appearance on the young woman's part was not hypocrisy, but the desire not to stain her name, not to be diminished in the eyes of the world. She had wanted to be free, but her liberty was not as great as before, since it was necessary to lie incessantly. Lie! She could no longer do anything else! She experienced the impossibility of extracting herself from that horrible duty. Sometimes, reflecting on herself, she was frightened by what she had done. Without amour, she had given herself to the least worthy for the pleasure of a new sensation, a discovery, or a surprise. Then, still warm from those sad kisses, she had held out her lips to Julien's lips.

He loved her, with joy, with ardor and with confidence. Merely in seeing her, he had the emotion of the entire being that makes the heart beat faster. His body, his mouth, the affection and caress of his gestures, went involuntarily toward her. No friction discouraged him, neither mockery nor insults, nor the corruption of the pleasures that he had desired. She could do with him whatever she wished, calumniate him, and abuse him; he remained hers, under the heel of her ankle boot.

To love that woman was necessary to him; he warmed himself upon her, he lived for her, he respired her. He had the temperament of beasts that ill-treatment attaches. And when she fell ill, he spent his days at her door, begging for news of her. He almost died of anxiety and despair.

It was Philippe who reassured him, with a scornful pity. What did that pure tenderness, so misunderstood and so scantly repaid, matter to him? If necessary, he would even have encouraged it, in order to preserve himself from less worthy treasons.

Julien did not suspect the Comte or anyone else. His idol was always upright and imposing on the pedestal of his faith.

In his disgust for life, Philippe took pleasure in seeing that child, in confessing him, in extracting from him the avowal of his tenderness. Julien talked about Camille as an unknown beauty from whom he had only had smiles, but beneath the reserve of his words, an infinite amour was transparent. He was too unhappy and, above all, too agitated, to divine his interlocutor's sentiments; a passion as complicated as the Comte's would have been incomprehensible to him, even if he had received the confession of it. His words were so little under the direction of his mind that he delivered himself entirely, while thinking that he was keeping the most absolute discretion. The danger that Camille was in and the idea that he might lose her robbed him of all faculty of reasoning.

One day, as Philippe was coming out of the house, Julien, who was on the lookout for him, ran toward him.

"She's getting better, isn't she?"

"Yes, it's only a matter of time now."

"What does the doctor say?"

"Oh, very little. Assiduous care will be necessary, and also, doubtless, a change of air. But why don't you go up to see the ladies?"

"I'm not sufficiently in their intimacy, and I sense that my presence is out of place."

"Bah! Would you be poorly received?"

"No, but coldly. Messieurs Chazel, Perdonnet and Gréville don't even seem to perceive my presence."

"Pure jealousy! They're old and ugly, you're young and handsome—don't seek elsewhere for the reason for their hostility."

"What do I care? I'd like to be in their place, even at the price of my youth and all the advantages you attribute to me."

"Ah! You're in love!"

Julien blushed to his ears. "In love? No, you're mistaken . . . but I don't understand Mademoiselle de Luzac's character, and I'd like to be informed. Why has she left it so long without giving me her news? Doesn't she know that I'm too close a friend not to be interested in the events of her life?"

Philippe laughed silently—which disconcerted the young man.

"Have no fear," he said. "Go up; she'll inform you."

XII

Julien was already in Camille's presence, in the small, brightly lit drawing room where she received visitors since falling ill.

He was about to fall at her feet, but she looked at him in a fashion so glacial that he remained motionless and silent.

"Why are you here?" she asked, harshly.

"To see you . . . to see you, Camille . . . I don't know what to think . . . you no longer write to me."

"Shh! Someone might hear you . . . Why would I have written to you?" she added, in an indifferent tone. "I didn't have any reason to write to you."

"But . . ."

"No reason . . . I no longer love you."

At that terrible blow, dazed by amour and desolation, Julien attempted to soften his friend.

Nothing was more absurd. Can one justify displeasure?

He remained there, begging, but Camille was no longer listening, entirely given over to a new thought, which darkened her gaze and contracted her lips.

That day, she was almost annihilated by the frightful idea of having given rights over her to men, of whom she was so profoundly scornful.

In bold and prideful characters, there is only one step from anger against oneself to rage against others. Enervated by her malady, exasperated by a scene she had just had with Philippe, she heaped Julien with marks of the greatest disdain. She had infinite wit, and that wit triumphed in the art of torturing self-esteem and inflicting the cruelest wounds upon it.

Far from thinking of defending himself, at that moment, the young man became scornful of himself. In hearing himself treated with so much irony, it seemed to him that Camille was right, that he had never been worthy of the affection that he thought he had inspired in her.

"Crush me," he said, finally. "I don't, in fact, merit the happiness you've given me. I only ask one mercy of you: not to deprive me of your presence."

"I'm leaving, though."

"Leaving?"

"Yes. My cure is far from being complete; the doctors have prescribed the air of the Midi, the most absolute rest . . ."

"I'll follow you wherever you go; it will be sufficient for me to see you."

"I forbid you to follow me. What would be the point, since I no longer love you? Have I ever loved you, in fact? I wanted to know everything about life. Today, I'm weary, disillusioned, discouraged, and infinitely sad. I haven't found what I was looking for. Nothing remains to me but the shame of my curiosities and weaknesses."

He could no longer find the strength to respond, so great was his distress.

The young woman spoke for a long time in the same tone of sarcasm and bitterness. After such a humiliating scene, in a person less sincerely infatuated than Julien was, amour would have become impossible.

Without straying for a single instant from what she owed to herself, Mademoiselle de Luzac addressed wounding things to him, so well calculated that they could appear veritable even when one recalled them coolly. He had, however, in order to sustain his pride, the memory of what had happened between them, not so very long ago. *No man*, he said to himself, naïvely, *can boast of a similar happiness*. And that idea gave him the courage to support all the affronts. His wisdom did not go any further; he had no understanding at all of the character of the singular person who was disposing of his destiny so casually.

He tried again to move closer to Camille and take her hand.

"No," she said, "it's futile. Go away, leave me alone. Your presence is painful to me. It's over."

He tottered, and went away like a drunken man. It seemed to him that the ground was disappearing beneath his feet, and that objects were spinning around him.

When she could no longer hear him, she got up, picked up a mirror from the table and looked at herself. After a few minutes of contemplation she closed her eyes with lassitude. *To be beautiful? To live? To be loved? Why?* she thought. *I no longer desire anything. It seems to me that I'm so old now!*

Disgust rose to her lips. She took pleasure in humiliating herself, in comparing herself to certain women whom she had seen fall under shame, beneath nature itself; she evoked an entire future of ignominy. Would she not be similar to those miserable creatures who pick up amour at hazard, use it up in a night and no longer need to give themselves the time to desire in their furious and sudden caprice? Avid for the first to come along, she would scarcely look at them and would not be able to recognize them. For those women, beauty and youth no longer existed; in all men, their gaze no longer saw anything but man, the ardent and brutal male.

Often, by night, with Nina, she had followed those errant forms that beat the streets, with the suspect and furtive gait of beasts, searching the shadows in the exasperation of a sharp hunger. She had seen them sniffing around, going toward impure ambushes in a waste ground, opportunities of darkness and solitude, hands that reached out, feverish and menacing. She had laughed then at all those unfortunates; now, it seemed to her that she was one of them, that her decadence had nothing for theirs to envy.

Her past horrified her, but she could not escape it, for Nina and Philippe scarcely quit her, intensifying the wound in her soul. At every moment of the day she had to suffer their presence, and she resigned herself to it, in the dread of a possible delation. Nina, perhaps, might have kept silent, in order to preserve herself from reprisals, but Philippe, whom she knew to be vindictive and unscrupulous, would not let a fine opportunity for vengeance escape.

And it was thus, in the midst of the attentions and homages of her faithful that she dragged the agony of a wounded beast. The sensation of having spoiled her life casually, even having lost the right to lament, obsessed and overwhelmed her. She had done nothing, succeeded in nothing, and obtained nothing. Her soul was vile! No good deed had ever rejoiced it; no devotion had ever ennobled and magnified it. Her sole heroic effort to conquer a vain liberty now filled her with regret and shame.

After a fit of coughing more violent than the others, she began to weep. The tears flowed down her cheeks and fell on to her hands. She had never felt her misery and impotence so intensely.

XIII

Camille thought herself doomed and Baronne de Luzac thought herself cured. In order to celebrate those two joys, there were, as on the good days of the previous year, a few intimate friends in the small house.

Philippe, Duclerc, Perdonnet and Michel Gréville arrived first. There was mention of Tissier, who was to bring one of his relatives, Georges Darvy, the well-known sculptor, whose recent successes had been celebrated in all the newspapers. He possessed, it was said, the traditions of the Renaissance, with all the modern impetuosity and sincerity. He was, according to Perdonnet—who was not easily enthused—the exquisite revealer of human strength and suppleness.

Those appreciations had been exchanged in all salons for months; Georges was the man of the moment.

The young woman listened with a distracted ear, indifferent to the eulogies and criticisms. What did the renown and talent of that artist matter to her, whom she did not know and doubtless would not invite again?

When he appeared, she was surprised. Rather tall in stature, with a blond, fine beard trimmed without pretention, he looked her straight in the face with his large, profound and slightly hard brown eyes. He was slim, with powerful shoulders and thoroughbred hands. Everything about him respired strength and determination. His haughty reserve was imposing; he lived in a narrow circle, disdaining elegant gallantry and great fashionable salons where others would have shone. He only wanted to go into interiors where his serious and veiled qualities were sure to be appreciated, and if he had consented to allow himself to be taken to Madame de Luzac's home, it was because Tissier, his only relative in Paris, was an intimate of the household.

He sat down after paying his respects to the Baronne, immobile in her armchair, and responded in a few words to the banal phrases that Camille addressed to him. He had scarcely seemed to notice her beauty, and yet she was strangely seductive with her discolored complexion, her bright eyes and the somber contusion of her eyelids. By virtue of a strange caprice, she had wanted to dress in flowers, and her bodice was nothing but a sheath of Parma violets that a few tea-roses halted at the shoulders, leaving the arms entirely naked. The perfume of all those corollas went to her head in a dolorous intoxication; she felt herself becoming even paler, and abandoned herself to the disquieting ecstasy.

Philippe examined his mistress and the newcomer by turns. For whom was that singular costume destined? For him, the lover, for the unknown visitor, or for Nina Saurel?

The door opened, and the young woman was announced.

Mademoiselle de Luzac ran toward her and, while keeping watch on her fragile flowers, she kissed her, her lips parted in a little lustful moue. It was an exquisite, desirable kiss, given and returned ardently by both mouths.

For the first time, Philippe shivered with jealousy. She had never kissed him like that. *Oh*, he said to himself, bitterly, *these women are no longer made for us.*

Georges Darvy was examining the hangings, the trinkets, and the rare furniture.

In order to create that interior, of which she was justly proud, Camille had drawn upon the knowledge and complaisance of all the artists she knew. They had found a multiplicity of charming and original things for her, which she had arranged with an innate artistry.

"My dear," said Tissier to Georges, in order to dissipate the species of awkwardness caused by the young woman's evident distraction, "I'll show you the treasures of this drawing room. Here, first of all, is an authentic Houdon bust, a group by Clodion, and Tanagra statuettes. Look at the delicacy of detail!"

Georges took the figurines and examined them closely, with a happy smile. He stated his opinion in sure and sober terms. His voice was soft, slightly veiled; people looked at him sympathetically.

A domestic announced: "Madame la Baronne is served." And while Madame de Luzac's armchair was rolled, Camille took Perdonnet's arm, in order to go into the dining room.

At table, the sculptor did not appear to pay any more attention to her. Urged by Tissier, who wanted to see him shine, he talked about old masters, criticized new tendencies delicately, recounted his impressions of all the works of art known to him, and rendered visible the intoxication that the grace of forms caused to enter his soul by way of the eyes.

I'm beautiful too, though, Camille thought, *but he hasn't even honored me with a glance.*

"Yes," he went on, "for five years I've traveled the world, contemplating marble, wood and stone metamorphosed into masterpieces, under the inspiration of great artists."

"It's necessary not to invite that fellow often," Nina murmured in the young woman's ear. "He's as severe as a rainy day."

But Camille was listening to Georges with interest. "He doesn't displease me," she replied. And she said to him, smiling: "You love your art above everything else, then?"

"Yes, Mademoiselle, above everything else, because I find a profound and durable joy in it. I endeavor to manipulate the beautiful in its purest and highest form. I never weary of my research, which suffices to fill my existence."

He stopped talking, and the conversation languished for the rest of the dinner. Philippe was nervous, hostile to everyone; the others ate distractedly, looking covertly at times at the young woman, who, concentrated and preoccupied, appeared to be in an entirely different place than her home. Inattentive, amiable in response, and then immediately frozen, she appeared to be thinking about something that interested her more than her guests and their commonplaces. At dessert, however, there was quarreling over political questions and all the discontentments dissolved into a discordant concert. Then they got up from the table in the midst of a great agitation, which suddenly disappeared in the freshness of the drawing rooms. The conversation became general and languid again, stifled by ideas that had fluttered without daring to settle.

Tissier took Georges Darvy away early and Nina uttered a sigh of relief as soon as they had gone.

"What do you say to that, Camille?"

"Nothing," replied the young woman, wearily.

"For a bore, he's quite a bore!"

"Get away," said Philippe, bitterly, drawing nearer. "Camille has never looked at a man as she's just looked at that sculptor. He scarcely admired her dress, though, and she's the only trinket he disdained. Isn't that humiliating, on the part of a man who seems so sensible to all manifestations of beauty?"

"Oh," the young woman murmured, "perhaps Monsieur Darvy found me ugly. Why should that matter to me?"

"It assuredly matters a great deal to you, for you care about the opinion of that artist."

"You're mad. I don't care any more about his than yours. Everything is indifferent to me. You know that better than anyone."

"You're going to come to see me tomorrow, aren't you, Camille?"

Her lips contracted, paling further. "I'm ill, as you see . . ."

"I have to talk to you. I want to see you."

Others were nearby, and in order not to attract attention, she promised to yield to the solicitations of the man she could not escape.

XIV

Camille lingered every morning in the bathroom. It was a large room, well illuminated from above, hung with fine Persian cloth with green designs on a soft pink background. Against the wall, furniture in pink marble bore everything that served for a young woman's toilette: large bowls, boxes, crystal cups with silver-crowned monograms, bottles of all dimensions and the mysterious implements and instruments invented by modern coquetry to serve a thousand complicated and delicate functions. In one corner there was an immense low divan, covered and surrounded by furs; in the opposite corner there was a profound pool in pink marble, into which one descended by two steps; a bronze woman kneeling on the edge poured hot and cold water into it from silver urns.

In the warm and perfumed water, the young woman remained motionless. She had been there for twenty minutes, her arms floating, her breasts brushing the surface with their delicate flowers, when the chambermaid knocked and came in.

"Mademoiselle, it's Madame Saurel."

Nina was already on her knees next to the bather.

Camille pushed her away, with annoyance.

"Leave me alone, you're tiring me."

"Again? Always, now! Truly, I don't understand you any more."

"So much the better."

"Why this Lenten expression? At least you'll come to our supper tomorrow? I have two new recruits, two adorable blondes . . ."

"What does it matter to me?"

"You don't know what you're refusing."

"I know only too well."

"Come on, you're crazy. Do you intend to shut yourself away in some cloister and do penance?"

"Perhaps. Anything seems preferable to the life I'm leading. I'm not cut from the cloth of a free woman, you see; I wasn't worthy of entering into the corporation."

"Since you entered it anyway . . ."

"I can get out."

"Well, after Richard's little operation, you'll always be lacking something."

"No one knows, and I don't want to know from now on."

"That will be difficult."

Camille made an angry gesture. "If I told you I wanted to die, you wouldn't believe me, and yet it's the truth. Death appears pleasant to me by comparison with the existence I'm leading."

"You're young, you're rich; men implore you and adore you. Isn't that a great joy? They can be suspicious, forewarned against the lures of coquetry, but the moment of capitulation always arrives. You're no longer one of those who allow themselves to be seduced stupidly, but one of those who chooses and takes. You see in your house the mendacious supplication of weak tenderness; you're able to give birth, with a feline skill and an inexhaustible curiosity, to the secret and torturing evil in the eyes of all those you want to seduce; you fear none, and you're scornful of the most redoubtable. If you knew how it amuses me to sense all those handsome messieurs invaded, conquered and dominated by an invincible power, to become for them the unique, capricious and sovereign idol! Truly, it's a facile game in our situation. And then, don't we all have the secret instinct that grows in us quietly and develops: the instinct of war and conquest? Only we're disarmed by nature and the brutal male has the right of the strong over us. So it isn't nothing, is it, my dear, to be able finally to treat with them as equals, and to have finished with all the miseries of our sex?"

"I don't know any longer."

"Oh, the pleasure of bending wills, of clawing resistances, and causing suffering, too! I was born wicked; I love pursuing and taming human beings, as a hunter pursues beasts, simply to see them fall! My soul is violent, not avid for emotions like that of tender and sentimental women. I disdain the unique amour of one man and satisfaction in a passion. I want the admiration of them all, the tributes, the prostrations, the submissions and the prayers, before the altar of my beauty. Once regimented in my troop of adorers, they belong to me by right of conquest. I govern with savant skill, in accordance with faults, qualities, the nature of jealousies, and I remain mentally indifferent and cold. Never, you see, never have I submitted to any traction of the imagination. I'm too scornful for that."

"Yes," Camille murmured. "I've followed your advice. Julien Rival might die of it."

"Let him. It's the definitive consecration of power, my darling. As long as a man hasn't killed himself for us, our glory is lacking something."

"Julien will commit that last stupidity, if he wants to. I no longer reply to his letters . . . he's obsessed with me."

"Good."

"But one remains of whom I can't rid myself. And if you knew how much I hate that one, how my whole being revolts at the mere thought of his caresses . . ."

"Philippe? Indeed, it's necessary to submit to him to buy his silence."

"So I have to incline before a man anyway! What use is that famous liberty of which you're so proud?"

"It's always necessary to incline before someone or something; liberty is only ever relative; above all creatures there's power, money, and the unknown. One can only avoid humiliating oneself for pleasure. Unfortunately, you have the soul of a poet, and I sense some mystery under this great disillusionment that you've been telling me about for some time."

Camille blushed.

"You receive too many artists," Nina went on. "Your mind works and you sense refinement, nuances and inner delicacies in them; they awaken in you the intermittent and outmoded dream of grand amours and long liaisons."

"What do you expect? I don't yet possess the eyes of the modern skeptic, which strip the greatest of men of their prestige in a matter of hours."

"Oh, they're as ridiculous as the others, though, our great men, when they abandon their poses of representation and pompous habits, in the disorder of their instincts. They're all alike, I tell you, those conceited and empty mannequins who only desire our bodies for the satisfaction of their vices. Personally, I only want them for the satisfaction of mine, and I render them disdain for disdain, insult for insult, satiety for satiety, when I've taken everything they could offer."

Camille shook her head.

"What you say is doubtless true, but I'm bored, for debauchery doesn't fill either the heart or the mind. And what can I do now, a spinster without hope, a woman without a husband, a lover without love? What use is my life? I sense that I would have loved a child."

"A child! A child who would have deformed you, aged you prematurely! A sly, cruel, egotistical child, a true little man! A child who would have taken your time, your health and your youth, only to abandon you later, ill and disillusioned, and who would never have had any sentiment of sincere gratitude or pity! You see, I'm not only in revolt against humanity, but against nature, which has given us all the suffering, all the pain, all the punishment, without any compensation, without any real joy. Oh, the world can end—it isn't me who'll encourage the conservation of the species."

"I'm right, then; the best thing there is down here is death."

"No, not for us who no longer fear anything. There's still pleasure . . ."

"Oh, Nina, what is it that you call pleasure? I've submitted to all our feasts with yawns stifled in my throat and sleep in my eyelids. I no longer have any curiosity for the embraces of our rendezvous, which leave me as indifferent as the flirtations of our salons. I'm sated with sensuality, sickened by vice; although my nerves are still tormenting me, my desires are extinct. Deprived of all the preoccupations of simple or ardent souls, I live in a bleak lassitude, without the common faith in happiness, merely in quest of physical shocks and carnal vertigos . . ."

"Come on, shut up!"

Nina had slipped off the China silk peignoir in which Camille was enveloped and led her toward the divan. She attached her to herself by the caress, a redoubtable bond, the most powerful of all, the only one from which one cannot free oneself when firmly enlaced by it, when it squeezes a woman's flesh all the way to the blood.

Camille went to Nina's house regularly, without resistance, attracted, it seemed, as much by the amusement of those rendezvous, the charm of the discreet little ground-floor apartment that had become a hothouse of rare flowers, as by the habitude of that culpable life, scarcely dangerous because everyone had an interest in keeping quiet. It was with Madame Saurel that she had savored the keenest joys, and of all her follies, none had left such a durable impression on her.

After a moment, Nina drew away slightly in order to contemplate her lover.

"You ought," she said, "to leave me a little souvenir of you in this little peignoir that I love so much. Let's see, which painter shall we choose?"

"A painter? That's very banal."

"A bust, then?"

"Yes, a bust," the young woman murmured, blushing. "I'll give you a pretty marble of me."

"And doubtless you've already found your sculptor? I'll wager that it's Georges Darvy."

"Perhaps."

"Be careful. You looked at him too much the other evening, at dinner."

"I assure you . . ."

"He interests you infinitely."

"Why would he interest me?"

"Because, of all the men you know, he's the only one who has resisted the suggestion of your beauty. For the moment, that's only a petty irritation of your self-esteem, but if you don't apply a remedy to it, the illness will aggravate quickly."

"Get away! An artist like the others . . . a little more absorbed, that's all. And then, I don't care about it, that bust—it's only to give you pleasure."

"Perfect. I renounce it, then. Let's not talk about it any more."

XV

When Nina had gone, Camille got dressed. She put on a small gray dress—light gray, as melancholy as twilight, and uniform, with a little old lace at the collar and the wrists. The bodice was tightened at the neckline and the waist; the skirt was tight about the hips, allowing everything to be divined without betraying anything.

The chambermaid handed her a letter from Julien, as she did every day. Without taking the trouble to open it, she slipped it into her pocket.

"Go fetch Miss Ketty for me," she said, adjusting an exquisitely formed black straw hat over her blonde hair.

The Englishwoman came in, calm and resigned, her conscience silenced by the munificence of her mistress.

"We're going to see a sculptor that I scarcely know, Miss Ketty. You'll go in with me, and keep yourself slightly apart."

The Englishwoman nodded her head.

"All this, of course, must remain between us."

"Yes, Mademoiselle."

Camille's coupé rolled at the fast trot of the two horses over the pavement of the Rue de Bac. The rain hammered on the window of the carriage and made puddles on the uneven causeway. The passers-by, under their umbrellas, were making haste, their necks hidden by the turned-up collars of their overcoats.

Her eyes half-closed, her back against the padded cushions, the young woman thought, painfully, that after visiting Georges Darvy's studio it would be necessary to take a cab to meet Philippe. A sharp desire to send a telegram obsessed her, but she had promised herself not to commit any more imprudences.

In reality, she had never felt, next to her lovers, those surges of the being toward another being that are born, it is said, when bodies drawn by the emotion of the senses unite. Those surges had never come. A fatigue invaded her and an impotence to deceive herself and others any longer.

She observed with astonishment that all kisses importuned her, even though she was not insensible to them. She had never felt, like so many other women, her flesh stirred by the troubling and desired expectation of embraces. She submitted to them, accepted them, involuntarily conquered and vibrant, but was never carried away.

Was it that her body, so fine, so delicate and so refined, retained unknown modesties, the modesties of a superior and aristocratic animal, of which her skeptical mind was unaware?

The carriage stopped in the Rue de Regard, in front of an old, tall house. Camille got down with Miss Ketty. It was there, at the back of the courtyard, in a bushy garden planted with a few beautiful trees, that the studio, which was very spacious, formed a square pavilion with two elevated perrons of several steps. The sculptor came to open the door, without recognizing his visitor right away.

She named herself, and, as he stood there, surprised and disconcerted, she added: "It's the artist alone that I've come to see; my visit has a purpose . . ."

"Come in, Mademoiselle, and be indulgent. I'm only a poor laborer, whom beautiful ladies generally disdain. The dwelling is modest, as you see, and scarcely worthy of the honor you're doing it."

Rather coldly, he indicated a divan in the corner of the studio.

There were plaster groups there, busts commenced, covered with damp cloths, buckets of water and spoiled clay. The walls only displayed a few sketches of friends, of outdoor scenes, and ancient arms hung up at random. A raw daylight fell upon all of it.

After a moment of silence she revealed the objective of her visit.

"A bust? I don't really have time at the moment."

"Oh, it won't take long. I'd like . . . to give my grandmother a surprise."

"It's of you, then?"

"Yes, Monsieur."

For the first time, he seemed to examine her with some interest.

Slightly dryly, she said: "Will you refuse me?"

He hesitated; then, seemingly making a decision, he said; "No, I consent. Would you like to begin right away?"

She blushed. "It's just that . . . I only have an hour to spare."

"Very good. You won't be posing in a high-necked dress, I assume?"

He showed her into a little room, soberly furnished. Two chaise longues and a few low seats for the repose of weary limbs and undressed bodies occupied it, as well as a large mirror formed of three panels, the two lateral sides of which, articulated on hinges, permitted models to see themselves face on, in profile and from behind.

Camille took off her bodice and slid down a little of the lace of her chemise. She seemed thinner thus, with her slender, rounded torso and supple arms. The nape of her neck and her adorable shoulders were pure milk, lovely white silk of an infinite softness.

She went back in, and Georges placed her immediately, draped her in a soft cloth, and arranged her hair with a light and adroit hand. Then, swiftly, he set to work, rough-hewing the formless mass that he had prepared, giving it the contours of the face that he had before his eyes. He worked with a perfect serenity, without asking himself what implications the young woman's visit might have that could flatter his self-esteem.

Georges Darvy was satisfied with the hundred and some thousand francs that he had earned and invested wisely. Reassured for the future, he scarcely devoted himself to anything but his art, simply keeping a clientele of friends who did not pay him a great deal. When one of them seemed less neglectful, he was almost tempted to refuse such munificence. But his exquisite groups, reproduced in multiple fashions, sold well. Without intrigues, without humiliations, almost without struggles, he had achieved celebrity—which could be considered, in our day, as an exceptional case.

Nothing existed for him outside his labor and the tender worship that he had for Beauty. His was a delicate and sensitive nature, but he was imprisoned in his dream. He passed through the life, the amour and the society of men and women without seeing anything except what he was shown, and he thought that everything was good down here, created for the happiness of all. Dawns were made to cradle the awakenings of soft light, days for ripening crops, rain for fecundating the soil and breezes for bringing the soul errant perfumes.

Georges saw a perfect accord between creatures and things, because he scarcely existed except in himself, and the habit of meditation had rendered him silent. He was entirely devoted, body and soul, to the realizations of his beautiful artistic visions; he had hidden his passions, the feverish fire of an ardent nature, beneath a deceptive appearance of coldness.

After an hour, Camille stood up.

"I'll come back soon," she said. "Fix the day yourself."

"The day after tomorrow, if you wish."

"So be it, the day after tomorrow."

She dressed hastily and then, on the threshold of the studio, extended her small hand to the sculptor. He shook it distractedly and let it fall again, without noticing the young woman's disappointed moue.

In the street, she dismissed Miss Ketty and took a cab.

XVI

Philippe was waiting for her, with a surly expression, his lips pale.

"You've been to see Georges Darvy," he said.

"How do you know?"

"I know everything. In Paris one is always informed . . ."

Through the window, he showed her a man crossing the street. "Look, that's the man who was following you. Tomorrow it won't be the same one . . . and whatever you do, you'll be unearthed."

She tried to laugh. "That's truly frightening, what you're telling me."

Already, he had removed her hat.

"Admit that I'm not a jealous lover. I've let Nina and Julien Rival pass, and many other inconsequential caprices, because I knew that your heart was free. I don't want a serious attachment."

"I've commissioned the sculptor to make my bust, it's necessary for me to go back to his studio. He can't come to the domicile like a tailor or a dressmaker." With a hint of bitterness, she added: "What a lucky man Georges Darvy is! He only loves one thing, his art, thinking of nothing but that, only loving for that, and that fills him, consoles him, cheers him up and makes his existence good. He's truly a great artist of the old school. Oh, he doesn't worry about women, that man, our women in ribbons, feathers and disguises. Plastic purity is necessary for him, not the artificial."

"It's certain that, for you, a bust by Houdon or Tanagra statuettes are only little adornments necessary to frame the masterpiece of nature that is you—you and your dress, for your dress plays an important role in your preoccupations; it's the new note that you give every day to your omnipotent charm."

"There's something better for me."

"Get away! As futile and personal as all your peers, you know and understand what will show you advantageously, in terms of adornment and jewelry, but you don't know what a rare and constant selection is, what a great and artistic penetration requires. You have incomplete senses, inaccessible to anything that doesn't directly affect the feminine egotism that absorbs everything in you. You only have the instinct of a savage, the instinct of cunning, deception and cruelty. And that absence of comprehension, which obscures your intellectual vision when it's a matter of higher things, often blinds you even more when it's a matter of us. It's futile, in order to seduce you, to have a soul, a heart and qualities of exceptional merit; you go, for preference, to the most unworthy, the most despicable . . ."

As he paused for breath, she said, without emotion: "Go on, my friend. You interest me infinitely. If you knew how amusing you are in the role of moralist!"

"I'm putting you on guard against yourself, that's all."

"I haven't changed since I've known you."

"Indeed, you're as affected as you were on the first day."

"Since you know that, why keep going?"

"To put myself at the level of the clowns you frequent. I desired to see you, and nothing more . . ."

"Then let's end it, now that your caprice is satisfied."

"No, you'd experience too much joy . . ."

"You know full well that I've never loved you, that I yielded because I was afraid."

"I know that; you're like those who formed you. Oh, the pupil does honor to the teachers!"

"Since men have organized pleasure like work, there's no longer any room for sentiment. The attraction that once impelled the sexes toward one another has disappeared. They approach one another as enemies, possess one another as enemies and quit one another with the intention of never seeing one another again. You've set the example, Messieurs; of what do you have to complain?"

"There are men who attach themselves seriously."

"Oh, yes, Julien Rival, But he's a child, who'll form himself in time and become similar to all the rest. By the way, here's his latest letter—read it to me."

She took the crumpled piece of paper out of her pocket and threw it at him.

Philippe moved to the window.

"There are tears on this sheet of paper."

"That's the final ridicule. Go on, read. What are you waiting for?"

"Nothing." And he read, in a grave voice: "*Camille, do you remember my first letter? I told you about my happiness, my gratitude, my intoxication. Today, I'm weeping and I'm bidding you adieu. I will have quit Paris when you receive my letter, for I can no longer live so close to you and so far from your heart. Men like me should never know women like you. If I were a poet or an artist, perhaps my dolor would give birth to a masterpiece and art would enable me to support existence, but I'm nothing but a poor fellow into whom has entered, with his love for you, an atrocious and intolerable distress.*

When I met you, I did not think I could feel and suffer in this fash-
ion, for you have only been able to torture me. I don't hold it against
you, I don't reproach you for anything, and I don't even think that I
have the right to write you these lines, but, in spite of myself, I still
hope that you might recall me by means of an affectionate word . . .
I'll wait . . . No, I sense that you won't respond. I no longer have
anything in the world but a cruel thought attached to me, which it's
necessary to kill. Adieu, Camille, thank you and pardon me. This
evening, still, I love you with all my soul."

Philippe folded up the letter and returned it to Mademoiselle
de Luzac.

"You'll let him leave?"

"Certainly."

"Without seeing him again?"

"What's the point? Haven't I been generous enough?"

"It's not for me to plead Julien Rival's cause; the role scarcely
befits me. However, I think that you've played an imprudent
game with him, as with me."

Camille looked him up and down, scornfully. "In any case,
it's a game of which I'm weary. Julien has had the sense to go
away. Do the same, and let's remain friends. That would be better, I assure you."

"Go away! Do you think so? You're too charming for me to
resign myself to such a sacrifice. I'll keep you. Until tomorrow,
then?"

XVII

In her mad life of pleasures, in the strangest places in the world
where people amuse themselves, Camille had discovered, in spite
of her skepticism, sometimes with an envious, jealous and almost malevolent surprise, people—men and women—in which
something unexpected was produced. With her anxious flair, she
sensed it and divined it in faces, in eyes and in smiles. It was a

gleam of ecstasy and rapture, a joy of the soul expanding in the body, illuminating the flesh and the gaze. A frisson of anger ran through her then, for the sincerely amorous had always annoyed her, and she qualified as disdain the dull hatred that people whose hearts were beating with passion inspired in her.

When she thought of that intoxication, that tender excitement into which the idolization of another person could throw someone, their vision, speech and thought, she judged herself incapable of feeling anything similar. And yet, many a time, weary of indifferent kisses, tormented by the nagging desire for change, which was perhaps nothing but the obscure agitation of an indefinite search for affection, she had wanted to encounter a man who would also throw her into that bewitching overexcitement of all thought and reason.

But that man had not come along; Julien loved her too much and Philippe not enough. Julien was too credulous and Philippe too suspicious. With everyone, she had observed that defects were more prominent than qualities, that even talent is a special gift, like good eyesight or a sound stomach, an isolated gift without any relationship with the ensemble of the individual.

Since her encounter with Georges Darvy, however, her opinions had deviated slightly. He interested her by virtue of his very coldness, his indifference, the pure ideal that was within him and caused him to scorn the habitual satisfactions of the flesh. He had interested her, because she thought about him incessantly, seeking to divine the enigma of that existence so different from others. He hardly ever went out, had no relations, no intimate friends, and seemed almost to repel the favor that went toward him—why?

For the first time, she felt a sincere desire to be something other than a seductive mistress for that man. Did she love him? In order to love, was it necessary for someone to appear endowed with rare attractions, different from others, in the aureole that the heart lights up around its preferred, or was it sufficient for them to please you, and for you no longer to be able to do without them?

For the first time, she had felt the inexpressible something that bears us toward someone almost involuntarily. She had had a great pleasure in looking at him in his studio, in following all his movements, in hearing the sound of his voice. She had experienced a bizarre desire to approach him, to lean her head on his shoulder, to give him the secret intimacy of her soul.

Two days later she dressed with enormous care for simplicity, and went to the Rue de Regard, accompanied by Miss Ketty.

Georges was working on a group, and did not seem to be expecting her. However, he immediately dismissed his models and lifted the damp cloth that was covering the sketch.

"When would you like the bust?" he asked.

"Oh, don't hurry. I want a finished work, a perfect resemblance. It will be difficult, won't it? I have such mobile features."

"No, I think I'll be able to seize your expression, and it's the expression above all that creates the resemblance."

"We have time."

"It's just that other commissions are arriving, which I can't neglect . . ."

She looked at him in a supplicant fashion, but he did not appear to perceive it, and set to work rapidly.

Georges imagined groups and statues by the hundred; he felt a power in carving marble like Canova, and the bust of a young woman scarcely interested him. Although he had not dared to refuse, he firmly intended to finish the unimportant work as quickly as possible, in order to get back to serious work, to the truly great and noble works that his dream caressed. They alone occupied his thoughts and held a place in his life; they alone had the power to animate him and move him.

But Camille became all the more attached the more one seemed to disdain her; for Georges she had her most gracious smiles, her most caressant voice . . .

He must still be ignorant of the fashions of the modern world, its scarcely dissimulated audacities and disdains. The art of loving consists enormously of paradoxes, mockeries, lies and poses.

Passion is a martyrdom; no one wants it any more! One does not even make a semblance any longer of aspiring to the ideal, to the infinite, to perfection; people amuse themselves by scratching one another gently, like cats in a gutter. Beautiful phrases were once a pretext for putting more ardor into practice, more rage into falls. Now, one falls limply, without conviction and without real desire; one falls often, and the wounds are not serious.

Camille had set up her batteries, believing that she had divined Georges' character. The comedy of sentiment might have for that savage the charm of novelty; she made herself thoughtful, gentle, innocent, with little girl confidences.

Miss Ketty, stiff and mute in a corner of the studio, could not get over it. She had witnessed so many mad escapades that she could not imagine such a transformation in Mademoiselle de Luzac.

Camille was now interrogating the sculptor about his preferences. She was delighted when she heard him talk with a profound scorn about some of our most praised masters, but she was surprised when she heard him express his enthusiasm and respect for some others.

For Georges it was a matter of taste, an artistic passion. He admired talent frankly when he encountered it, and was severe for the charlatans of art who beat the big drum in the newspapers and only arrived at notoriety via advertising and intrigue.

In those questions he emerged from his indifference and put a great deal of passion into defending his opinions. It seemed to Camille, however, that something was lacking in that powerful organization: the heart was no longer beating therein. Perhaps it was simply asleep, and perhaps it was about to awake to the luminous daylight that a woman's gaze pours into life.

She examined, waited, and collected all the artist's words and thoughts in order to carry them away into her silence; and with all of that laborious youth, of that love of the beautiful, of that admiration for true artists, she began to create for herself one of those idols to which women devote themselves and which crush them under their debris when reality causes them to crumble with a breath of wind.

She would have laughed at a tender word, responded to an audacious gaze, shrugged her shoulders before an attack, but here, everything seemed strange; she alone made the path that took her away from her repose without bringing her any closer to Georges.

The most attentive mother could not have been disturbed by his composure; the man was perfect, as splendid and hard as a diamond.

The young woman wished ardently that her bust might be wanting. She tried to seek a quarrel with the artist over the slightest details in order to pose for longer, but how could one criticize in the presence of such a work? It was Mademoiselle de Luzac idealized and transfigured, with an expression of tenderness and joy that she had never known!

She no longer sought to intrigue Georges; she listened to him patiently when he told her about his hopes for the future, and approved of him having no goal but power and glory, without remarking that the thought of a generous affection, a worship of the heart, never mingled with his grandiose ideas. He scarcely granted a place, in the life for which he was ambitious, for exterior luxury; what people called society only inspired his disdain.

She did not perceive that the opinions, like the actions, of men, have very different appearances in accordance with the point of view from which they are seen. She believed that she had placed herself, in order to see and judge the sculptor, in the terrain of skepticism, when she was at the opposite point: that of interest and belief.

She dismissed Miss Ketty, under some pretext, and drew nearer to Georges, letting the cloth that he had draped over her shoulders slide; but he was only thinking about his work, continuing to knead the clay. She stood behind him, her breast almost touching his back, and her chagrin became such as to extract a tear and a muted exclamation from her.

Georges turned round and looked at her, finally, and remained motionless, as if struck by a sudden inspiration.

"Oh!" he said. "Stay like that, so I can look at you . . . if you knew!"

"What?"

"Well, you're divinely beautiful. I'd like to lend to the face of the Virgin the expression that you have now."

"What are you saying?" she asked, thinking that she had misheard.

"Would you like to pose for a moment for my group of holy women. I'll make the physiognomy of Mary after yours. That can't displease you?"

She was seized by a nervous laugh that shook her from head to toe; then, letting herself collapse on the divan, she burst into sobs.

He remained standing next to her, disconcerted, not understanding that unexpected crisis at all.

"Are you in pain?" he asked.

When she was able to speak, she murmured, effortfully, glad to find the pretext: "Yes, I'm in pain. I've been very ill recently. The physicians might not be able to save me. So the slightest fatigue . . ."

"Go home, quickly. I'll help you."

He did, indeed, help her, awkwardly, but without trouble. Then, as soon as she was ready, because she had sent her carriage away, he ran to fetch one for her.

Her face livid, her eyes swollen, Camille left without a word of adieu; then, furiously, without worrying about the artist, who was still on the sidewalk, she gave the coachman Philippe's address.

XVIII

Two days later, however, she knocked on the door of the studio. Georges removed the cloth covering the bust tranquilly, but after a few moments he turned to her, smiling.

"Oh," he said, "I've worked, and I hope I've succeeded this time."

She did not reply.

"You'd be very kind," he said, "to permit me to see you as I saw you the other day."

"Of what use would that be to you?"

"To make a masterpiece."

She went frightfully pale. "No, no, I beg you, don't ever talk to me again about that moment of weakness, which I want to forget. If you knew . . ."

"That's all right," he said. "I won't insist, but it's a pity. I didn't think I'd offended you . . ."

They remained silent, disconcerted and discontented.

Finally, she got up, and came to place her hand on his.

"I consent," she said.

"Really?"

"Yes, it will be infinitely original." And her dolorous laughter took hold of her again. As he seemed anxious, she made an effort. "Forgive me; my nerves have been playing these ridiculous tricks on me for several days. I laugh, and I want to weep."

For three weeks, Camille returned to Georges' studio in order to pose, in spite of Nina's mockery and Philippe's threats. Already, she was no longer the mistress of her impressions; curiosity spoke more loudly than her pride in the sovereign language of the arts, which excites the imagination so ardently. Her soul began to open to pleasant and rare sensations, to the sentiment of the enjoyment of the Beautiful. She understood that the pleasure of amour is first to love, and that one is more joyful in the passion that one has than the passion that one inspires.

Finally, she had a goal in life, a goal toward which everything brought her, and which changed the face of everything. Her thoughts cast nature entire before her eyes with its charming aspects, like a novelty invented the day before. She was astonished never to have seen that adorable spectacle. People and things seemed different and better.

The misfortune of inconstancy is ennui. The coquette has an empty heart and only knows how to pass the time; the woman in love trembles to displease, and that dread occupies every minute of her life with memory. Ennui takes everything away, including the courage to kill oneself; amour gives everything, including the pleasure of death.

Previously, while being scornful of them, she had glimpsed those great surges of the entire being toward another being, born, it is said, when bodies drawn by the emotion of souls are united. Those surges had not come. She had, however, wanted to draw Julien's passion, to multiply their rendezvous and to prove to herself that she loved him sincerely—but fatigue had quickly set in, leading to the impotence of deception. She had renounced deceiving herself and deceiving him more, observing with surprise that the kisses she received importuned her. She had submitted to the embraces, imagining every time that she might find the desired sensation, and always came away disillusioned.

Now, Julien no longer existed for her; she did not know what had become of him, and scarcely cared. How he had adored her, though! How hard and how long it would be for him to get over her! Oh, how badly she had bruised that heart, and dug her cruel hands into the wound to enlarge it. Then she had rendered it incurable by plunging her mortal indifference into it, like a knife. Too bad; he would suffer for the others.

While Georges was absent, Nina had come to the studio with Rose Mignot and Claire Delys. On seeing the group of holy women, and recognizing the face of Camille in the Virgin, they had uttered exclamations and bursts of laughter.

Rose had let herself fall on the divan in a crisis of merriment, and Nina had murmured, with a jealous irony: "He has a temperament, your sculptor! Having not found a model chaste enough, he chose you! Truly, he isn't boring."

"Why shouldn't he have chosen me?" Mademoiselle de Luzac replied, sadly. "Don't we die a little every day? The Camille of yesterday no longer exists."

"Nothing in life is effaced."

"Nothing is effaced in memory, it's true, but everything metamorphoses in sentiments. My former existence has become incomprehensible to me."

Nina took a cigarette from a cup and lit it. "Our poor friend is lost," she said, gravely. "What I feared has happened."

"What's that?" asked Rose.

"It's quite simple; she's in love."

"But that's insensate!" cried Claire. "In love . . . and with a man!"

"A man who doesn't want her."

"A man who scorns her."

Camille's eyes flashed. "In a month, I'll be Georges' wife," she said, proudly.

She had just glimpsed the future. Only that man could save her from others and from herself. By means of Georges alone she could attempt the work of renovation. Her decision was made.

Nina shrugged her shoulders. "He won't marry you."

"He doesn't know anything."

"What about Philippe?"

"Philippe will keep quiet.,"

"That's not certain—unless you remain his mistress."

Camille put her fists to her temples, despairingly. "Oh, if you knew how I hate him!"

"Well, he's been cleverer than you."

"I'll take Georges away; we'll travel."

"Philippe will easily be able to catch up with you."

"In that case . . . in that case, I'll kill myself."

"If you like. In any case, we won't talk, although it's not very nice of you to abandon us."

"Shh!" said Rose, who had opened the door slightly. "Here comes the artist. Let's be women of the world."

Georges did, indeed, return, with a bunch of carnations that he had bought in the street. At the sight of his visitors he was nonplussed.

"They're my friends, Mademoiselle de Luzac explained. "They wanted to express their admiration for the bust that you made of me."

"And also for the statue of the Virgin, which is truly marvelous," said Nina.

Their faces had become impassive, their manner perfectly correct.

Georges accompanied them to the gate of his little garden. When he came back into the studio he found Camille in tears.

"What's the matter?" he asked.

"You'll never see me again. You'll have to finish the group without me."

"But that's impossible!" he exclaimed, desolate.

"It's necessary. People are beginning to talk. My long sessions here seem singular. People are saying . . ."

"What are they saying?"

"What's the point of repeating such things? What does it matter to you?"

In a changed voice, he stammered: "You're treating me harshly, Mademoiselle. I didn't think I'd merited such severity."

Bitterly, she continued: "I'm nothing to you but a young woman like all the others. Art alone occupies your thoughts."

He looked at her and suddenly felt drawn to her. His heart, which he had thought insensible, began to beat precipitately. He understood that he loved her, and had, perhaps, for a long time.

"You're rich," he said, "and I have nothing."

"You're richer than I am, since you have genius. If you were less indifferent, you could make a great deal of money."

"That's true. In future I'll work for you, and one day, my fortune will equal yours. Would you like to become my wife?"

She uttered a cry of joy, and almost knelt before him.

"Would I like it! For days I've been looking for a tender word from your lips, a word truly from the heart. Would I like it! Take me, keep me, make of me what you will. I'm yours, Georges, yours entirely and forever."

PART THREE

I

As if Baronne de Luzac had only been waiting for her grand-daughter's marriage to quit this world, she was found dead in her armchair the day after the ceremony.

Camille, in full mourning, quit Paris without informing anyone. They embarked in Cannes, early in the morning, on a yacht chartered expressly for the voyage. It was a twenty-tonne boat with fine canvas sails. The feeble breezes exhaled toward the sea by the gulfs impelled them gently, taking them toward the Italian coast. On that summer afternoon, the cruel sun filled the sky over the Mediterranean, making the water a blue-tinted mirror, devoid of clouds and almost devoid of ripples.

In the interior, it was cool. The boat was profound, constructed for navigating on the northern seas, and standing up to bad weather. Slightly narrow, six or seven people—passengers and crew—could live in that little floating dwelling.

Camille was sitting beside Georges, her head on his shoulder, and both of them remained silent, full of their happiness. They savored the idle sensuality that invades a happy couple in a narrow space, the tender and insinuating emotion going from one to another, a kind of soft magnetic penetration of their two bodies, their two minds, in a languid and charming meditation. They tasted a physical and spiritual intimacy in the discreet half-light in which the veiled rays of the sun passing through the portholes played in the shade with the woman's hair, her long eyelashes and the silky pleats of her dress.

They loved the rocking of the waves that swings beings and minds, throwing them against one another. And without a single amorous word, the two spouses abandoned themselves to their reverie, Georges holding Camille's hand in his own, playing mechanically with the warm, slender fingers, caressing her soft skin, of which a little of the life seemed to be transfusing into him.

They dined in the smoking room, on a very small table, without the service of domestics. Camille found her first lover in her husband. For the first time, she was in love, she finally gave herself body and soul. They had stupidities of sentiment in complete liberty, apropos of nothing and everything; the emotion of that passionate intimacy, in that box of varnished wood, made it resemble a student supper in a mansard. They both ate while looking at one another and smiling. From time to time, Camille put down her fork, and, after a moment of religious contemplation, murmured in a grave voice: "You're beautiful, my Georges."

And she truly saw him as beautiful, tall and transfigured by his amour. He was no longer a man, but the man she had chosen among all of them, who bore the superb aureole of that distinction. And it was curious and amusing, the spectacle of Georges' embarrassment and emotional confusion before the court paid to him by the woman who had seemed so disdainful only a month before. He could not find words to respond to the attentiveness and the enveloping grace of that unexpected passion.

Dinner was over. Camille knelt before her husband, brought his mouth to her lips, and said to him in a kiss—one of the kisses that she had not had for Julien, or for Nina, or for anyone— "Come."

In the narrow cabin, undressed in a second, she summoned him again, proud of the tenderness that she could admit in the face of everyone, proud of the exquisite sensations that she finally experienced, banally, like any amorous woman.

What was the point, then, of so much depravity and so much shame, to end up here?

The passion that she had previously sought in vain emanated from her vibrant body like an electricity, a plenitude of pleasure going all the way to the extremities of the organism of the man clutched in her arms. And amid the sensual transports of her intoxication, there were, at the same time, the ingenuous caresses of a young woman and the libertinage of a courtesan: restraints and immodesties. Sometimes, moaning in a spasm, her childhood rose up again within her and put puerile words between her chattering teeth; then, for fear of something enclosed in the depths of her soul, she enveloped Georges with her entire body, like a panicked and delirious protection.

Outside, they could hear nothing except the ticking of the little clock suspended from the wooden partition; only that minuscule beat troubled their indescribable embraces, and the immense repose of the elements gave them, at times, when they awoke from their ecstasy, breast to breast, the surprising sensation of unlimited solitudes in which the murmurs of worlds, stifled a few meters from their surfaces, became imperceptible in the universal silence. It seemed to them that something of the eternal calm of space was descending and spreading over the motionless sea on that warm summer night.

And always kisses, kisses and more kisses . . . and the mingling of those two bodies dissolved in one long caress lasted until dawn.

Georges brought his wife a brand new soul, which was abandoning itself thus for the first time. He was surprised and charmed by that plenitude of happiness, which he had never dared to imagine outside his divine art.

II

The entire sky was veiled by clouds. Gradually, however, the vapors paled, thinned out and seemed to dissolve. One sensed that the sun was burning them, drinking them with all its ardor, and that they were about to be annihilated by the enormous force of light. The air was refreshed by the night; the frisson of a breeze caressed the sea, causing it to quiver by tickling it, its blue waves striped with brightness.

The yacht went into the port of Savone. A group of factory chimneys and foundries that alimented four or five large steamships laden with coal every day, projected a tortuous vomit of black smoke into the sky through their giant mouths. Rapturous, Georges and Camille gazed at the small Italian town full of agitated merchants, and fruits spread on the ground: scarlet tomatoes, golden or amethyst grapes and crimson split watermelons.

All day long, as on the previous day, they remained next to one another, enclosed in their happiness. Then evening came. The waves, slightly heavy although the wind over the open sea had dropped completely, trailed the regular and monotonous sound around them; and the violet firmament—a lustrous violet silvered by an infinite dust of stars—allowed a gentle night to fall lightly into their gaze.

The young woman was dreaming as in the convent, the charming dreams that she had had in the white dormitory before going to sleep. In the depths of her bruised heart, poisoned by incredulity, the first beliefs awoke, with their naïve songs and fluttering wings.

They visited Genoa, which retained them for two days. From the port all the way to Porto-Fino there is a chaplet of towns, a scattering of houses on beaches, between the blue of the sea and the green of the mountains. The yacht was tacking in the breeze, inclining or launching forward like a runaway horse. As it tacked, it drew away from or drew closer to the shore.

The captain, who was consulting the horizon in order to know, by means of the sail carried and the maneuvers undertaken by the ships in sight, the force and direction of the air currents, decided abruptly to bring down the topsail in order to avoid any danger. The long inflated canvas descended from the summit of the mast and slid, palpitating like a wounded bird, along the mizzen, which was beginning to sense the imminent squall. Everything was still calm, though; only a little foam was seething before them. Suddenly, however, the water became completely white in the distance, and when that pale line was no more than a few hundred meters away, the sails received an abrupt shock, and the fleecy water agitated, rising under the invisible whistling assault of the squall.

Lying on its side, the rail drowned, the hawsers taut and the mast creaking, the yacht departed on a crazy course, seized by a vertigo, a fury of speed.

Camille, huddled against Georges' chest, abandoned herself to that intoxication, with the hoarse breath of sensuality.

"Again! Again!" she murmured. "Oh, to die thus!"

But he closed her lips with a kiss.

"Die? No, no, we're too happy."

The tempest only lasted an hour, and suddenly, when the Mediterranean had recovered its beautiful tranquility of precious stone, the sky no longer had anything but smiles and the gaiety of the sunlight expanded broadly through space.

They went past Porto Venere at the entrance to the gulf of La Spezzia, Santa Margherita, Rapallo and Chiavari. They stopped in a little village full of flowers and fruits. The place seemed so delightful to them that they wanted to spend a few days there.

They had never felt an impression of bliss comparable to that of the repose they savored in that solitary and silent green cove. The yacht remained motionless in the middle of the minuscule harbor, and they roamed along the coasts in a dinghy, going to explore that land of dreams.

They found mysterious cool grottoes, reefs at the level of the water that bore manes of seaweed. Under the water, in the undulations of the waves, they saw pink and blue plants floating, where immense families of newborn fish were gliding. Boys with bronzed bodies were diving to pick up coins or gamboling madly from rock to rock. When they had rowed enough they went ashore and wandered overland.

Innumerable little paths separated gardens of olive groves and fig trees garlanded with brown clusters. Through the foliage they perceived, as far as the eye could see, the changing sea, capes, white villages and somber fir-woods on slopes, and summits of gray granite. Tall women with dark and profound eyes watched them pass by.

A week later, they were in Florence. Georges had a particular veneration for that superb city, into which the great men of the Renaissance had thrown treasures by the handful. The same reflection of imperishable beauty appeared under the brushes of painters and the chisels of sculptors, growing in lines of stone on the facades of monuments, and the churches were full of works by Lucca dell Robbia, Donatello, Michelangelo, Giambologna and Benvenuto Cellini. The artist was conquered, intoxicated by that section of the voyage in a forest of human marvels, and nothing equaled his admiration.

He took Camille gladly in order to associate her with his joy. He showed her the virgins of the primitives with innocent features, bright hair, ideal and mystical, and compared them with the one he had composed after her, which seemed to him to be equal in beauty. Every day there were surprises; he saw things that were not commonly indicated to travelers; he discovered on the walls at the back of choirs inestimable paintings by the masters of old, who had lived in poverty and without the hope of fortune, with the divine consolation of their genius.

One evening, as they were returning to the hotel, Camille was handed a letter, which she crumpled angrily.

Astonished, he asked: "Aren't you going to read it?"

"I don't know the handwriting. It's of no importance."

Even so, she opened the envelope. As soon as she read the first lines she was seized by a tremor.

"Bad news?"

"Yes."

"May one know?"

"Of course. A friend is ill."

He took the room key and went upstairs without further insistence, while she held on to the rail in order not to fall.

The letter was from Philippe and contained these words: *I've finally been able to pick up your trail. Whatever you do, you won't escape me. I'm in Florence and I'll come to your hotel at three o'clock tomorrow. Send your husband away.*

"Are you in pain?" Georges asked, when he had closed the door behind them.

"No," she said, making an effort. "I'm simply saddened by what I've just learned. Let's go away, my love. Let's leave tomorrow, if you like."

"Leave? We still have so many things to see."

"We'll come back and see them. I need to numb myself, to forget. Do you understand?"

"Can you grant me another day or two?"

"No, I beg you, do this for me." She put her arms around him, calm and supplicant.

"All right," he said. "We'll leave."

"Tomorrow morning?"

"Tomorrow morning."

III

Camille had become another woman, all tenderness and grace. She took pleasure in, and was delighted by, the unexpectedness of her femininity; she received particular impressions from contact with people and things, the expression of which was translated in an original fashion. She felt, she saw and she judged better than in the past, and with a greater benevolence.

Among socialites and bourgeois women, the feminine being is, so to speak, still the same, and the sensitivity of both seems established on an identical pattern. Under the action of external cause they have repulsions, sympathies, commiserations and revolts that escape men. In all of them, the initial movements of the soul are attenuated by a sort of fearful reserve that corrects them, amends them, renders them decorous, and in all of them, save for slight nuances brought by temperament or an exceptional nervousness, everything is dissimulated by virtue of pride or prudence. Camille's impressions, by contrast, had the bitter taste of a soul in revolt and at war. She disdained pretense and showed herself in the first impulse of her opinions. It had required that sudden passion to inspire the idea of dissimulation in her, and she only resigned herself to it reluctantly. Still, however, she remained the creature of election, endowed aristocratically for superior elegance, informed more by virtue of a faculty of intuition than received education.

Georges did not worry for long about his wife's inexplicable caprice; she had become charming again and did not mention the letter that had caused her so much emotion. Several times, he tried to interrogate her about the friend about whom she had never spoken, but after a few banal phrases, she changed the subject, speaking to him in turn about his past life, his commencements and his struggles. And his confidence in her was fortified, increasing in spite of the warning.

By contrast, Camille began to awaken from the beautiful dream she had created. In spite of her apparent tranquility, a secret anguish gripped her heart. She would have liked to flee to the ends of the earth, to put the silence of the tomb between her past and her present. She had made the resolution to cure herself, even of memory, and her entire being quivered with rage at the thought that the enemy was on her track and still pursuing her with the same obstinacy. She would have become criminal in order to escape him, but how could such an adversary be punished? She was desolate at the endless situation and uplifted herself by talking about her plans for the future and her joy with tears in her eyes.

Georges sometimes asked her: "Why do you love me, Camille? It seems to me that I have nothing of what is necessary to seduce a woman . . ."

She interrupted him, animated by reasons and reasoning. And when he smiled, incredulously, she said: "I love you because you don't resemble the others, because you have thoughts higher than your desires, because you don't only seek the slaking of the senses and the satisfaction of vanity . . ." Then she added, anxiously: "Will you always be the same?"

"Yes, Camille, in many years, I'll be the same. But will you? Are you not similar to the majority of passionate women with violent caprices, who simply put all their life into romance? Until now, I've preferred art to amour because art isn't deceptive. You've taught me that tenderness is better still. The heart needs a hidden companion. The ambitious appetite for success doesn't prevent a man from being devoted and faithful, from giving all his thought, if not all his dreams, affection, sincere attachment and the absolute confidence of his soul, in order to receive in exchange the impression, so rare and so sweet, of not being alone in life. I beg you, always be the same, and let me lean on you with security, as on the most loyal and the most worthy friend."

She went mortally pale, shivering from head to toe, so ill did those words make her feel.

They had departed the next morning, as she had desired, and he had taken advantage of that caprice to go and visit a distant region in which other artists had left memories more faded but as eternal.

People in France are convinced that Sicily is difficult of access, and if a few courageous travelers sometimes venture as far as Palermo they come back from there satisfied, without taking their visit any further. The island, the pearl of the Mediterranean, is not in the number of countries that it is customary to explore, and snobs like nothing better than to abstain from it, everything in France being a matter of fashion.

However, the natural and artistic beauties of Sicily are particularly remarkable and certainly merit retaining the attention. All peoples desired and possessed that charming country, ardently coveted like a young and beautiful mistress. As much as Spain, it is a paradise of golden fruits, the florid soil whose air, in spring, is nothing but a perfume, and every night, above the sea, the mysterious beacon of Etna, the greatest volcano in Europe, lights up.

There is born a special, original art in which an Arab influence is dominant, in the midst of Greek and sometimes Egyptian memories. The severities of the Gothic style, brought by the Normans, are tempered by the charming ornamentation of Byzantine decoration. And it is an incomparable pleasure to seek, in its exquisite monuments, the special mark of each art, to discern the detail come from Egypt, the lanceolate ogive that the Arabs brought, the vaults in relief that resemble the stalactites of marine grottoes, the pure Byzantine ornamentation, or the Gothic friezes that awaken the memory of tall Northern cathedrals.

Georges enabled Camille to see all those works, which, belonging to different eras and origins, nevertheless form a harmonious and powerfully original whole. He showed her specimens of ancient Greek architecture in the midst of adorably sunlit landscapes. Everywhere, they were conquered and moved by something almost sensual that color added to the beauty of forms. The admirable effect of churches comes in Palermo from the mixture and opposition of marbles and mosaics. Although the lower sections of walls are ornamented by delicate stone arabesques, the upper parts have an unexpected richness, with their gigantic subjects in dazzling colors. One might think that an inspired artist, a more colorful, more forceful and more naïve Puvis de Chavannes had made them in an era of violent faith.

No one resembles a Neapolitan less than a Sicilian. The latter has the gravity of manner of an Arab combined with the intellectual vivacity of an Italian. His native pride, his love of titles and the arrogance of his physiognomy also likens him to a Spaniard. The streets of Palermo are wide and beautiful in the rich quarters, and, in the poor quarters, resemble the narrow tortuous and colorful back streets of Oriental cities. The women, enveloped in brightly-colored rags, chat outside their houses and watch strangers passing by with their dark eyes, which sparkle under the forest of their black or russet hair. Whatever is said about Sicilian brigands, one can walk the streets in that country day and night unarmed and without an escort; one only encounters people full of benevolence for visitors.

Georges and Camille installed themselves some distance from the city in a place that overlooked the entire valley full of flowering orange trees. A continual breeze rose from the embalmed forest, which intoxicated the mind and troubled the senses. That scent enveloped them, mingling the delicate sensation of perfumes with the joy of their amour, casting them into a wellbeing of thought and body that was another happiness.

They perceived around them high mountains with soft lines, classical lines, and on the summits, the severe, doubtless somewhat heavy, but admirably imposing temples that one encounters throughout the land. The railway follows the shore, a shore of red terrains and orange rocks; then the track inclines toward the interior of the island through raised fields, like a sea of monstrous and motionless waves. The road climbs between two lines of flowering aloes, and as far as the eye can see it is flanked by the infinite troop of those sharp warrior plants, armed and armored to the tips of the leaves. One proceeds, contemplating in the distance the profile of a Greek temple: one of the powerful monuments that the divine people erected to its human gods.

IV

For a fortnight, Camille had thought herself safe and had relaxed into the softness of that new existence, when a second warning came to throw her back into alarm.

After a few others, she had wanted to visit the temple of Segesta, which stands out, with its thirty-six Doric columns, between two mountains linked together by a slope rounded out in a crescent. It is alone in that limitless country, and one senses, when one sees the grandiose and simple landscape that surrounds it, that one could only place a Greek temple there.

130

Masters of genius who had learned the art of humanity showed in Sicily, more than elsewhere, the profound science they had of scene-setting.

Georges and Camille saw the summit of the mountain on which the temple and the theater stand. Every day they undertook excursions, going forth alone most of the time, without fear of brigands, glad of the surprises they encountered at every step. They had been there since morning, in the center of the rocky amphitheater, and did not weary of contemplating the imposing masses, ringed by green forests, and the carpet of blue sea that extended at their feet.

Suddenly, on turning round, Camille uttered a scream. Philippe was behind her. His ironic smile chilled her with terror.

"Do you know one another?" asked Georges.

She stammered: "No . . . that is to say, yes . . . it's Comte von Talberg, who came to play whist in our house. Would you like me to introduce you?"

"Certainly. One is always glad to encounter a compatriot. Besides, I believe I've seen Monsieur von Talberg before."

"Yes, the first time you came to dinner with my grandmother. Do you remember?"

Philippe had approached. He replied to Georges' amiable words quite naturally, and waxed ecstatic over the beauty of the country. He had deserted Paris, he said, to console himself for an unhappy love affair, and had not brought anyone, in order to isolate himself more, in order no longer to hear any voice already heard, no longer to see any face already seen.

"You must be cursing us, then, Monsieur!" Georges exclaimed, cheerfully.

"No, I assure you. Since my departure, my thoughts have taken another course. I'm cured, completely cured."

"Your passion didn't have very profound roots, admit it."

"No, my God no. I loved an unworthy creature, and scorn finally got the upper hand."

Trembling, Camille sought to read the gaze of her former lover, but Philippe's eyes remained cold and impenetrable. He did not seem to perceive her presence, and chatted tranquilly with Georges about his latest works and projects.

The delighted sculptor delivered himself without any afterthought, declaring his joy in having found a companion like Camille, and that he was counting on her intelligent support.

In their company, the young woman asked herself: *What does he want? Why is he pursuing me so obstinately?* Her soul shivered with impotent wrath, her limbs would no longer sustain her, her heart was beating madly, and her body seemed afflicted by an inconceivable curvature. That crushing sensation came from the hatred that she felt weighing upon her, which she could neither appease nor withstand.

Why does the past keep returning incessantly? she asked herself. *Before knowing Georges I had not been subject to any attraction; I only had instincts, curiosity and appetites; I wanted to know everything without risking anything, and I have, in sum, only harmed myself. My senses savored without ever being intoxicated; I understood too much to lose my head; I reasoned and analyzed my inclinations too much to submit to them blindly. And now this man who is threatening me today has imposed himself upon me, in spite of me, in spite of my repulsion and my resistance, he has dictated his will to me and is still subjugating me by his presence alone. By what right, after all?*

She approached Philippe resolutely.

"I order you to go away," she said, in a low voice.

He responded in the same way, without looking at her: "I'm not going."

And as Georges drew away slightly to contemplate the collapsed columns, fallen side by side in the sand like dead soldiers, she said, rapidly: "What are you hoping for, then? More than ever, I don't belong to you. Why have you followed me all the way here? It's all over, go away. We must no longer be anything but strangers to one another . . ."

"Why? There's only your husband between us."

"Oh, shut up!"

"Is my conduct more culpable than yours?"

"I have my amour for an excuse."

"Perhaps my excuse is the same."

"Get away! You're incapable of love, and anyway, you know me too well for that."

"Be careful. Your husband might hear us."

In fact, Georges was considering them with some astonishment, unable to explain the alteration in their faces.

"I believe, my dear Monsieur," said Philippe, loudly, and with the greatest calm, "that Madame Darvy is suffering from the excessive heat here. The leaden sun and these bright colors are not made for a Parisienne who has scarcely known anything but the spring fogs of the Bois du Boulogne and the capricious warmth of Trouville or Ostend."

"That's true," said Camille. "I'd like to go back."

The return journey was long and difficult. As soon as she was back home she lay down on the bed and closed her eyes, scarcely responding to her husband's anxious questions.

"Would you like to see a doctor?"

"No, I beg you. I only need calm. You were wrong to invite Monsieur von Talberg."

"Why? I thought he was one of your friends."

"I don't want to see anyone. I only have one friend, and that's you."

There was a tone so true, a dolor so bitter, and something so stifled and heartbroken in that voice that moved him to pity.

"What's the matter with you today? You seem not only to be suffering but saddened."

"You're mistaken."

"Then why do you say that you have no friends. At your age, you ought not to know anything of existence. You've lived like all young women . . ."

She smiled wanly and did not reply.

"A young woman knows nothing of real chagrin," he said. "She has had neither bitterness, nor disillusionment, not conflicts. Once married, her husband, if he really loves her, ought to continue the sketched dream. Isn't that so?"

She took his hand and placed it over her moist eyes.

"Oh, yes . . . I assure you that I don't desire anything more than the present happiness. Why alarm yourself over this malaise, which will pass as it came?"

"You've felt feverish and weary for some time?"

"Yes."

He knelt before her.

"Camille," he said, "is it really true? I daren't believe in so much joy."

She sat up, astonished. "What do you mean?"

"Tell me that I'm not mistaken. This state of fatigue, of vague malaise of which you speak, is it . . . ?"

"I assure you, my friend, that I don't understand you."

"Come on, you really don't know? Oh, it that could be, how I'd thank you! How I'd bless you!"

She was seized by a nervous tremor, and he murmured in her ear, with a rapturous stammer: "If I could be a father . . ."

She looked at him with her large, dilated eyes, went mortally pale, and lost consciousness.

V

Extremely anxious, Georges spent the night in an armchair next to his wife's bed.

She was delirious, agitating feverishly, putting her hands to her throat, seeming to want to extract the sensation of a sharp pain within her. He tried in vain to make her breathe ether; the waves of pain that were passing through her body continued to pass, shaking her, for hours. Then, suddenly, tears—a deluge of tears—escaped her eyes and bore away the terrible crisis. Her distress was no longer anything but an intermittent shudder, soon appeased by a lassitude, a general exhaustion.

After that ordeal, Camille fell into a great melancholy. A child! How sweet it would have been to have a child by the man she adored with all the strength of her being. Coldly, inexorably, she was condemned to eternal sterility. By virtue of what vertigo of folly had she committed that crime? A voice murmured to her that a child to love would have been her Providence; everything that she still feared would have gone away if it had had that head to sanctify it. It seemed to her that she could feel her maternal heart pacifying and purifying her horrible past. She saw a child as something celestial, which consoles and heals, a little angel of deliverance emerged from human sins in order to redeem them and efface them.

When she began to vanquish the initial annihilation of her despair, when the perception of life returned to her, she looked around with eyes that were still troubled, searching for Georges in order to throw herself into his arms, but, fatigued by that night of insomnia, he was walking in the garden.

She called to him in a coaxing voice: "Forgive me, my love."

"How do you feel now?"

"Much better . . . but what about you? You haven't slept for an instant."

"Oh, me, I'm strong!"

"You must rest."

"No, I don't want to leave you. You assure me that you're no longer suffering?"

"Not at all. But . . . never speak to me about . . . what you said to me last night . . ."

He considered her with a dolorous astonishment.

"Why not?"

"I'll explain to you later. Yes, later . . ."

"Oh, Camille! Am I mistaken? Aren't you woman, true woman, with all her tenderness, all her devotion?"

"Yes, I am that woman . . . now. You can see that."

"And you'll love your child . . . your children . . . ?"

She interrupted him, shivering. "If you knew the harm you're doing me! I'm no longer sufficient for you, then? You need something else to interest your thought?"

"You're the only adored, today as yesterday, but I'm thinking of the future, of what must necessarily happen."

She shook her head in a melancholy fashion. "Don't think of anything but our amour. It's great enough, believe me, to fill our life!"

Completely reassured about the state of Camille's health, Georges went out for a moment after lunch, desirous of making the choice of some original curio or trinket to take back to Paris.

In the garden of the villa, the young woman respired the perfumed breeze. The shores of Sicily exhale such a powerful odor of orange blossom that the entire strait is impregnated like a lovenest. She received those sensations over the whole surface of her flesh, as well as through her eyes, mouth, nose and ears. That nervous excitability of the epidermis and all the organs was a rare and redoubtable faculty in her, which made an emotion out of physical impressions, and which, in accordance with temperatures, the odors of the soil and the color of the daylight, imposed sadness or joy in her.

Half lying on a marble step, she listened to a distant music. The faint but clear sounds, of a charming sonority, cast an operatic murmur over the dormant countryside.

A voice spoke nearby, and she uttered a cry.

"You! You again!"

"It's necessary for you to listen to me," Philippe murmured. "What I have to say to you is serious."

"I'm listening . . . get on with it."

"I still love you, Camille, and I can't resolve to lose you. It's necessary that you belong to me, as in the past."

She sat up, wildly. "Never!"

"It's necessary. Remember that you're not free . . . that your past . . ."

"Oh, always my past! So I shall drag that shame after me until death?"

"Yes, until death. Remember . . . I too have offered you my name; I too have loved you fearfully and purely. Why did you reject me?"

"Oh, how do I know? I wasn't then the woman I am today. My thought had been perverted and my soul polluted. Having made, by a sort of fatality, dangerous acquaintances in the feminine and Parisian society in which the most incredible depravity hides under the correction of manners and apparent life, I had to succumb. Not knowing anything yet, I learned evil as easily as I would have learned good. Is it my fault if I was left an orphan at an age when the surveillance of a mother and the protection of a father are indispensable?"

"The causes don't concern me; I only want to see the results."

"You're unjust."

"Everything in existence is injustice. You had enough discernment to understand and choose. Good examples were no more lacking than bad ones."

"It wasn't the good examples that were lacking but their advice."

"Why recriminate, since nothing that has happened cannot be annihilated?"

"What if I want to remake my existence, to become an honest woman?"

"That's no longer possible."

"Really?"

"No. I won't resign myself to losing you."

"You have no rights over me. I can expel you at any moment."

"Try."

"You'll tell Georges everything? You'd have that infamous courage?"

"Perhaps."

"What kind of man are you, then?"

"A man who desires you to the extent of crime."

"Julien loved me as much as you, and he resigned himself."

"Julien resigned himself because he thought you were a woman like the rest, tender and weak. But I revolt, because I know your hypocrisy and your indignity."

"Oh!"

"Yes, yes, I revolt, for your temporary repentance doesn't inspire any pity in me. Your sins are among those that can't be expiated or forgiven. You're a monster in nature, and if you didn't have youth and beauty in your favor, it would be necessary to kill you like a harmful beast. But I love you because of that youth and that beauty . . . and perhaps also because of that perversity, which flatters my evil instincts. We're equals, Camille, and nothing can separate us but my pleasure."

He took her by the wrists and shoved her toward the door, which was still open. She struggled and fought with an unusual strength, but she dared not cry out.

In spite of the insults that she hurled at him, in a voice strangled by hatred, he did not yield, circling her waist and maintaining her rebellious body. She felt herself carried, dominated, conquered, and the idea that she was about to be possessed once again by that man that she hated with all her strength gave her the temptation to commit a crime; red flashes passed before her eyes; her hands clutched her torturer's neck.

Suddenly, the garden gate opened, and Philippe, suddenly sobered up, got up and drew away from the young woman. When Georges came in, he had recovered all his composure, while Camille, livid, was leaning on a table in order not to faint.

The sculptor advanced, his hand extended.

But she said, ironically, challenging her former lover with a cruel glance. "That man is not your friend. Throw him out!"

Philippe shuddered under the insult. "I believe Madame Darvy is mad. What have I done?"

She repeated, in a vibrant voice: "Georges, I tell you to throw that man out!"

The Comte made a menacing gesture. "No one throws me out! If you weren't a woman you'd expiate those words harshly!"

But, her lips quivering and her eyes gleaming, she said again: "Get out! Get out!"

"No, not before having recounted what you are, what . . ."

"Recount, then!" She had folded her arms, and was challenging him with an expression of supreme disdain. "Speak, then!" she repeated. "You're hesitating? Are you afraid? Afraid of a woman? That's scarcely in your habits!"

But Philippe, his mouth taut and his face contracted with fury, headed for the door.

"No," he said, "I'll keep silent this time, once again." He turned toward Georges. "Forgive me for having prolonged this painful scene, Monsieur. I don't know what Madame Darvy can have against me, and I don't want to know. I don't hold you responsible for the insults she has just addressed to me in a moment of dementia."

Georges had taken his wife's hand. "Explain yourself! Why that scene? Have you something of which to complain? Speak. I'm here to avenge you."

But she uttered a nervous, halting laugh. "No, no, a simple caprice . . . I was certainly wrong . . ."

"And you, Monsieur? You've said too much, or not enough. I want to know!"

"Pardon a moment of involuntary indignation. I know absolutely nothing."

"However, just now, you accused . . ."

"I accused in order to defend myself. Believe, Monsieur, that I deplore that unfortunate scene as much as Madame Darvy, who was not the mistress of her nerves. I regret anything that I might have said . . . unconsciously."

Philippe had closed the door again, and when she heard his footsteps draw away over the sand of the garden, she took her husband in her arms, pressed herself to his breast and crushed on his lips the questions that he was about to ask.

"Don't interrogate me, I beg you! I have nothing for which to reproach myself . . . nothing! You don't doubt me, do you? I only love you, I swear it! If anyone seeks to turn you away from my affection, resist, protest—all the accusations will be calumnies. I'm sincere . . . with you, I always have been. How can one not be sincere when one adores? Only, you see, society is wicked and jealous; purity of sentiment wounds it and makes it indignant. Whatever people say about me, you won't believe it, will you? Repeat that you won't believe it?"

Stunned by that flood of words, he only responded to Camille's kisses with kisses; but doubt had entered into him, and if he was not suffering from it as yet, he already sensed it vaguely, and it installed itself slyly in his soul.

VI

Philippe turned over a thousand projects of vengeance in his head. However, vengeance was so easy that he rejected it. His amour disintegrated, turning into hatred without weakening his desire. He began to detest his mistress, and to search for anything that could make him detest her more, in order to cure himself of her. And, as his thought returned to the young woman's sins, to her frightful previous existence, he convinced himself that she was playing an unworthy comedy once again, and he was horrified by her, running away from her as if from a curse.

He could not succeed in forgetting her, however, and when he returned to Paris one of his first visits was to Julien Rival, whom he knew to be as inconsolable as he was. In spite of his rancor, he experienced the need to talk about her and to calm his suffering by means of the suffering of another.

As Philippe had foreseen, Julien had returned to the apartment that he had furnished and decorated for his amour. He spent hours before the little bed of black wood where he had held her in his arms; he contemplated a lace handkerchief that she had forgotten, a small veil, a glove: precious relics, the sight of which caressed and bruised his heart.

Increasingly, he lived reclusively, only receiving a few friends at intervals. The combat was still going on; the internal dispute was frightful. For weeks, and months, he had felt neglected by everything that he had cherished; he suffered from the privation of the words of affection, the silences of caresses with which the beloved absentee had once cradled him all day long by means of hope and memory. He no longer had any of the warmth of tenderness that was the air vital to his soul.

At length, a sentiment of fear of himself came to him in confrontation with his mental obsessions, as if before a danger. He recoiled from his evocations as if from temptations, forbade himself the images they created. An immense sadness drowned his days and his interminable nights.

When Philippe came to see him he was glad to be able to talk to someone who had known Camille and who might be able to inform him regarding her new existence.

Comte von Talberg had smiled on seeing the young man's dejection and melancholy. "You can't forget her, then?" he asked.

Julien blushed under the penetrating gaze that searched his consciousness and stirred his dolor.

"Oh," said Philippe, "there are women that one ought to kill! If my pain can console yours, I'll confide it to you. In spite of all my skepticism, I'm no more valiant than you."

The young man took his hand eagerly. "Oh, how I sympathize with you!"

"It's singular; I'd never felt anything similar, and the present state of my soul fills me with astonishment. I have more judgment than instinct, and fundamentally, I'm just a demanding and capricious pleasure-seeker. I loved the things of life with the senses of an expert who savors without being intoxicated, and who, rationalizing his tastes, was able not to submit to them blindly. And then, without preparation, without any reason, a woman imposed herself on me, in spite of myself, in spite of my fear and knowledge of those like her. The woman is a coquette, a vicious, dangerous creature whom I was neither able to esteem nor cherish, and yet, she holds me by a thousand powerful bonds that I can't break. I hate her, I despise her, and I desire her madly!"

"Personally," said Julien, "I love an adorable creature who no longer loves me. But at least I have the consolation of gratitude and respect."

Philippe had an evil smile.

"Yes, you've already told me that, and I don't want to take away your illusions. Your mistress is no better than mine."

"I swear to you that I have nothing for which to reproach her but her indifference. Did she not act honestly in telling me that she no longer loved me? And then, there was another reason . . ."

"I know. The marriage."

"The marriage . . . yes. You see that I can't hold anything against her. I'm unhappy, that's all."

"I admire your confidence," said Philippe. "Personally, I lost faith a long time ago. The one I possessed, after many others, can no longer count her falls. What has she to fear, anyway? Has she not visited the clinic of Dr. Richard, who has preserved her forever against the risks of maternity? She no longer has anything of womanhood except that which intoxicates and maddens, the perverse charm that takes the male and subjugates him in spite of his experience and scorn. She has fallen lower than shame, lower than nature itself. From fall to fall, she has collected the amours that dissipate in one night, which pass, which one encounters, which the hazard of a soirée or a dinner allows the creature who seeks to find . . .

"She has corrupted young girls and has spent indescribable moments with them. She no longer needs to give herself the time for desire; her caprice is furious, sudden, instantly ignited. Avid for a woman or a man, she scarcely looks at her conquests and wouldn't be able to recognize them. In all beings, her eyes no longer see anything but sensual prey; the individual is irrelevant to her. The last modesty and the last human sense of debauchery, preference, choice, she has lost, and even what remains to prostitutes by way of conscience, disgust.

"Amour has been nothing for her but the satisfaction of an unhealthy curiosity, and she has never brought anything to her caprices but the cold instincts of evil awakened by bad books, dangerous confidences and the first breaths of impurity, which deflower. What the woman puts around the man she loves—the veils, the caresses, the amusing words, the imaginations of tenderness—nothing of that exists for her. Once again, amour is nothing in her eyes but an obscene and forbidden image . . .

"There are a whole band of them in Paris. One encounters them, veiled, in evil places; they seem to have thrown themselves outside their sex, having no fear of attacking, soliciting, and amusing themselves with drunkenness—and it's to them that one yields! They march, breathing in the air, sniffing around them, going toward what there is of the covert and the impure, sinister, quivering or frightfully cheerful. They slither and crawl, skirting the darkness with the physiognomy of madwomen and sick individuals, who cause the heart of the thinker and the thought of the physician to labor over abysms of sadness."

"Oh," said Julien, "that isn't possible; one doesn't encounter those unfortunates in our world!"

"One finds them in all worlds."

"How sorry I feel for you for having loved one of those poor creatures!"

"Your mistress, you say, is worthy of all respects? Mine has all the vices. Yours is good, tender and sincere; mine is cruel, insolent and a liar. Yours had only had a single lover? Mine has given herself to anyone who came along. And yet, your mistress and mine are one and the same woman."

Julien leapt up and stood before the Comte. "You're lying! You're lying!"

Coldly, Philippe repeated: "Your mistress and mine are one and the same woman, whose name is . . ."

But he did not have time to finish. Julien's hand had fallen upon his face.

VII

A duel was decided. However, Philippe did not want to kill Julien, who inspired an immense pity in him. He was already regretting having talked, having yielded to the criminal folly of that confession. Involuntarily, he had experienced the need to wash his wounds with the blood of another, and, cruelly, he had inflicted new wounds to soothe his own.

It was eight o'clock when the seconds of the two adversaries came to fetch them in order to take them to the combat terrain.

Philippe had exercised the day before in a fencing school, not in order to be better able to strike Julien, whom he knew to be inexperienced, but in order to be able only to inflict an insignificant wound on him. *How pointless it is to fight in these circumstances! What do two men gain by risking their lives for a hussy?* His mind, vagabonding in the night, meditated on the poverty of people's intelligence, the mediocrity of their ideas and their preoccupations, and the stupidity of their morality.

Having gone home after dining summarily in a boulevard restaurant, he had felt anxious and ill at ease. A single idea filled his mind: *A duel tomorrow with Julien, who has never done anything to me and might have become my friend.* He had started to reflect on that strange event, which he had not sought, which he had not foreseen. His hands shook slightly, with a nervous tremor, when they touched objects; his mind wandered, his thoughts turbulent, chopped, fleeting and dolorous. And incessantly, he repeated to himself: *I don't want to kill that child!*

Then, distinctly, he had seen Julien lying on the carpet of his room; he had seen the hollow visage that the dead have, and the whiteness of hands that will not move again.

With one bound, Philippe had stood up and had opened the window in order to drive away the frightful vision. He imagined, now, his own attitude and the bearing of his adversary. He imagined the slightest details of the duel, and promised himself to stay calm, to parry the attacks without riposting, and only to scratch

Julien. But the horrible dread came back, along with remorse for his futile denunciation.

He had opened a cupboard, seized a bottle of brandy and drunk a few long gulps avidly. A heat like that of a flame had soon burned his stomach, had spread into his limbs, had reaffirmed his dolorous soul, and he had stayed thus until morning, in a vague somnolence. Then, when he had heard distant locomotives uttering shrill and repeated appeals, he had slowly begun to dress.

Two hours later, there was a knock on his door and his seconds came in. In the carriage they had found the physician, asleep on the cushions.

A damp fog enveloped things, giving everything a uniform and melancholy hue. Rotting leaves adhered to the wheels of the landau, splashes of mud sprang up on to the windows. The paths of the Bois were deserted at that early hour. They had turned right into an avenue, then right again, and taken a little path that terminated in a clearing.

The other carriage was already stationed there, and Julien, very calm, watched his adversary coming. He saluted his adversary with a grave courtesy that pleased Philippe.

After the preparations, the witness pronounced the sacramental phrase: "Go, Messieurs!"

The first engagement was very lively, and yet produced no result, thanks to the Comte's composure, but the combatants put themselves *en garde* again, and Julien soon rolled on the ground with a feeble cry. Philippe's blade had penetrated his left breast and frayed a path straight into the lung.

As they tried to bring the young man to his feet, he said: "Don't touch me. I sense that the slightest movement would hasten my death. Go away; I would like to talk to Monsieur von Talberg."

The latter was already kneeling in the grass next to the wounded man; the witnesses stood aside respectfully.

"I'm glad to die," Julien continued. "I threw myself on your sword, and you certainly made every effort to spare me. I'm glad to die, for I know now that you told the truth. The indignity of that woman is certain, and I no longer understand my blindness. It's for her that I'm dying . . . it's her that has killed me."

"Oh, I greatly regret having spoken . . ."

"No, no, don't regret anything. Sooner or later, I would have learned the truth, and you've only abridged my suffering. Give me your hand."

The Comte took the hand that Julien no longer had the strength to hold out to him. The wounded man tried once again to speak, but a convulsion cut off his voice. He was coughing now, and spitting blood, which ran from the corners of his mouth at each cough. His neck, his breast and his clothing seemed to have been steeped in a red tub. He closed his eyes, out of strength, panting frightfully, and a sinister gargle was audible in his throat, all the way to the depths of his lungs.

Philippe got up, and, darting one last glance at the now motionless body, he murmured: "Oh, Camille! The crime you have made me commit will not go unpunished!"

VIII

Shortly thereafter, Dr. Richard was denounced, as well as Nina Saurel, who had recruited patients for him and taken perfectly healthy young women, and even girls, to his clinic. They had all submitted to ovariectomy, and had returned, healed and expert, to the ground-floor apartment in the Rue Blanche.

The judiciary investigation brought that high society affair into the daylight. There were instructive surgical discussions, and the revelation made in public of the existence in Paris of dubious dispensaries where, without any control, certain physicians carried out bizarre operations uniquely destined to earn them large sums of money.

The details were raw, repulsive and frightful. Bottles full of pieces of evidence were passed from hand to hand, along with forceps, probes and long flexible needles. Letters of thanks were read out, requests for meetings and promises of money.

A multitude of sinners filed through Richard's premises from morning until evening; he received them without distinction, gave long consultations, which all concluded with the necessity of an operation. The crackbrains who came to see him mingled debauchery with amour, vice with questions of interest. The magnitude of the sum to be paid out did not frighten them, however, so much in haste were they to rid themselves of all anxiety and all inconvenience.

Nina touted for clients, brought them to her associate, and had a share of the profit—hence the origin of her luxury, still largely inexplicable. The physician found an immense advantage in employing a woman who was entirely devoted to him and who proved, at the same time, more adroit and less exacting than a colleague. Science mingled with depravity, and all the unhappy wives removed there the mask of hypocrisy that they put on in society in order to hide their perverse passions. For the young women, the initiation was more delicate, but Nina fascinated fearful consciences, enlightened them, almost brutalized them, and generally ended up reckoning with their last modesties. Without the harvest of ovaries, it would have been difficult for her to satisfy her expensive tastes; it was therefore necessary to bring new victims to Richard every day. Sometimes there were cries, tears and protestations, which she calmed with a caress and a kiss, and the most timorous abandoned themselves body and soul to her.

Grateful patients convinced their friends to follow their example; sometimes, chambermaids and governesses, richly paid, waited at the door. Finally, there was the supper of the "demi-sexes," over which the doctor deigned to preside. To him, all smiles were directed, all actions of grace; he had only to choose his mistresses from the gracious flock that he had formed.

Richard was arrested immediately, but Nina, warned in time, was able to escape the research.

The trial of the affair had an enormous resonance. The judges multiplied interrogations, the experts reconstituted the productive thrusts of the scalpel, which, unfortunately, were not always devoid of danger for those thirsty for pleasure and liberty. Witnesses related what they had seen, indignant relatives filed through the court; the terror of chloroform and the lancet reigned momentarily over souls, for beneath the flowering bushes, a few frightful cadavers were found.

Austere moralists attacked the power of the physician, which, in our days, has become as unlimited as that of the executioner, and it was perceived—without seeking, however, to remedy that state of affairs—that only a physician has the right to be mad, sadistic and criminal, to vivisect, to torture, to claw, to quarter and to exsanguinate: in sum, the satanic conceptions of the most deregulated imagination. Whatever he does, his folly is considered as a theory and his hecatombs as sacrifices necessary to the progress of science. An unparalleled power has been constituted for him, made of egotism, avidity and human stupidity.

Thus the medical band had been able to prosper whom the denunciation of Richard suddenly came to strike. The innumerable mutilations and the murders that were committed with impunity every day in the handsome Richard's elegant clinic were displayed in the light of day. Women had rushed in hundreds toward that dispensary, where, according to the advertisements of Nina and her fellows, a little thrust of a knife could rid them of responsibilities, without danger and without pain, and exonerate them from fatal original suffering.

IX

In spite of her condition of weakness, Camille had wanted to return to France. Georges was no longer the same for her; beneath his saddened reserve she sensed him detaching himself and disaffecting himself from her person. That violent amour had only been a surprise, an almost unhealthy transport of the imagination and the senses. Little by little, his worship of art, his conception of genius, had to regain the upper hand and vanquish all the rest. In any case, now that his suspicion had been awakened, he became unjust, not knowing enough about women to disentangle the true from the false in them.

In Camille's sincere tenderness it seemed to him that he discovered the fabricated phrases dragged out in feuilletons, books and plays. He thought that in all of that there was nothing of her, nothing of the individuality of her heart and her intelligence. And then, he would have liked a child. Why did she impose silence on him, with horror, every time he raised the subject? For him, a child would have been a rival adoration for his art; he would have seen, in that masterpiece of nature and humanity, a better goal for his existence, a reason to become the great artist that he could be.

Why did Camille never talk about the hope that all women ought to caress, the hope of maternity that occupies the heart of the humblest and gives them the strength for sublime sacrifices? Why was his wife not similar to others? She even turned away from children when she encountered them in passing, and Georges sensed that those little beings were excluded from her thoughts and her desires; he suffered from the privation of the futile tender words that strangers address to babies in the flowery pathways of public promenades. He would at least have liked the tender silences, the smiles, the warmth of pity that announces the little mother and reanimates the ardor of infantile gaieties . . .

And, by virtue of a sort of indignation or unconscious hostility, he returned ten times a day to his preoccupation, offering himself the bitter pleasure of confession.

"You don't know what I'm thinking about?"

And, when she did not reply: "I'm thinking about our future, the long winter evenings in the warm studio, with a little child at our feet, who, all rosy, will roll on the carpet like a flower of flesh."

"Yes," she repeated, "a little child . . ."

And tears flowed from her eyes.

"Is it painful for you, then, to talk about such things?"

She inclined her head sadly, and remained silent. He did not insist, but a rancor remained in him. He told himself that his wife was too egotistical for maternal devotion and she seemed to him henceforth to be incapable of a serious affection. When she spoke to him, encouraged him or caressed him, he found the voice as false as the heart, and convinced himself that nothing moved or softened her except the folly of the senses.

She walked with him, preoccupied and weary, scarcely admiring the masterpieces that he showed her. She was there, beside him, with the resigned expression that no longer quit her, and he told himself that with such a companion, he would not be able to conceive or execute a truly beautiful and powerful work. The illusion had fled; he found within him and around him, in his flesh and in his soul, in the air and in the entire world, a kind of disappearance of the joy of living that had sustained and illuminated him for a time.

What had happened? Nothing . . . almost nothing. She had not mentioned Philippe von Talberg to him again, and he had not interrogated her on the subject; however, he felt that she had just made him revelations of which he would have liked still to be ignorant.

Certainly, she was beautiful, well-born, made to please, to receive tributes and hear bland compliments; among everyone, she had chosen him, united herself with him and his life, boldly and regally . . . He would remain, even so, the grateful servant of her caprices and the resigned spectator of her frivolous existence; but many things were suffering within him, in the mysterious cavern of the depths of the soul where singular sensibilities are huddled.

Undoubtedly, he was wrong, and he had always been wrong, to know nothing of worldly customs, living as a savage for the sole glory of making beautiful statues. Now, he no longer understood what was sufficient for other men. He was not made either for amour or for marriage; his susceptibility was too keen in juxtaposition with his inexperience. The kind of isolation into which he had retreated, for fear of painful contacts, suited him very well; why, then, had he emerged from it?

Frictions almost always come from what one does not admit, from what one cannot tolerate in others, a nature opposed to one's own. He knew that, having sometimes observed it, but he could not modify at his whim the special vibration of his soul.

In sum, he had nothing for which to reproach Camille, who always showed herself as tender as on the first day. Why, then, had that pain entered his heart? Oh, it was because he had believed her to be entirely his, and he had just recognized, or divined, that there was something that she was not telling him.

During the return journey, that painful impression increased instead of diminishing, and he sought in vain for the origins of the further malaises of his thought. They came and went, passing like little gusts of icy air, awakening in him an anguish that was still slight and distant, but singularly tenacious.

He was not jealous, his affection being one of those that cannot exist without esteem; he was unaware of that disposition, while observing it in others and scorning it as a folly unworthy of him. However, he was suspicious by instinct, by virtue of a sudden impulse of mistrust, slid into his veins rather than his intellect by the almost physical discontentment of a man who is not sure of his companion, and he was exasperated by that weakness . . .

How she had impressed him with a discreet authority at the little door of his studio! How she had entered, without emotion and without hesitation! How she had felt at home, immediately, in that suspect dwelling into which so many other women might have come! Would a young woman, even a bold one, superior to the stupid customs of false prudery, disdainful of prejudices, have maintained that tranquility in penetrating as a novice into the utter unknown of the studio of a painter or sculptor? Would not physical hesitations and mental turbulence have persisted after the first words exchanged, and would they not have hastened the departure?

Disturbed by the irritating fever that anxieties of the soul awaken throughout the body, Georges was agitated, becoming nervous, impressionable and moody. Sometimes, he tried to halt the march of his suppositions; he sought, found and savored just and reassuring reflections; but a seed of fear was within him that he could neither destroy nor hinder in its growth.

Camille, for her part, was suffering even more, because her amour was greater. Precisely what had charmed her in that enthusiastic and upright nature was about to be lost to her. Georges was detaching himself from her, and once the work of separation was accomplished, nothing in the world would be able to return her husband's heart to her. She was the idol that it was necessary not to touch, the one that could only be accepted pure of any suspicion, as impeccable and immaculate as supreme beauty. The fall would be all the more rapid because she was falling from a higher altitude, and nothing would remain of her past power.

She struggled to conserve her gaiety and apparent confidence, but the depths of her heart were full of sadness and fear. Certainly, a day would come when dissimulation would no longer be possible, when the truth would burst forth, when all the infamy of her former existence would rise again to the surface of her new existence, as the mud of a pond rises again and troubles the water when a stone is thrown into it.

She shivered at that thought, and ideas of suicide haunted her brain.

At present she brought into her tenderness a kind of madness, of delirium, of despair; her amour summoned dolor, drove her as far as heartbreak. In the paroxysm of excitement in which she found herself, her head, her nerves and her imagination no longer sought even forgetfulness in possession, but something more bitter, more poignant, and in a whisper she invoked death, burning in the embrace in the agony of her transports.

Georges was frightened by that exaltation, and sometimes pushed her away. "Where have you learned such things?" he demanded.

"You no longer love me," she replied, sadly. "I shall always love you . . . Once, you found quite natural what surprises you today . . ."

"Perhaps . . . I'm unjust, forgive me."

He tried to console her, but she could see clearly that the tender words he was murmuring were scarcely sincere, that the sentiment that dictated them was more akin to pity than affection.

X

On returning to Paris, Camille learned, at the same time, of Julien's death and Dr. Richard's arrest. She lived, then, in a frightful trance, expecting a denunciation at any moment. The witnesses cited numbered nearly three hundred, in addition to the doctors and experts; the list of those having undergone the operation was even longer. A few disastrous experiments had already attracted attention to the operator, Nina having failed to put the habitual discretion into her latest negotiations, and Philippe, in sum, had only brought forward the hour of reprisals. Young women had told everything to their parents, and if the latter had remained silent for fear of scandal, they had nevertheless acted in secret.

There had been curious revelations regarding certain aspects of Parisian life that were not generally known, or of which people feigned ignorance. Public opinion finally became indignant against the charlatans with diplomas and the manageresses of apartments who turned a blind eye to the crime and debauchery practiced there every day. The public prosecutor obligingly placed before the eyes of the jury the professional lives of those butchers of flesh and conscience, whose sinister misdeeds so often went unpunished.

In order to try to distract herself, Camille employed her nervous activity in the installation of her new dwelling. She had bought a charming house near the Parc Monceau, and she furnished it with feverish haste. People were hammering nails and washing things down everywhere. At the back of a vast and elegant garden was Georges' studio, very spacious and well lit. She went shopping, buying trinkets to make the interior of the dwelling flowery, as the gardener had rendered the exterior florid with his pale autumn blooms.

She arrived early in the morning, presided over the placement of furniture, climbed ladders, hanging pictures herself or changing the drape of a curtain. In her need to forget, she had the impression of doing the most important thing she had ever done.

Continually, she checked the clock, calculating how much time still separated her from the time when *he* would come in and thank her with a caress for having divined his tastes so accurately.

While waiting for the installation to be complete, they lived in the Faubourg Saint-Honoré, in Baronne de Luzac's former townhouse. Camille's bedroom, with its slackly draped soft fabrics and its pale green lacquered furniture, had become the conjugal bedroom, and every evening, after the day's labor and excursions, Georges came to join his wife.

He treated her with generosity, seemingly having compassion for the torments he divined in her without knowing the cause, and she suffered more from that vague pity, which humiliated her. Hatred is a tonic that stimulates life by means of the hope of vengeance, but pity kills, for it further enfeebles weakness. An ardent imagination makes a poem, terrible or joyful, of everything, in accordance with the events that strike it; its exaltation only seeks the vivid and trenchant nuances, the exaggeration in everything.

For Camille, that pity was a threat, a sinister death-knell.

For a while, she had lived with her husband in a charming dream, savoring the pleasures of a second childhood; she had forgotten her past sins and, in her happy insouciance, she had thought herself saved. A profound egotism had overwhelmed her, in which the universe had been engulfed; in her eyes, there was no more universe—the universe was her amour!

Sadly, she thought about that brief intoxication, which had momentarily enabled her life to blossom in the banality of marriage.

Georges was about to return. She was waiting for him in her bedroom, by the fireside, for the evening was cold and damp. She remained motionless, sunk in the mists of her melancholy. The flight of the minutes, however, was heavy and dolorous.

She picked up a book at random and tried to read, in order to ward off her apprehensions, for her nerves were vibrating terribly and the solitude was becoming intolerable to her; but she could not fix her attention on the volume she was holding, her eyes alone were following the aligned characters over the white page.

She listened to the clock chiming the bleak evening hours, and at that sound, although so natural, she slumped against the back of her armchair with an inexpressible anguish.

Why was Georges not with her to console her, and to defend her?

Suddenly, the door swung slowly on its hinges, and Nina appeared on the threshold.

"You!" cried Camille, leaping to her feet.

"Me . . . Does that astonish you? I've been able to escape the research, as you see . . . and here I am."

"Get out!"

"You're going to listen to me first."

"What do you want, then?"

"To demand that you account for your denunciation."

"I haven't denounced anyone."

"You're lying!"

"Why would I lie?"

"Anyway, someone has talked . . ."

"I don't know . . . what does it matter to me?"

They looked at one another, very pale, with a tremor of anger at the corners of their lips.

Nina, her throat contracted, murmured in a hoarse voice: "It's bad, what you've done!"

"Once again, I haven't done anything," Camille said, scornfully, "but I'm glad it's happened. I hate you! You've spoiled my life, soiled all my beliefs, and destroyed everything good and pure that there was in me. The punishment you've merited is above human judgment, and I wish ardently that it will reach you one day, in this world or the next . . ."

Nina started laughing. "Words! Words!"

"Words that kill."

"Get away! We both have beautiful years of pleasure before us. Your husband knows nothing of the past?"

"No . . . how would he know? I haven't been compromised . . . You're not replying? Oh, Nina, I beg you, reassure me . . . tell me that Georges doesn't know anything . . ."

Nina was still laughing. "He doesn't know anything today; tomorrow he'll know everything."

"Tomorrow?"

"Yes. I thought you'd denounced me, and I denounced you in my turn."

"You've done that?"

"At present, the law knows your life as well as mine."

"And you've come . . . ?"

"To tell you the good news."

"Oh!"

Camille had the strength to smile, but her fingernails were digging into her clenched hands. Nina did not divine her horrible anguish.

"Listen," she said, drawing nearer. "You can't stay here. Let's leave, let's unite our fortunes and recommence our former existence elsewhere . . ."

"Really?"

"You weren't made for marriage, you see. The little experiment has lasted long enough, and I assume that you're weary of playing the role of honest woman?"

"Yes, very weary . . ."

"You see! When one has savored certain joys, one returns to them incessantly, they're so attractive! I foresaw everything. My carriage is waiting to take us to the railway station. In a few hours we'll be out of danger. Come on!"

"What about Georges?"

"Georges no longer exists for you. Tomorrow, doubtless, he'll know everything, and you'll horrify him. Do you understand? It's better to leave before then. You think you love him, but deep down, you're incapable of love. Do women like us have a heart? You've been playing at marriage, that's all. You wanted a husband, a real one, because you didn't know that sensation yet. Now, the comedy has gone on long enough . . . you're becoming ridiculous."

"Yes."

"You're weeping? Go on, weep a little, it will do you good . . . and then, you're so pretty when you weep . . . Your lips!"

She took her hands, and tried to draw her to her. Camille was wearing a light peignoir of muslin silk and lace. Nina clutched her friend, pinned her mouth in a kiss as violent as a bite, and, recoiling unwittingly, caused the hem of her dress to jump into the fire. In a minute, they were surrounded by flames.

Nina tried to scream, but, imprisoned in Camille's arms, with the living gag of her mouth over her lips, she could only find strangled sounds in her breast, each aspiration of which, increasingly hollowed out, seemed to depart from her entrails.

When help arrived, it was too late. The bodies of two women were found enlaced, devoid of clothing, the flesh entirely charred. Under the action of the fire, their cadavers were so strangely diminished and twisted that it was impossible to distinguish one from another. When the attempt was made to separate them, they fell to pieces.

The world believed that it was an accident, and Georges remained ignorant of Camille's past. He mourned her sincerely, and extracted from the grave melancholy that enveloped his life the courage for the struggle, and the tender inspiration that makes masterpieces.

THE ANDROGYNES

I
The Confetti Ball

Fiamette Silly, one of the prettiest girls in the studio of Pascal—the painter of subtle elegance, fervent about sunsets and moonrises—had spent that Mardi-Gras evening at the Master's house. A joyful company was generally to be found there, but invitations were very rare and much sought after. They were only sent to disciples, friends and postulants of note, who were only permitted to enter on showing a pink and white card, as at certain sensational marriages—except that here, there was no crowd to dread; the vicinity of the temple and the corridors remained deserted, with the consequence that the faithful members of the congregation, some of whom only adorned their pure nudity with a simple ermine or rabbit-fur mantle, were able to penetrate discreetly, without delighting gazes or offending modesty.

Public morality, which had not, on that day, any outrage to suffer, found itself very morose and chagrined, as was also the case with a few individuals of grim virtue but vivid imagination, but in the hermetically sealed townhouse of the feminist, people were enjoying themselves greatly.

When Fiamette nonchalantly allowed the sumptuous sable mantle that enveloped her blonde beauty to fall away, there was only one cry of admiration. On her body, as nacreous as that of the Anadyomene, a frail necklace of diamonds was radiant, which her young breasts caused to glide in their voluptuous flux and reflux.

In truth, Fiamette scarcely possessed anything except for her sable and her necklace, but she maintained the faith of her eighteen Aprils and the good humor of joyful creatures who, no longer having anything to lose, have everything to gain.

The ball became very animated in the large studio, florid with a profusion of tea-roses, anemones and mimosas with delicate electric pistils, dissimulated in the heart of clusters, caressed with enfevering gleams. Japanese masks with gilded eyes and teeth grimaced among the ivories and jades on the silk of Mikado hangings. Nude studies borrowed from the adorable models who were crowding around the Master appeared, by contrast, slightly fixed and dull, not being, like the living masterpieces of that festival night, animated by the desire to dance and by kisses.

"Personally," said Ninoche, a beautiful girl who was holding forth in the middle of a group of pupils, her shoulders pecked by greedy lips, "I pose, principally, because one only really enjoys oneself at Pascal's."

"You think so?"

"Well, he chooses the most beautiful models, and he isn't as demanding as many of the failures who denigrate him."

"You go the extra mile for him?"

"Like all those he's created!" declared Ninoche, brazenly, lifting up the pink gauze that veiled her breasts.

And, in fact, the voluptuous swarm that was buzzing around the painter comprised the most suggestive of Montmartrean hives. The guests were gleaning a kiss here and there, attempting a friction, a pressure or a more direct caress, imploring a rendez-vous, trying to draw the laughing lovelies away.

On cushions in the corners, lively couples were confessing their desire, their eyes dilated, their impatient hands searching, and clutching one another for a long time.

Tigrane, the star of the Folies Perverses, who was to create the principal role in a ballet by Jacques Chozelle, had taken possession of Pascal and a prominent financier. Old rakes clustered around her, providing elytra and antennae at random.

"You know," she said to the artist, "I want you to paint my portrait. You understand me, you sense everything there is in my soul of ungraspable tenderness, of noble impulses suppressed by base realities, of aspirations and flights toward an utterly distant ideal." And as Chozelle was already having an unfortunate influence on the young woman, she added: "I'm the sphinx with blue-green eyes, the succubus exhaling morbid amour . . . I'm . . ."

"Personally, I'm a little pressed for time," declared the financier, disappearing into the crowd of pretty girls.

Pascal, a trifle slyly, examined the forty-two rings that were climbing over Tigrane's various knucklebones.

"There are enough of them today to finance it then?"

"No, I also like you a lot; you have a certain something that pleases women, which incites them to stupidities. I want you to paint me in a green spiderweb! You understand—so, thin threads, then, but growing, entangling against a mysterious background, in such a fashion as to form a velvet niche, in which I radiate like a glaucous star. A prodigious apparition, divine and terrible!"

"We'll talk about it again in a month's time."

"No, no, right away. I want my spiderweb."

"You already have it, my child," said Pascal, with a soft smile.

Here and there, there were notable literary men and others in search of attention, and names were being whispered with respect or malice. Legends were circulating about the former and the latter. There were celebrities of the criminal fraternity with reputations to make deportees to Noumea shiver, but the heroes of those . . . regrettable adventures seemed to be standing tall in their turpitude, glorying in their fall, and wearing their petty corruption like a flower in the buttonhole.

Fiamette drew close to a friend, a redhead with skin that was a little too pale, long feverish dark eyes and a dolorous face framed by rutilant headbands.

"Have you seen André? He quit me at the beginning of the soirée."

The friend with the misty eyes smiled enigmatically. "André? Yes, he's chatting with Chozelle."

"Oh! Where are they, then, Nora?"

"Back there on the divan."

Fiamette peered through the groups. "No, they must have left the studio."

"Are you jealous?"

"Jealous? Why?"

"Well, Chozelle is a bad acquaintance for André . . ."

Fiamette shrugged her shoulders disdainfully. "What do I have to fear? My amour has already triumphed over so many obstacles; it will triumph again."

Nora adjusted her gilded belt, the clasp of which was bruising her, over the light gauze of a scarf knotted around her loins.

"If I were in your place, I'd let go. André can only hinder your future . . ."

"I love him!"

"He has no fortune, no situation, and no influential friends."

"I love him!"

"He doesn't even have the I-don't-know-what that conquers women of the world. He's timid and weak. A pretty face, but no chic, no brio. A half-tone lover, in fact."

"I love him."

"As you wish . . . what I'm telling you is only for your own good, and for love of the art. I think it's a pity to spoil so much youth and beauty, to the profit of a fellow of such scant importance . . ."

At that moment, Pascal's pupils separated the two friends, and Nora, seized by impatient arms, found herself perched on a table and invited to mimic the transports of houris, as she had done for six months at the Egyptian theater of the Exposition. Meekly, the young woman seized the ends of her scarf and delivered herself to extraordinary quiverings of the belly and hips, while the audience imitated the cicada-like squeals of little flutes and the hoarse hiccupping of delirious drums.

During the Exposition, many unemployed young women had substituted for the insufficiency of exotic dancers. They were better able than them to agitate their bodies in voluptuous frissons, to offer themselves, refuse themselves and swoon by turns, in the vehement and precise mime in honor of the lands of the sun that is imprudently authorized on our Parisian stages.

Nora, supple, ardent and sinewy, had embellished the lascivious and monotonous dance of Montmartrean fantasy, more perversely spiced than the habitual simulacrum of amour, and certainly unexpected in its effect. Her success almost surpassed that of Sada Yacco, the dainty doll with the hooded eyes and the cooing voice of a Japanese turtle-dove.[1] All Paris had wanted to applaud the frenetic bacchante with the fiery eyes, and drink the wine of voluptuousness from her lips. She had made a fortune there, and contracted a pulmonary phthisis that slowly undermined her.

A sudden intoxication burst forth in Pascal's studio. The entire room quivered with a swell of swaying bodies, while girdles and golden ornaments leapt on tumultuous rumps and white breasts.

Nora spun recklessly, and then launched her slender leg into the air like a rocket, and the spangles of her little shoe caught fire above the heads. Holding the pink satin heel in one hand, she pivoted lightly, and suddenly fell like a scythed corolla, one foot here and another there, in a fantastic split.

"Bravo, Nora! Nora the Comet!"

And the supple girl with the mat skin, seemingly animated by an interior light, with the rutilant russet mane, did indeed resemble a wandering star describing audacious parabolas.

At the first light of dawn, the painters realized the amiable whim of dressing their lovers with a tunic of confetti, a rain of roses having become too expensive since the days of Roman orgies. Then, from the height of the long ladders of the studio, there was a hail, an avalanche, a deluge of light, gummed disks, which stuck to the bodies of the women in rosettes, arabesques and dazzling mosaics. Serpentine girdles and the headdresses of barbarian chieftainesses completed the metamorphosis.

Only the Tanagrean beauty of Fiamette still remained in its initial splendor, when a dauber decided that that lily-white body

---

1 The Japanese dancer Sada Yacco (1871-1946), a former geisha, performed at the 1900 Exposition Universelle in Loie Fuller's pavilion.

demanded an immaculate fleece of white confetti, and within a minute, the pretty girl personified well enough the Frost Fairy, crowned with snow and circled with long ribbons of frost. As she laughed, tickled by the silk of the paper stuck to her skin, Nora whispered to her malevolently: "Only, André isn't here to admire it . . ."

"André!"

The young man on the divan appeared to be asleep. His head supported on cushions, his eyes closed, he was motionless, lost in a dream . . .

Fiamette parted the crowd and, all white, her hair undone, leaned over her friend, who suppressed a movement of ennui.

"Come on, look at me, then!"

"Oh, leave me alone."

But she lifted up his head and stuck her lips violently to his. "You belong to me! I want you! Let's go home!"

Pascal intervened. "Yes, take him away. What is he thinking, not to be able to see that the most precious thing he possesses is in peril?"

"Come on!" Fiamette repeated. "I'll keep my confetti; there'll be room even so for your kisses."

André pushed her away. "No—why did you wake me up? I'd lost the notion of stupid reality . . ."

"Be polite," Pascal interjected.

" . . . Of reality, simply, if you wish, and it's a good opportunity not to be able to think about it any longer!"

"I can understand that, when one has spent an hour in the company of Jacques Chozelle!" riposted Fiamette, aggressively.

The artists laughed, almost all being hostile to the disquieting esthete that name evoked.

"What woman here would swallow such a specimen?" snapped Fiamette, parading her gaze over the tightly pressed ranks of pretty girls, whose young nudity did not make them immodest.

There was a buzz in the room, as of pollen-gathering bees at the departure of a useless male expelled from the hive of amour.

"Me," said Nora. "The man I love is a handsome fellow who knows how to draw upon all the resources of sensuality without ever baulking at the task! I'm his until death!"

"And he cheats on you with all your friends," murmured a painter. "That's what gives you a proud idea of his temperament."

"Oh," said a girl with cleavage scarcely blossoming under the mesh of a corselet of blue pearls, who posed as "Innocence" for Pascal, "there's nothing like painters for giving pleasure."

To thank her, Pascal kissed her bright eyes, and passed an Egyptian necklace around her neck, formed of enamel scarabs and stolen from some ancient sepulcher.

People were beginning to leave, and the most obstinate, taking one another by the hand, gathered frenetically round the master. Shaking off the multicolored spangles of confetti and curly serpentine ribbons, the women were resplendent in the pure glory of their youth, their slender bodies, nacreous or gilded, delectably polished, with the pink nipples of breasts erect in the battle of sensuality.

Then couples formed, gliding toward the exit, in haste for an embrace.

André got up, yawning, traversed the staircase, slowly put on his overcoat, and distractedly aided his mistress, who was shivering in the antechamber.

II
Return to the Love Nest

They set forth, leaning on one another in order to warm up, and reached the Rue Caulaincourt, the sinister street that passes over the dead[1] and climbs toward the butte, dear to poets and the poor. It was there that they had suspended their nest, on the fifth floor of a house of bourgeois appearance.

---

1 The Rue Caulaincourt includes a viaduct that passes over a corner of Montmartre Cemetery.

For their six hundred francs a year, they occupied three small sunlit rooms with a cabinet that served as a kitchen. From their balcony, they contemplated the garden of the defunct, which scintillated with all its glass flowers in the gold of its immortelles, and, further away, the swarm of the living, obstinate in their brief, futile struggle. A little earth above, a little earth below; truly, the living are always close to the dead, and it is pitiful to see them striving madly for an illusory goal of quietude and justice.

Fiamette had disdained a commencement of opulence in order to follow her seductive chimera, and the infatuation, entirely cerebral at first, had gained her heart sinuously but irresistibly. Fiamette, a creature of amour, sincere in the gift of herself, had necessarily to commit the stupidity of loving, and, by virtue of that, inspired scorn in her triumphant lover, by suppressing the pride in the struggle. That unfortunate generosity was aggravated by a certain education, too easily acquired, and a great deal of natural intelligence.

André Flavien possessed talent and arrogance, the imperious desire to succeed, and the awkwardness of all those whose real merit prevents them from indulging in base intrigues and productive speculations.

She and he often skipped meals, supping on dubious cooked meats, thinking that they were having a feast and living like vagabonds.

André still possessed a small sum of money, originating from an inheritance, and two notebooks of verses copied in a feverish handwriting redolent of dreams.

For her entire fortune, Fiamette had her sable and her necklace.

"What have I done?" she asked, when they were back in their cramped room, encumbered by books and feminine knick-knacks thrown randomly on to the furniture.

He moved aside a velvet cap and a mauve surah skirt, and was able to sit down on the edge of an armchair. Then, drawing her toward him, he said: "Are you courageous, my little Fiamette?"

She went pale seeing the distress in his gaze beneath his blond eyebrows, while he slid a caressant hand under her fur, testing the softness of her skin.

"What do you have to say to me?" she murmured.

"You know how much I love you, darling?"

"When you're close to me, like this, I certainly don't doubt it, but there are hours of anguish and frightful jealousy that you'd spare me if you could understand the distress of my soul."

André's lips strayed over the blonde hair of his mistress, and she closed her eyes, already reconquered, stirred delectably by his savant caresses.

"Oh," she said, "I no longer have the strength to scold you. Every kiss collects from my lips that reproach that is burning them and changes it into amorous words. We women are doomed, you see, when we're in love!"

He pressed her against himself more forcefully, and she nestled in his arms, utterly frail beneath that male will, happy to annihilate herself against her lover's heart.

For a long time he cosseted her, like a suffering child that it was necessary not to cause to weep; then, by means of specious reasoning, he became firmer in his resolution.

"Darling, listen to me courageously."

"Again!"

"Yes, it's necessary to think about the future."

"What's the point. Let's profit from the present. Aren't we happy like this?"

"Life has its necessities."

"You're leaving me?"

As she weakened, utterly pale, he tried to attenuate the dolorous impression that his words had produced on his mistress by means of a banal explanation.

"I'm not leaving you. I'm trying to get out of a rut and create a situation for myself. It's not by declaiming verses in Montmartre brasseries that I'll get out of difficulty. Truly, I'm weary of so much vain effort."

He spoke volubly, fundamentally unconvinced.

"Has someone offered you something?" asked Fiamette, impatiently.

"Yes. Oh, I'll see you anyway, and it will be even better . . . but living together has become impossible."

She tried to put a little order in her ideas and to reason calmly.

"Your family, no doubt."

"No."

"Who, then?"

"Jacques Chozelle has offered me a secretarial position."

"In his house? You're going to live with him?"

"No, not with him, obviously, but in the vicinity, in order to be there at a moment's notice."

Fiamette uttered a bitter laugh, in which all her amorous rancor burst forth, at the same time as her pity for her lover's naïvety.

"You don't know what people say about Jacques, then?"

"Calumnies of no importance! He's envied, like all successful men. We'll collaborate on fine and strong works . . ."

"Really?"

"A grandiose and superb idea that he's submitted to me. I'm going to set to work on it right away."

"He'll doubtless get you to write his novels and pay you in fine words . . ."

"What an invention! It's Pascal who's put it into your head . . ."

"Pascal judges without acrimony; his disdain, I assure you, is full of sincerity. He thinks that Jacques Chozelle is as empty as a coconut, and that, physically and mentally, he's only held together by paint. Cracked, worm-eaten, mildewed and crumbling, I tell you!"

"A rage of idiots to denigrate him . . ."

"Get away. His reputation is only made by the scandal he kicks up, and he uses it, exploiting the taste for the morbid, the adulterated and the corrupt that reigns at present in a certain society . . ."

170

"My little Fiamette, these appreciations aren't yours . . ."

"You judge me too futile and too ignorant to accord me a personal opinion? Well, yes, I'm only bringing you the faithful echo of what people were saying this evening. They must have said many others things too, which I didn't hear, because I was far from expecting the intrusion of Jacques into our pretty nest, so pleasantly closed until now. Oh, my poor darling!"

André did not reply. Either out of weariness, or the settled determination to follow his plan, he pulled Fiamette toward him again, seeking the seductive pressure of her lips.

She was still covered, here and there, by a capricious snow of confetti. He amused himself following the elaborate design on her body, lingering over mysterious coverts where the accumulated flakes mingled with a little gold. Passive, she put up no resistance, invaded by an unconscious lust.

"You know very well that I love you," he exclaimed, as she thanked him with a happy smile, "but life is hard. I don't want you to sell your necklace for me."

III
Nora the Comet

The morning light was subdued in the narrow room that the drawn curtain left mysteriously in shadow. Fiamette, her eyelids hazy and her lips blanched, was asleep on the thick silk of her hair, weary of having made love or wept. André, with an elbow on the pillow, remained pensive and indecisive, drawn toward a literary labor that he hoped might be brilliant and remunerative, but held back by the certainty of hurting his friend.

"Come and find me," Jacques Chozelle had said. "I find in you the abundant and supple talent for which I'm searching for a collaborative work; I'll show you my notes and we can begin immediately."

Chozelle had thrown the young man the gilded mat of his praise, and with the cajoling voice that he was able to adopt when the occasion demanded, he had caused a glorious future to flash before his eyes.

André Flavien gazed at his mistress sadly, brushed her hair with a kiss, and proceeded to get washed and dressed in the next room, trying to make as little noise as possible. When he was ready, he returned to contemplate the sleeper, who had not budged, and left the apartment with a velvet step.

Nora, who was coming up, bumped into him on the stairs.

"A louis says that you're going to see Jacques!"

"Perhaps—but that doesn't concern you."

"Is Fiamette still asleep?"

"Go in if you want."

"And what would you say if I took your mistress away?"

"Are you working for yourself?"

"I'm working for her."

"Then take her away, if you like; let her follow her whim or her fortune . . . both, if possible."

"I admire your philosophy. You take events with serenity."

"It's them that take me, and I let them do it. It's necessary not to oppose destiny."

"Good luck, André!"

"Good luck, Nora. One last kiss for Miette . . ."

He was at the bottom of the stairs. Nora knocked gently on the door of the forsaken girl.

After a moment, Fiamette came to open it, with a poorly fastened peignoir over her round shoulders.

"You, so early!"

"Yes, I need to talk to you about something serious, and it's reason that will speak through my mouth . . ."

The two women, leaning on one another fondly, went into the dressing room, devastated by André's impatient fever, which had thrown paper towels everywhere. A small divan draped with Japanese fabrics in exquisite hues, garnished the back of the narrow room, under a bric-à-brac of arms, slippers, fans and sketches by friends: a bizarre and yet harmonious assemblage of disparate objects grouped by artistic hands.

Nora stifled a fit of coughing with her handkerchief, and the delicate linen cloth was tinted pink.

Fiamette put her friend's pale head on her breast, gently.

"You ought to be asleep, dreaming about amour."

"Or death . . ."

"Would you like to shut up? At your age . . . and with such pretty eyes!"

"My eyes see further than life; perhaps that's why they're so beautiful . . . but it's not a matter of me . . ."

"So it's a serious reason that brought you here?"

"My step would be poorly judged in the bourgeois world, and a vile epithet would be thrown at my head. Believe, however, that it's my amity alone that has impelled me here at this moment."

"Go on."

"After your departure from Pascal's soirée I had a long conversation with Francis Lombard. He loves you and he asked me to tell you so."

With an abrupt movement, Fiamette pushed her friend away. "Oh, that's bad! I'll never leave André, you know that very well."

Nora's smile was tinted with indulgence. "In fact, you won't have that trouble; it's him who'll go away."

"No, you don't know my influence over him. I assure you that André is more tightly bound to me than he thinks."

"I met him on the stairs; he's going to see Chozelle."

"So what?"

"He believes the word of that schemer, who has promised him his protection; he's proud and suffers from seeing you in need. He's authorized me himself to talk to you as I'm doing."

"He told you . . . ?"

"That you could follow your whim . . . yes."

Fiamette shivered dolorously; then, trying to adopt a cheerful tone: "You're offering me an astonishing situation, then?"

"A little house, horses, correct domesticity and the heart of a worthy fellow who's worth as much as his fortune, which is rare.

Come on, doesn't this rag dishonor your young royalty?" With a disdainful fingertip, Nora uncovered a section of pink breast beneath dubious lace. "We should have English and Bruges needlepoint, and precious guipures! A woman, my dear, only has fifteen years of her existence to roll and gather moss. After that, she can still roll, but she no longer gathers anything. I can at least die tranquil, having myself pampered as if someone really loved me. It's the Exposition that brought me that, the dance of Mahomet and the Moulin Rouge."

"Oh, you make good progress . . ."

"As much as I can."

"You've conquered independence, that's something."

"It's everything! Don't seek for anything beyond it. Oh, I've known more poverty than you, and the disdain of imbeciles, and the rebuffs of boors, and the proposals of handsome monsieurs who pretended to be guiding me and lived at my expense. That's what gives one a fine idea of the other sex! Come on, my little Fiamette, think about the marvelous opportunity that I'm offering you. Yes, I seem to be playing a rather shady role, but you know me, you know that I'm incapable of a bad action, and that I'm only acting in your interest."

"I know."

"Then say yes and I'll run to take the news to the amorous fellow who's waiting for me downstairs . . ."

"At my door?"

"Look!" Fiamette leaned over her balcony curiously, and perceived a blue coupé harnessed to a chestnut horse, with a coat as shiny as gold, and an impeccably stuffed coachman on its seat.

"Your carriage!" said Nora, laughing. "Quickly, put on your prettiest dress, your sable and your necklace. It's Opportunity calling!"

Fiamette blew a kiss to that Opportunity, always in such a hurry, which was trotting through her life, and then went back into the warm room, took off her frayed peignoir and slid between the sheets in the place of the lover she cherished too much.

"I'd rather sleep," she said.

174

IV
Foetuses and Salamanders

I love you, my mistress, as much as the blue sky,
Breezes, perfumes, mountains, woods, waves,
Laughter, songs, profound ecstasies,
     And fiery kisses.

I love you, my mistress! From your mouth my desire
Is incessantly suspended, an enchanted butterfly!
And I have known through you the ardent sensuality
     Of possessing my dream!

I have closed my heart recklessly on your caress,
In order that in memory, imprisoned and vibrant,
It gives me still the intoxicating shock
     Of your victorious spasm!

If amour is reborn in heaven for the faithful,
My mistress, I want to die on your lips,
In order to keep the kiss that causes to flourish
     Eternal roses!

Jacques yawned in the green silk wing-chair in which he was sprawling idly.

"Amour! Always amour! Oh, my boy, it will be necessary to change that!"

"No more love?"

"A different kind of love; the love of the superior being, the divine Androgyne, which forms a perfect whole in itself."

"I don't understand."

"Woman, my child, cannot satisfy us, because her inferior nature does not respond to the aspirations of our intelligence.

Our artistic temperament suffers from her incomprehension, the brutality of her passion, always exaggerated, and at the same time, from her excessive submission to our desires. Woman has more instinct than rationality; she is too close to animality."

"It's her weakness that makes her charm. Are we not happy in protecting her mentally while she caresses us with her maternal or amorous tenderness? Doesn't the strongest man love to forget himself in the supple arms of a mistress?"

"Base literature, my dear. Initiation will enable to you judge differently. Real amour can only exist between two equal beings, and I mean by amour, not only the intoxication of the senses, but the adorable communion of two similar souls. The Androgynes knew the plenitude of happiness. Not being able to have, like them, the double apparatus of generation, let us at least try to possess mentally the force of fecundation and creation."

André smiled.

"Don't you know, Master, that the Androgynes were superior beings, but filled with pride; that they wanted, like the Titans, to scale Olympus, and that it was Jupiter, in order to punish them, who brought about the separation of which we complain today. Having two faces, four arms and four legs, they could be cut in two with no difficulty. The incomplete man searches eternally for his dolorous other half, for the universe is so large that he has little chance of finding her!"

"Man, my boy, should try to regain his primitive state by being self-sufficient."

"That would be the end of the world."

"So much the better. Such as it is, the world isn't worth a mass, and could be extinguished in impenitence, even if good and evil exist. A matter of appreciation . . . come on, read me something other than songs of amour!"

André chose other sheets, laid bare his nostalgic poetic soul, and Jacques, smoking tobacco paler than the gilded crumbs of true hosts, listened distractedly.

The young man, his scroll of paper between his fingers, waited anxiously for the judgment that the authorized lips of the Master was about to let fall. His astonished gaze wandered over the walls, where amazing paintings were displayed, representing vague foetuses swimming in alcohol. After a more attentive examination, he perceived that they were flower-children, little hydrocephalous boys growing leaves outside a vase with glaucous reflections, tilting their bloodless and monstrous heads like morbid corollas. On the ground, on cushions, snakes and salamanders with ocher and cinnabar pustules, and also worm-flowers, were displayed, and André had the desire to flick the Master, motionless on his armchair, in order to assure himself that he was not also a flamboyant reptile asleep in the hallucination of that marsh in a room.

"You're looking at my dream studies? They're beautiful, aren't they? One can scent the penetrating and seductive odor of charnel houses before those violated adolescent heads. And the fixed swarm of those larvae seems to be caressing the decomposed bodies under the surface when one dives among the nenuphars. Oh, the green nenuphars and the black irises! Oh . . . !"

André was ill at ease; he would have liked, nevertheless, to say something amiable—but Chozelle did not give him the time. He launched forth and spoke abundantly about his talent, his genius, his beauty and his fragile health.

"Your little verses, my dear André, are not 'artistic': too much sentiment, clarity and bourgeois emotion. You see, it's necessary never to try to express the meaning of things, or the state of your soul; only writing, the grouping of words, retains some importance. Be esthetic in form; ideas fatigue readers, troubling the digestion."

"But esthetics change, while ideas remain."

"Pooh! Our paintings are less outdated than our writings. Make up your palette, my dear, with rare tones, of all poisonous vegetables, aquatic herbs and beached medusae. Don't fear to dip your brush in the putrefaction of stagnant water and overripe flesh. Reread the divine Baudelaire's *La Charogne*. A masterpiece!"

"Certainly, but there's more in that piece than words grouped like earthworms around a porous root."

"I don't want to see anything in it but words and horror; since you desire to work with me, penetrate my morbid essence, my demonic charm, my disquieting strangeness . . ."

"I'll try. Would you care to listen to this other little piece, in which I believe there's an image?"

André chose another poem.

"It's a sunset," he said. "I'll read it rapidly." And when he had finished, he asked, with an imploring anguish: "Is that better?"

"No. It's not my style. Too much clarity. People only truly admire what they don't understand."

"Will you counsel me?"

"Call me dear Master, my child. I'll be glad to support myself on your young and robust shoulder. Your fine head and large eyes will add to my glory. We'll be seen together and people will think about that other Master, so much calumniated, who showed himself sometimes in all the radiation of his genius, with his companion of election. Oh, how beautiful he was, that lover of form and poetry!"

"The master?"

"No, the friend."

And Jacques pulled back slightly, in order to consider André at length, with severity; then drawing closer, he tapped his back and his chest, as horse-traders do with a thoroughbred colt.

"Broad shoulders, slim waist. You're badly dressed, my dear, but I divine, beneath that humble jacket, exquisite sinuosities, a rare epidermis . . ."

Surprised, André had paled slightly.

"Oh," said Jacques, laughing. "I want my disciple to do me honor; I'm an artist before everything else."

The young man darted a discouraged glance at the salamanders, the pustules of which were bursting over the furniture, and the foetus-flowers fixed in the rancid oil of a painter who was naïve in spite of his pretentions.

Jacques, with his slender moustache, and his lashes lowered over his troubled blue eyes, pinched his earlobe in order to redden it.

"It's an artist of great intuition who made me these studies, after the Dream . . ."

"Oh!"

"An opium dream that lasted for an entire night, and held us in its powerful claws. Oh, that was an unparalleled anguish and voluptuousness, I'll initiate you . . ."

Wan and melancholy, André told himself that life was hard and that a few louis would make things better, but he dared not broach that down-to-earth question, and waited impatiently for the generous offer of collaboration.

"And the urgent work?" he finally asked, in a bland voice.

"I haven't forgotten it, my young friend; it's necessary, in order for you to devote yourself to it fruitfully, for you to know my genre, my style, that you put on, if I might express it thus, my skin. In my works, I speak, above all, about myself, and that awakens the curiosity of the reader, interesting him much more than an adventure of the imagination, about which one no longer thinks when the book is closed. I'm not entirely what you've been told, what you might believe . . ."

"I don't believe anything. Would I be here otherwise?"

"In this time of excessive fame, it's necessary to create an almost disquieting personality, and it's used up quickly, for imitators abound."

"Oh, I know . . ."

"Yes, you've seen many young writers copying me in a deplorable manner. Well, André, my good friend, my dear disciple, it's necessary for my talent to be inimitable and . . . that concerns you . . ."

"Me!"

"Certainly. When you've lived in my intimacy for a while, you'll understand me, and you'll write beautiful and great things."

"Ah!"

"For that, my dear, you'll have two hundred francs a month. I'd like to do more, but I'm poor, you know. Is that agreed?"

André reflected that he owed two months' rent to his landlord and truly did not know how he would live in the coming month. With tears in his eyes and his throat contracted, he accepted.

Jacques escorted him to the door fraternally, with a hand on his shoulder.

"Master," said André, blushing, "could you advance me a little money . . . I'm embarrassed at the moment, and I have a mistress . . ."

"A mistress! Damn! You don't, I see, have modern ideas. Women dishonor us by their physical and mental inferiority."

"In your books, however . . ."

"Yes, I put them in my books, because it's necessary to satisfy the reader, who is also a coarse being, but I don't put them in my life. In any case, my literary women are exceptional creatures who can have some charm. I make them thinking corpses, astral lovers, desexualized, so to speak, and in my articles I avenge myself for that concession accorded to the poor taste of the crowds. When you can, you'll imitate me. By the way, yesterday's attire suited you very well. Come and pick me up on Saturday at seven o'clock; I'll take you to a dinner of men, where a few of the arcana of mystery will be revealed to you."

Negligently, Jacques plunged his fingers, ringed with aquamarines, into one of the pockets of his waistcoat, and handed his confused disciple a louis.

V
Between Lovers

"It's you," said Fiamette, raising herself up on the pillow. "I knew you'd come back."

"What, still in bed! It's two o'clock."

"I didn't have the wherewithal to buy lunch, and I needed sleep."

"I haven't had anything to eat either. Look, here's twenty francs."

Joyfully, the young woman leapt out of bed, bathed in cold water, put on a skirt, threw her sable over her shoulders and, putting up her hair in a golden helmet, ran down the five flights of stairs. She was singing, and André could hear her lovely voice, with the accompaniment of her little heels on the steps.

A woman, a friend, an attentive and discreet companion who cares for the heart and body with witty gestures and the friction of comprehensive caresses—is there anything sweeter, down here? he asked himself, thinking of Jacques' bitter and vindictive words. And, instinctively, he mistrusted the fop with the troubled eyes and disdainful lip, slobbering eulogies and bile. But what could he do? It was necessary to live, and in the métier of letters, one takes what is offered, with the hope of splendid revenges when fruitful success has arrived.

After ten minutes, Fiamette came back laden with provisions, and on the corner of a table they devoured them with a terrible appetite, the fine hunger of healthy and robust youth.

"You've seen Jacques Chozelle, then? What is he like at home?"

"Quite something, in the ensemble, with bizarre details. I imagined the interior of a poet quite differently. My word, it's better here."

"Bravo! You'll stay here."

"My poor Miette, I'd like that very much . . . alas, it isn't possible."

"Oh, the wretch!"

With the plaint of a little girl, she threw her arms around his neck, rubbed his chin with hers, closing her eyes like a cat drinking milk. And all the slight caresses of loving women came to trouble the young man delectably.

"André, I don't want you to work for that man!"

"But we have nothing, nothing but valueless knick-knacks that we wouldn't be able to live on for a month. Jacques is offering me two hundred francs."

"Are you sure that someone else wouldn't offer you more and be less demanding?"

"I fear, in fact, that Jacques has neither personal merit nor acquired talent. With the bitter desire to succeed, however, he's tried to create a genre, and he's exploited the improper sides of certain souls: the taste for literary and moral gaminess, or simply the snobbery of imbeciles. The man is neither an artist nor a poet, since he's ignorant of the love of the beautiful. He's a skilful plagiarist who, in his stubborn labor, scorns the ideal, to think only of the practical and commercial side of things."

"Then again," said Fiamette, "has he ever indicated a real talent, aided a writer or artist of value to emerge from the shadows?"

"No, he's not so stupid. He's only ever celebrated pretentious nullities, voluntary eccentrics devoid of any future, who can't bear him umbrage."

"We're slandering him! So, it's agreed, you'll go and knock on other doors."

"No, I was mistaken on Jacques' account, but the study of the person and the special milieu in which he moves interests me, for the moment. To succeed elsewhere, it would be necessary to take steps, perhaps humiliating ones, to wait for a long time in the antechambers of seigneurs of mark or countermark, and to expose oneself to rebuffs. I don't have a supple enough spine to bow down to that extent."

"Then at least promise me to come back every evening. You can't leave me like this. You don't know, then, what has been proposed to me?"

André had a tremor in his hands, the abrupt clench of someone who would like to knot his fingers around an enemy's throat.

"Yes, I know," he said, very quietly. "You're free, Fiamette . . ."

"How can you say that to me?"

"Fortune is doubtless offered to you; it's necessary not to let it draw away. You've made me a sacrifice that has lasted long enough. Remember, my little Miette, that old age is hard for women, and that you won't always remain the flower of amour that you are today."

Fiamette scowled, and nestled on her lover's knees.

"That's my business, and if it pleases me to end my days in a concierge's lodge or a student garret . . . I'm free, I think?"

André forgot himself, respiring the voluptuous softness of his mistress' stray hairs behind the ear, a place where she was particularly sensitive.

She undid the silky skein, wrapping it round the young man's neck like a golden serpent.

"Now you're a prisoner!"

And the faces of the lovers, thus united, must have resembled those of the heroes of Longinus, in the flower of their desire and their youth. But André pushed his friend away, his eyebrow suddenly furrowed by an anxiety.

"Have you examined my coat?"

"Your coat?"

"It had a little tear under the arm, in a place corroded by mites; I'm sure that it's enlarged. If only you knew how to make an invisible repair . . ."

"I'll ask the concierge for a lesson. Have you been invited to the home of a princess, then?"

"Perhaps . . ."

The coat that Fiamette held up, front and back, was less damaged than one might have thought, after Carnival night. It was silhouetted almost elegantly against the Japanese hangings of the room. André relaxed.

"It was a chic tailor who made that for me!"

"Come on, let me in on the big secret. Who's the conquest at which you're aiming?"

"Oh, you don't have to be jealous. I'm going to a soirée of men."

"How bored you'll be, my poor darling."

"Even more than you think. A session of bitter denigration for the absent, and sticky flattery for the attendees."

"Why are you going?"

"I'm accompanying Jacques."

Fiamette's delicate features took on a nasty expression. "Oh! I'd prefer to see you spending the evening with women!"

VI
Old and New Games

"You haven't taken a cab, then, my young friend? Your shoes are dirty . . . and that knot in your cravat!"

Jacques did not seem to be delighted with his new disciple's attire. He poured a few drops of an aggressive perfume into his handkerchief and carefully slid a glaucous orchid with black-striped petals into his buttonhole. Then he stepped back a few paces, in order to contemplate his work.

"That's already better . . . do you like flowers?"

"Yes, very much . . . but all flowers, while you seem to me to have a predilection for hybrid and poisonous species . . ."

"What, not the slightest ring, and fingernails cut short! Where have you come from? That's horrible!"

"I prefer not to wear rings. As for my fingernails, I'll let them grow if you think it desirable, although it seems to me that it's of no great utility."

184

"It's capital! No more than a woman, a man ought not to neglect any means of seduction. Know, too, that when I permit a newcomer to accompany me to the houses of my friends, I want him to do me honor in every fashion."

Jacques had perfumed and powdered his thin hair; a little rouge animated his cheeks; one would have sworn that a hint of kohl elongated and emphasized his eyelids, giving his fugitive gaze an enveloping softness.

André preferred not to examine the Master's make-up more profoundly. "Would you like me to go down and hail a cab?" he asked, in a slightly dry tone, which earned him an acquiescence full of forbearance, for Jacques had scant esteem for those who spoke to him timidly.

Having thrown an address on the Avenue de Messine to the coachman, the Master installed himself in the fiacre, carefully raised the glasses, his bronchi being unable to support the cold, and said in the singing voice that was habitual to him:

"My friend Paul Defeuille, whose acquaintance you are about to make, sometimes invites us to dinner, as he has this evening. He's a man of great worth and refined manners. I hope that you recognize the favor he is doing you, for his door only opens judiciously and his invitations are very rare. At these little feasts, of a very particular character, the conversations roll over all subjects with a complete liberty, as is customary in gatherings from which women are excluded. Those pretentious creatures talk about everything without knowing anything, admiring and chattering with a comical assurance and an unparalleled naïvety!"

"You certainly detest them!"

"My God, no, I'm merely scornful of them. I see, painfully, that you still follow the old errors, and I truly dread that you'll cut a sorry figure this evening . . ."

"Why?"

"Well, your candor might suffer a few assaults . . ."

Jacques had an ironic crease at the corners of his lips that displeased the young man.

"I believe I have a few things to learn . . ."

"So much the better."

The carriage stopped in front of a house of fine appearance, and Jacques, leaning on the arm of his new friend, went up one floor and penetrated into an antechamber hung with old tapestries and ornamented with Venetian mirrors with precious frames. Carefully, he repaired the slight disorder that the journey had inflicted on his attire, straightened the petals of the orchid that ornamented his coat, and clouded his features by means of a powder-puff hidden in his handkerchief.

In the drawing room, with vast divans strewn with rose petals under lustrous iridescent tulips, a dozen men were chatting nonchalantly in poses that demi-mondaines expert in the art of pleasing would not have disavowed. Waistcoats with sparkling nuances tightened figures, rings with enormous bezels covered fingers and heady gusts of multiple extracts mingled with the perfume of the flowers.

The master of the house stood up eagerly as Jacques Chozelle entered, gave him the accolade, and shook André's fingers affectionately. The latter paled slightly, sickened but resolute.

"An expressive head," Defeuille said, after having examined him with a connoisseur's eye, "With nice teeth and eyelashes . . . but look at those eyelashes, as curly as a little girl's! Scarcely twenty-three, yes?"

"Twenty-four."

"Bravo! What do you think, Messieurs?"

There was a flattering murmur. Jacques turned up his moustache. "He's my pupil."

"Where did you pick him up?"

"In Pascal's studio, which was dishonored by female nudities."

"Pooh! These artists truly never understand the beautiful. What is comparable to the forms of the Antinous, or the Apollo of the Vatican? The vigor, the elegance, the majesty, a perfect harmony of lines . . . whereas even the ancient genius was unable to idealize the ridicule of feminine roundness: bags for reproduction and milking."

"Woman is only a blind instrument, an imbecile organ designed to fill a necessary function . . ."

"Man is the expression of intelligence in strength. He is the psychological and physiological Master of creation. He is the divine Androgyne who ought to be self-sufficient."

André, having decided not to be astonished any longer by anything, gazed with a mocking curiosity at those bearded and moustached faces blossoming in the adoration of themselves, and thought about fakirs in perpetual ecstasy before their atrophied sex organs ornamented with flowers.

A correct and grave valet announced that dinner was served. In sympathetic couples, with nonchalant arms around waists, the guests went into the dining room and took their places around the table, decked with narcissi and roses. Gem-studded Bohemian glass goblets, delicate and nacreous, like precious jewels, were only disposed at every alternate place-setting, with the result that couples took communion throughout the meal, in the same thought of election. André observed that it would be necessary for him to drink from Jacques' cup, and his displeasure was mingled with a certain anxiety when it was filled with the warmly scented wine the color of sunlight and topaz that was to seal their entente.

"I drink," said Chozelle, "to our esthetic union and the success of our legitimate ambitions!" He inclined his moustache over the fine crystal, which misted sadly, and then handed the half-empty cup to his friend.

But André, incapable of vanquishing himself, contented himself with a gesture, although the wine seemed to him to be appreciable.

The dinner, delicately organized and sumptuously served, was morose for the young man. No abandonment of soul, no affectionate confidence, was evident there. Everyone was playing a role, wanting to testify his independence and his intellectual superiority by means of thoughts and actions unknown to the vulgar—the filthy crowd. Unfortunately, those pretentions were scarcely realized; ideas deserted those amorphous brains; the conversations, in spite of the over-elaboration of expressions and the preciosity of the mannerisms, remained painfully banal. And in spite of everything, those enemies of women returned to women invincibly, with bitter remarks and bilious persiflage.

André thought that, in the circumstances, those insults constituted a fine eulogy.

When the extra-dry was sparkling in the brains, in will-o'-the-wisps of blond gaiety, the poet requested authorization to recite a few verses, sand he placed a sonnet dedicated to woman in the midst of an evident hostility.

> *I sing of kisses.*
>
> *Kisses have the hues of skies, lakes and flowers!*
> *Some, the color of autumnal roses,*
> *Weep over the past of people and things,*
> *Tears of distant mournings, charms and dolors.*
>
> *Others, of light azure, others bewitching,*
> *Vervains with golden hearts, feverishly blooming,*
> *Sing of amour, life and metamorphoses.*
> *Others slyly set the traps of bird-catchers.*
>
> *A few have the discreet hue of violets;*
> *Those, almost effaced, soft, frail skeletons,*
> *Seem to me a swarm of great gray moths.*
>
> *Those, on the tombs, burn like candles.*
> *But the royal kiss, with which my heart is smitten.*
> *Is the snowy kiss of souls and Virgins.*[1]

---

1 I have simply translated the meaning of the lines without endeavouring to reproduce the rhyme-scheme and the scansion, even though it is those features that attract Jacques' scorn. In the same way, I have translated the meaning of the words that Jacques employs to signify false rhymes, since there is no need to retain the original terms to signify their disharmony.

"Pooh," said Jacques, "your verses have twelve feet and supporting consonants. You know very well that we've changed all that. Squarely, we make *seaweed* rhyme with *flame* and *murder* with *egg*. As for feet, the more there are, the better. The thought ought to remain obscure, misted with the Beyond; you ought not to understand it yourself, in order that every reader can give to your strophes the meaning he prefers. That way, everyone is content."

"Readers are mugs," declared Defeuille.

"The public want to be amazed, that's all," agreed a green-tinted young man with a monocle and a stye, the one sustaining the other. "Listen to this unequaled morsel . . ."

But no one was listening any longer, the conversations having taken a very intimate tone. Other silversmiths, sculptors of words and demolishers of rhymes, were able to launch the little pebbles of their inspiration without hitting anyone, and that was entirely to the benefit of the art.

The coffee being served in the drawing room, they resumed, supporting one another along the road already traveled. André, who was dying of thirst, emptied three cups one after another and inundated himself with kummel, communion in liqueur-glasses not being obligatory.

Defeuille busied himself lowering the light of the chandelier, pulling the curtains and distributing fresh orchids taken from baskets garnished with moss. Those Messieurs did not smoke. It was in bad taste, Jacques had declared, to smoke anything but hashish or flowers, and one desired to remain in the perfume of strawberries steeped in ether.

Voices became languid, whispered words dissolved mysteriously.

The Messieurs gathered around the Master resembled worshipers of some malefic god, awaiting the sacrifice.

In fact, cassolettes were lit, and Defeuille invited his guests to visit the well-appointed bedrooms of his apartment . . .

"Come on," said Jacques, nudging André, who started.

"I'd rather smoke a cigarette outside. It's stifling among these roses and that incense."

But Jacques smiled.

"I was about to propose that to you . . ."

VII
Esthetic Sensuality

In the street, the two men looked at one another.

"Truly, it's better here!" André declared.

The Master breathed in the icy air with dolorous nostrils.

"Pooh! What I like, you see, is the reek of the faubourgs, the odor of vice and human beasts. I've spent exquisite hours in certain suburban quarters of Paris. And what handsome fellows! Defeuille is full of good will, but, outside the regal delicacy of the intelligence, there's little joy to be gleaned in his home. Morbid civilization has bridled the instincts of man there, and nothing is sadder than effort for the sake of pleasure . . ."

"You always leave before the end, then, Master?"

"Almost always. Then again, I forbid myself to stay up too late. I've demanded too much of my nerves in recent years; I'm broken down, neurasthenic . . . an etheromaniac . . ."

Jacques did not speak of his fatigues without pride and the word "etheromaniac" flowered on his lips like the purulent orchid in his buttonhole. He did not notice the ironic tone in which his disciple was interrogating him, and André, understanding that he was not dealing with a subtle psychologist, scarcely dissimulated.

"I'll come tomorrow to obtain your advice about the work you mentioned to me, my dear Master."

"Oh, the work! That's the only truly sweet thing in life. When one has vanquished the untamed Word, one feels the same delectable lassitude as after amour."

"Certainly," declared André, "before literary labor the brain is animated by the same transport as the heart before possession. The desire to create is manifest in all its vehemence. But it is, in my opinion, poetry that procures the rarest sensations. The sonnet, for example, represents for me the embrace, complete in its measured and graduated perfection. To begin with, there is the soft caress of the first eight lines, of which the rhyme recurs, as persistent as the initiating kiss, savant, penetrating, tenacious and magnetic. Then the tight enlacement of two briefer strophes, more sinewy, of a profound acuity that excites reliably, uplifting the entire being with impatient ardor. Then, finally, the last line, whose rhyme springs forth like a golden nail and fixes the adorable poem irresistibly . . ."

Jacques deigned to approve. "It's necessary to put that in my novel. Make a note of it immediately."

"Oh, there's no need; I'll remember it."

"You'll take as the title of the first chapter *Esthetic Sensuality* . . ."

". . . ?"

"To start with, you'll describe this evening's scene."

"Completely?"

"No, only what you've seen . . . we'll place it in a worldly newspaper."

"Oh."

"My dear, in knowing how to set about things, one has to accept many things. The art of saying nothing while saying everything is much to the taste of people in society. And it's the passages least flattering to them that make the little women swoon most effectively . . . they adore me, you see."

"That's true."

"Who is the feminist writer who could compete with me? Who is the man who is able, with more mastery than me, to awaken their perverse streak? They come to me as the snobs go to Bruant, in order to be insulted. And that's what gives me a fine idea of their stupidity."

"Perhaps they'll avenge themselves one day?"

Chozelle pouted ineffably. "I'm sure of myself."

"What if it's only to experience new sensations?"

"The Faculty has affirmed that I'm safe from impulsive actions."

André, who was only wearing a light autumn overcoat, was beginning to shiver. He thought about the warm bed where Fiamette, curled up like a sensitive cat, was waiting for him. Already he thought he could sense the pressure of her supple arms on his shoulders, and the sweetness of her small, melting mouth, ever-ready for a kiss, on his lips. He took his leave of Jacques and drew away, murmuring lines that Lausanne, the singer of caresses, had just set to music for him, on a dance tune.

> *Waltz, lovers whom nothing wearies,*
> *Waltz, to the rhythm of kisses,*
> *Waltz, unappeased lovers;*
> *Life is just a fleeting kiss!*

> *Waltz, waltz, life is brief;*
> *But what does tomorrow matter?*
> *Inebriate yourselves, hand in hand,*
> *Waltz, beautiful lovers of dreams.*

> *Drink, narrowly united*
> *The philter of demented lips,*
> *Make of the hearts of your darlings,*
> *Lovers, the silkiest of nests.*

> *Love, lovers whom nothing wearies,*
> *Love to the rhythm of kisses,*
> *Love, unappeased lovers;*
> *Life is just a fleeting kiss!*

VIII
The Evil Influence

That night, Fiamette was a sad, amorous woman—not that she doubted André, but it seemed to her that something had darkened in his soul, that the naïve and tender poet had given way to the resigned and perverse skeptic. He experienced less pleasure in her tender cajoleries, showed himself demanding, irritable and almost cruel in his singular caprices. It was no longer sufficient for him to have her completely, to cradle her in his arms like a great blonde doll, to listen to the fervent canticle of her adoration. His curiosities went beyond the habitual caresses; he had acquired the unhealthy need to make her suffer in order to feel more himself. The wild beast was quivering in the shadows, the exquisite poet became a man, and perhaps less than a civilized man.

"André," she said, "you don't love me as you did yesterday, and tomorrow, you'll no longer love me as you do today."

"You're complaining about . . ."

"Oh! You hurt me . . . nothing more."

In fact, he had been brutal, without real amour, willful, complicated and disdainful of habitual intoxications. She rediscovered in him the malevolent vanity of first lovers and their need to humiliate the woman who has given herself, by means of gazes, gestures and facial expressions even more than by words.

For his part—a strange reversal of the human spirit—André, who had coveted Fiamette madly a little while before, told himself that ardent, complete, durable amour is impossible, that the most beautiful playthings break and tarnish, that the most burning desires are extinguished as soon as they are realized, that there is nothing in nothing.

The leaven of hatred that ferments in the hearts of all lovers, was manifest confusedly within him. He almost held against his mistress the joys that she had given him in too complete a submission. And that sentiment, common to almost all men, creates the supposition that the great scorn that they have, fundamentally, for themselves, falls back logically on those who love and admire them. That is so true that certain women, in life, can only count on the constancy of a lover who pays them, because, in such circumstances, the gallant runs after his money.

Fiamette wept in silence, and the disciple, after having stirred other evil thoughts, went to sleep, with his back turned to his happiness.

It was necessary, the next day, to think about Jacques' novel, *Esthetic Sensuality*, to adapt himself to the genre that he had adopted, to grind the strange within the reach of snobs.

After half an hour, André was writing Chozelle fluently, and he softened again before the weary eyelids and dolorous eyes of Fiamette.

"Forgive me, Miette, I've behaved badly."

She kissed him softly. "Why must I cherish you more after your insults? Do women in love lose all dignity, then?"

"Doesn't the dignity of forgiveness count for anything, then? God doesn't act otherwise with sinners."

"I don't want you to leave."

"Have I ever wanted to?"

"Well, you told me last night that the pleasure I gave you wasn't worth as much as the work I caused you to lose—that everything that amour offers to writers is lost to literature. The fecundating seeds rise up to your brains, and you procreate without the help of women!"

André started to laugh.

"All the great authors have been chaste, my little Fiamette."

"Imbeciles or madmen!"

"What about success?"

"Success? A word! Doesn't Ninoche, or Nora the Comet, have as much as you? And me, if I wanted to?"

"Certainly."

"Success goes to the most infimal, the worst and the wicked, it's only ungraspable for those who are above it."

"You're right, Miette."

André held his mistress against him, pressed her forehead to his heart, and savored for a long time the joy of being utterly small and frail beside such great affection.

IX
An Article by Chozelle

"Here, dear Master, is the requested chapter of *Esthetic Sensuality*."

The disciple had written, with a fluent pen, the story of what he had seen at Defeuille's. It was mainly a question of the amity that two men might experience for one another. That profound amity had to be pursued in the midst of the vexations of the literary struggle; the novel, in sum, was nothing but a passionate story unfurling in the banality of Parisian life. But, the perverse idea being attached to everything, and the imagination of the reader evoking lascivious images at the slightest obscure passage, the adventure could be ornamented with a certain equivocal charm.

There and then, Chozelle crossed out words, added rare adjectives, blurred a few phrases that were too clear, and sent it to the copyist.

"My friend," he said, "I'm satisfied by that first endeavor. Continue in that direction, trying to make me clearly recognizable in the principal character. The intrigue scarcely matters, everything ought to be in the detail. About twelve thousand lines; the publisher is waiting. But for tomorrow, I need an article."

"On what subject?"

"Oh, my God, the theater. Talk about the ballet being performed at the *Folies Perverses*—my ballet—and slip in a few snide remarks about Ninoche."

"Ninoche?"

"She displeased me during Pascal's soirée."

"She's a good girl."

"I don't like good girls. You'll say that she's grotesque on stage, that at her age, retirement is required. Anyway, you have the choice of epithets, provided that they're stinging."

André baulked. "No; even if I thought what you say about Ninoche, I wouldn't say it."

"Why not?"

"Because I don't attack women."

Jacques wrinkled his nose and eyebrows. "Even that one? A creature who gives herself to anyone?"

André could not repress a mocking exclamation, which Chozelle did not understand, or did not want to understand.

"Write the article anyway. I'll add what pleases me."

"That's your right, since you're signing it. Permit me to say to you, however, dear Master, that it would be preferable to exercise that combative humor on those who can defend themselves. You have enemies, I agree, but you count fewer among women than among men. Address yourself to the latter."

"Men sometimes fight," Jacques confessed, naïvely.

"So?"

"I don't want anyone to damage my skin. And then, in speaking ill of a woman, I'll have all the others with me. They're so jealous! Are you still with that whore? Fiamette Silly, I believe?"

André shivered, and replied dryly: "My mistress isn't a whore. She loves me sincerely."

"All right, don't get annoyed about something so trivial. Come on, sit down there and get started on that article: the pantomime, the seductions of my work, the charm of Tigrane, the star dancer who created the Bat in my ballet . . . got it?"

"I don't know Tigrane."

"That's of no importance: the exsanguinated head of a drowning victim, or a prophetess drunk on ether, supple serpentine movements: 'a snake dancing on the end of a stick.' She has all the bewitchments and all the black magic."

"She's a woman who pleases you, then?"

"Not at all, but she's useful to me. The uncomprehending public isn't content today with mimes chosen uniquely among men. It's necessary, when one can't do otherwise, to make sacrifices to bad taste."

While the pupil worked meekly, Jacques dozed blissfully in his soft wing-chair.

The salamanders on the cushions resembled jewels of amber and beryl, the snakes huddled in some hole. All morning the rain had been tapping on the muddy window panes with its multitudinous little simian fingers. A wet day is sadder than snowy days, which, at least, dress everything in a delicate cotton wool, setting people and things like gems in caskets padded with white velvet; the roofs sparkle at the slightest radiance; the gutters are decorated with crystal pendants; the branches shake like pearly powder-puffs. In the rain, by contrast, everything becomes faded, decomposing, bringing out the senility of stones and trees, and the soul also loses its garments of dream, remaining naked before reality.

"Have you written it?" Jacques asked his disciple, who, paling in the green-tinted daylight, was leaning nervously over his sheet of paper.

"Yes, as you see."

"Fabrics, gemstones, flowers! It needs to be rutilant, serpentine, writhing, bursting like dazzling fireworks . . . I like to roll in gemstones and perfumes! I'm the ultimate manifestation of our delectably rotten civilization! Oh, the reek of the Parisian dives where vice swarms!"

André handed him the article that he had skimped, in the manner of the Master, easy to grasp with a little craftsmanship and flexibility, and Jacques Chozelle scanned it with a severe eye.

"I've put into it for your satisfaction my most alarming verve, my most complicated cerebral gaminess . . ."

"It's not bad."

Chozelle seized his pen, made a few deletions, and then, between two compliments to Tigrane, insinuated a little of the verjuice that he kept in reserve for common mortals: "As for Ninoche, the critic has been occupied too long with her over-ripe flesh. That old she-monkey, as tenacious as she is talentless, offends the eye and the other senses. Are there not cages at the Jardin des Plantes for her peers?"

It was devoid of humor, but Jacques laughed for a long time at that lucky find, the vehement savor of which the disciple was obliged to praise.

X

A Theater of Women

The following evening, in her dressing-room at the Folies Per-verses, Ninoche confided her distress to her lover.

"Have you read this filth?"

"No."

"Look!"

She stuck the paper under his nose, and underlined the in-sulting passage with a furious finger.

"Pooh," said the other. "That's of no importance."

"You think so?"

"No one gets annoyed any longer by what Chozelle writes."

"Everything is permitted, then? Well, I'll get my revenge on my own."

Ninoche was performing a serpentine dance that evening for the All-Paris of premières. Standing before a mirror broadly bathed by beams of electric light, she draped herself in an im-mense fleecy sheet of fabric, made it undulate over sticks, arched her loins and leaned over, supple and phantasmal. She was no longer a woman but a gigantic corolla, undulating in the slightest breeze, turning and tucking up her nacreous petals. Then, the flower became a butterfly with crimson wings illuminated by two golden eyes, in a dust of diamonds.[1]

---

1 This description clearly recalls the costume of a famous dance performed by Loie Fuller, which, because it was filmed by Georges Meliés, can nowadays

The dresser hastily fixed the floating veil and lifted up the silk leotard, which had slid down over the thighs, overcoming the feverish impatience of the dancer with difficulty.

In the dressing room, hung with mauve liberty, flower baskets with handles lightly bound with ribbons and lace emitted an agonizing breath. Jules Laroche, the lover of the day, disappeared under a heap of Parma violets, devastated by a vengeful hand; it reeked of powder, woman and the blood of roses.

"A good crowd," said Ninoche, passing a brush lightly coated with kohl over her eyelids and eyebrows. Then, with a blotter, she drowned her gaze with an amorous languor, and insinuated on to the cornea of the eye a little of a mysterious powder designed to dilate the pupil and communicate a strange flame to it. The mouth was bloody in the naturally pale face; she corrected the overly rigid design, rounding out the lower lip with crimson, and then touched up the nostrils.

The make-up she was using spread a violent perfume of tube-roses; each of her movements dislodged more violent effluvia.

"And do you know why Chozelle has a grudge against me?" Ninoche demanded, pursuing her idea.

"No."

"Because I declared, at Pascal's soirée, that everything in him is fake: the wit and everything else: showing off, of which even women of the world no longer expect anything."

Jules Laroche shrugged his shoulders. "In the business you're in, one ought not to attack anyone."

"Why not? In 'the business that I'm in' one also knows how to make oneself respected, as you'll see in a little while."

Her nostrils quivering, Ninoche braced her harmonious upper body, and, with a wild gesture, threw back the short and thick curls of her hair, which gave her something of the appearance of a savage.

---

be seen on YouTube. Another dance by Fuller was the basis of a eulogistic description by Jean Lorrain, in an article adapted as a chapter in *Monsieur de Phocas*, attributed there to a fictitious character.

"On stage for number twelve!" shouted the stage manager, while a dozen acrobats went past, panting, their arms and faces inundated with sweat, their muscles standing out under pink leotards. Tigrane, who was beginning the second part, was trailing a long, sable, quilted garment in the dust of the corridors and humming in a shrill voice.

"The Bat!" whispered the mime, with a street-arab gesture. "Out of the way! Let me past—they're calling me back!"

In the hall, people were arriving to see Chozelle's ballet, which was said to be delightfully staged, with a host of pretty women. The boxes were resplendent, occupied by stars of the first and second magnitude of gallantry. There was nothing but an undulation of pearls, streams of jewels, so crowded that they seemed from a distance to be imprisoning busts in the carapaces of prestigious turtles. Flesh offered milky hues; hair, expertly powdered, made golden, jet or copper aureoles for the feverish faces. As befitted princesses of joy, laughter rang out impertinently, shrill or hoarse, in accordance with age or fatigue, the debuts often having been difficult and disheartening.

What was striking, at first, about the display of skin and finery, was the resemblance that there was between all those painted dolls, which appeared to have emerged from a huge factory in Nuremberg: playthings for old, naïve and vainglorious children. All of them were showing their teeth in the same fashion, in a febrile and artificial gaiety, their hair crimped by the same capillary artist, wearing similar corsets, which caused them a slight pain in the pit of the stomach. "The corset and amour! Oh, my dear!" Two chores of which they would be well rid! "But one has to live, doesn't one?" At the racecourses, and theater premières, at Trouville, at Dieppe, at baccarat and roulette tables, the fragile dolls crowded, tintinnabulatory and hollow, with a louis sounding the chamade beneath the armature of the corset.

A man exhibits his mistress as he exhibits his carriages and his racehorses; he is not jealous, and sometimes even dispenses with a more direct homage. For that care there is the head coachman, if he is a handsome fellow, the butler, some passing artist, a wrestler or a second tenor. It is agreed that the lover who pays is never loved, but as often as not, he does not care.

Behind the boxes, noisy with renowned parasites, humbler whores pass by, in quest of a rapid embrace, a fatiguing but inconsequential whim. The latter, their cheeks creased, bloodless or marbled with pink, ornament themselves with garish dresses, and their hair, poorly done-up, reveals frequent stations in the furnished hotels of the surrounding area. They maintain a bored, indifferent expression, only approaching seated men, soliciting a punch or a peppermint cordial that will turn their stomachs. Many have not dined and fear that they will go without supper. Over the flood of liquid imbibed, there will then remain the resource of some dubious cold meat kept in reserve for workless evenings.

Young men were amusing themselves talking to them, and, when there were two of them, inviting them together, fond of their intimacy. They were pleasant households where everything was in common, good and bad luck, kisses and blows. Some adopted masculine appearances, wearing cravats and short hair under a felt hat; some had a friend, smaller, thin and languid, who spoke in a soft voice, playing with her skirt. And that entente, more simulated than real, sharpened curiosities and awoke the desires of hunters of rare sensations.

Isolated matrons, laboriously refurbished with a cement of cold cream, ceruse white and powder in the wrinkles of their skin, swung ostrich-feather fans and powerful rumps. They were seen emerging with novices escaped from some college, desirous of conciliating their voracious appetite with the exigency of their resources.

In the first hall, where tankards of beer were being emptied amid lascivious quarrels, where the livestock of lust was circulating freely, an orchestra of Viennese ladies girdled in blue over white muslin dresses was toiling away in a melancholy fashion.

André Flavien arrived slightly late with his mistress. Nora the Comet was waiting for her friends in a ground-floor box, and, either out of malice or unconscious frivolity, she had asked Francis Lombard to accompany her, without warning him about the dangerous proximity to which he would be subjected.

Fiamette with her cornflower eyes and her tenderly ashen hair, caused a sensation when she entered her box. Her delicate face contrasted, by virtue of an entirely personal charm, and an ideal expression of intelligence and mildness, with the doll-like or bestial faces of the renowned prostitutes. There was no defect to trouble the joy of the gaze in the harmony of her shoulders and arms, and the whole of her charming body, white and velvety as a magnolia flower, exhaled the perfume of youth.

On perceiving André, Francis Lombard shivered, and got up to leave, but Nora retained him imperiously.

"My friend Francis Lombard," she said, with her most feline smile, "had the keenest desire to meet you, my dear André. I hope that all three of you will be kind enough to keep me company."

"Oh," murmured Fiamette, "since he's been working for Chozelle, André quits me continually, and I fear that he won't be any more faithful to me tonight than any other evening."

"Chozelle? A bad acquaintance," said Nora, "but André is too good a psychologist to let himself get caught by the piping of that bird-catcher."

XI
The Luminous Dance

Darkness had fallen in the hall; from the height of the balcony, three electric eyes lit up fantastically. The velvet curtain drew aside slowly, and Ninoche emerged from the darkness like a luminous phantom. From all the corners of the stage, other Ninoches appeared at the same time, reflected infinitely by a set of mirrors, giving the impression of a ballet of nuns resuscitated for some *danse macabre*. Swiftly or softly, the mime agitated, beneath the fabric, the long sticks that, by means of their rapid and precise movements, gave the mysterious woman the appearance of an inverted calyx, a parachute, a meteor or a swirl of foam. With tiny steps she changed place, fluttering, while the light fabric inflated, deployed in smoky spirals, and then fell back like nonchalant snow or a guttering flame. There were also pyrotechnic surprises, silver girandoles, spinning roses, Vulcan's rings, diamantine glories, Pyrrhic fans, stars of Venus, eruptions of flowers, mirrors of Diana, rutilant mosaics and golden sunbursts and rosettes.

Fires rose like Roman candles, silver lilies burst forth in light rockets, and cascades of precious stones streamed over the fabric. The woman disappeared; she was nothing but a fugitive vision, her mouth smiling like a crimson heart, her burning gaze piercing the electric furnace in which she was moving.

The spectators, however, remained frozen, accustomed to the spectacle that had held the stage for several years. When the curtain fell back in heavy folds, people applauded the skill of the dancer and the harmony of her attitudes with their fingertips. Then laughter ran around at the memory of that morning's article and the terrible irony of its epithets.

Ninoche reappeared as an emerald scarab with golden antennae. She caressed an imaginary corolla, went to sleep in the flower, and then mutated into a crimson butterfly, a steel dragonfly and a fantastic moth. After having beaten her wings against the black drapes, she ran around the stage with the intoxication of an increasing terror and disappeared into the friezes.

Finally, after a last metamorphosis, she came back in a white tunic, feet and wrists tied, to be delivered to the pyre. Admirably simulated, the blaze lit up in thick smoke. Blue-tinted tongues brushed the martyr's knees, flanks, breasts and face. Frenzied, the flames running over her shoulders made her an aureole of glory and rose up like chimeras and wrathful dragons all the way to the heavens. Ninoche, her face dolorous, writhed under the bites, and her febrile movements stimulated the fury of the monsters.

Crimson shreds were still floating, like an immense royal mantle, seemingly weeping bloody lilies. Then the avid teeth of new blue and green flames finished ripping the august veil. The woman, her entire body clenched, rejecting death, bounded on the spot and, her mouth open as if to utter one last scream, she had an expression of tragic, almost superhuman suffering.

A higher sheaf of flame rose up in a dazzling fury, floated momentarily, enveloped the voluptuous flesh in its turbulence, and then the conflagration diminished, vanquished by its own power. Like a torn rag, the body of the mime collapsed, and darkness fell.

XII
The Bat

Jacques Chozelle, who was installed in a proscenium box with Defeuille and a few fervent admirers, got up when the curtain fell and went into the wings.

As he passed by, the women smiled with indulgent simpers, while he turned away sullenly. In the corridors, a dozen streetwalkers surrounded him, and, as he pushed them away brutally, formed a cortege for him.

Little chorus girls with thin arms offered the gracile nudity of their torsos in a savant state of undress. Their bodices, open to the waist, came up just high enough to imprison the delicately-tipped breasts as if with hands. Their backs emphasized freely their voluptuous furrow, and the down of the armpits darkened the gold of corselets, split like the elytra of ladybirds.

Seen at close range the forms appeared vulgar, deprived of the harmony that the prestige of the footlights and movement gave them. The eyes, overly charcoaled, reduced the savor of the blonde wigs and the swollen feet crammed painfully into bright pumps.

"Is Tigrane ready?" Jacques asked the little girls.

"You can knock; her old man isn't there."

"And even if he were," said a sly fourteen-year-old, "one isn't jealous of Monsieur."

"Tigrane's old man and Monsieur Chozelle! O la la! She must sleep tranquil in her grotto, the Bat!"

"Monsieur isn't afraid of being violated? It's dangerous to wander in the wings."

"A kiss, my handsome blond?"

"I'll have you all fired!" cried Jacques, who had to defend himself against twenty audacious hands and lips mockingly extended.

"What! For a peck?"

"You won't die of it!"

But Tigrane's door opened and the young woman, laughing, had the author come in, a trifle crumpled.

"Damn!" he said. "You've brought out your gems!"

"Yes, I've brightened up this sinister costume."

Tigrane was charming in her gray leotard and dark velvet corselet. Long wings of spidery gauze were attached to her wrists and ankles by aquamarine fibulae, so that, when she threw her arms wide and glided softly, she gave the impression of flying over mysterious corollas.

Languorously, she leaned over, also trying to kiss him, either out of mischief or curiosity, but he turned his back on her in order to examine a painting by Pascal newly hung up under floods of Japanese silk.

"Why, it's this evening's costume . . . and you're catching golden flies!"

"A symbolic portrait. I love to catch flies, you see, but they need to be in gold."

"You're right; if I were a woman, I'd do the same."

"A woman? Aren't you, a little?"

With a conquering gesture, Jacques passed a hand through his hair.

"By the way," said Tigrane, "look out for Ninoche; she hasn't digested this morning's article."

"Is her lover with her?"

"They were together when I arrived."

"Ah," said Jacques, thoughtfully.

And he went out a moment later to go in search of André Flavien.

XIII
The Vengeance

In Nora's box, André was listening with an indifferent ear to the dancer's sallies. Increasingly, he deplored the morning's article and Chozelle's malevolence.

Ninoche had not created luminous dancing, but she demonstrated that she was an innovator by the great intelligence of her attitudes. To the Folies Perverses, where scarcely any but loose women drunk on renown were exhibited, she brought a real sentiment of art, a rare consciousness of means and effects.

A writer, whoever he might be, ought never to occupy the readers with his personal grudges. His judgments are only valuable insofar as they are stripped of all prejudice. Now, Chozelle had punished the poor woman for a few imprudent words, and chastized her vilely for an innocent mockery, while he slipped away meekly before the direct attacks of his colleagues. But Ninoche was disarmed, because the lover of an actress rarely comes to her defense, and Chozelle, sure of impunity, had free rein.

André made these reflections, and others, which showed him the "Master" in a very bad light. The latter had never taken advantage of his notoriety to launch a remarkable talent. His praise went to clowns who were quickly stifled, tricksters who, having only a few uninteresting numbers in their bag, could not even reap the benefit of his condescension.

In any case, Jacques sold his adjectives dearly, and it was necessary to have the password and silky bills to shake a few of them loose.

"There's a very particular enjoyment in abuse and lies," he had said to his disciple. "I rarely keep my promises and never my oaths, for I find in the indignation of honest imbeciles a tasty stew that I prefer to gratitude."

Twice already, Fiamette had felt the light caress of Francis Lombard on her shoulder. Nora, with her apparent frivolity, was chatting about everything and nothing, and her whim brushed twenty subjects, as nimble as a bird fluttering from branch to branch. Her eyelids, however, were more bruised than usual, and her long slender hands, covered with rings, sometimes posed, burning, on those of her friend.

"Chozelle's beckoning to you," she said to André, who had not unsealed his lips.

"Stay with us, I beg you," Fiamette implored.

But André was already quitting the box, and was lost in the floods of amorous locusts undulating from one corridor to another, threatening to submerge everything.

"Are you jealous?" Nora asked the young woman, laughing.

"Yes, I'm jealous, and I don't want anyone to take my property."

"Oh, it'll be returned to you without any great damage. What do you say, my dear, to that amour that is proof against anything?"

"I say that I'd give a great deal to be loved like that," murmured Francis Lombard, with a sigh. "What is it necessary to do to merit such good fortune?"

"Nothing," said Fiamette, dryly. "I'm neither for the taking nor for sale."

The curtain went up for the first part of the ballet and Chozelle, accompanied by André Flavien, went back into his box.

Tigrane, the Bat, was huddled in a corner of the stage, reigning over her court of buzzing flies; and it was an enchantment for the eyes, that farandole of golden insects with long iridescent wings. The dragonflies were braced by corselets of sapphires with lunar reflections, over black leotards; the ladybirds, beneath their elytra, had coral-studded capes; the plush bees, the orange-striped asps and the scarabs with carapaces of beryls and peridots, filed past in a stream of pearls and metallic wings. The somnolent, happy bat was waiting for nightfall to capture the imprudent insects. She was asleep, cruel and lascivious, dreaming of murders and kisses. She was asleep, like a morbid orchid, a floral succubus, the eternal courtesan of whose poison people and plants die.

Into that lustful ballet, Chozelle had been able to put a little symbolism and psychology, with the glorification of the cruel and perverse woman, created by God for the punishment of crimes of amour. A delicate poetry, an artistic thought, might have been able to sustain that subject, too often deflowered, but Chozelle did not have such high aims. Always attracted by bizarre ugliness, he had put a bat on stage, and a long-eared owl appeared to vanquish the enchantress. In her turn, the poor creature made amends, begging, and was vanquished by the charm of the bird of prey. In the moonlight there were excursions of lamias and empusas, combats of hideous gnomes, and then, a virtuous enchantress appeared and, as in all tales for little children, rendered the amorous their primitive forms.

The prince married the princess.

Such was the banal work that the theater director had hastened to put on; for, as soon as a poet shows real merit, as soon as an author strays from the beaten path by staging some truly literary manifestation, it frightens the hidebound businessman, the dishonest grocer who only wants to serve his clients the habitual brown sugar and the various jams of the old manufacturers.

Chozelle delighted in the flattering belches of his fervent admirers, who found a prodigious originality in the fact that he had dared to put to stage a bat and a long-eared owl!

Two people had just come into the box, white with admiration, which they expressed in curt phrases, like hiccups of ecstasy:

"Truly, it's a marvel!"

"Tigrane has grasped all the bewitching charm of the writer!"

"What deftness of touch!"

"Admirable! Suggestive! Enveloping! Alarming!"

André examined the couple, who, by virtue of something out of the ordinary, retained his attention. The man, tall and slightly bloated, with soft flesh and livid skin, might have passed for a fairly good-looking fellow; the woman, also tall, and bony, with drawn and slightly discolored features, had excessively bright eyes, a feverish expression and a wide mouth afflicted by nervous tics. Her hair, very abundant, was arranged artfully. Her thin stature gave her flat chest and broad shoulders a certain androgynous elegance. Her white costume, veiled with guipures, was in perfect taste. André was astonished to hear her speak in a hoarse voice, ripped at moments by shriller notes.

The orchestra was playing furiously for the dance of the lamias and empusas; Jacques leaned over and whispered in André's ear: "They're both men."

"Impossible!"

"One wouldn't think so, would one? For three years they haven't quit one another, and the police close their eyes. Anyway, the secret is well guarded"

Sickened, André had a desire to flee, but he was able to vanquish his repugnance, and studied the couple who offered themselves so ingenuously to his observation.

After the first tableau, a singular incident threw the hall into turmoil.

Ninoche, shoving the door-openers out of the way, came into the box, and, before anyone could stop her, threw herself on the "Master" and jammed his hat all the way down to his chin; then, beating the sides as if it were a Basque drum she said: "That's for the article . . . and do it again, if you like!"

There was a fusillade of laughter, a firework display of gibes, whistles, applause and the frantic stamping of feet.

Jacques, at first mute with surprise and shock, had straightened up, trying to free his face. He succeeded, after bizarre efforts that brought the joy of the audience to its maximum. His lips were trembling, his eyes misted by terror. The fervent admirers had deserted the box, fearing ridicule, and André had great difficulty holding back the laughter that was hovering on his lips.

"That whore! That whore!" murmured Chozelle, who was finally able to speak.

Then he took the young man's hand. "You're a friend, André? I can count on you, can't I?"

In a halting voice, André affirmed that he was utterly devoted to the Master.

"It's necessary not to think of writing another article . . . that fury would do it again. But she has a lover . . ."

"So?"

"It's necessary to demand a reckoning from that man for the offense. The scandal has been too great."

"You want me to challenge Ninoche's lover on your behalf?"

"Yes."

"And you'll go to the terrain?"

But Jacques smiled softly. "Not at all, my friend—it's you who'll fight."

XIV
That Which Settles Everything

André, finding the idea comical, did not reply.

Jacques caressed him gently with his fingers and said: "You're my pupil, the elect of my heart; isn't it natural that you would undertake my defense? Go, and know that you're fighting in beauty."

In her dressing-room, Ninoche was having a crisis of nerves, and two ladybirds in coral pink corselets were dabbing her face with napkins steeped in essences. In their haste, the girls had upset the bowl full of soapy water, and were paddling in a puddle.

André, avoiding the porcelain debris, asked for the dancer's lover, but Jules Desroches had fled. Retracing his steps, the young man encountered the androgynous couple who, surrounded by Chozelle's friends, were commenting on the incident.

They stopped him; they asked, with a feigned interest, for further details. What had the Master said after the unfortunate adventure? It was regrettable, certainly; however, the article had been very nasty, and they criticized Jacques for putting himself in a ridiculous position.

André replied that he had the intention to fight in order to avenge the insult.

They begged him not to do so. There had been no insult; the eccentricities of a Ninoche were of no account; a duel would give a further resonance to the story . . .

"No," said Defeuille, "I'll have a few echoes appear in the newspapers, and people will learn that the girl was simply drunk. What do you think?"

That ingenious idea was approved, and André drew away, utterly sickened.

✳

In Nora's box, Francis Lombard had drawn closer to Fiamette, while the dancer, lying back in her chair, her eyes half-closed and her thought absent, abandoned herself to the mysterious disease that weakened her more every day.

"Your lover scarcely loves you," Francis murmured, running his fingers through Fiamette's blonde hair. "I know, personally, that I would never quit you!"

"André quits me because he can't do otherwise; he's Chozelle's secretary."

"Truly, you're at that point! Can't your friend work without the help of others, then? I thought he had talent . . ."

Fiamette blushed, and replied hotly: "André has more than talent, and I hope people will soon know it. But don't you know how difficult it is at present to acquire a situation in letters? I could cite you the names of writers full of merit who work for others because their works are refused systematically by the good periodicals. They haven't had any luck, haven't been able to get past the editors, are too independent to become part of a coterie, and too proud to flock round an eccentric personality. But as it's necessary to live, they still have the resource, after having failed everywhere, of selling their work to a known novelist, who'll pay dearly for the same prose that everyone else rejects disdainfully."

"And those fashionable writers accept to sign the work of others?"

"It's done routinely."

"In commerce, if we're less glorious, we're more honest."

"Perhaps you're better defended . . ."

"Then your lover . . . ?"

"What do you expect? He's taken what was on offer: a secretarial position."

"And you assist in the generation of these works of elevated taste! How tedious that must be for you, my poor Fiamette! These unhealthy lucubrations are doubtless read to you, and you're called upon to throw delicate morsels of flattery between two stifled yawns?"

"Oh," she said, laughing, "André isn't doing himself much harm. He got a grasp of the Master's gamy genre right away, and he writes fluently with the pen, saying that there will always be enough blank verse at the end of the hook to catch the snobs . . ."

"Fiamette," said the young man, "you're a burden for your lover, and you'd both be happier by taking back your liberty. I'm rich. If you wanted . . ."

"No," she said, gently. "Don't go on."

"Tell her, then, Nora, that she's being stupid!"

Nora sat up on her chair, passed her hand over her damp forehead, and murmured: "How rich she'd be in money if she were less rich in love!"

"Not love for me!" said Francis, laughing.

"Bah! It's so easy to love when one isn't in love!"

"Perhaps that's true."

"Personally, I've never wanted to have a dog or a grand passion . . . it always ends badly."

Pascal, who was exchanging skirmishes with a debutante decked out like a basket of wedding-presents, stopped in front of the box, and held out his hand to the two women.

"Where's André?"

"He's with Chozelle . . ."

"Ah! You know the story?"

"What story?" asked Fiamette, who had not attributed any great importance to the tumult in the hall, thinking that it was a dispute between women.

"Ninoche has had a 'reckoning' with Jacques."

"Really? Talk, quickly!"

"André will recount the scene to you. Personally, I'd like to talk to you about an idea I had just now, seeing you so pretty against that gold and crimson background."

"Speak."

"Would you like to pose for my Salome? A blonde Salome, about whom I've been dreaming for some time. I hope your friend won't oppose it?"

"Oh, he knows that there's nothing to fear from you."

"Anyway, you'll be so covered in gems and flowers that only little corners of your flesh will be visible. It's agreed?"

"I'll talk to André about it, and if he accepts, I'll be very happy to do it . . ."

"Tomorrow, Fiamette, for it's necessary to take advantage of inspiration, which flirts, plays and slips away like a true woman! When one holds her by a flap of her tunic, it's necessary not to let her flee."

He put a kiss on the darling's fingers, and resumed his gallant pursuit in the corridors.

"You'll be adorable," said Nora.

"A model!" sighed Francis. "You only lacked that humiliation! You're going to pose before that fellow, then?"

"Many great ladies would be flattered to be able to do as much . . ."

"That's not a reason!"

Francis Lombard had risen to his feet. "One thing is certain," he said, ironically, "and that is that you won't go to Pascal's studio tomorrow."

"Why not?"

"You haven't heard what's being said in the next box, then?"

"No."

"Your friend is fighting a duel."

"He's fighting a duel!"

"Yes. Is he not the man of the association?" And Francis added in a scornful tone: "It's his duty to defend Jacques."

"How can you think that?"

"I don't think anything. There are certain individuals that one doesn't frequent with impunity. Undoubtedly, your friend, whom I esteem in spite of everything, didn't weigh all the consequences of that intimacy. He doesn't pass for Jacques' secretary but for his . . ."

"Shut up!"

✳

André Flavien found Fiamette weeping on Nora's shoulder.

"Are you going to fight a duel?" she demanded.

"Who told you that?"

"Everybody knows."

He shrugged his shoulders. "No, it would be too ridiculous."

A smile illuminated the lover's features. "Truly? You swear to me not to commit that folly?"

"Oh, with all my heart."

All three of them went out, while the curtain drew aside for the final tableau: the final round of ghosts, stryges and lamias around the Bat.

In the hall, people were talking about the incident, and laughter was bursting out in all directions. Chozelle and Ninoche were the heroes of the night—the brief Parisian night that passes over sorrows and miseries like moths with crimson wings over a field of death.

XV
Holy Intoxications

Fiamette's sorrow was no longer one of those that act and struggle. She was weary of fighting, weary of hoping for unrealizable things. So she no longer interrogated her lover about his actions or his projects, content with his meager confidences. He was not going to fight, that was the essential thing; it mattered little to her to know how things had happened and why, Ninoche having insulted Chozelle, it was André who was demanding reparation for the offense.

Amused by the ludicrousness of the adventure, the young man recounted the facts to his mistress and described humorously the androgynous household that Ninoche's entry had put to flight.

"A man dressed as a woman! Is that possible?"

"Well . . ."

Seductively, she put her arms around him. "Aren't my kisses better than all their affectations?"

"Dear Miette!"

"Don't you love my embrace and the softness of my mouth?"

"Yes."

"There isn't any little corner of my body that you don't know . . ."

"Every charming cranny has been the nest of a kiss, and those kisses have made you laugh or cry out with joy. And there will be other kisses still, rare and precious kisses, kisses as light and silky as the petals of lilies; there'll be so many that if our good fay had the power to make precious stones of them, they'd cover you with a fulgurant mesh . . ."

"And I'd borrow on them," she said, laughing, "and we'd be rich."

He had knelt down fervently, like a Brahmin before the triangular stone that penitents bear to their lips, and, closing her eyes, she abandoned herself . . .

"André," she said, after a long silence, "it's necessary not to see that vile man any longer. Pascal has asked me to pose for a Salome that he destines for the next Salon."

"A blonde Salome?"

"Yes, and that will transform our nocturnal eyes and moonlight hues . . . I'll have a naked torso, covered with turquoises and pearls. You'll permit it?"

"I have no fear of Pascal . . ."

"I'll also have rings on all my fingers, heavy rings, necklaces and sculpted clasps. I'll scintillate like a star in the darkness with my milky skin and my golden hair!"

"You'll be divinely pretty."

"And I'll earn large sums . . . for I'm not posing for just anyone, you know."

"Well, you'll be able to buy dresses."

But she thought about the bad days, and found a delectable lie. "And another thing. Pascal, who wishes you well, has placed your reports in a major periodical. He doesn't know yet when they'll appear, but he's been paid right away."

With the insouciance of poets, André did not ask for any further explanation. "Oh, Miette, Miette! You're my little Providence!"

"Love me then, love me well!"

And the adorable duo recommenced, in accordance with the desire of nature, which has done well what she has done, and has only permitted the revolt of men in order to better establish, by contrast, the beauty of her teachings.

Fiamette had filled the bedroom with violets, and the whole gloomy landscape seemed revivified, with its verdure, its waters and its forests, in the golden yellow of a branch of mimosa. The young woman recalled a similar joy when, as a little girl, she had woken up on the edge of a wood, in the house of a relative who was a gamekeeper in the environs of Paris. She had had the same impression of felicity and quietude, and that impression had not seemed new to her then, as if she were subject to the influence of distant memories anterior to her birth, memories that something trivial had sufficed to resuscitate, and which were singing mysteriously in her soul.

Moved, the lovers looked at the little sunlit branch on which yellow studs were trembling. They believed they could scent the odors of renewal and apple blossom behind that luminous cluster, which made a kind of screen for their kisses. They listened to amour singing within them and around them; it seemed that the afflux of the life of plants was invading their veins like a flow of honey. Oh, the black hours of solitude! Oh, the nights of doubt and funereal joys in fashionable cabarets and the smoky halls of theaters of women! Fiamette's soul of old was certainly not the same as it was at this exquisite hour; it was then a corpse lying under the shroud of frost and snow in universal desolation; now it was reborn, having retained nothing from its long slumber but a passionate and suffering fragility.

"I won't leave you again, Fiamette."

She shook her head. "If only I could believe you! But you're only a poet, a flame that launches forth, palpitates, inclines, flares up or goes out at the whim of the wind."

"Perhaps . . ."

"Anyway, let's not think . . . today, I'm happy."

"Me, I'm afraid. Why is Destiny obstinate in harassing the meekest and the best? It's necessary to accept the evident hostility of people and things. Once, folded up in myself, I tried to penetrate that mystery of hatred; I wondered of what sin, what crime, I had rendered myself culpable."

"What's the point?"

"Yes, what's the point? Reflection exasperates the sense of justice that we have within us. Reflection is bad, for it takes away the impassiveness of the brute and the unconsciousness of conquerors."

Fiamette kissed her friend's eyelids gently, and put her cheek against his, with a maternal tenderness.

"Was your childhood sad?"

"As far as my memory goes back, I can see nothing around me but disdain and indifference. But I was sustained by the eternal Chimera that put me above the calculations, the discussions of interest and the baseness of those who surrounded me. I caressed the enchantress with the glaucous eyes in order to forget, to hope for I know not what, which never arrives, but which, all the same, sustains you until the final collapse . . ."

"Now we can both hope, and we'll be happy, since nothing exists except by virtue of imagination."

"Yes, the thing most ardently desired is only a fragile canvas on which each of us embroiders the flora of wishes; all joy is in that action of embroidery with the golden needle of the mind and the crimson silk of the heart. What does it matter if, in the dazzling frame, a man has left parcels of energy, and if every rose of election has cost him a drop of the purest of his blood? The canvas, even if it is woven from the very fibers of his flesh and the silky skeins of his living arteries, will still be a felicity for the man who embroiders thereon the sparkling and perverse lie of the Dream!"

XVI
A Princess of Dream

Fiamette is posing in the warmth of the heater.

She has blackened her eyelids, and her eyes have an uncertain gleam, like the green of the foliage of nympheas under the troubled waters of a pool. Over her luminous skin falls the ardent mantle of her hair, a sunset over a moonrise.

André, who is proceeding to dress his mistress, has sheathed her in sardonyxes and chrysoberyls, with a turquoise clasp at the place of his desire. He has tightened a cobweb tissue around her breasts and her knees, and has put rings with glaucous bezels on her toes. She smiles, happy to feel upon her the hand that is caressing her and the gaze that is admiring her.

"Lift your arm," says Pascal. "No, not like that." And he climbs on to the stage to indicate the movement that he desires. "You've just danced, Fiamette, and your entire body is twisted voluptuously, offering itself, seemingly abandoning itself . . . you're expressing amour, cruel perversity, the joy of triumph . . ."

The young woman lends herself meekly to the artist's demands.

"That's marvelous," he says. "It's forbidden to be so beautiful!"

André has scribbled something against an easel.

"Read us your verses, poet," Pascal demands. "That will inspire me. Give me the color of your dream and the soul of tenderness."

In a sonorous voice, André launches the scintillating lines, which seem to fix themselves in clusters of fireflies on the gem-studded body of his mistress.

> *Maleficent princess of strange beauty,*
> *The master who made you both blonde and brunette*
> *Blew you kisses of sunlight and moonlight;*
> *You seem darkness and daylight by turns.*
>
> *One seeks the regret of your divinity*
> *In your somber gaze, which life importunes,*
> *In the arrogance, amour and rancor of your lips,*
> *Which declare your power and fragility.*
>
> *Symbol of desire, of cruel sensuality,*
> *Woman, strix, bacchante, eternal tease!*
> *What is that flower, then, sad among flowers*
>
> *Whose already distant soul you want to respire?*
> *That anguished flower, streaming with tears?*
> *Virgin, that lily of blood is a human head!*

"After that, I can leave my brushes!" exclaimed Pascal. "Your Salome is more alive than mine."

Fiamette, having come down from the stage, had taken a cigarette from a jade cup covered with Hindu divinities, and her blonde head was clouded with blonde smoke.

"André has made me a promise," she said, "but I fear that he can't keep it."

"He's promised you not to see Jacques again?" said the artist, smiling.

"Yes. How do you know?"

"Oh, it's not difficult to guess; it's the only thing you have in your heart."

"Am I not right?"

"You're so right that you're wrong. Don't forget, darling, that it's necessary not to affirm one's superiority too much, and that the rarest of senses in man is common sense. André will go to see Chozelle again, because it's absurd."

"No," said the young man.

"Pardon me, my lad, but you'll go back there in spite of yourself—without pleasure, perhaps even with disgust—but it's fatal."

Very pale, Fiamette placed herself in front of her lover.

"I swear to you that if you see Jacques again, you won't find me when you return."

She was trembling so much that the bracelets on her arms were clinking.

"Madwoman!" he said. And he put a sincere, very soft kiss on her lips.

They spent exquisite hours in Pascal's studio, forgetful of everything that had separated them.

Outside, a hostile, aggressive rain was stinging souls with melancholy, drowning desires and determinations, communicating its evil intentions to people. And the liquid specks intersected, became confused, dragging sonorous pearls over umbrellas, escaping in cascades, seeming to imprison the pedestrians in sentry-boxes of glass thread.

It was good in the warmth of the large room, so hospitable with its large divans and its carpets with rare hues, disposed like flower-baskets under the feet of visitors.

And Salome was animated on the canvas, became disquieting with temptation and perversity in her hieratic sheath studded with sardonyxes and chrysoberyls, pieces by the pink nipples of her breasts. The gemstones on her naked flesh seemed to live and move like prestigious scarabs and reptiles of flame. She was upright, palpitating, with her low girdle strung with pearls, and she extended her arms, her head slightly tilted back, in a pose of challenge and lust.

"I believe that I have a success," repeated Pascal, who was perhaps the happiest of the three.

In the midst of that quietude, they had a visit from Tigrane, who often came to take the air of the studio and seek advice for her costumes.

The mime shook André's hand.

"It was you who was assisting Jacques on the day of . . . the incident? He was too spiteful, though."

"Oh yes, the next day's little note: *A drunken woman in the corridors of the Folies Perverses has permitted herself to insult one of our most popular colleagues, and it was only with great difficulty that the fury was mastered.*"

"Ninoche has been weeping with rage for three days."

"What could the poor thing do in the circumstances? There are too many of them!"

Serpentine and seductive in her fashionable furs, Tigrane admired the painter's work.

"Oh, Master, how inspired you were to choose Fiamette for your Salome! A subject that you've been able to rejuvenate, and which will be the glory of the next Salon!"

But the mime had not only come to compliment the artist and the model. Her visit had another purpose. While Fiamette resumed her pose on the stage and Pascal was absorbed in the mixing of his prestigious colors, she drew near to André.

"Oh, what a lovely triptych," she said. "Is it, at least, of the Venetian school? Inform me, I'm very ignorant."

He examined the item of furniture, finely carved in copper and ivory, ornamented with subjects after Veronese and Tintoretto. As they turned their backs on Fiamette, Tigrane murmured; "It's for you, Monsieur Flavien, that I've come."

"For me?"

"Yes. Jacques wants to talk to you."

"It's futile," said André. "I don't understand Chozelle, and I prefer not to see him again."

"Oh, he's not a bad fellow, fundamentally. I assure you that he's very kind to his friends."

"That's possible, but he chooses them so singularly that he's wrong to be kind to them."

"Yes, some bureaucrats have ink in the heart."

"And they're easily nauseated."

"My God!" sighed the Bat. "I've known a great many men . . ."

"Certainly," said André, with conviction.

"Well, I assure you that they're almost all similar, morally, with only a few different manias. I'm grateful to Jacques for not demanding anything of me. It's so tedious, the simulacrum of amour, when amour is absent."

"So, Jacques . . . ?"

"But you know that very well."

"I didn't want to believe it, especially with you, Tigrane."

"Well, you were wrong. Not that!"

And she clicked the tip of her pink fingernail against her teeth.

XVII
The Divine Mirage

Next to Fiamette, André set to work again—a work in accordance with his reason and his heart, bright with hope. He told his mistress that he had been insane to want to forget her and he understood now that all his strength and courage came from her.

His confessions, his prayers and his promises had been punctuated by kisses, tender follies, and, teasingly, she scolded him or delighted herself with him and his imaginations.

Was it not everything to be confident, reassured, and free, with the charming future that she would make for him? Was it possible to create torments for himself when he only had to let himself live, let the hours flow by, as limpid as the beads in a crystal rosary?

And the flow never dried up of the sweet words that sing the eternal hymn of resurrection in the hearts of poets.

The beautiful romance of caresses recommenced.

André's only occupation, after his labor, was adoring Fiamette, and he had the illusion of loving her with all the ardor of prime youth. She no longer had gazes, no longer seemed to have thoughts, except for him. He saw her as a tragic princess in the flames of her precious stones, motionless and almost immaterial on the stage of crimson velvet, and she was not only a woman but the incarnation of his dream. Through the mesh of her gorget, he caressed the fresh cups of her breasts, and placed his lips delightedly on the voluptuous dimples that the golden network uncovered.

He often took her away in her sidereal costume, in order to possess her thus, and the luminous verses sang so madly in his head that he seemed to be juggling with stars.

He had bought a delicate antique silk from a second-hand dealer, patterned with carnations and roses on a soft gray background, and that fabric had covered the walls of their bedroom, which was cheered up every day by new flowers.

Thus, with their tenderness, they possessed spring in their home. Their paradise seemed to them to be vast, and the world very small, lost in the mists of distance. Nothing around them was not themselves, there was no hostile gaze between their gazes, no discordant voice between their voices. In the evening, while he was writing, she huddled in the bed, making a warm place for him. The lamp poured out a white light, illuminating a corner of the table, an armchair and a patch of carpet. The rest was in blonde shadow, brightened here and there by a fleck of gold on a picture frame, a glimmer of silk or a gleam of copper.

He turned toward her, the ink still damp on the sheet of paper in his hand, and he read his verses slowly, in quest of approval, but also ready to make corrections in accordance with the sentiment of his mistress.

> *. . . And in the obscure sky where I see nothing,*
> *I discover, bewildered, the aerial nest*
> *Of confused kisses, crazed, avid kisses.*
>
> *What does the wing of my victorious love wrap?*
> *What does the awakening to livid mists matter?*
> *I have hidden the sun entire in my heart!*

The time passed as water flows through the fingers, leaving nothing but an impression of fluid softness. The dream impelled the dream in an ever-renascent intoxication, and the memory of happiness succeeded the hope of pleasure. No bitterness, no dread, no cares, no doubt, no threat; was it sufficient, then, to be happy to allow oneself to live and to allow oneself to love? How simple it was!

André, by virtue of the contrast he had seen and divined in an unworthy society, found charm in the slightest details of his placid existence.

"You see," he said to Fiamette, "I've emerged unscathed from all the ordeals, because I never ceased to cherish you, and nothing in me or around me could ever extinguish the sacred fire. Miette, pardon the imprudence! I swear to you never to see Chozelle again. Your patience, your sweetness, has not been exercised in favor of an ingrate. I know that you've sacrificed a fortune for me—Nora has told me everything—and I adore you for loving me so much."

"Poet," she murmured, kissing his eyes, "you're sincere today and I'm joyful, but God knows where your chimera will take you tomorrow. You're like those children who build palaces on sandy beaches. Nothing is lacking therein, neither the opaline life of medusae, nor the nacreous treasure of seashells, nor the sunlit horizon. The builders install themselves in their kingdom like monarchs, and then everything crumbles, swept away by the tide. But I don't want to know what tomorrow will be. Tomorrow is forgetfulness, suffering and death. It's necessary to enjoy the present moment, to close the eyes and block the ears. Tomorrow, others will have taken our place and we'll be in the past. Embrace me well, my dear lover, and let our souls be linked, like our bodies, for the supreme ecstasy!"

"Tell me, Miette, that I'll always be able to count on you."

"Undoubtedly," she said, in a hesitant voice, "but it's necessary not to tempt nature, and dolor is very close to need. If you quit me again, I don't know what I'd do . . ."

"I won't quit you again."

"Even if you were offered marvels?"

"No. And then, I have confidence in myself. I'm working with an ardor and a liberty that I haven't known until today. I must succeed, because I have the determination. If I weaken, you'll be there to sustain me with your amour. Do you think that there's anything else in life but amour? Do you think that it's easy to make oneself loved as much as one loves? Many people die with souls unsated because they haven't been able to give what they had in them of tenderness, in exchange for an equal tenderness. Often, a person of delicacy and sensibility remains unknown, misunderstood, and emerges virginal from all embraces and all sensualities. Oh, when hazard brings together two caresses and two sentiments of equal value, it's no longer necessary to desire or to hope for anything else on earth, for happiness is nothing but the fusion of two individuals in a kiss!"

And Miette, smiling, put her soul on her lips in order to offer it to her friend.

He went on, feverishly:

"You've sensed that in me there was more than the artist and the companion of a day. If you doubted my present love I would doubt your past love. You haven't chosen me out of pride, so you won't abandon me out of egotism. Miette, Miette, think what I'd lose if you left me . . ."

Slightly sadly, she replied: "I won't leave you. Why torment yourself?"

"Oh," he said, "I'm not made for happiness, and when destiny gives me brand new playthings, I break them to see what there is inside!"

XVIII
Nora's Lover

It was the final day of posing, and Fiamette was going to Pascal's studio. The air was cold, the frost crackling under the feet of the passers-by who were hurrying through the thin morning mist. On the bridge of the Rue Caulaincourt, a maidservant stopped the young woman.

"Ah, Madame, I was coming to see you."

"What's happened, then?"

"Madame Nora is very ill today and would like to see you."

"All right, I'll come with you."

In a few minutes, Fiamette was in the delightful house where the Comet resided in the Rue Clapeyron. Domestics were running around in alarm, because the dancer, who had not gone to bed until very late after a night of carousing, had just had a fainting fit.

Very frail, almost diaphanous in a froth of lace and lawn, she seemed no longer to have anything alive except in her large eyes, like somber embers. Fiamette threw herself into her arms.

"My darling!"

"Ah! Yes, I have a funny look, don't I. But again, it won't be today."

"Shut up!"

"You see, I'm all nerves. An old scrawny cat that can't be destroyed! When I think it's all over, it all starts again. I had supper last night . . ."

"You had supper!"

"And I never laughed so madly . . . Three men and three women . . . They told stories about the band, you know. Before long, that whole jolly society will be compromised in a nasty affair. I tell you that so your André won't go back there."

Fiamette had a fine smile of disdain. "He won't leave me again; everything is forgotten."

"What will you live on, then?"

"I've sold my sable and my necklace. That will last for some time, and then, Pascal is paying me for posing. Don't say anything to André—he thinks it's the money for his reports."

"That innocence!"

Again, Nora fell back, utterly white. Between her eyelashes, the corneas of her eyes glistened in a slender nacreous ribbon; the thin nostrils gathered again, and all the blood had withdrawn from her dry lips.

Frightened, Fiamette made her friend respire salts, and the Comet came round.

"You see, darling, I'm very low; however, would you believe it, I've never had so much success with men. They're seeking the macabre at present. If I listened to them, I wouldn't have a moment to myself."

"What about your lover?"

"He's not jealous—on the contrary. He's a man full of abnegation; you see, he wants me to quit him without regrets."

A slight bitterness creased the Comet's mouth, and her large eyes had a darker gleam. "You're wrong to sacrifice yourself to your amour," she said. "If you knew men, you'd no longer have any more sentiment."

"I'd rather love."

"They love to be loved. That's the difference."

"Well, everyone gets what they want, then."

The soubrette who had been to fetch Fiamette appeared at that moment.

"Monsieur is here, Madame."

"Do you mind if I let Georges in?" Nora asked her friend.

"If I'm not in the way . . . but Pascal's waiting for me to finish his work . . . and since you're no longer alone . . ."

"Stay a moment. It might be instructive."

The Comet's official lover came in, and immediately, without even paying any heed to his mistress, smiled at Fiamette, took her hand, and examined her in the light from the window, the curtain of which he drew. Satisfied with that inspection, he said to the dancer: "She's nice, your friend."

"Even more than you think."

"Shall we have supper this evening, the three of us? Mademoiselle will consent, won't she?"

"You know that I nearly died!"

"Bah! You know the remedy. You'll only be more amorous; the pretty eyes of this little one will cure you."

Fiamette got up with disgust. "Adieu, Nora," she said.

"Stay a while, Miette," moaned the dancer. "I really do feel very ill."

And as Georges, very bored, went away, she leaned her moist forehead over the young woman's breast and remained thus, nestled against the friendly heart, while a small tear filtered gently between her eyelashes and ran down her hollow cheek.

"You see," she murmured, "what men are. I give myself to all of them, in order not to love any of them."

"But you love all the same, poor Comet!"

XIX
The Chimera Flies Away

André Flavien put a scroll of papers under his arm and went to Pascal's, where he expected to find his mistress.

The master was waiting, putting slight retouches to his work. From time to time he stepped back in order to assess the ensemble, squinting, tilting his head, and, dissatisfied with some detail, took a savant glaze from his palette with the tip of his sable brush.

"Where's Fiamette?" asked André, after shaking Pascal's hand.

"I was about to ask you the same question."

"What?"

"I've been waiting for two hours . . ."

A little shiver ran between the young man's shoulders. "Fiamette left me in order to come and join you."

"I haven't seen anyone."

"Then . . ."

"Don't worry; perhaps she's run into a friend and is playing truant. There's also the milliner, the hairdresser, the dressmaker . . . what do I know? A pretty girl needs so many things."

André breathed out. "That's it. She'll have gone to buy flowers or some bauble to ornament the apartment . . . as if her presence weren't sufficient!"

"People like change."

"Since we're alone, my dear friend, permit me to thank you . . ."

"Thank me for what?"

"For your precious recommendation with regard to my influential colleagues."

Pascal opened his eyes wide. "I don't understand."

"You've placed verses and a few reports in periodicals that are going to publish them imminently, it appears. In any case, the editors of the periodicals have been generous."

"Ah!"

"And I'd like," André continued, blushing, "to give Fiamette a surprise."

"So?"

"So, for that, I need money, and I thought that you could get another advance on these articles . . ."

André unfurled his scroll.

"I've dealt with current affairs, and I think the subject is interesting."

"Oh," said Pascal. "What are you saying to me?"

"I'm asking you for a service similar to the one you've already rendered with regard to periodical editors."

"I haven't rendered you any service of that kind."

Very pale, André wiped his brow. "Fiamette told me . . ."

Seeing the young man's contracted features, the painter regretted his frankness, but it was too late to repair the damage.

"I don't know what your friend might have told you. I count on indemnifying her handsomely for her kindness, because, thanks to her, I've made a masterpiece, and I'm ready to acquit the debt right away, if you wish."

"Don't say any more," said André, confused by the artist's slightly brutal offer.

"If you were my pupil," Pascal went on, "I could doubtless be useful to you; as for aiding you with the placement of your articles, that's scarcely possible for me; I humbly confess that I don't have any influence in the literary world."

"In that case," the poet murmured, "I don't know what we've been living on since I quit Chozelle."

The painter had a slightly ironic smile, which was like a revelation to André.

"No, that's impossible! I'm hardly ever apart from her. But . . ."

And André, doubly unhappy, sensed his beautiful dream of amour and his beautiful dream of glory agonizing within him.

XX
Rupture

When Fiamette came back she found a letter from her lover.

You have deceived me, he wrote, *and you have made me play a despicable role. I won't debase myself by interrogating you. What would be the point? You're able to pretend and lie, like all women, and I wouldn't be able to believe anything you could say to me. Adieu, Fiamette; don't regret me. Destiny will be good to you, for I was only an obstacle in your life.*

André Flavien

The young woman was devastated. She shut herself away in the little bedroom, still florid and perfumed with cherished memories, and remained thoughtful for a long time. Everything in her was monochrome sadness, without the relief of tears, which could not rise as far as her eyes. Henceforth, life would be uniform in its indifference, gray, painful and devoid of purpose. To what could she attach herself now that her lover had gone? To whom would she murmur the litanies of tenderness that all women have in their heart? Between what she had wanted and what had been realized, in spite of her devotion and her abnegation, there was the distance that separates illusion from experience, enthusiasm from disenchantment.

It was the story of almost all liaisons, which begin in canticles and actions of grace and end in laments of mourning. She knew little of life, being so young, but human ingratitude already astonished her like a monstrosity, a neglect of nature, which has perfect forms and colors without worrying about souls. The appetite for sentimental emotion that was the dominant trait of her character was exasperated in the void. She was not consoled for her woes even by their grandeur, as happens in malady, the disasters of fortune or the death of those we cherish. Her adventure had been banal, almost despicable, and for that reason alone, it seemed more difficult to bear.

And her entire childhood of an innocent and free country-dweller returned to her memory. She saw once again the stone path full of bees and mulberries, the squat apple trees with green fruits that she picked in secret on already misty September mornings. She returned from her raids with her skirts heavy with chestnuts and mushrooms, stopping here and there to pick a campanula or a scabious, and sometimes going to sleep under a high, dense, somber vault of greenery, holed by little white sunbeams, which the wind agitated above her head like a luminous cobweb.

Behind a few thinner trees, to the left, she perceived hedges of sorb and hawthorn displaying their coral beads, and to the right, the glaucous mirror of a pond with a patina of black insects. Fear came to her at dusk and she resumed her route at a run, pursued by the caressing voice of the breeze and the voluptuous buzzing of wasps. At the bends in the road she perceived the red-tinted countryside or the wall of a farm building, which, framed in a gap, seemed to fill in the sky. The solitude impressed her childish thoughts. She only recovered confidence in the courtyard of her little house, where the domestic cat and the guard dog welcomed her tenderly.

Then, glad of that protection, she lay down under an acacia, which, reflowering in autumn, let its fleecy petals fall on her. The centenarian bark of the tree had the metallic patina and the roughness of animal hide. Under half-closed eyelids her gaze sought the fantastic forms of dragons or chimeras, the profiles of ogres and malevolent spirits.

Sometimes, she sat on the edge of the well, contemplating the hole of cold shadow, in which dead water shone. Behind the little garden rose a regular colonnade of large Italian pines, raising the majesty of their nave to the daylight, and as she approached that monumental wood, with resinous trunks and interleaved parasols of violet branches in the warm fur of moss and gray ash, she felt full of an inexpressible wellbeing.

Thus her early years had gone by in the midst of the smiles of nature; then she had lost her parents, and an aunt had collected her and had put her in school in a suburb of Paris. She had made rapid progress, being very intelligent, and, little by little, by virtue of the frequentation of perverse companions, evil had entered into her and withered the roses of her heart. Bruised before having lived, lost before having loved, she really was the hasty flower, morbidly blossomed, of extreme civilizations.

André alone might have been able to save her from others and herself, but André had not wanted to, or had not understood, and now she was about to fall back into the gutter of vice, regretful of having glimpsed the reflection of the stars for a brief moment.

Alone in the apartment, Fiamette stirred dolorous thoughts, allowed herself to be cradled by enervations comparable in their bleak languor to the semi-sleep that morphine provides. Then, shaking everything, emerging from that laxity, she recovered her ardor, her strength, the exasperation of her will. The hallucination of the last embrace passed back and forth in the darkness of her nights. She reignited her feverish desires, reanimated her thirst for amour. And it was not the voluptuousness of the senses that she desired but the voluptuousness of the heart, a thousand times more vivid, the supreme voluptuousness in which all human joys seemed to be exalted and annihilated . . .

In those alternatives of dejection and revolt, the time dragged slowly, only bringing a little repose in the early hours of the day. She interrogated herself in vain, seeking to understand her disgrace, and not knowing what to conclude.

Had she not been a submissive, humble, delicate, fervent and passionate lover? Of what neglect, of what fault, could she be accused?

Oh, she said to herself, *Nora was quite right; it's necessary to put everything into amour but sentiment!*

But she was too broken-hearted to think of distracting herself, of escaping her pain. The mysterious labor of renewal that gradually effaces our despair, as the epidermis replaces itself, scarring the rawest wounds, had not yet commenced within her.

Agonized and nostalgic, she remained in her little apartment for eight days, respiring the flowers that she had given him, arranging his pens, his inkwell, his books and his bottles, her soul communing with his cherished memory, in all the passages that he had jotted down. Pieces of paper trailed everywhere, covered in the poet's anxious and nervous handwriting. She gathered them together, put them under her pillow and reposed on those relics of amour for a week. For eight days she had no other thought, no other hope and no other desire than his distant caress, and she bit her sheets in crises of jealousy and passion.

Finally, on the ninth day, when she could scarcely stand up, and seemed to feel within her skull a tolling bell that was detaching her brain therefrom, she thought that Nora was even sicker than she was, and went out.

XXI
A Parisian Orgy

As desperate as Fiamette, André had rented a modest room in a furnished house and, trying to vanquish his pride, had returned to the editorial offices of newspapers where he had left copy. In one place, he was kept waiting for two hours nursing fallacious promises; in another he had been sent away, asking him to come back in a few weeks. In any case, no one read, no one had the time to read, and no room remained to insert all the articles he sent out on a daily basis. A few editors of more modest periodicals had deigned to scan André's reports or short stories, and had returned them to him, admitting that his excessively literary genre would put off the ordinary clientele of the paper.

One evening, having dined on a bread roll and a glass of milk, the poet sought a refuge with Chozelle, who welcomed him as if he had seen him the previous day.

The Master was attending scrupulously to his toilette.

Standing in front of a table laden with small pots and mysterious instruments, rounded or pointed, he was making delicate use of pencils, pastes and pads, effacing a wrinkle, accentuating a shadow, reddening or blue-tinting here and there. On the shelves there were lotions for widening the eyes, foams of crimson and ceruse white for heightening the complexion, oils for making the skin supple, unguents and balms for the hands and concentrated perfumes with delicate floral tints in crystal vaporizers.

Jacques, bare-chested, had just finished depilating himself, and he was passing a powder-puff scented with vervain over his shoulders and chest. A black satin corset was waiting on a chair, in the company of long, mauve silk stockings and fluffy garters.

In spite of his sadness, André could not help smiling.

"These . . . feminine objects are for you?"

"Certainly. I've always protested, you know, against the carelessness and ugliness of men's garments. I'm setting a good example."

"Who will know?"

Slightly nonplussed, Jacques replied, warily: "Well . . . you, for a start. . ."

"It's necessary not to count on me for propagandas. I'm a savage, you know."

Chozelle shrugged his shoulders.

"We'll civilize you. Here, a mist of white heliotrope in a cloud of Chypre—that makes an appreciable mixture."

He turned his back on the poet, who was obliged to press the rubber bulb of a vaporizer and spread the perfumed mist over the Master's back and shoulder blades.

"Pass me that mauve lawn chemise . . . oh, and my little gold chain with the talisman; I have a mania for fetishes and amulets, you know."

Mechanically, his soul in mourning, André obeyed Chozelle, who blew kisses to himself in the mirror, rounding his arm and raising the little finger in a precious fashion.

"Are there going to be women?" asked the poet, with the vague desire to numb himself, to drown the memory of defunct intoxications in other intoxications.

Jacques turned round indignantly. "Women? It's quite enough to have to put up with them at the theater! Have I ever taken you among women?"

"In sum, where are we going?"

"That's true—it's two months since you quit me and you don't know anything about my life. We're going . . . but you're not thinking of accompanying me dressed like that, I suppose?"

"I've taken a room nearby; it will only take me ten minutes to get dressed."

"Go on, then—and be beautiful."

Chozelle took André to the house of a friend of Defeuille's, very luxuriously installed, who hosted . . . esthetic soirées. The room into which the newcomers were introduced was surrounded by low divans with gilded amours on marble pedestals, holding electric wheatsheaves, in the corners. Other amours, kneeling or recumbent, were presenting baskets of fruits and flowers.

Pipes and thin green pastilles were disposed on trays. A few opium-smokers were already installed for the fiction of amour, forgetfulness or oblivion.

Heating long needles in the flame of pink wax candles burning beside them on little tables, they introduced them into the paste, which fixed a light ball thereto, and then garnished their silver pipes. The ignited opium cooked slowly, sending clouds of acrid smoke toward the ceiling, where the shadows of the dreams evoked were designed.

André felt a surge of joy. He would be able, then, to intoxicate himself, to forget, to drown his dolor in morbid fiction!

"Come on, Jacques," said Defeuille. "We're only waiting for you."

Chozelle shook his fingers, made a tour of the room, naming each guest, who returned his handshake idly. The bruised eyes had disquieting gleams, the hands, laden with rings, were agitating in feverish impatience. A little to one side, the androgyne couple only seemed to be living for one another. A single pipe served for two ecstasies, and interlaced fingers bore it from the lips of one to the lips of the other.

There were very young men there, almost children, who had curious and frightened gazes, an expression of disgust and pride, dread and audacity. Their curly heads, blond or brunette, reposed on velvet cushions; their voices had a strange resonance and their vague, murky, disquieting ideas retained nevertheless a destructive charm.

The perverse nonchalance, and the cruel and cold complication of all those crackbrains troubled them reciprocally with passions and morbid desires.

Children passed by, throwing rose petals into glasses of champagne, which they presented to the guests. André emptied his in a single draught and asked for more, his soul anguished and tortured by amour.

"I see, young friend," Jacques observed, "that you're in an excellent disposition. You'll see that one doesn't get bored here."

Smokers were agitating on the divans. Hallucinated gazes were scintillating or dying, ecstatic pupils moving upwards in the nacre of the eye, and sighs occasionally escaped from panting throats. Breasts inflated, under soft silk shirts, arms apart as if to seize the shadows of dreams. A few sleepers with features contracted by a mysterious terror seemed to be creatures of nightmare, the exhausted participants in some macabre round-dance.

The flames of the pink candles vacillated under feverish breaths, and it seemed to André that the gilded amours were agitating on their pedestals. But that was certainly a hallucination produced by the first puffs of opium that rose to his brain. He was lying on a divan and had cooked the green paste, following the example of those surrounding him. A pain drilled his temples, and he thought that a clod of earth was rising beneath his skin. The impression was disagreeable; he was unaccustomed to it, and an initial nausea followed his effort. But the alert passed and he recommenced, wanting to numb himself at any cost.

There were young men there from good families, gone astray, handsome lads devoid of scruples, sick people, madmen and cunning individuals avid for fame. The mystery with which the latter surrounded themselves, the scorn that they affected for the bourgeois and women, made an aureole of strangeness for them, and in a land where nothing any longer surprises anyone, they could inflate the poisonous mushrooms of their souls "esthetically."

Even more so than at Defeuille's dinner, attitudes were free and mannerisms singularly provocative.

Chozelle, however, had disappeared with a dozen young men. André remained in the company of the smokers and a few knights of doleful countenance who were drinking silently. Acrid smoke drowned the electric jets, which no longer illuminated any more than vague Argand lamps in a distant fog.

The poet no longer knew what was real in that décor; his imagination wandered in the troubling fields of dream. It seemed to him that magical eyes were shining like embers in the night, and that Chozelle's stryges and empusas were descending from the ceiling to kiss him on the lips.

Those caresses had a viscous and bitter flavor; disgust nauseated him. The larvae and the vampires, which like blood, spread out and populated the shadows, fleeing the trenchant edge of the sword,. He told himself that they were not spirits but fluid coagulations that one could cleave or destroy, and tried in vain to get up in order to chase them away.

However, he added, mentally, with a residue of lucidity, *human thought creates what it imagines; the phantoms of superstition project their real deformity into souls, and live the very terrors to which they give birth. The black giant extending his wings from the Orient to the Occident, the monster that destroys consciences, the frightful divinity of ignorance and fear—the Devil, in a word—is still, for an immense multitude of children of all ages, a terrible reality.*

At that moment, he saw, distinctly, membranous wings, terminated by claws, palpitating above him, and a fleshless face with hollow orbits and a lipless mouth leaning over his.

238

The hallucinations of opium, he told himself, *are not playful. Everything that overexcites sensibility leads to depravity or crime; tears summon blood! Great emotions are like strong liquor; making habitual use of them is abusing them. Now, any abuse of the emotions perverts the moral sense; one seeks them for their own sake, one sacrifices everything to procure them; they erode the heart and crush the skull!*

He waved his arms to drive away a colossal toad with red pustules and phosphorescent eyes, which had just leapt on to his breast. For a minute he was suffocating, but then the monster disappeared.

Continuing to analyze his impressions with a singular clarity, he observed, mentally: *One arrives at the deplorable and irreparable absurdity of committing suicide in order to admire and pity oneself in seeing oneself die. Manfred, René and Lélia are type specimens of perversity all the more profound because they rationalize their unhealthy pride and poeticize their dementia. The light of reason does not illuminate insensible things for closed eyes; or, at least, it only illuminates them to the profit of those who can see. The word of* Genesis, Let there be light! *is the victory cry of the intelligence triumphant over darkness. That word is sublime because it expresses the most beautiful thing in the world, the creation of intelligence by itself.*

André, who had closed his eyes, opened them again, and his gaze fell upon one of the torch-bearing amours. Was it another hallucination? He distinctly saw the child move, hang the electric tulips on the wall and descended from his pedestal, shaking off the gold powder that covered his skin. The other amours did the same, and, holding one another by the hand, led a farandole around the smokers.

Their bodies shone under the gilt, they laughed, and sometimes let themselves fall on to divans.

André lifted the little pipe to his lips again, and a freshness descended and ran through his veins. He felt a great wellbeing invade him; a thousand new thoughts whirled in his head. He smoked and smoked again; then he spoke in a voice steeped in tears; an extraordinary sensibility gripped him, as if all his other sensations had dissolved, saturated in an immense desire to weep.

He tried to get up, but an intolerable pain drilled his temples. Everything around him was spinning: the tables, the drinkers, and the amours sighing on a bed of roses and gold powder. Specters agitated, laughing. Then he heard his voice, which had a sound like a cracked bell, and he did not understand what he was talking about. He was increasingly duplicated, his thinking and reasoning being witnessed, mute, gagged and confused, the decline of the other.

The doors opened very wide, and he saw Chozelle advancing again, dressed as a woman, and displaying, under a short skirt, his mauve silk stockings. Other men followed in analogous disguise, causing gauze corsages to seethe over flat chests, rounding out the biceps of wrestlers while simpering, and quivering like voluptuous gypsy women.

It was too much. André was seized by frenetic, inextinguishable laughter, and then everything was abolished within him.

XXII
The Quat'z'Arts[1]

The fay of opium is a mistress who refuses herself at first, but soon lavishes her lovers with the most intoxicating caresses. Almost every day, having finished his work, the poet plunged into the hallucinating inebriation. Thus, his nights, populated by phantoms, did not have the banal bitterness of reality. He lived a double life, caressing in dreams a smiling and faithful Fiamette,

---

1 The Bal des Quat'z'Arts was first organized in Montmartre in 1892 as a celebration for students at the École Nationale Supérieur des Beaux-Arts, and became an important annual event and spectacle, modeled on the Mardi Gras Carnival.

who did not sell her kisses, but put her soul on her mouth in order to offer it to him, like a flower in a virginal cup that no other lip had brushed.

But the young man's nerves were exacerbated by that game; he had continual vertigos, stiffening in the street in order to maintain a firm stride, and sometimes, on the sly, leaning on walls in order to recover his strength. His memory, once marvelous, had lacunae; he often required a fatiguing mental tension to recall the simplest things. In those dispositions, he put up a vague resistance to the caprices of Jacques, whose demands took on an increasingly aggressive character.

They went out at hazard, when the sun's rays, like golden baldrics, striped the narrow streets of the quarters of vice and misery. They went past sordid boutiques, abattoirs black with coagulated blood where quarters of meat hung from iron hooks, along with the livers and hearts of cattle with huge protruding blue arteries. Water from flower pots dripped on their heads and "seamstresses" leaning out of mansards laughed on seeing them shake themselves like dogs under the overly impetuous jets of their watering cans.

But Jacques welcomed those feminine whims without amenity, and fled toward more discreet dens of misery, eclipsed behind the door of some hovel that stood ajar, while André continued walking at random, searching for he knew not what: appeasement or dolor, visions of idylls or murder.

In the mills of Montmartre, Pascal tried to stun his young friend, showing him masquerades à la Gavarni, displays of women for the taking or for sale on tumbrils decorated with flowers and pennants, collapsing the naked flesh, as in pedlars' trays offered to lovers of spicy delicacies. Neurasthenic corteges of Bacchus and Pan blew pipes and ran out of breath behind the laughing beautiful girls, and a wind of dementia caused the plumes of barbarian chiefs and enchanted Lohengrins to oscillate, in the midst of a crowd drunk on cries and animal odors.

Volleys of laughter became so loud that the orchestra some-times stopped, losing the key and the measure.

There were Romans with naked arms and proud torsos, slaves with strides impeded by chains, their hands bound; and tortur-ers brandishing pincers, boots and flesh-tearing scissors. Hindus dressed in white, Talapoins coiffed with cords and beautiful Moorish women tinkling with barbaric jewels were delivering themselves to epileptic tremors while awaiting the principal pro-cession. Under the raw light of electric tulips, all the neuroses of the Parisian festival passed by, supremely made up.

As at the Folies Perverses, androgynous couples were circulat-ing, enlaced, and in the near effacement of sexual nature, the thought of disquieting anomalies took increasingly deep root.

Journalists were taking notes, collecting fruitful publicity; demi-mondaines were showing off their jewelry, more enthusi-astic for renown than homages. Only the artists and the models were really amusing themselves, without posing, happy with their well-earned success. And there truly was an entire bouquet of pretty girls there, with fine limbs and breasts offered in volup-tuous cups.

"Take your choice," said Pascal. "Life is short and you're still young enough to be loved for yourself. I can see gazes fixed on you, and they're not grim. If you wanted . . . !"

"No," sighed André. "I don't have the heart for pleasure . . ."

"Bah! Try anyway."

"I wouldn't know what to say. Amorous words freeze on my lips . . ."

"They'll love you more for it, disdainful beau!"

"Isn't it better to love than to be loved?"

"Pooh! Those are big words for very little. An hour of sweet embrace doesn't commit you to anything. One drinks from a cup of flesh as one drinks a little amontillado from a cup of crystal when one is thirsty, and one goes to sleep without regret. There's no question here of sentiment, and the girls with firm breasts who offer the wine of amour don't want you to give them your

242

soul in exchange. They wouldn't know what to do with it, poor things!"

"I believe, friend, that you're mistaken. A woman requires even more tenderness than caresses, and her laughter is always near to tears."

"Poet!"

"Perhaps . . . and even more so today than yesterday, because I'm more unhappy."

Pascal shrugged his shoulders. "Go back to your Fiamette, then."

"No. I don't want to. I can't."

"Because you love her too much. When I told you that amour only makes people do stupid things."

The bays of the great hall of the Moulin Bleu[1] had been converted into boxes decorated in a bizarre and charming fashion. Women were emerging from floral sprays, showing a corner of their nudity, and the corollas of roses were mingled with the corollas of breasts, summoning the butterflies of the kiss.

At midnight the procession was organized, in which Gaul, Egypt, India, Assyria, Persia, Phoenicia, etc. were all represented. Prehistoric times were rendered with a fortunate abundance of imagination, and an ironic fantasy that always attained the unexpected.

There were Hindu pyres there, surrounded by bayaderes with gauze langoutis, tragic mourners and Brahmin sacrificers. Egyptian houses, boats of flowers, gallant guinguettes, Byzantine palaces and prehistoric grottoes offered women of all colors, all sellers of lust.

---

1 Although the text has already referred to the Moulin Rouge (where the Bal de Quat'z'Arts was held after 1893) by its real name the author seems to have thought a substitution more appropriate, as she had in the satirical transformation of the Folies Bergère into the Folies Perverses. She made the same substitutions in many of the short stories she produced for *La Lanterne*, which frequently offer a flippantly satirical depiction of the love lives of dancing girls, and which occasionally feature characters mentioned in the present novel, notably Ninoche.

The Moloch of *Salammbô* reared up in a corner, gigantic and terrifying, and the faint sounds of kisses departed from niches where cardboard gods raised their murderous arms. The priestesses of amour, always ready for sweet sacrifices, only had to disturb their jewels to offer their flesh to caresses.

A young man of almost supernatural beauty was leading the Phoenician bull, and prostitutes threw him flowers, begging for a glance from his wild velvet eyes.

André could not help admiring the harmonious arrangement of everything, and if the lover was still suffering, the artist, fond of beautiful forms and beautiful décor, experienced a secret contentment. He did not admit it, however, fearful of Pascal's skeptical smile, and his slightly humiliating consolations of a man blasé with regard to the promises and the disappointments of the heart.

"You see," said the artist, "the man who is in love is like a torture victim turning on that wheel. Every foreseen turn brings the same tortures. Amour is always similar, and he does not pardon his victims."

He was pointing at an enormous wheel on a cart preceded by barbarians clad in animal skins, armed with steel blades to butcher the body. All around, the condemned charged with chains were groaning; two supple young women were agitating the curls of their hair in the flames, and the heads of virgins, freshly severed, opened their languorous eyes on the ends of golden pikes. A Buddha mounted on a frog brought up the rear of the cortege.

Pascal had dragged André to supper. Installed beside a pretty girl of fifteen, he was frightfully drunk, and had no idea how he was going to get home. Only the sound of a soft voice remained in his ear, and he had discovered in a pocket of his carnival costume a red poppy similar to the one that the child was wearing in her hair.

XXIII
The Ladybird Cabaret

In that epoch the disciple had a very regrettable adventure.

Jacques had the custom of going to a mysterious location, elegantly perverse, about which he only spoke in a low voice, with alarmed and glorious expressions of very pleasing effect.

A considerable number of those equivocal establishments exist in Paris, which the police tolerate because important people frequent them and the scandal of an arrest would have a great resonance. The descents of the law are thus only habitual in houses of the second rank, the more modest clientele of which cannot protest.

Outside, nothing denounces the special seductions of the place. Honest shop windows display, through transparent curtains, a few rows of tables and a counter where a woman of mature years—the only one in the place—is enthroned. Pale esthetes are drinking bitter wines the color of mahogany or amethyst, and chatting politely about one thing and another. At the back, a felted door that closes of its own accord gives access to a luxurious and barbaric salon, which recalls those of brothels. No pretty women, alas, but a display of special absurdity. English types, above all, flock there, displaying the awkwardness of tall clergymen in frock-coats, with varnished shoes and rings with large bezels on every finger. There are also aggressive bulldog faces with ears devoid of lobes, surprising baboons, flaccid individuals with bloodshot eyes and idiots with the faces of cut-throats, flashy foreigners and lunatics.

At midnight, the fête begins, and the program scarcely varies. As among Defeuille and his friends, the interpreters of the "drawing room comedies", decked out in feminine costumes, put on abundant curled wigs with reflections of gold or flame, rub themselves with ceruse, oils and balms with subtle essences, to give themselves the illusion that they are exactly what they scorn. Very young men truly resembling women, who almost have the right to be proud of their slim stature and their large dark-ringed eyes, are the most surrounded, the most pampered.

Full of resignation, André laced the Master's corset, fastened his mauve satin garters and fixed verbena cushions to all the futile hollows of his feminine armature.

Jacques stretched his arms, struck poses, and smiled at himself in the huge mirror with three faces, in which he could see himself generously.

"Am I at my best this evening?" he asked, pinching his ear-lobe, after having passed a moist finger over his eyebrows in order to fluff up the velveteen.

"You're full of seduction, dear Master."

"Why don't you want to be one of ours, my child?"

"I don't know," the young man murmured, with a discreet irony. "I don't have the vocation."

"Alas, in spite of my lessons, I haven't found in you the docile pupil for whom I was searching. You don't have the soul of the divine androgynes who, alone, bring some charm to life! If you were even a faithful companion, a submissive and comprehensive disciple!"

Resigned, André did not riposte; his brow was dolorous and his thoughts vague, almost always blurred by the abuse of narcotics, and Jacques softened.

"It would be so pleasant, however, to be only one, only to exist for that ardent union of heart and soul! Look, the scarab of this clasp is scratching me, and this whalebone is digging into my ribs . . ."

"Yes, Master."

"This evening, I'm no longer, and better than, your Master, I'm . . . but why that hangdog face? Are you ill?"

"Indeed . . ."

And the young man, paler than the ceruse paste the covered Jacques' cheeks, let himself fall in to an armchair, experiencing something akin to a shock to the heart, followed by the breakdown of a poorly-greased machine.

"What's the matter, then?"

"If you'll permit, this evening I'll stay at home."

"No, I want you to come with me, in order that I can lean on your shoulder and mirror my eyes in yours. You'll inspire me with a few harmonious verses on the grandeur of our absolutely superior esthetic mission. Here, get my clothes, and put this gold powder in your hair."

André had therefore known, after many other nostalgic gatherings, the rendezvous of the Labybird, the honest cabaret with the banal provincial front window. He had witnessed, in an elegant stupidity, the gallant tourneys of florid knights; then, drunk on peppery wines, mingled with extracts of tuberose and acacia, his soul still capsized by his opium dreams, he had lost the notion of time.

Old readings came back to him, especially that in which Petronius recounts in the *Satyricon* the debauched life of Rome. Pigs crowned with myrtle and roses had the same curiosities and strange ruts as our enervated Parisians. In hospitable houses open to amorous passers-by, one glimpsed, between placards, indecisive nudities and brief couplings to the chords of barbaric music. There were disquieting incubi with the heavy finery of courtesans, plastered with white greasepaint, primped and perfumed, asexual individuals, plump and unhealthy, with wide empty eyes circled with kohl.

Those scenes, cut out in the quick of ancient mores, were almost the same as those played out there in paltry fashion for a few initiates. Adulterated joys of Sodom, unrealizable desires of new sensualists, disgust of a decrepit civilization, unconsciousness of vice become necessity, all the aberrations of our modern literature are found in the *Satyricon*, and André remembered its enticing debauches and erudite hysterias.

In his sleep, he now saw singular things: an elevated throne rose up before him, enameled with polychromatic tiles, encrusted with beryls and opals. Sprawling on the steps were adolescents with naked, imprecise forms, with slender limbs decked with jewels, and Jacques, seated on the broad seat, caressed them one by one, and then cut their throats slowly without a muscle in his face twitching. Blood spattered the steps; the bodies, in brief spasms, rolled down one after another.

His jaundiced, parchment complexion striped with wrinkles, his gaze fixed with cold cruelty, Chozelle reddened his hands in that work of butchery, lingering over warm touches, in the perverse joy of the agonies that he had determined.

Then there were other scenes, lascivious dances of naked young men, whose loins undulated under girdles of sardonyxes and emeralds, whose necklaces spat sparks, swarming over flat chests like chameleons of flame.

And a hermaphrodite detached himself from the group, displayed pale limbs, of a perfect beauty, and mimed Salome's dances before Herod. André thought he was seeing Fiamette, but a mutilated, strange, vengeful Fiamette.

It was not only a swooning dancer that was reanimating the senses of an old man by means of sighs and soft flesh, quivering with lust; it was Sin itself, an adorable, hybrid and venomous corolla, swelling for the annihilation of a race.

Fiamette—for it was her—mounted the steps of the throne, bent over the tetrarch, offered him her scarcely-emerged breasts, the nipples of which were bleeding, and the enlaced couple disappeared in swirls of mist, and then flew away, to be lost in the ceiling, while André uttered a cry of rage.

And other hallucinations, after a moment of anguish, populated his semi-slumber.

From time to time, he emerged from his nightmares, exhausted, worn out, his thought capsized in terror, and he heard, above the noise of poorly closed bedrooms, the dull, regular and feverish shock of arteries that were beating madly beneath the skin of his neck.

"André, I assure you that this russet wig would suit you marvelously, and this girdle of peridots with the enamel scarab would fasten without difficulty around your loins. You can sing to us, in a soft voice, the amorous chants I've taught you. Do you want to?"

"Leave him alone; can't you see that he's drunk and can't hear us."

"Then let's put these gold lamé veils on him ourselves."

Jacques took André in his arms, and the disciple, continuing his dream, allowed himself to be undressed without resistance. Under the rain of flowers that submerged him, he heard, confusedly, the light plaints of syrinx flutes and ewe-skin drums, the fury of sistra of iron and ivory, and he thought he was at a Roman orgy in which the games would unfold in floods of wine and blood.

He was Heliogabalus, and the Priests of the Sun were dancing before the obscene symbol of the Black Stone, brandishing torches whose perfumed drops were falling all around him. He did not refuse the adorations, conscious of his august role, and smiled while an entire people prostrated themselves, awaiting a word from his painted lips.

The priests of Cybele kissed him on the corner of his lips, and invited him to take part in the fête of voluptuous Nature.

He was lying on a very low bed in the form of a gondola, his breast and legs naked, with a curly wig that covered his forehead. Cassolettes were burning beside him, and he was rolling the pink beads of a coral necklace between his fingers. His eyes filled with an incessant mirage, he respired warm aromatic smoke that exasperated his desires, and he felt procreated for the advent of the androgyne intermediate between woman and man: the definitive triumph of the principle of life. He thought that he had both sexes, and he rejoiced in the idea of engendering himself in the glory of his omnipotence.

Supplicant arms were extended toward him, however; if he disdained the caresses, he did not repel them, generous in his triumph, and his hallucinated gaze was lost in a tumult of shimmering silks and gemstones in which fragments of flesh blushed.

Jacques leaned over him, and hugged his shoulders more and more narrowly, while a slave fanned them with a large flabellum. And there was a softness that the disciple would not have dared to suspect. His thought floated randomly; he no longer imagined other delights.

"My child of election," said Jacques, "how I'm quivering in sensing you here, in my power without revolt. You have finally understood the goal of your existence, the mystery of your destiny, and nothing will separate us henceforth." He did not cease kissing his eyes, hugging him, palpating his body with a nervous impulsiveness, similar to a delirious crisis.

The slave agitated the flabellum more limply in the thickened air, and the golden wax candles let their burning tears fall on the white tunics of the priests of Cybele, kneeling as for a sacrifice.

Docile, André allowed himself to be manipulated. Then there was a noise in the corridors; the witnesses suddenly rose up to the ceiling, and everything disappeared in floods of mist.

The disciple recovered consciousness under a rude fist that was striking him, and an unknown voice enjoined him to put on his clothes, which men were throwing at him disdainfully.

He got dressed, without understanding, as if in a dream. It was only later that he learned that a police raid had disturbed the esthetic fête at the Ladybird cabaret.

He was incarcerated, along with the proprietor of the establishment, but thanks to Chozelle's influence, he only spent a few days in prison.

XXIV
The Little Streetwalker

André recommenced roaming the dives of Paris, the disreputable taverns on the waterfront, the shady terrains of distant constructions, the suburban quarters black with people and poverty.

Jacques claimed to be making curious encounters there, and to prefer the spicy vice of the faubourgs to the classical and slightly insipid perversions of his friend Defeuille. He touched callous hands with brown fingernails and spatulate fingers; he smiled at greedy criminal faces with basely ferocious expressions, and everything that was vile and vulgar in the depths of his nature delighted in those frequentations.

Sometimes, they arrived in the middle of a battle. Drinkers formed a circle around the combatants, who, foaming at the mouth, their eyes bloodshot, rushed to death with bestial cries. People around them laughed, exciting them with voices and gestures, or applauding in accordance with the value of the blows. An ear, or a shred of flesh, often bloodied the teeth of the more ferocious, and knives, twisted in wounds, brought out bloody fluids.

When the police did not intervene, the combat only ceased with the fall of one of the men, and the victor was seen to get up again, his hands sticky, wiping his butcher's knife on his shirt.

There were few women in those filthy hovels. Jacques visited the special houses that female sellers of amour avoided, knowing that their charms were not appreciated there. At the most, on occasion, a streetwalker came to look for her brother or her son, rarely her lover.

Chozelle offered a drink to the most handsome fellows, and made his choice, while André, half-asleep on a corner of a table, dreamed about Fiamette. In his rare moments of lucidity, he horrified himself, and it seemed to him that each of his feverish nights aggravated his decline, pushing him irredeemably into the shameful path. A kind of suggestive force dominated his will, which had been suspended under the influence of the poison; he submitted to the quotidian torture with the resignation of an invalid.

In his cowardice, Chozelle feared unfortunate adventures, and if he had his young disciple accompany him, it was less out of amity for him than always to be assured of an efficacious protection.

Sometimes, in fact, a jealous or cunning male intervened, spitting the most horrible threats or proposing a settlement, and that recalled the customs and actions of barrière pimps; only the livestock differed. It is true that those professors of infamy principally recruited children or adolescents, and Jacques preferred ripe fruit to beginners.

One day, however, the disciple had put himself in front of the Master and had received a punch in the chest that had knocked him down. He had come round leaning against a lamp-post, and Jacques, kneeling beside him, was stemming the blood flowing from his nose and mouth.

Those dangers pleased the poet, causing him to find a morbid attraction in those nocturnal expeditions, and an excuse. He tried to forget his sad amour, and, when he had enough presence of mind, he made notes for a novel of contemporary life that he was meditating.

Thus the time passed; he had no news of his mistress and thought he would be able to forget her. In spite of the sadness of his heart, he followed with an indulgent eye the errant forms, soft under their tawdry finery, who roamed the streets with the suspect and furtive gait of beasts, who stopped passers-by, humble and promising, searching the shadows in the exasperation of their obstinate pursuit. And while Jacques turned away scornfully, André smiled kindly at those creatures of joy, who knew neither joy not laughter, those daughters of amour who knew no more of amour than the gesture.

However, his being was afflicted by wanting to love and having nothing to love. He sensed the chill that forms around a sterile youth, a youth disinherited of tender protection and seductive grace. In spite of himself, he lingered over the depiction of the ardent and pure face of Fiamette, and the adorable contours of her body. He saw her again in her robe of dreams, strung with flames, with the proud tips of her breasts lifting up the mesh of the pearl gorget.

One evening, a prostitute took his hand in the darkness and drew him away while Jacques was drinking with his chance friends. The child could not have been older than fifteen. She had thin limbs, superb hair and peridot eyes that enfevered her face. Her slender hips undulated beneath a red skirt; an artificial poppy was bleeding in her hair.

"You look sad," she said. "Come."

He smiled. He had recognized the child of the Moulin Bleu

"You know love, then. How do you like it?"

"I cradle chagrins in my heart as I cradled my dolls not long ago."

"You have a heart, then?"

"So it appears, and I suffer when people mistreat me,"

"How long have you been following this profession?"

"Two years, but it's necessary not to say so, because I'm not old enough."

"It's dangerous to go with you, then?"

"Oh, you're not risking anything. It's big Charles who . . ."

"Charles?"

The child swelled with pride. "Yes, my lover . . . the man who makes me work . . ."

Sadly, André contemplated that eglantine of the pavement, not withered yet but paled by the fatigues of amour and perverse embraces.

"And this big Charles . . . do you love him?"

She shivered, and replied in a whisper: "No."

"Then why stay with him?"

"Because I'm afraid of him."

"He beats you?"

"Often."

"When you don't bring back enough money?"

She lowered her eyes, and answered with a melancholy nod of the head.

"It's necessary to run away, to try to find a place somewhere."

"I've thought of that," she said, swiftly, "and you can help me!"

"Me?"

"What do you expect me to do on my own? I'm not strong enough, and I don't have any money. Charles takes everything I'm given. Call me Zélie . . ."

As André considered the child thoughtfully, she tried again to draw him away.

"Come with me, and if I don't please you, I'll go to find my sister, who's already a woman . . . my sister Lucienne . . . she's very pretty . . ."

The young man smiled palely, with a mixture of pity and disgust. But a kind of unhealthy curiosity overtook him.

"Since you're agreeable," he said, "you can take me home."

"Should I fetch Lucienne?"

"No, just you."

She leapt joyfully, and marched in front of him to guide him through the sordid back streets. Her little red skirt stuck to her hips, and her superb hair was rutilant when a street-light caressed it in passing. From time to time she turned her head to see whether he was still following her, and, reassured, she showed her kittenish teeth in a burst of laughter.

"I'm happy! Happy!"

They went up an abominable stairway in which all the reeks of misery were confounded, and penetrated into a small room with no fire and no carpet, furnished by a large bed draped with andrinople, a few chairs and a chest of drawers, with the indispensable bowl, soap and a bottle of Lubin water.

"My home isn't beautiful, you see," she said, "but it's all that Charles has given me, and I never have money to buy flowers and other pretty things that would give me pleasure."

André took a chair, and the child came to rub herself against his legs, kissed him, and, as he remained pensive, sat on his knees.

"Tell me why you don't want to play with me, like the others?"

He looked around. "We're alone, at least?"

"Yes, they're drinking at Père Philippe's."

"Charles and your sister?"

"They always wait for me there. They must have seen us go past."

"Ah!"

"They won't come up; you can be tranquil."

His heart constricted, André put his cheek against the child's cheek, and remained like that. Tears filtered between his lashes, and Zélie, infected by that emotion, also began to weep, for her and for him, because she was a good little girl who ought not to have to follow such a profession.

"You'll take me away, then?"

He sighed. "I'm not rich, alas."

"What does that matter? I'll look after your house, and you won't have to do anything."

He remained silent, not knowing what to do in order to disillusion that poor thing.

She had recoiled, chagrined. "I can see that I don't please you. You didn't see me very well just now, you thought I was better developed. Oh, I'm a meager treat!"

"No, Zélie, I prefer you as you are. Stay with me, kiss me as you'd kiss a cherished comrade. I only want a little affection; you'll be my little friend—and I'll pay you anyway," he added, seeing a cloud of anxiety passing through the child's eyes.

He put in her hand everything he had on him, and, as she hesitated, looking at the silver coins, he said: "It's for you."

"But I haven't done anything for . . ."

"You've done enough if you love me a little."

"Oh, yes, I love you!"

And, laughing and weeping, she threw herself into his arms.

XXV
Nightmares

Slightly consoled, André rejoined Chozelle in the shady tavern where he had left him. As soon as he went in he noticed a couple installed in front of a bottle of cheap wine, and divined that the man and the woman, who were examining him suspiciously, must be the torturers of his little friend.

Lucienne was wearing a red skirt like her sister, and a poppy similar to hers in her hair, which was crinkling in the smoky light of the Argand lamps. Doubtless they wore the same livery to seduce clients, to entice them with a more perverse promise.

Zélie bore no resemblance to the creature of vice who was laughing, sprawling on the benches of the infamous dive. The child's eyes had been full of a sad softness, while those of the whore shone with a flame of intoxication or crime, searching, cruel and provocative, those of the drinkers who were rubbing shoulders with her.

"Go back to see what he's given the kid," big Charles said to her in a low voice.

But Lucienne protested. "She'll come and tell us."

"She's an idler . . . and one day, she'll give us the slip."

"Thin and weedy as she is!"

"Fresh meat. There are old ones who prefer them like that."

"Bah! Let me drink; we'll see tomorrow."

Big Charles clenched his fists, while the whore clicked her teeth on the rim of the thick glass, tipping her head back voluptuously. "Drinking and sleeping, that's all there is!"

But Charles, who had been staring at Chozelle for a moment, jogged his companion's elbow. "Try to get hold of the other one."

She shrugged her shoulders. "Nothing to be done. Can't you see what that fellow is? Didn't you see him go out two days ago with Frizzy?"

Jacques took his disciple away, somewhat embarrassed by the man's mocking gaze. He was in a bad mood, discontented with himself and others, having wasted his time. So he demanded, without amenity: "Where did you run off to while I was stuck with those brutes?"

André blushed. "I felt ill and I went to get some air."

"For two hours!"

"Two hours? It seemed to me that I'd only been walking for a moment."

"I can see that the time passes quickly when I'm not there."

The Master still had many things on his mind, but he disdained further complaint and promised himself to demand extra labor the following day. André's works were successful, and Jacques applauded himself for his fortunate choice, without allowing his pupil to experience an imprudent satisfaction in that. It was necessary not to spoil the game.

When the two men did not go out the Master deigned to give some advice, to relieve the insipidity of an article with amusing and rare words stuck in here and there. Thus, all of André's productions had a family resemblance: the Chozelle genre, which—so his admirers claimed—was recognizable as soon as the second line of a review or a short story.

Jacques lived on men as certain of his colleagues lived on women, and, a very typical thing in this era of moral corruption and homicidal struggle, he gloried in it, recounting his good fortune and displaying his vices at the club, the theater and in the middle of the boulevard. Everyone, critics, gossip columnists and society reporters, praised his merit, his originality and his ingenious and mordant turn of mind. There was an apotheosis of epithets to demonstrate his value, which perverse petty women obligingly repeated to one another.

In the evening, clad in his formal jacket, with a white cravat, Jacques cast a glance over the enticing gazettes, while his disciple, nestled by the fireplace, where a red-hot copper plate shone, heated by an invisible gas jet, was dreaming sadly. And his life was like that ardent plate, a criminal red, devoid of the joy of vagabond flames, free flames that rose up at the liberty of their caprice and crackled madly, like amorous cicadas. His life was feverish without purpose, burning sinisterly, without hope and without tenderness, futile and artificial.

While he was dreaming, his cheek applied to the warm marble, Chozelle, who was reading, made approving exclamations over some eulogy that caressed his authorial vanity more particularly.

"I've been lucky, all the same," he said.

"Certainly," said the poet, with a weary ironic smile.

"How many men of talent struggle without being able to succeed, spending their time wishing for impossible revenges! You, for example, my friend."

"Alas."

And, with a cruel frankness, Jacques went on, with a need to torture the nerves of the other that procured him delicate enjoyments and artistic sensations as he said: "Thus, these articles, if signed by you, wouldn't have any success, and I challenge you to place one with a newspaper. You see, it isn't sufficient to have talent in order to succeed; in our profession, it's knowing what attracts the client. Impose or buy good information, be adroit or rich—that's the key to everything."

The petty harvest of glory concluded, the Master stretched himself out in his green silk armchair, and did not take long to fall asleep, while the young man, approaching the window, contemplated, beneath the metallic sky charged with snow, the roofs of a neighboring house, on which large flakes were palpitating like the white feathers of a fan agitated by an invisible hand . . .

But he had his opium pipe ready at hand, as always, and he warmed the paste of forgetfulness feverishly, installed it, and took a few liberating puffs.

Gradually, the décor changed, the walls vacillated; Chozelle rose toward the ceiling like a figure painted on canvas that was being pulled. Clouds of mist swirled, like the black rings that blur the trajectories of rockets at the end of a firework display. Then everything dissipated and Pascal's studio appeared, luminous, as on the evening of the confetti ball. Two by two the models circulated, almost naked under their jewels, displaying white shoulders, rumps bouncing under the arching of backs, limbs nervous, gloved in black silk, with darts embroidered in bright colors, and flowers thrown like kisses around ankles, kisses climbing in seed-beds of clematis and roses.

Nora, her waist contained by her belt with glaucous studs, leaps like a clown, pirouettes, and is disarticulated, one leg here and the other there. Then, without the aid of her hands, she stands up again, and with the tip of her dainty foot lifts up a glass of champagne, which Chozelle bears to his lips. There she is, legs in the air, spinning like a golden scarab in a cage; she stretches and folds herself up, becomes a snake, puts her head between her legs, sticks a mocking tongue out at the audience; and suddenly her features contract, her eyes grow wide, hollowing out, retreating into the depths of their orbits, and her flesh decomposes and desiccates. She is a skeleton dancing on the end of a string!

Couples pass by; Cythera and Lesbos, pupils cloudy, lips bruised, smile vaguely in a stupidity of embraces and kisses. Here are the foestusards of chic and check, the chevaliers of mark and countermark, the vermicular etheromaniacs, the ataractics with cotton-wool legs and molten marrow, all the force-fed and all the starvelings, as livid as one another and equally macabre.

Red-haired, brunette and blonde girls show off their armpits, where a little sweat is shining like a diamond dew; a musky odor of skin and fur excites the senses, and puts covetous glimmers in the eyes of men.

The gouges of sensuality take one another by the hand for a mad round-dance around a newcomer who makes the most famous pale. It is Fiamette, Tanagrean and unreal in her corselet studded with sapphires, which trembles and sparkles on her flesh, stirred by the haste of her breasts.

André sees himself next to his mistress; he is morose and does not respond to her coaxing expressions or her kisses. Then she draws away, drops the network of gems that covers her, appears unveiled under the arrested gaze of men. All of them, trembling with desire, study her, scrutinizing the mystery of her loins, stirred by her attitudes. All of them want her, judging her beauty flawless, and they throw themselves upon her in a sudden frenzy.

André, his heart hammering with great sonorous blows, makes vain efforts to get up, to stop the amorous scramble, the raucous breath of which grates in his ears. He begs, weeps and writhes, impotent, while the avid pack passes over Fiamette, feeding on her lily-white flesh.

At times, he perceives the rosy crown of a breast, the flowery star of her navel, and divines another flower that everyone can pick except him.

The opium dream becomes a nightmare. His muscles contract, his heartbeat accelerates, and, in a frenzy of rage, he finally stands up, unhooks a weapon at random from the wall of the studio and, bounding into the heap of males in rut, strikes those lustful faces, those throats gasping voluptuous sighs, plunges his hands into the bloody mass of breasts and bellies, and then faints on top of Fiamette's body . . .

When the young man recovered consciousness, he was mortally weary, and bizarre tics were running over his face. The poison was slowly acting on his organism, exasperating his nerves, and breaking down his health, already tried by late nights and privations.

XXVI
Zélie Dances

At Père Philippe's tavern, André found his little friend again. Usually, she waited for him at the door in order not to attract Jacques' attention, and quickly took him home with her, told him about her projects, and confided in him as if he were an affectionate elder brother. She did not want to stay with Lucienne and big Charles any longer, that was decided; placed in a clothing store with the aid of André Flavien, she would work, and would be able to conquer the respect of people. Did not all problems vanish at her age?

The young man smiled at the twittering of the little bird, felt better in the company of that little soul, amiable and fresh in spite of the ignominy of her entourage.

Similarly, he had told Zélie about the past, and how he had left his mistress, who wanted to make him live on the money of others. He had fled, full of shame and indignation; however, his heart was still suffering, his lips retained the imprint of old kisses and were not able to savor new caresses. A bewitchment of memory attached him to the unworthy friend that he adored and cursed by turns.

"And you left your love nest?"

"It was necessary."

"Why?"

"Because . . . because . . . you wouldn't understand, little Zélie, if I told you."

"Oh. What was it like, your home?"

"Banal, for others, no doubt, adorable for my loving heart. Moss and flowers . . . just room for our double tenderness . . ."

"You'll go back to your Fiamette."

"Never!"

"Bah! You imagine that everything is finished, and then everything begins again. Sadness flees like joy. You're unhappy one day and consoled the next, without knowing how it has happened. Sometimes, I want to kill myself, and then, in the evening, I dance like a lunatic, and life seems very amusing."

"You're still only a little girl, Zélie. Later, chagrins will leave a more profound imprint on you."

"You think so? In any case, talk to me about Her; that gives me pleasure, because I sense that it consoles you."

And the poet told her all about his life, and that of his mistress, knowing full well that the little friend who was listening to him would not betray him, enclosing in her, as if in a tabernacle, the holy ciborium of his defunct amour.

"But now, you see, I want you to help me forget that past, the memory of which is doing me too much harm."

And Zélie, who was already a woman, tried to cure him with a woman's means. Having nothing to offer but her frail, amorous body, she offered it ingenuously, telling him that it was of no consequence, that she was resigned to being nothing but a little animal of joy, without hope of happiness. She did not want anything except to console him, to sow a little forgetfulness in brief minutes.

He did not respond, his soul distant, and she knelt at his feet, holding his hands prisoner, and, looking at him with her large, pure eyes, asked him why he did not want her.

"What does it matter, since you'll go away immediately afterwards?"

And he found arguments in order to distance himself.

"If I took you, I wouldn't love you any more."

"I don't want you to love me, since I love you for two. Only take pleasure; that will calm your heart."

"No, Zélie, it's not necessary. I'm all right like this, my mind is confident. It seems to me that I'm breathing in a wood of roses, after having traversed feverish plains and pestilential marshes that produce malaria."

She shook her head, laughing, and, in order to distract him, tried even so to awaken his lust, having no other felicity to offer him. With an impatient hand, she took out her hairpins, shook off the red poppy, which slid to her feet like a murderous flower, agonizing and malefic, a flower of shame that declared her profession, attracted the attentions of seekers of kisses at street corners. Her loose hair enveloped him then like a warm, magnetic fur, into which he plunged his forehead gently.

She also knew dances, perverse and naïve dances, which Lucienne had taught her, tucking up her skirts. Like her, pinching her scarlet skirt, she lifted her leg, pivoted on the tip of one foot, and, with her fingers splayed, passed the bow of an imaginary violin over her thin calf. Her gestures, unconsciously precise, summoned the brutal embrace, the embrace of the male devoid of any simulacrum of amour.

She was gracious, however, in her vulgar dances, with a certain skill. To make her more supple, big Charles had stood her against a wall with her leg in the air, and recommenced the exercise every day, pushing harder, making the bones creak, until the line was straight, to the point of complete dislocation.

In certain suburban establishments, people formed a circle around her in order to see her flutter in the light of Argand lamps. Charles had no one like her for the splits. He picked her up with a single thrust, with the flexibility of a clown, and his perverse imagination suggested new figures to her, which her rivals hastened to copy.

Lucienne agitated next to Zélie, enlaced her, spun with her, more immodest, more devil-led, and their scarlet dresses made bloody patches in the thick air of dives. Neglecting the bowls of cheap wine and punch with serpentine flames, the drinkers applauded, demanding more vehement dances.

And they were those poses of the amorous possessed that Zélie tried out before André, not so much to conquer him as to distract him, glad when her effort brought a smile to the poet's lips.

"Oh," he said, "your demonic leaps are the leaps of a fallen angel, and if your wings are reddened by the fires of the Sabbat, little Zélie, your heart has retained the color of the sky!"

XXVII
Knife-Thrust

One evening, as the young man was returning to Père Philippe's tavern, he heard irritated voices. Very pale, Chozelle was reproaching big Charles for the bad behavior of Lucienne who, being drunk, had dared to imitate his tics. He demanded that the whore be thrown out, threatening to find another location for his habitual rendezvous.

On the prudent observations of the tavern-keeper, who doubtless "knew stories," the couple left without resistance, sly and full of hatred.

"You see how I talk to them," said Jacques. "They won't come back."

"Perhaps you were wrong."

"You know that I'm not afraid. That gallows-fodder will make themselves scarce. They don't want to be caught."

André shrugged his shoulders, slightly anxious, however, about the fate of his little friend, whom he feared that he might not see again.

Having thrown a silver coin on the counter, Chozelle headed for the door.

The weather was very foggy, and the widely spaced gas laps illuminated the sidewalk, which was barred in places by houses under construction, very poorly.

"Your arm?" Jacques requested.

They walked uncertainly along the road, looking for a cab.

Black holes suddenly opened alongside them, full of mysterious fear; bitter breaths of corruption reached them through doorways, as if from the mouths of sewers. They stumbled in cracks, slipped on sticky peelings, increasingly lost in a maze of obscure back streets.

Sometimes, the sound of a fight dominated the other noises of the faubourg; the moans of choking prostitutes echoed like the hooting of owls; then there was the thick laughter, insults and obscene words that the poorly closed window of some dive sent to them as they passed by. They went past plots of land for sale, cluttered with plaster and detritus, in which some domestic cat was mewling sadly. The reek of the abattoir mingled with the reek of poverty, and from so much hidden distress an invincible sadness emanated, and an infinite physical and moral malaise.

André did not speak, having some trouble steering his companion, who was leaning heavily on his arm. The fog was so thick that the line of the houses was scarcely discernible without the indication of the street.

264

Having stepped in a puddle, Chozelle broke the silence.

"A nightmare, this city of mud and soot, this quarter of murder lost in the City of Light!"

"A nightmare that we know only too well. Why not seek more pleasant spectacles? The love of the macabre will do you a bad turn, dear Master."

"You think so?"

"One does not confront the hatred and hunger of the poor with impunity."

Jacques shivered.

"Perhaps you're right. I'm sick of this poverty, which no longer has even the attraction of the unknown. At least Defeuille has elegant vice, and one doesn't risk having one's throat cut on emerging from one of his little fêtes. I'll persuade him to invite my new friends. Only the décor will have changed."

It seemed to André that they were retracing their steps, and a sort of nervous anxiety agitated him involuntarily.

"We'll never get out of here," murmured Chozelle, with discouragement.

"Let's try to find Père Philippe's house again, and ask to spend the night there."

"Yes, you're right. I'm horribly tired."

He had scarcely finished when a man threw himself upon them, brandishing a weapon.

Instinctively, André had stepped forward, struggling hand to hand with big Charles, whom he had recognized. The other tried to move him aside, to knock him down; unable to do that, he plunged his knife into his chest. André opened his arms, staggered, bumped his head against a wall, and then collapsed on to the viscous pavement.

"Quickly! The other one!" cried the hoarse voice of Lucienne.

And the wounded man heard the noise of galloping feet in the fog, which closed over Jacques' frantic flight.

XXVIII
Fiamette Forgives

Fiamette, who had been looking after the Comet for two months, had just received a letter whose address was written in large, childish handwriting, unknown to her.

"What's that?" Nora asked, turning a waxen face toward her friend, only illuminated by a strange inquisitive and tender gaze: the gaze of the dying, which interrogates incessantly, seeking in the gaze of another the hope of a recovery or the certainty of an imminent end.

"A letter that doesn't say anything good to me."

"Are you afraid to open it?"

"I'm afraid of everything at present. Some anonymous note, no doubt."

Tremulously, she opened the envelope, and a cry of anguish expired on her lips.

"What is it?" asked Nora. "Bad news?"

"Yes. André has been wounded, last night."

"Wounded! A duel?"

"I don't know—look."

She passed the letter to the Comet, who made an effort to raise herself up on her cushions.

"It's signed *Zélie*. You know her?"

"No."

"The letter is touching, though badly spelled," the invalid murmured, and she read it aloud, slowly:

"*Last night your friend received a knife thrust that wasn't intended for him. He lost consciousness and was taken to hospital, because he has no one to care for him at home. I know that he still loves you; I'm telling you so that you can go to cure him. I love him too but I'm only a friend and I only desire him to be happy through you. Zélie.* The address of the hospital follows."

"Zélie!" sighed Fiamette.

"She's a worthy little soul," said Nora. "It's necessary to go and find André."

Fiamette was ready to leave. Hastily, she kissed the Comet, who smiled in a melancholy fashion.

"I'm going."

"You'll come back though?"

"Of course."

"You know . . . it won't be for long . . . don't abandon me."

But the young woman was no longer listening. She went through the antechamber and down the stairs at a run. The door to the courtyard was open, a fiacre was passing by. Rapidly, Fiamette gave the address to the coachman and threw herself on to the cushions, where she remained, annihilated, her eyes fixed, following her dolorous chimera. She never knew the route that she had taken, and when the carriage stopped she got down mechanically in front of a large building with prison walls, which, as soon as the threshold was crossed, expressed despair and the end of things.

The surly concierge indicated a rectangular, rigid inhospitable room with chairs and benches grouped at the back in front of a glazed window. Unfortunates were already waiting, holding oranges in silk paper, pots of jam, bottles of fine wine and delicacies for the condemned whom they had come to see.

Fiamette joined the queue; then, when she reached the little window, asked for the necessary information. Another employee indicated to her, without benevolence, the ward where André was lying, and after a few detours in the corridors, reeking of phenol and chloroform, she found what she was looking for. Bed 18, which her friend occupied, was the last on the left of a vast room, bright and cold. His shirt open, André seemed to be asleep. He was very pale, having lost a lot of blood. Freshly applied bandages covered his breast.

Fiamette leaned over him, took his hand gently and, as he did not move, murmured his name.

"I've come to care for you, for you've forgiven me, haven't you? You've forgotten? You know that I'm not culpable, that I never loved anyone but you?"

The wounded man could not hear her. She went on, in a tremulous voice, thinking that he was persisting in his unjust rancor.

"Answer me, tell me that you don't hold anything against me. I was only seeking your benefit, and if I acted imprudently, it's necessary to absolve me, for I didn't have any bad intention. My heart, then as now, was full of you. Yes, the money for which you're reproaching me? Well, to get it, I sold my necklace—you know, the beautiful necklace that went down so well at Pascal's fête? I also gave up my sable, which was too luxurious for my woolen clothes. I didn't have anything else. What could I do? But you would have refused the sacrifice. So I lied, I said that Pascal had managed to place your articles and that the papers had been generous. Yes, you were wounded in your just pride; I should have found another pretext. Stupidly, I made use of what was dearest to your heart, not thinking about the cruel revelation, the double disillusionment that awaited you, since, one day or another, you were bound to find out. Of that fault, alone, I'm guilty. Have pity, my André, it was still out of love for you . . ."

The wounded man opened vague eyes, and looked at his lover with a pale, unseeing gaze.

A passing intern shook his head and put a hand to his forehead.

"He doesn't recognize you, Madame. The shock was too great."

"Ah!" Fiamette sighed. "You'll save him, though?"

"Undoubtedly, if complications don't set in."

"The wound?"

"Oh, it's not serious . . . the killer's blade slid over a rib. Another, in that young man's place, would already be out of danger."

"What do you fear, then?"

"My God, Madame, the patient is very weak—late nights, excesses, perhaps cerebral labor. He's a neurasthenic, an etheromaniac . . . when he was brought in, he was delirious. It's necessary to expect a relapse. See, his hand is burning, nervous tics are tugging at his face . . ."

Fiamette wept, not daring to say to that stranger the words that were burning her lips. She would have liked her soul to be caressed by a little pity, to draw from the experience and the sympathy of the other the strength to support the ordeal. But the intern was seeing in her, above all, the pretty and elegant woman; his male sentiments, instinctively jealous, would become hostile to the wounded man. She understood that, and remained silent, while the other, in order to linger in that amorous atmosphere, brushed against her silky skirt, arranged the pillow under André's head, and adjusted the bandage covering the still bleeding wound.

"Oh, it will need time," he said. "The recovery will be very difficult."

Fiamette dabbed her eyes, ready to soak. "Can the patient be transported to my house?"

"A week from now, doubtless."

"Thank you, Monsieur."

She kissed her friend, put a bouquet of violets that she had brought in his feverish hands, and left, stifling her sobs.

XXIX
The Agony

And for ten days there was a calvary. Always with one of the two dying individuals, Fiamette knew the heaviest hours of her existence.

Nora thought she might die at any moment. Frightful crises of coughing tore her lungs; she could no longer support herself except by an extraordinary tension of her nerves.

A void had formed around the sick woman. The last lover had fled, not caring to witness that end, to contemplate that frightful visage of amorous death, in which the eyes were still imploring tender charity.

"You see what men are!" said Nora. "That one, however, I cherished well, and never asked him for anything. Yes, he's the one I loved the most, and he's the one who made me suffer the most! Keep your heart, child!"

"Bah!" Fiamette answered, sadly. "It's better to give oneself and weep. Life is too ugly without love."

"Perhaps you're right . . . then again, one always believes that one's loved anyway, that sacrifices bring gratitude. It's necessary to die to lose the last illusion . . . fortunately, one only dies once. One would be so happy, though, with a little justice and kindness . . ."

"Don't talk," said Fiamette. "The doctor has forbidden it."

"Yes, because it makes me cough, and I'll die in a worse crisis."

"I assure you . . ."

"Oh, don't try to lie. If you knew how little I care . . ."

After a moment's silence, filled with melancholy reveries, she asked, "And André?"

Fiamette told her about her daily visit, giving the details untiringly.

"Can you imagine that Jacques hasn't gone once to ask for news of him—and yet, he owes him his life. That knife-thrust was intended for him."

"How do you know?"

"From little Zélie, who has told me everything. Oh, the charming and tender creature! It appears that André always talked to her about me. She's been very unhappy."

"I could do something for her, if she really is so interesting."

"More than you could believe."

And Fiamette told her about the streetwalker's odyssey, the ill-treatment to which she had been subject, the demands of her sister Lucienne and big Charles, who beat her when she had not accomplished her shameful work. But the Comet was drowsy and her earthen face, already covered with the mask of death, distressed the young woman, who knelt down beside the bed, closed her eyes in order to forget the frightful vision, searched her memory for a few fragments of prayers, and fervently implored heaven for the cure of those two dear individuals: her lover and her friend.

XXX
The Comet's Testament

The Comet passed away on a somber rainy day, amid the sadness of people and things. She spat out her soul in a deluge of blood—the indomitable soul that had only served to enable her to suffer more—and Fiamette, after closing her eyes, put a sincere kiss on her forehead, which, with a bunch of roses, flowered her final slumber.

A few vestals of lust followed the hearse, similarly emplumed, and almost jealous of the dead woman, who had the wherewithal to offer herself a luxurious convoy of empty carriages. At the church, they wept more for themselves than for the fortunate companion who had departed while still young, without knowing disdain, wrinkles and white hair.

On Pascal's arm, Fiamette went back to her little apartment in the Rue Caulaincourt, where a housemaid had been cleaning and tidying for two days, because André, finally out of danger, was to arrive the next day.

It is thus that chagrins and joys balance out. Death incessantly being repaired by life, renews everything and effaces everything, the heart as well as the earth opening indifferently to good or bad seed, to hope or revolt.

"This time," said Pascal, on quitting his model, "hang on to your lover."

"That won't be difficult," Fiamette sighed. "André, you know, no longer recognizes me. He lives in a perpetual dream."

"Dreams have merit. In your place, child, since your friend isn't malevolent, I wouldn't want him to wake up."

"But he's mad!"

"We're all mad. It's just a matter of knowing whether it's him or us that's more so."

A few days later, having put on her Salome costume once again in order to please the poet, who was singing while poking the fire with an idle hand, Fiamette learned that she had inherited Nora's fortune.

"André," she said, "we're rich."

But he did not understand, continuing to construct palaces of flame in the hearth, and the golden rhymes took flight harmoniously, filling the room with the flutter of sonorous wings.

And as he kissed her on the lips, unconsciously, as a butterfly alights on a flower, she said: "Oh, if you understood, you'd no longer like it. Stay like this, dear amour. Only those who *don't know* are happy."

A PARTIAL LIST OF SNUGGLY BOOKS

CPSIA information can be obtained
at www.ICGtesting.com
Printed in the USA
LVHW050033231122
733810LV00003B/268